PRAISE FOR *PANDEMONIUM*

"*Pandemonium* is a biological battle royale: Fahy is a monster-making machine."
—Scott Sigler,
New York Times bestselling author
of the Infected trilogy

"An expertly crafted, heart-stopping tale of darkness and danger that I will not soon forget."
—Whitley Strieber,
New York Times bestselling author of
Alien Hunter

"*Pandemonium* is probably the best high-tech thriller I've read since *The Mote in God's Eye*. My heart was pounding (literally) from page one. Can't wait for his next tale."
—David Hagberg,
New York Times bestselling author of
Castro's Daughter

"If you thought *Fragment* was exciting, Warren Fahy manages to double down with *Pandemonium*!"
—Greig Beck,
author of *Beneath the Dark Ice*

PRAISE FOR *FRAGMENT*

"Fahy takes readers on a wild ride through a parallel universe where evolution has run amok—think *Jurassic Park* but scarier."
—*The Wall Street Journal*

"Fahy's novel is one of the most remarkable adventure stories to come out this year. He makes the fantastic believable to the point that you'll think you're reading nonfiction."
—*RT Book Reviews*

"Few debuts are as explosive . . . A story of evolutionary horror that leaps off the page and grabs for your throat. Think *Jurassic Park* on steroids. This is one helluva ride!"
—James Rollins,
New York Times bestselling author of
The Eye of God

"Fast-paced action adventures with a speculative scientific edge."
—*Library Journal*

ALSO BY WARREN FAHY

Fragment

PANDEMONIUM

WARREN FAHY

A TOM DOHERTY ASSOCIATES BOOK • NEW YORK

PANDEMONIUM

Map and illustrations by Michael Limber

A Tor Book
Published by Tom Doherty Associates, LLC
175 Fifth Avenue
New York, NY 10010

www.tor-forge.com

ISBN 978-0-7653-6946-8

Tor books may be purchased for educational, business, or promotional use. For information on bulk purchases, please contact Macmillan Corporate and Premium Sales Department at 1-800-221-7945, extension 5442, or write specialmarkets@macmillan.com.

First Edition: March 2013
First Mass Market Edition: February 2014

Printed in the United States of America

0 9 8 7 6 5 4 3 2 1

ACKNOWLEDGMENTS

Thanks to Don Lovett, chair of the biology department at the University of New Jersey, for helping me design another roller coaster; Michael Limber for bringing the visuals to life; my agent, Peter McGuigan at Foundry, for greasing the rails; and Bob Gleason, for being just crazy enough to open the ride to the public.

CONTENTS

Pandemonium the Palace of Satan rises,
suddenly built out of the Deep.

—JOHN MILTON, *Paradise Lost*

PANDEMONIUM

PROLOGUE

We think of the underworld as a place for the dead. Yet beneath our feet teems a world of life more vibrant, diverse, mysterious, and resilient than anything clinging to Earth's fragile exterior.

Our deepest drills, boring a mile below the ocean floor, found *life*. Three miles down the shaft of a South African gold mine, life was waiting for us. Even inside a body of water the size of Lake Ontario locked two miles under the surface of Antarctica, researchers found an entire ecosystem of life they never imagined.

In the depths of the Earth dwell organisms impervious to boiling heat, freezing cold, intense radiation, toxic salinity, noxious gases, extreme pressure, and total darkness. Far from fragile, these communities of extremophiles have proved themselves hardier than any surface life in the temperate zones that we call home.

Indeed, after sampling the depths of our planet,

scientists now believe that even cataclysmic impacts from extraterrestrial bodies could not eradicate life on Earth. Subterranean species would undoubtedly survive. Life might even have endured the death of other planets and traveled trillions of miles inside meteors to seed our islands and seas, resulting, three-and-a-half billion years later, in scientists who question life's endurance.

With all the shifting, layering, and folding of our planet's geology, the variety of microorganisms evolving inside its crust must be impossible to guess. Whole worlds separated by an inner space of solid rock have been adapting for millions and billions of years, each in entirely unique conditions. Most organisms in these isolated ecosystems grow very slowly, some dividing only once a century. Others devour rock and, over geological ages, they have created some of the world's largest cave systems.

When exposed and then sealed, caves capture samples of life from the surface and carry them forward on diverging evolutionary pathways across inconceivable spans of time. The Movile Cave in Romania, isolated five million years ago, contains today thirty-three species found nowhere else. A recently unsealed cave in Israel revealed unique shrimps and scorpions whose ancestors must have entered from the former Mediterranean shore millions of years ago. Newly discovered caves of Sequoia National Park revealed twenty-seven new species, some of which had evolved to live in only *one room* of the cave.

Over a quarter of a million caves have been documented, so far, and the number grows more rapidly each year. Humans have explored only a fraction of these subterranean worlds, each of which contains a different atmosphere of gases, a unique mix of minerals, and a collection of species that have adapted to its conditions descending from different epochs in our planet's history.

And yet, for all the exotic species that we know must dwell beneath the Earth, the species closest to the underworld, both physically and spiritually, may be us.

Researchers excavating a South African cave recently discovered evidence that our "caveman" heritage stretches back at least two million years. Caves were, indeed, the cradle of mankind.

Stone Age Europeans and ancient peoples in the Americas frequented caves that stretch for miles, as modern-day spelunkers have discovered to their astonishment. Such dangerous journeys were undertaken for mysterious purposes, and certainly not practical ones, suggesting a fearless fascination with the infernal regions that may run deep in our psychological heritage.

During their long Stone Age, humans accumulated an intimate knowledge of Earth and its layers that would lay the foundations of our future progress. Along the way, the fossils borne up by the earth were like bas-relief friezes of gods and monsters. The odd shapes they saw in the stones, spiraling symbols and complex forms, leaped out of the rock like words into the brains of primitive hominids. The fossil record of the Earth was a premonition of art, mythology, and geometry. We now know that Neanderthals were the first to paint symbolic animals on a cave wall, and we know that they collected fossils. These first paleontologists actually sorted them by species like religious relics. The pages of Earth's own history book thus instructed our ancestors' intellectual evolution.

As far back as 15,000 B.C., in Turkey, humans began to modify caves. And it is there that centuries later cave dwelling reached its apex in the underground cities of Cappadocia.

Over the course of the Stone Age, accident and insight fused fire with rock. And at the end of that long precursor to human history, the principles of metallurgy emerged. The smelting of ore produced copper, equipping humans with tools that could cut limestone and construct the pyramids that mimicked mountains riddled with tunnels and caves. Bronze forged from the earth enabled men to chisel marble into cavernlike temples supported by stalagmite pillars of marble built of disks resembling the fossilized vertebrae of crinoids.

We left our caves behind for freestanding dwellings aboveground, and yet we humans have continued to return to the underworld long after to mine its mysteries and treasures. With new technology, our species has drilled and blasted vast subways for us to travel beneath Moscow, New York, London, San Francisco, Paris, and Hong Kong. Whole underground cities have been carved under Seattle, Montreal, Sydney, Buenos Aires, Santiago, Beijing, Kish, Osaka, Tokyo, Kawasaki, and Nagoya, and they are currently occupied by millions of people every day. Yet even these titanic excavations shrink before the future engineering projects already grinding their way into our planet's crust.

Particle accelerators that spare the surface from the consequences of quantum physics, sensors buried deep under mountains to detect cosmic rays, earthquake sensors miles beneath the ocean floor, and even more ambitious underground engineering projects to divert surface floods, span channels, cross mountain ranges, or hide secret military operations are under way around the globe every day. Deep oil-drilling techniques will soon bore five miles into the Earth's crust and, as oil grows ever more scarce, drill ever deeper.

We know we are not the only exotic creatures expanding their niche in the vast inner space beneath us. Whatever the earth yields up, whatever its shape, story, and strategy, it will certainly prove more incredible, perhaps more infernal and diabolical, than all the myths our ignorance has conjured.

—from the afterword of *The Underground History of Planet Earth* by Anastasia Kurolesova, Moscow Geological Institute Press

1957

JANUARY 28

12:02 P.M.

"*Poékhali!*" bellowed Taras Demochev, Guard No. 114 of Corrective Labor Camp No. 479. He pushed through the men in the tunnel as he walked beside a mining car carrying a load of blasting powder. "Why aren't we *moving*?"

For nine days, prisoners had struggled with faulty pneumatic jackhammers and pickaxes to widen the last fifty yards of the tunnel so that a newly arrived boring machine could gnaw through a stubborn layer of dolomite. Tethered by straining cables a hundred yards up the grade behind Taras, the borer steamed like a locomotive on wide-gauge rails.

Taras barely regarded the half-starved prisoners clogging the tunnel ahead, casting them aside like scarecrows as he bulled forward. The wretched convicts, even the ones in their twenties, were already *dokhodyaga*, "goners," buying their last hours of life by digging their own graves. "Move your asses!" Taras yelled. "Out of my way!"

A young subordinate guard rushed to meet him.

"What's the holdup, Yvgeny?"

"Some *zeks* fell out of the airshaft."

As the men parted before him, Taras saw five men sprawled on the ground under a hole in the ceiling twenty yards ahead. He had sent the men up that morning to continue drilling the ventilation shaft. Their heavy pneumatic drills had battered and mangled them on the way down, and the men lay tangled under the heavy equipment and hoses in a pitiful heap. Taras strode forward and fired his revolver into the groaning pile, shocking the younger guard. Many of the prisoners doubled over at the earsplitting gunshot, though most could not hear.

Since they had come under Taras's command, none of these men officially existed anymore. Once they were sent to Corrective Labor Camp No. 479, their lives were erased. Sixty thousand ghosts labored in this ancient salt mine near the village of Gursk in the Kaziristani highlands. Criminals and lawyers, rapists and poets, murderers and doctors, all were now *zeks* to the guards. Like ants, they worked until they died and were carried away.

On the mountainside above, the *zeks* slept in rough wooden barracks slapped together with timber from the foothills of Mount Kazar. Each of their dormitories was the size of a double-wide trailer and housed 120 men by day and 120 by night. Hundreds of the ramshackle dormitories dotted the mountain slopes around the salt mine that, until now, had provided the nearby town's sustenance for seven centuries. Since their new rulers confiscated the mine four years ago, the villagers of Gursk called the mine that once fed them, "Stalin's Mouth."

Over twenty thousand men had been swallowed by the mine. Convicts continuously arrived, but the camp's population never grew. The townspeople rarely saw salt harvested these days. Instead, an endless stream of mining cars and conveyors disgorged a miniature mountain range of pulverized rock at the foot of the mountain.

More bewildering to the villagers was what they saw going *into* the mine. Endless shipments arrived by train and were taken by truck and mining car into the mountain—cement and ceiling fans, bricks and marble bathtubs, Persian rugs, alabaster pillars, terra-cotta tiles, bronze streetlamps, bicycles, beds, even baby carriages. Some whispered that they had seen crates of French champagne, beluga caviar, even ZIS-115 limousines straight from Automotive Factory No. 2 in Moscow, all fed into the mine's mouth.

Taras fired another round at the hesitating prisoners, this time dropping one with a gut shot. "Get going!" he shouted at the rest. He had outlived 61 guards who came before him and 122 guards after. He knew he would be executed along with any convicts who tried to escape on his watch. This had never become a problem for him, since most of Taras's *zeks* were dead after only a few weeks. His superiors did not complain about this. In fact, they began deliberately assigning certain prisoners to his detail, which Taras Demochev took as a compliment.

Taras waved away the smoke of his pistol, questioning his eyes: instead of running away from the bullets, this time the *zeks* were running toward him. A terror rehearsed in his dreams gripped him. He backed away, but as he turned to run, he noticed blue and green sparks gushing out of the unfinished ventilation shaft. An oval of light oozed from the hole and glided like a flashlight beam over the ceiling. Then it peeled from the roof and landed on the back of a screaming convict.

Taras decided to hold his ground. He fired his gun, and two men fell as the rest retreated. But one of the *zeks* leaped like a gazelle over his comrades' heads, shrieking and soaring with superhuman force. He landed on all fours at Taras's feet, his back covered by a glowing mass. The convict jackknifed upright, and as he recognized Taras, an expression of relief came over his face. Taras was horrified, having never provoked that response in a *zek* before.

The convict reached forward and clutched Taras's arm. Two white ovals glided down the prisoner's wrist, over Taras's gun, and under the guard's sleeve.

"Shit!" Taras yelled. He felt tongues fringed with needles sliding up his arm. *Leeches!* he thought. With urgent strength, the *zek* jerked the barrel of Taras's pistol to his own forehead with pleading eyes. Taras obliged him, squeezing the trigger and blasting his head apart. Then he pulled himself away as the prisoner dropped like a marionette whose strings had been cut.

Half a dozen glowing ovals were now sliding over the tunnel's ceiling toward him. Hundreds of glowing red and yellow goblinlike creatures poured from the ventilation shaft onto the men. Taras turned and ran as the tunnel was filled with shrieks. *"Let the Grinder go!"* he screamed at the men in the tunnel up ahead.

Rising on all fours behind him, the dead *zek* leaped into the air.

Taras did not look back as he made it to the narrow-gauge rails beside the tunnel borer and shouted, *"Cut it loose!"*

As the dead *zek* landed on all fours in front of the hissing machine, Taras reached the far side and the convicts there uncoupled the cables, unleashing the machine's two hundred tons of mass, which gathered a terrible momentum as it rumbled down the tracks.

Taras scratched at his chest as he charged up the tunnel, past laborers who were plastering and tiling the walls. "Out of my way!" Taras snarled, kicking them aside.

The boring machine accelerated as it mowed over miners and smashed into the mining cart that carried the blasting powder. Driving the cart like a warhead through a forest of flesh and bone, it finally crashed into the dolomite dead end of the tunnel and detonated its payload, rupturing the tunnel like a backfiring cannon.

6:39 P.M.

When the first inspection team arrived, the only human remains visible at the edge of the rubble were Taras Demochev's hand, disembodied, still clutching his Tokarev pistol.

It was soon determined that it was more practical to cement over this tunnel and memorialize the loss of men with a plaque, and then try drilling in a different direction.

Guard No. 321 took the undamaged gun and pushed some gravel over Guard No. 114's hand with his boot.

PRESENT DAY

JANUARY 29

6:11 A.M.

Toughened and tanned by salt spray and sun, the mummified corpse of Thatcher Redmond resembled beef jerky. His formerly red hair and beard were now snow white. The remains of the zoologist had meandered across the open sea in a partially deflated raft for 134 days.

As though conveyed by a series of belts, the sagging Zodiac had drifted on Pacific currents for thirty-five thousand miles. Sucked east into the Peru–Chile Current, the raft was slung around the South Pacific gyre to the west along the top of the South Equatorial Current, where it was sloughed by the remnants of a storm into the North Equatorial Current. Now it glided on an eddy of the Kuroshio Current, passing the spray of volcanic islands north of Japan.

As it wandered too close to a rocky islet, a large wave caught the Zodiac and pushed it out of the sea, depositing it high up a pebble beach on a colorful tide line of trash.

6:20 A.M.

The first sand flies from the island arrived. As they scribbled the air around the beached raft, a wasplike creature with five wings like a whirlybird emerged from the mummy's mouth. Its five quivering legs gripped the man's chin as it basked in the sun to warm its copper blood. Its five upper legs opened and snapped like praying mantis claws, methodically snatching sand flies two at a time out of the air and feeding them like popcorn into a mouth at the end of its distended abdomen. From each of the corpse's eye sockets two more of these bugs emerged, emulating the first as they stood on each of his cheekbones.

6:31 A.M.

Beach fleas and crabs began invading the Zodiac.

Like a sand dollar fringed by a centipede, a disk the size of a dime rolled on its edge out of the zoologist's ear. . . .

6:33 A.M.

Drawn by a scent signal from the scout, a few dozen more of the rolling bugs emerged from the watertight corpse, which had been hollowed out like a leather flask by the creatures that had sought refuge inside it.

Like discuses, the bugs launched at the advancing sea roaches, sand flies, and crabs. Generations of juveniles unloaded from the backs of the disk-shaped bugs and gnawed through the joints of the island's native arthropods, consuming them from the inside, and recycling them into more of themselves, each one of them an assembly line.

10:02 A.M.

The zoologist's bony hands clutched a jar on his chest. A breeze moaned in the jar's mouth as a winged creature with three legs took flight from the jar, drawn by the smell of land. A single green scale of what appeared to be lichen clung to one of its three legs.

11:21 P.M.

Out of every thousand juveniles clinging to the sides of the rolling bugs, one dropped off and extended legs on one side like mangrove roots. Then their disk-shaped bodies expanded into tiny cylinders as their upper legs morphed into fronds. Multicolored egg clusters formed like coconuts under the fronds. Within each color of egg, a different species of "tree" began to incubate. . . .

FEBRUARY 21

10:14 A.M.

Clouds colored the sea gray like the shore except for a spill of vivid hues on the rocky coast of a tiny island Captain Tezuka was studying with his binoculars. His crab boat, the *Kirishima,* had been poaching the contested waters north of Japan when his crew drew his attention to the strange sight on the shore. It looked like a melted circus growing out of the island. He rubbed his eyes and smoothed back the white stubble on his shaved scalp, stumped.

This fragment of the Khabomai Rocks was one of a hundred islets dotting a political limbo claimed by both Russia and Japan. With both countries' navies asserting their authority over them, it was effectively a no-man's-land, where a fortune in snow and king crab could be harvested for a gambler like Tezuka.

"Captain, we shouldn't stay here any longer," his first mate implored.

Captain Tezuka knew he was right, but in all his

travels, he had never seen what he was looking at now. "Send three men in for a closer look, Hiro. Have them bring back some of that stuff," he ordered. Tezuka had a gut feeling this might be a lot more valuable than crabs, to the right buyer. And he knew the right buyer. Telling the authorities was out of the question, of course. After all, it was illegal for him to be here in the first place. "Tell them to use your camera case!"

Hiro sighed. In that camera case was his new video camera, which he was hoping to use to make a reality show pilot of their crab-fishing adventures and sell it to one of Japan's television networks.

"Empty the case and give it to them," Tezuka ordered.

Hiro sadly removed his camera and the foam forms inside, placing them inside an empty ice chest. Tezuka threw the empty aluminum case down to three men in the inflatable launch, who gunned the outboard engine and whipped a creamy curve across the sea toward the eruption on the shore of the island.

When they hit the shore, one man dragged the launch above the surf onto the gray pebble beach as the other two men trotted toward the lurid garden growing on the rocky shelf above.

At the base of the ledge, they found the remains of a large Zodiac, half-buried in seaweed. Oddly, no swarms of flies rose as they approached to inspect it. Inside the raft was a corpse wearing a bleached cargo vest, jeans, and shriveled Nikes. The mummy's bearded face was frozen in a scream and its eye sockets followed them as they passed.

The younger man took the aluminum camera

case and lunged up footholds in the escarpment to the ledge. He reached out to a purple coral-like growth and broke off a branch, throwing it into the open case. Reaching down with his other hand, he scooped handfuls of some kind of flat-leafed square-edged moss into the open case, along with what looked like two hard brown dates and some skittering white bugs that suddenly appeared all around him, crawling over the rock.

Transparent blue flower petals popped out on the branches of the coral tree next to his face, startling him. The heel of his hand burned suddenly, and pain scorched the skin on his legs. The three-petaled flowers shot out of the purple branches, revealing insect bodies hanging under three beating wings, hovering a few inches in front of his face, like whirligigs. Before the young man could react, two inch-long bugs had bitten into his neck.

A five-winged creature dived into his cheek and bounced off into the case as he slammed it shut. The case banged down the ledge as he dropped it, where his shipmate caught it and saw the young man collapse, blood spraying from his neck. His mate was about to climb up to help when an angry swarm of strange bugs appeared and instantly covered the young man's body as he screamed.

His older crewmate turned and ran, embracing the suitcase. Thousands of tiny disks rolled, bounced, and hurled after him like miniature Frisbees. They caught up to the veteran crabber, who had come ashore barefoot with pants rolled up above his knees.

Seven of the pale disks stuck like Chinese throwing stars into his calves, and he ran twenty more steps before falling in crippling agony, dropping the case. It slid down the pebbled beach toward the water as he shrieked and the bones of his calves were exposed as his flesh melted off his legs before his eyes. Attracted by his screams, two flying bugs shot down his throat, silencing him.

The third shipmate, who had stayed with the launch, heard his muffled scream as a wave embraced the camera case and sucked it into the surf. A number of large flying bugs headed toward him, buzzing loudly as he shoved the launch into the water, leaping in. He saw the case floating near the boat and pulled it aboard, throttling the launch toward the *Kirishima*.

The flying bugs turned away, heading back to shore.

10:28 A.M.

Through his binoculars, Captain Tezuka saw the body of his crew chief rolling in the surf. "*Kuso!*" he cursed.

"We must report this, Captain," said Hiro.

Tezuka scoffed. "And get ourselves arrested?" The captain rubbed his head. "Rikio is coming."

They saw the weeping man in the raft, holding the aluminum case over his head.

"He got it!" Tezuko shouted.

MARCH 12

5:27 A.M. CENTRAL EUROPEAN TIME

Otto Inman heard the e-mail *beep* while he was typing his notes. He had been up all night, working on a book about his experiences on Henders Island.

Several of his colleagues had made a bundle off book deals and product endorsements since the species they discovered on the island had added an entire branch to the tree of Earth's evolution. All the creatures that had evolved on that isolated, crumbling fragment of an ancient supercontinent had been sterilized with a nuclear weapon—except for the incredibly alien and astonishingly sentient "hendros," who were now kept in an undisclosed location.

Though virtually imprisoned since their public debut on the reality TV show that had first encountered them, the five surviving hendros had become world famous. Even in their seclusion, they had each made a fortune in sponsorship deals, their likenesses appearing in comic books, movies, trading cards, action figures, board games, children's cartoons, and commercials for hundreds of brands around the world.

Otto was one of the first scientists to encounter life on Henders Island, and was instrumental in designing the doomed NASA mobile lab the navy had flown in to investigate the island, yet he was having trouble spinning his story into gold, as so many others had. He did appreciate, and accept, a lucrative fellowship at the University of Berlin to study the legacy of Henders Island and the vast array of animals from its now extinct ecosystem, but he knew he was letting a golden opportunity pass.

Bored with his ideas, Otto welcomed the distracting e-mail. At first, it seemed like an offer to help an African prince withdraw money from a frozen bank account:

Dear Dr. Inman,

It is with the greatest respect that I solicit your expertise on a matter I believe to be of professional interest to you, and to the scientific community at large. We are prepared to make your acceptance of our offer quite lucrative, in the amount of two million American Dollars to be discreetly deposited into a private Swiss bank account with appropriately exclusive access.

I hope you will meet me at 5 o'clock this afternoon at Maruoosh restaurant in Charlottensburg to discuss the project, which, you should understand, we expect you to keep in perfect confidence.

I look forward to making your acquaintance and to discussing this matter further. We hope very much you will be agreeable to assisting us in this important scientific investigation, which promises to be very much more than professionally rewarding.

Very truly yours,

Galia Sokolof
Human Resources Procurement Director
GEM Worldwide Holdings

Well, why not, he thought, and replied:

See you there!

MARCH 14

6:59 P.M. EASTERN STANDARD TIME

The placard onstage in Lillie Auditorium read:

TONIGHT'S
FIRE-BREATHING CHAT:
What Is Human?

The cozy theater in Woods Hole, Massachusetts, was packed as people continued to crowd in, standing behind the seats.

"Good evening, ladies and gentlemen."

Nell stacked her index cards on the lectern, pushing back a strand of her auburn hair, which was trimmed after her first trip to a hairdresser in three months. Tall, slender, with engaging mahogany brown eyes and an easily freckled complexion, Nell surveyed the crowd. "Tonight I must start with the confession that I am not an anthropologist. However, I would like to discuss a new force in evolution, which I believe may explain the rise of sentient life on Earth. My husband, the founder of the Fire-Breathing Chat, who seems to be late, informs me that this audience, above all others, might welcome such an unconventional proposal as I am about to propose, if only to rip it to pieces." She smiled wryly, and the audience congratulated itself with applause.

A few wolf whistles pierced the humble auditorium where three dozen Nobel Prize–winning scientists had spoken over the last century. Nell scanned her cue cards and kicked a leg out of the hula skirt she was wearing, which got a big cheer. "Now, now." She arched a brow and waggled her finger at the audience of rambunctious nerds. The Fire-Breathing Chat tradition required her to wear a random garment of ethnic origin, so she had chosen a *pa'u*, or Hawaiian "hula skirt," as well as her husband Geoffrey's torn CONSERVE ISLAND HABITATS T-shirt, which had somehow survived Henders Island.

"I have spent the last six months with hendropods, the marvelously intelligent species that my colleagues and I helped rescue from Henders Island. And during this extraordinary time, I have concluded that there is something unique about the development of sentient beings that both of our species share despite the vast biological differences that separate us. Indeed, a unique evolutionary force distinguishes us, in a very real way, from all other life on Earth."

Nell peered over the audience but still saw no sign of Geoffrey. Though she and her husband enjoyed a very special relationship with the hendropods, it had not come without a cost. Shy of human contact, the hendros interacted with only a very exclusive group of humans. For any biologist, it was the greatest opportunity in history to be one of those they had chosen. These intelligent creatures inhabited the Earth and yet were not of human, primate, or even mammalian origin. Their mere existence was the most exciting discovery of all time, even more astonishing than would be the discovery of intelligent life on another planet. Nell and Geoffrey treated this privilege, moreover, as a solemn duty, vowing to protect the brilliant beings who now depended on them.

But the responsibility had proved exhausting, and this brief furlough away from the hendros was their first separation since encountering them on Henders Island. Even so, apart from getting married in a quick wedding ceremony in New York two days ago, attended by Geoffrey's rushed parents, she and Geoffrey had so far spent their marriage separated from each other. Geoffrey had had to attend several high-level meetings at the United Nations to lobby for the hendros' freedom while Nell departed for Woods Hole to give this lecture. Both of them realized, however, that their fates were inextricably intertwined with that of the hendropods. The sooner the hendropods won their freedom, the sooner Nell and Geoffrey would regain theirs.

An athletic man with a coffee and cream complexion, handsome African features, and pale blue eyes burst through the doors at the back of the auditorium. With relief, Nell recognized her husband, despite his new haircut. Geoffrey's dreadlocks were shorn, and she noticed the pleasing shape of his cranium in the soft light. "Hi, husby!" she said.

A round of laughter and applause acknowledged the newlywed scientists. He waved back as an audience member offered him his seat near the back. After dealing with UN diplomats for two days, Geoffrey had been flown from LaGuardia to Logan Airport only three hours ago, racing in a government limousine to get here. He thanked the man and sat, sighing, as he waved at her.

"Now, then," she said. "To the topic of tonight's chat. Most scientists claim no special origin for human beings out of a desire to acknowledge that the same evolutionary processes that created all life on Earth produced us, as well. I believe, however, that this bias might have obscured an essential factor in the understanding of human evolution, one which may well explain the spectacularly rapid rise of our species in such a relatively short time. In fact, I think that humans and hendros, unlike all other species, share a unique and powerful evolutionary dynamic: We are both the product of *intelligent design*!"

The feisty first row harrumphed, ready to pounce, as she knew they would, and catcalls rose in the back of the auditorium. Geoffrey braced himself.

Nell smiled and squeezed the clicker to project an image of a cute wallaby. "Kangaroos and this Henders species helped retire Plato's definition of human beings as the 'featherless biped.' " A series of images showed a furry biped with an anvil-like head bashing the window of a doomed NASA lab abandoned on Henders Island. The pictures elicited gasps, as did all pictures of Henders organisms. "Benjamin Franklin defined man as the 'tool-making animal.' " Nell put up a photo of a wise bonobo ape with penetrating eyes. "Jane Goodall disproved his definition by discovering toolmaking chimpanzees. We now know that some birds, like crows, also fashion twigs into tools. After the discovery of the hendros, however, I believe that an entirely new distinction redefines 'humanity.' Humans, I suggest, are the only animals that *create themselves*."

The theater hummed with tension as she projected an image of a primitive stone ax. "Nature still had to provide the raw material: DNA sequences that produced a brain that could conceptualize, a vocal apparatus that could create sounds to symbolize concepts, and coordinated hands with opposable thumbs that could facilitate creativity. But this potential was all nature could provide. When a human ancestor with these innate abilities made the giant innovation of assigning a vocalized sound to an abstraction—a specialized grunt symbolizing 'lion,' for example—that creative act connected these aptitudes in a new way and introduced a unique evolutionary force to the animal kingdom, and this new force could operate over generations just like DNA. Creative behavior that required specific physical aptitudes was transferred by language from generation to generation, creating a new evolutionary pressure."

Nell gauged the audience as she took a breath and they settled back in their seats.

"Language required aptitudes for conceiving, communicating, and implementing ideas and at the same time set conditions for selecting those aptitudes over generations. It would not have mattered if the ancient genius who thought of the first word had the best vocal cords or brain specialization to fully exploit speech. The invention of language conferred benefits on those equipped to take advantage and pass those genetic traits to their descendants. In this way, humans created themselves as their own *ideas* influenced their evolution."

Nell clicked to a close-up of a gibbon gripping a branch. "When a prehuman ancestor suited to tree-swinging thought of a new use for hands—making tools—an idea, once again, became an adaptive force. Without language, such a creative breakthrough could not have been passed through offspring long enough to have an evolutionary effect. But *with* language—the DNA of ideas—a toolmaking culture could be transmitted from generation to generation over a sufficient amount of time to select for improved opposable thumbs, hand-to-eye coordination, geometric thinking, and a host of other complementary adaptations."

Nell clicked through a series of primitive stone axes now, all of which appeared roughly the same. "This identical style of stone tool was made by *Homo erectus* for nearly one-and-a-half million years with no significant variation. But the hands and the brains making them over that time were changing and adapting to the task at hand along with the teaching of it. Just as Edison, Einstein, Ford, or Gates did in the modern day, one person finally improvised, long ago—and that innovation could be passed on through language, changing and focusing the pressures of adaptation." Nell clicked to an image of a diverse collection of stone knives, spearheads, tools, and adornments made by *Homo sapiens*. "By the time we appeared, an explosion of biological and technological adaptations had already occurred."

Nell clicked through a gallery of skydivers, spacewalkers, ballerinas, and Olympic swimmers. "We recognize in our hands, our mouth, our mind, our face, and our feet customizations that serve the needs of the spiritual, creative, inquisitive, and intellectual being that we are. There *is* something unique about human evolution, something that has made our bodies specialized vessels for the human spirit. Unlike any other animal, we ski on snow, skydive through air, swim in water, and walk in space. Something tells us that our origin could not simply be the result of purely mechanical or physical forces acting on the randomly mutating sequence of nucleotide bases in our genes. Our evolution is most profoundly of intellectual origin, expressed and carried forward, I submit, through *language*. Speech joined with DNA to complete a unique feedback loop between our minds and bodies, which over time accelerated and directed our own evolution. The intuition inspiring creationists—that humans must be different in some special way from all living beings and that there must be a conscious plan in our design—is not mistaken. Strictly physical theories of evolution are blind to an empirically obvious truth: We are the product of conscious design in almost every way that distinguishes us from other living things. But the designer we have searched for from time immemorial is *us*."

The audience churned like waves kicking up ahead of a storm. Nell showed an image of the famous biologist Richard Dawkins, whose picture elicited cheers, boos, scolds, and laughter. "The eminent evolutionary biologist Richard Dawkins has introduced a corollary to my hypothesis with his theory of 'memes.' His genetic metaphor suggests that ideas, or *memes*, are selected in the same way mutations are selected, leading to the evolution of human cultures. Good ideas have a way of surviving, along with their hosts. Bad ones perish, taking their hosts with them. I propose that not only do ideas select for or against their human hosts, as Dawkins postulates, but that successful ideas biologically alter their hosts over time, leading to the seemingly miraculous creation of both humans and hendros."

Nell clicked on a photo of a heavy-browed man wearing thick-framed glasses and shaggy hair. "Jacob Bronowski, in his seminal book, *The Ascent of Man,* postulated that the first step in the rise of humans was the 'biological revolution,' in which our ancestors domesticated the living world. Bronowski noted that wheat was created by people plucking the plumpest grass grains from the surrounding countryside, accidentally concentrating them at their campsites, where they cross-pollinated into a superproductive hybrid. The hybrid's high yield enabled our ancestors to establish permanent farming communities. At the same time, humans selected other species, changing them, too, over time, into crops, chickens, dogs, and cattle." Nell flicked through images of livestock and vegetables "domesticated" by humans. "Nobody would argue that wheat, pugs, corn, or Secretariat evolved naturally. But I propose tonight that Bronowski's observation applies to humans, as well, over the millions of years of our own evolution. Just as we domesticated horses, pigs, and peas based on criteria we created, we 'domesticated' ourselves, as well. And we have been domesticating ourselves to suit our purposes far longer than any other species."

Nell clicked to an image of Michelangelo's God touching Adam's finger. "The final blasphemy I offer tonight is this: The failure to acknowledge a role for intelligence and its innovations in our physical evolution is often ridiculed by science's detractors. What is probably most controversial about this proposition is that I agree with them. Yet I believe they, along with the scientific community ignore the true origin of the divine spark they insist must exist: we are animals that invented ourselves."

Nell cued an image of one of the six-limbed hendros. The strange creature stood between Nell and Geoffrey with four arms stretched around them, grasping their arms with four hands. Gratified *ooh*s and *ah*s swelled in the audience as she clicked through a succession of hendro family photos.

"Many have expressed confusion about how such intelligent, civilized, and gentle beings as hendropods could emerge from the biological slaughterhouse of Henders Island. Some wondered how they could have deviated from such an environment to develop the anatomy of speech, which their crustacean ancestors never exhibited."

Nell watched the awe-smitten faces in the audience as they looked at images of the colorful hendropods playing video games, drinking from mugs, using laptops, cooking on a stove, eating popcorn, and waving at the camera with multiple hands.

"Many have questioned whether or not hendropods—or 'sels,' as they prefer to call themselves—should truly be considered 'people.' Lawsuits and petitions are wending their way to the U.S. Supreme Court and the United Nations as we speak." She glanced in Geoffrey's direction.

Geoffrey nodded back at her and grinned, eager to give her the news after the lecture.

"The ecosystem on Henders Island began its separate evolutionary trajectory over half a billion years ago on a much larger landmass," Nell explained. "It was completely isolated from the rest of life on Earth. The same adaptive force *that* accelerated and distinguished *Homo sapiens* in only five million years from all other mammals also acted on *sels* to shape a species that is just as human in its own way—spiritually, physically, intellectually—millions of years before us." She clicked on an image of Geoffrey and Hender hunched over a chessboard like mismatched bookends.

"Yes, they play chess." Nell nodded. "And they mostly win. Those who are incredulous that a species from Henders Island could be sentient or civilized, I would point out that some of the most inhospitable environments, the Congo and the Amazon jungles, have given rise to some of the most peaceful cultures of *Homo sapiens*.

"Species that innovate take control of their evolutionary destiny and steer it in a unique and special way toward their own purposes. I propose tonight for your consideration that *this* is what distinguishes humanity and is the true definition that separates us from the rest of the animal kingdom. And we share this with only one other earthly species: our hendropod cousins."

Nell flourished a hand over the audience. "And so, without further adieu, you may attack my proposition without mercy." She bowed, inviting the post-lecture scrum that traditionally followed Fire-Breathing Chats.

Applause rose and hands ascended in front.

Nell pointed to a questioner stretching her arm in the third row. "Yes?"

"Don't you regret that it was your own human

curiosity that caused the destruction of an entire ecosystem on Henders Island, Dr. Binswanger?" the frowning woman accused more than asked.

A nervous gasp audibly spread over the audience.

Nell tilted her head toward the lectern. It was odd hearing her new last name. She realized that she and Geoffrey would both be taking this heat from now on, and she caught Geoffrey's eyes looking back at her ruefully. "That's an excellent question, and one I think about every day. Henders Island was sterilized with a nuclear weapon, as you all know. All I can say is that I do not regret it. I'm glad there is not even the slightest possibility that any species, other than the sels, of course, can ever reach the rest of our planet from Henders Island. Any species from that ecosystem would have eradicated all life as we know it. I hear that half of Henders Island has already crumbled into the sea, as nature itself seems to be bringing that evolutionary detour to a dead end. If we had not intervened, it would have been destroyed in short order, and nothing from Henders Island would have survived. If Hender, one of the five surviving sels inhabiting the island, had not figured out how to activate an emergency beacon on a beached sailboat, and if we had not been there to answer, they would have been lost, too, along with everything else. And we would have all lost what they can teach us about ourselves." She called on a man in the third row.

"Dr. Binswanger, considering the fact that the hendropods are intelligent beings like us, don't you acknowledge the fact that they might be the most dangerous creatures from Henders Island?"

"Well. That was certainly the belief of Thatcher

Redmond, one of my colleagues who was lost at sea while we were rescuing the hendropods. As sentient beings, hendropods are as capable of good and evil as we are, I suppose. It depends on whether one is a pessimist or an optimist about the power of autonomy. But I would say they are no more or less dangerous than we are."

"My very point!" the man answered.

The audience punctuated his point.

"It's a risk we take every day with our own species. It's a risk I believe is worth taking." Nell called on an elderly woman in the tenth row.

"Is this how you are spending your honeymoon?" she said, to spluttering laughter.

"We are flying to one of the Hawaiian Islands tomorrow for two glorious weeks of seclusion. We've always wanted to check out wolf spiders in lava tubes." Nell nodded. "Really!" She called on another.

"Is it true that sels see much better than humans can? And do they close their eyes?"

"Yes, they see millions of colors we cannot see, much like modern-day stomatopods, or mantis shrimp, which might be distant relatives and may even have originated on Henders Island, or at least the continent that Henders Island used to be. And yes! Their eyes are dry and they shed periodically like crab shells, but they can close them and also extend them on three-inch stalks. It's a bit disconcerting, like a Tex Avery cartoon, but it seems perfectly natural after being with them for a while. Yes, you in the blue shirt?"

"Do the hendros have any body odor, and if so, can you describe it?"

Nell smiled as laughter twittered. "They smell

sweet, like pennies. Perhaps that's because they have copper-based blood. Yes?"

"Do the hendros have Internet access, and if so, what do they think of porn?"

"Uh, no, they don't have access yet. Our own bashfulness may be why, but I'm not sure. We're working on it, though. They really want it. And I'm not sure what they'll think of porn, now that you mention it. . . . Yes?"

To Geoffrey's frustration, virtually none of the questions were about Nell's topic. The audience wanted to hear about the sels: What did they eat or drink, had they tried alcohol, did they have any favorite video games or favorite movie stars or television shows? Geoffrey sighed and realized that this was the way it would be—probably for the rest of their lives.

9:24 P.M.

Geoffrey hugged her behind the curtain. "You knocked 'em out, sweetheart." He handed her a dry airport rose. "Congratulations!"

She smelled the pink bloom. "That was *so* much fun. Thanks for arranging it, sweetheart."

"Don't mention it. You were brilliant."

"What's the news?"

"Well, we got them high-speed Internet." He smiled tentatively.

"Thank God! And?"

"And . . . Hender has been invited to London for a party in his honor."

"Fantastic . . ."

"It's a step."

"So . . . that's it?"

"Sort of."

"So it's . . . a trial, then?"

"More like a debut, I think."

"Oh."

"Come on, let's get out of here! I made some arrangements." He whispered in her ear. "We can give the Secret Service the slip and tell them where we are later. Or just take a cab to the airport in the morning." Geoffrey shouldered his bag and grabbed Nell's suitcase, which had been stowed backstage.

"OK! Sounds like fun."

Geoffrey whispered to a stagehand, "Keep it on the down-low." The man winked back as they slipped out the emergency exit and ran down the alley behind Lillie Auditorium.

They sneaked down the tiny streets of Woods Hole to Brick Dorm, the old dormitory of the Marine Biological Laboratory. Inside, they found the room Geoffrey's friend had reserved for them. Geoffrey was disappointed to find that the room's window faced a Dumpster in an alley instead of Eel Pond, where they could have watched the sailboats. At least no one knew they were here, he thought.

Nell sat on the bed and reflexively called Andy to check in, and Geoffrey stammered belatedly in protest. She looked at him apologetically as she answered. "I know they miss us, Andy. Could you just tell them that we miss them—? Oh, hi, Hender!"

Geoffrey sighed and stretched back on the bed next to her, placing his hands on his forehead. All five sels demanded to speak to her in succession. By the time she finished, the sleep-depleted Geoffrey snored loudly.

She decided not to wake him up and curled up beside him, still coming down from the high of delivering her first Fire-Breathing Chat at the legendary Lillie Auditorium.

MARCH 15

9:01 A.M. EASTERN STANDARD TIME

Geoffrey and Nell woke to a loud noise that sounded like the screech of a spiger, the most terrifying predator of Henders Island, and she jolted upright, peering out the window. She recoiled at the image of a garbage truck raising its spiked arms as it hoisted a bin. Adrenaline jolted her body as her groggy mind reacted, and she instinctively grabbed Geoffrey's arm, breathing hard.

He jerked awake and noticed that both of them were still dressed on top of the bedspread. "Oh, no," he said. "You let me sleep?" He noticed the terrified expression on her face. "What's the matter? Did you have a dream again?"

"The garbage truck," she sighed, mad at herself. "I thought it was a spiger!"

"Sorry."

"Damn," Nell said, trying to shake it off.

"It's only natural. We'll probably have nightmares for the rest of our lives. But we're safe now. I wish you hadn't let me go to sleep. I wanted to attack you, too." As he reached out to tickle her, the phone rang. Geoffrey answered and listened for a moment. "OK," he said, and hung up, dropping his head. "There's a limo out front. They found us."

"Surprise, surprise. I need a shower. I can't wear this hula skirt on the plane for nine hours."

"But we're going to Kauai."

"Ha."

"I'll go down and stall them."

He kissed her and dragged their luggage downstairs.

9:07 A.M.

In front of the dorm sat a huge black limousine. The Secret Service must have tracked her cell phone signal and, in the most annoyingly polite way, were waiting in front of the dormitory to escort them to the airport for their honeymoon. Geoffrey plucked a pink beach rose from the hedge bordering the sidewalk outside Brick Dorm. Then he peered into the open back door of the limousine.

Inside the cavernous cabin, which was far more opulent than their usual ride, he saw a large man reclining with his back to the driver and stretching telephone pole legs toward him, crossed at the ankle on the spotless black carpet. He wore expensive loafers on his feet. Geoffrey smelled strong cologne. Long black hair was combed back from the man's sharp widow's peak, and his massive, jutting face was overhung by bushy eyebrows, his jaw framed by a beard with snow-white brackets on his chin. He wore a stylish charcoal suit with a white dress shirt opened at the collar. Leaning forward toward Geoffrey, he grinned, flashing a gold tooth, his ice blue eyes strangely magnetic. "Come, come!" he boomed with a prodigious voice. He waved Geoffrey in with one hand and extended a drink with the other: *"A mimosa for groom!"*

Geoffrey accepted the fizzing mimosa and noticed a gold ring set with what looked like a 20-carat diamond on the man's pinkie finger. "Is this the right car?"

"Yes, Dr. Binswanger, this is *right car*!" laughed the man. His voice was not only deep but also *explosive*—like a Gatling gun inside the broad barrel of his chest. "Come, come! Let me introduce myself. I am *Maxim Dragolovich*!" He reached out hands as big as goliath tarantulas to grasp Geoffrey's hand. "You cut your hair, yes?"

Geoffrey winced as the man nearly crushed his hand and pulled him inside the car. He sat on the nearest seat and smiled. "Did you say Maxim Dragolovich?"

"Yes. You heard right." With his jutting jaw and nose like the broken ram of a trireme, and his six-foot-five-inch frame, the man was imposing in a way that handsome men cannot be. Geoffrey had certainly heard of the legendary Russian oligarch. His celebrity-adorned rooftop soirees in his Upper East Side mansion on Fifth Avenue were frequent grist for the "Page Six" gossip mill. The billionaire's latest investments were headlined in *The Wall Street Journal*. His hobbies were sports teams. His homes were feature spreads in *Time* magazine. For a man with such an outsized profile, Geoffrey thought, he certainly lived up to the hype.

"Congratulations on your wedding! Here is *to bride*!" With a sweep of his long arm, Maxim toasted Geoffrey so lustily, the biologist felt obliged to lift his glass. As he sipped the drink, he felt a kick of vodka in the "mimosa."

"Don't worry, Doctor. I have come with *wonderful proposition* for you!" The billionaire peaked his eyebrows apologetically, softening the natural threat of his countenance.

"Oh, yes? What would that be?" Geoffrey asked.

"Being capitalist, I promise to make your cooperation quite agreeable. I require expertise only you and your bride can provide. I am prepared to pay two million dollars for not more than few months of your time. Maybe only few weeks, perhaps." He shrugged. "With condition that you leave today. Right now, in fact."

Geoffrey laughed. "My wife and I are going on our honeymoon today. And due to other extremely pressing obligations, I'm afraid we couldn't possibly commit to that kind of time. I'm very sorry. It's really out of the question."

"But it sounds very interesting," Nell said. She climbed into the limousine wearing faded jeans and a fresh T-shirt. She pecked Geoffrey on the cheek, took the pink rose that was still in his hand, and sat next to him, facing Maxim Dragolovich.

Maxim laughed. His entire body quaked. *"Mimosa?"* He poured a glass and handed it to her, clinking their glasses in another toast. "I will pay you same amount as your husband. Two million dollars."

"Wow!" Nell tasted the surprisingly powerful drink. "What would we have to do for all that money?"

"I would rather not say before you agree, for reasons you will understand later. That is part of reason for high price. For now, let me say that only scientists with your expertise may be able to identify some species. Species that you will be able to take full credit for discovering. You can name some of them after yourselves. I don't care! So long as you name one of them after me." As he spoke, he removed a bottle of vodka from the refrigerator in the limo and spiked his own drink, downing it like fuel or medicine.

"Where?" Nell and Geoffrey asked simultaneously.

"Kaziristan." Maxim wiped his mouth on the back of his hand. "Former satellite of Soviet Union near Kazakhstan. I own city there." Maxim reached out and swung the door of the limo shut, decisively. He rapped on the glass partition behind him, and the limo pulled away from the curb. "Unfortunately, that is all I can tell you." He reached inside his jacket pocket and produced two envelopes, fanning them like a winning hand. "I have checks made out to both of you already."

"Wait, our luggage is back there!" Geoffrey said.

"Don't worry!" Maxim gestured a magician's hand. "It has been loaded into the trunk, Dr. Binswanger."

Geoffrey was incensed. "I'm sorry, Mr. Dragolovich. We can't do this. We're going on our honeymoon today. Please turn the car around immediately."

"We would have to have time to consider your offer, anyway," Nell said. "Please, turn the car around now!"

Maxim opened the bar and produced a jar, which he held up in front of them. Inside was a squirming centipede.

"OK," Geoffrey said. "Please—"

Maxim chuckled and flicked the jar with a fingernail. The "centipede" broke into a dozen pieces. Each segment raced around the jar independently pointing long mandibles. As Nell and Geoffrey watched, the segments came back together, coupling again like a train.

Nell gasped, squeezing Geoffrey's wrist.

"What is it?" Geoffrey said.

"*You* must answer that!" Maxim laughed.

"Can I see it?" Geoffrey asked.

Maxim handed him the jar. "Don't open, please."

He and Nell gaped at the long-legged creatures that had joined into one. "It's pale. Long legs, huge eyes on each segment . . ."

"A subterranean species?" Nell asked.

"With at least some light . . ."

"Very good! I see that I have best experts in world for this job. If you would like to see more, however, you must accept my offer first. Or, you can look for wolf spiders in lava vents in Hawaii. Yes, I attended your lecture last night, Doctor. It was quite intriguing! I tell you what. I know that you have two weeks set aside for your honeymoon. Why don't you come with me, instead? I promise first-class travel and accommodations. Plus chance to discover more than you ever found on Henders Island. In perfect safety, of course. And if you want to return after two weeks, I will fly you back home or to Hawaii, if you wish." Another confident laugh rocked his ribs.

Geoffrey and Nell looked at each other. "Why not?" she said.

Geoffrey pursed his lips, then shrugged and smiled involuntarily.

MARCH 16

8:29 P.M. PACIFIC TIME

"They are usually on time, Your Eminence. And they like very much for others to be, as well. Are you ready? We don't want to be late."

"I'm not sure how I could be ready," the cardinal answered irritably. "Do they speak English?"

"Yes. The one called Hender speaks English fairly well, I'm told. The others are learning."

"How many will there be?"

"Only two. Hender and another named Kuzu."

"I don't understand why you can't come with me."

"They don't like to meet more than one human at a time, Your Eminence."

The cleric drew in a deep breath, trying to steady his nerves. He was aware that the pope himself had declared that Revelation established that God made only man in his own image and for his own sake. And yet he was also aware that the pope's official astronomer declared intelligent life from alien planets should be treated as brothers who were equally the children of God, since there could be no limits on the creativity of God and such beings would necessarily be part of his creation. Yet these intelligent alien creatures were said to have evolved on *Earth*, long before humans. They were a living paradox, and the greatest trial of his faith he had ever encountered or imagined.

"Are you ready?" his aide asked again.

The cardinal took a deep breath, humbled by the test God laid before him. "As I'll ever be, Franklin," he said.

8:30 P.M. PACIFIC TIME

Kuzu and Hender arrived at the visitors' lounge, consulting the wristwatch on one of their eight wrists, both of which were synchronized to atomic clocks four times daily through a radio signal broadcast from Fort Collins, Colorado. The watches were accurate to within a second every million years. The sels were precisely on time as they entered the visitors' lounge through the air lock. Joe let them in.

Joe was sure to be there at the precise moment, knowing the sels took punctuality very seriously. Indeed, the sels seemed to fetishize their human timepieces. Joe assumed their compulsion was born of necessity on Henders Island, where life and death could be decided by nanoseconds.

The plush dining and meeting lounge had been constructed for VIPs just inside the western edge of the sels' Mylar dome. Over the polished mahogany table, acrylic windows arched, through which visitors could observe the sels' lifeless habitat: a circle of five cement trees connected by rope bridges under an artificial silver sky. On the conduit- and cable-snarled cement floor between the fake trees were scattered labs and trailers.

The two hendros strode through the vestibule of the air hatch on four springing legs. The one called Kuzu was a full third larger than the one called Hender. Kuzu's bristling fur coat shone black and purple. Hender's fur shone shifting patterns of blue, pink, and green.

Andy Beasley, a marine biologist who had been the first human to encounter the hendros on their isolated island in the South Pacific, rose from the table and greeted them. Skinny and narrow-shouldered, with frazzled blond hair and tortoiseshell eyeglasses, Andy looked more nervous than usual to Hender.

"Hi, Andy," Hender said. "OK?"

"Hi, Hender. OK."

According to sel tradition, as soon as they arrived, dinner was served by Joe and Bo. They were both warrant officers in the navy and wore dress whites for the occasion. While in Hawaii, they had been assigned guard detail over the sels and had not left their sides since, at the sels' request.

Hender and Kuzu sat down and immediately began eating. They did not rise with Andy to acknowledge their guest when he arrived a minute late through the opposite hatch of the lounge. Both sels pointed one eye in his direction as they sipped their soup from spoons.

Steadying himself with a cane, the bent human shambled along, dressed in a black cassock studded with crimson buttons and bound at the waist with a crimson fascia. A large gold crucifix dangled on a chain, bouncing on the cardinal's potbelly. A scarlet zucchetto domed the wispy cloud of his white hair. The clergyman's green eyes bulged as he saw his dinner companions. He had seen photographs—but nothing could prepare him for seeing the hendros in person.

Each of them used four hands to eat, holding four spoons that they lifted to their mouths in an unbroken succession. Rising like shoulders to each side of a cylindrical trunk, their arms bent down to a second joint that acted as an elbow from which forearms emerged. Their long boneless necks stretched and shortened under large heads with pronounced brows jutting over wide eyes the size of avocados that popped out of their sockets on stalks as they moved independently.

Cardinal Carnahan was told that they were related to crustaceans. But they were covered with a shining mammal-like fur that changed color in front of his eyes now. The old man cranked open an unconvincing smile as he approached the table, and he raised his cane in a brave, benevolent gesture. "I see that I'm late!"

Kuzu unfolded a six-foot-long arm across the table and pointed a few inches from the cleric's mouth. "Teeth yellow," he rumbled like a muffled truck engine. *"Like!"*

Bo sharply cleared his throat. "Excuse me, Your Eminence. May I introduce Hender and Kuzu. Hender and Kuzu, may I introduce you to Cardinal Michael Carnahan." The Texan pulled out their guest's chair.

The sels did not rise and kept eating, watching the cardinal with alternating eyes.

The cardinal seemed flustered now, which Andy

Beasley noticed in dread, and he reached out a hand to the clergyman. "It is an honor to meet you, sir." Andy shook the cardinal's hand inappropriately, hoping to distract him.

"For the sels, discussion comes only after food has been shared," Andy whispered with urgency into the cardinal's ear.

The cardinal nodded with a polite smile. He gathered his cassock as he sat down on the chair and waved Bo off, preferring to skooch his chair up to the table himself. He crossed himself and placed his hands in his lap as he regarded the strange beings across the table.

Andy quickly seated himself to the right of the cleric and eyed both hendros anxiously.

"The lobster bisque is very good, Your Eminence," Joe said, setting a bowl in front of the cardinal.

Cardinal Carnahan wrinkled his nose, nodded, and then drank all his wine. Joe served dinner and replenished his glass as the clergyman sipped three spoons of soup, swallowed one ravioli, and nibbled half a brussels sprout before he was finished with his meal. Joe placed a grappa on the table near the cardinal's empty wineglass. The cleric snatched the digestif and tossed back the snort of clear brandy, staring at the creatures from under his bushy white eyebrows as his cheeks flushed.

"Others came to talk about God."

It took a moment before the cardinal realized that Hender had said it while one of his four hands wiped his wide mouth with a napkin. "Ah?" The cardinal pulled back, shocked to hear one of them speak even though he was told to expect it. "Are you addressing me?"

Hender nodded. "Someone came before and told me very funny things."

"Ah." The high cleric quailed as he glanced at Andy to make sure that he was in control of the situation. Andy's expression did not persuade him. He turned back to the sels across the table. "What did this person say?"

To Andy's relief, the old man's voice sounded gentle and kind. All guests were shaken, at first, to hear the hendros speak. Andy was grateful that the clergyman was using the right approach so far.

"I did not know this man," Hender said.

Carnahan thought the hendropod's voice sounded like a woodwind, with melodic inflections. Speechless, he decided to listen.

"He told me what I should think. . . . He told me God would hurt me if I didn't." Hender's coat sparkled pink and blue as he seemed to *laugh*.

The cardinal found the staccato vibrations that emanated from the animal's cranial crest shocking and vulgar. "What religion did he represent?" the old man inquired.

"I don't know," Hender said. "What religion do you 'rep-ree-zent'?"

"That's a new word for Hender," Andy explained. "He's not mocking you, Cardinal!"

The old man nodded at Andy. "I represent the Catholic religion. *Represent* means that I believe in this religion, Hender. I believe it is true. Do you understand?"

"Catholic? OK," Hender said, waving two hands.

The cardinal smiled, though he found himself deeply horrified by the intelligence of the creature before him. "Why do you ask me this question, Hender?" He asked God at the same time.

"It confuses me."

"Why?"

"Because a sel never tells another sel what to think."

The cleric was taken aback. He was clearly dealing with a sophisticated mind and not the primitives he had expected. He dabbed his forehead with his napkin, trying to look into Hender's independently darting eyes. They were huge eyes, the size of guavas, and resembled tiger opals with three horizontal stripes, each of which seemed to have a pupil that looked straight into his soul, no matter which way the eyes swiveled. The cardinal chided himself as he tried to regain the initiative and closed his eyes. "Do you believe in God?"

"What god?" Kuzu's voice rumbled the air like a chain saw being stroked.

Carnahan flinched, startled. "Any god."

"Sels believe different things at different times," Hender intoned, his fur flushing red for a moment as one eye turned to Kuzu. "Long ago, sels tried to make other sels believe. Bad happened."

Joe poured the cardinal more grappa, and the cleric downed it like a tequila shot. The old man smiled then, careful not to show his teeth, and after a long moment Andy wondered if he were in some sort of physical distress, as he seemed frozen.

Kuzu's fur surged with purple and orange streaks as he pushed aside his plate and leaned over the table, his head tilting forward on his stretching neck. In a deep, rumbling voice like an engine, he purred: "Who is your God?"

Cardinal Carnahan seemed suddenly relieved by a question that made sense and that he had an answer for. He answered by reaching down and raising the ornate gold crucifix around his neck toward the alien being.

Kuzu and Hender both examined the golden symbol.

"What's the human doing?" Hender asked.

"Dying," the cleric breathed.

"Why?" Kuzu asked.

"For our sins." Carnahan's heart pounded in his throat.

Hender fluted with a low note. "*Why?*"

"He is the son of God." The cardinal closed his eyes.

"Why he die?" Kuzu growled.

"For our sins." The old man suddenly looked very fragile and pale, and Andy placed a worried hand on his arm.

Both the sels appeared confused as they glanced at each other with one of their eyes.

Andy waved at Hender to take things down a notch. He had seen the effect of communicating with the hendros on visitors many times and didn't want to have the cardinal taken out on the stretcher they had made handy.

"OK." Hender raised four hands, spreading their three fingers and two thumbs. "This is your religion, Michael Carnahan."

The cleric nodded.

Hender closed all twenty fingers on his four hands and nodded back at him, closing his eyes respectfully.

"Are you planning to have children?" the cardinal asked.

Andy's heart sank at the ominous question.

Hender shrugged his four "shoulders" and spread his long arms in four directions. "Here?" He frowned wryly at the old man.

Kuzu honked what seemed like a rude laugh.

"Well, Your Eminence," Andy interjected. "Who can blame them? This is hardly the place to have children."

Kuzu stretched over the table to the crucifix on the cardinal's chain, pinching it with two fingers and lifting the sacred icon up to one of his colorful eyes. "How God die?"

The cardinal gasped and whispered, "Crucified."

"Cru-ci-fied," the hendro said in a table-vibrating bass, as if memorizing the word. "How old your god?"

"Jesus Christ, our Savior, is immortal."

"He meant how old your religion?" Hender said.

"Two thousand years," the cardinal answered.

"My god is—" Kuzu whistled and buzzed strange sounds.

Hender translated: "Kuzu's religion is thirty-nine million years old."

Kuzu spoke more to Hender again in his language.

Hender said, "Kuzu is ninety-one thousand years old." Hender noticed the human turning red. With one outstretched hand, he patted the human's hand delicately. "OK, OK! So now you want to tell us your religion. Yes?" Hender was alarmed to see Andy display more concern suddenly, which he had learned to read on Andy's face.

"It's interesting to contemplate, Your Eminence," Andy interjected. "Sels have a very long history and culture, which go back well over a hundred million years. I know that's hard to grasp."

"Would you like more grappa?" Joe asked.

"I think dessert is coming right now, actually," Bo said.

Cardinal Carnahan waved them off, bowing his head. "Thank you, no. I believe I've had enough for now." He rose from his seat and steadied himself with his cane. "I'm not sure that there is anything more to discuss, at this time." To the sels, he added with a nod: "It was the most extraordinary moment of my life meeting you. I pray that God blesses you, and me, as well." The cardinal turned and headed for the visitors' air lock, escorted by Bo and Joe.

"Good-bye!" Hender fluted.

Kuzu glowered after him, hunched over the table on four elbows with his wide chin resting on three palms as the hatch closed behind the clergyman.

"Not so good, Kuzu." Hender's lips pursed into a frustrated bunch over his wide jaws. "Humans will hate us now!"

"So?" Kuzu said.

"We are *waku* to some humans," Hender said. "Humans need to know we mean no harm."

"No harm?" Kuzu asked. "They trap us. They kill us, too, maybe."

"There is no 'they,' Kuzu. There is only one, and one, and one. No 'they.' Remember?"

"That is how you win, *Shenuday*." Kuzu laughed like a cannonball bouncing down a stairway. "I learn from you!"

"This is not chess," said Hender, referring to Kuzu's favorite human game.

"Yes," Kuzu said. "It is."

Andy could swear Kuzu looked at him with chilling contempt then. The young marine biologist had learned to associate the sels' expressions with their emotions over the last six months. He watched warily as the mighty sel looked meekly out the window then. "Thank you, Joe. Delicious," Kuzu purred. "Love bisque!"

"Yes, thank you," Hender agreed.

"You are both very welcome," Joe said.

"Remember, there are many humans, and they believe many things, Kuzu," Andy said. "You don't have to believe what they believe, OK?"

"We believe *you*, Andy," Kuzu said.

"Thank you, Kuzu. I'm not perfect. But I'll never lie to you."

"You lie many times." Kuzu fixed one of his eyes on Andy. "But not too bad. Never to hurt."

Andy reached out a hand to Kuzu, and Kuzu grasped the human's hand with his upper right hand and shook it up and down, as was the humans' custom, his foot-wide lips curling up at the corners in an imitation of a human smile. Andy felt the supple filaments of short fur on Kuzu's palm and the rough pads on the digits of his fingers and thumbs as two of the hendropod's hands overwhelmed his. For an instant the crushing power of Kuzu's grip chilled him before Kuzu let his hand go with a tilt of his head.

"All right," Bo said. "Let's all go to bed. We'll all see each other in the morning."

8:48 A.M. KAZAKHSTAN EAST TIME ZONE

The Gulfstream V jet touched down on a dirt airstrip on a high mountain plain, jolting them awake. Nell and Geoffrey deplaned with Maxim and climbed into a waiting Range Rover that drove them to an empty train stopped on the tracks between stations in the field near the airstrip.

They climbed into the last car, and Maxim disappeared again, going forward and leaving them in the caboose. The train proceeded to pass every station along the way without stopping for the next two hours as it snaked into the mountainous highlands that stacked up against what they deduced was the northern horizon.

Geoffrey and Nell sat upright in the uncomfortable seat of the empty antique train car as they observed the tumultuous landscape piling higher and higher around them until a man finally entered the train through the forward vestibule. He was middle-aged, lithe, and well groomed with elegantly cropped silver hair that matched his expensive dove-gray suit. His sunken face and hollow eyes reminded Geoffrey of Boris Karloff. Maxim entered behind him. "Let me introduce you to my right hand. This is Galia Sokolof. Galia, these are the scientists."

Galia smiled. His cadaverous eyes brightened as he clasped both their hands. "I am so happy you decided to come. It is so very nice to meet you. Now, if you'll excuse us both for a while longer." He and Maxim departed to the front of the train car and spoke to each other in rapid Russian.

"God, I hope we're not crazy, honey," Geoffrey whispered.

"Oh, we're crazy," Nell said. "But that's why I married you, darling." She squeezed his hand.

9:16 A.M.

At last, after a long and circuitous haul up mountain grades past peaks, lakes, rivers, and gorges, the train reached a village named Gursk and exhaled an expulsion of steam as if announcing the town's name. To the left of the tracks, Geoffrey saw a row of shops and restaurants boarded up along the bank of a rushing blue river. To the right, a majestic mountain rose over the town, its peak flashing the sun's rays like a pyramid's capstone. Rusted mining equipment, teetering conveyors, mountains of tailings, and hundreds of dilapidated barracks swathed the foothills of the mighty peak.

The town was a curdled mix of well-preserved ancient and run-down modern buildings, with half-timbered façades next to cinder blocks and tin roofs.

"*This* is Maxim Dragolovich's city?" Nell whispered.

"Oh, we are definitely crazy, sweetheart. . . ."

9:21 A.M.

They arrived at the train station of Gursk, which blocked off their view of the city and the mountain to the north as they came to a hissing stop. The station was one of those patronized buildings in third-world countries that leap out of their surroundings with fraudulent promise, a chunk of propaganda dropped in like a leaflet from a bomber. The cracked concrete roof was supported by a dramatic colonnade of cement columns with alcoves along a back wall displaying Russian revolutionaries, now chipped and sprayed with graffiti. The bronze lampposts were dark as molasses, their glass domes shattered. The ceiling had dripped rivers of rust across the cracked marble platform.

As they stepped off the train, Maxim waved his arm cheerfully. "This way!"

They followed east along the platform. Nell and Geoffrey could not see anyone inhabiting the town in either direction and wondered if it was abandoned. They breathed the cold fresh air as the chill of apprehension froze into a panic.

Maxim and Galia led them to the east end of the platform, where the roof was missing and heavy pillars reached skeletal hands of rebar into the azure sky. There they turned at a railed-in stairway that descended in the opposite direction. Urging Nell and Geoffrey on, they went down the stairs, at the bottom of which was a steel hatch facing north. Galia produced a key and turned it in the door. Then he cranked a wheel like the ones on submarine hatches, and the stubborn hinges shrieked as he pushed the door open.

Inside, Maxim pulled down a large switch on the wall, and halogen lamps hanging from the ceiling flared to life over what appeared to be a small subway station. An antique subway car sat on rails perpendicular to the tracks of the train station above.

After closing and locking the door behind them, the older man turned to Geoffrey. "All aboard," Galia said, smiling.

"Please, Doctors," Maxim said, climbing into the subway car ahead of them and holding out a hand for Nell.

"OK," said Nell as she climbed in and Geoffrey

followed her. Galia headed to the front of the car. The carriage rocked, and they were suddenly zooming forward—and then *down*. The glazed white tiles lining the tunnel reflected the car's blazing running lights as they accelerated. Geoffrey saw heavy insulated electrical cables running along the tracks to either side as they plunged deeper into the earth and their ears popped.

"Where the hell are we going, Maxim?" Geoffrey blurted.

Nell nodded. "Yeah?"

"You'll see," Maxim said, watching them now with an abstract smile as they rattled through the glittering tunnel, which enlarged suddenly, a sign hanging from the ceiling that answered Geoffrey's question in both Cyrillic and Latin alphabets:

ПОБЕДОГРАД
POBEDOGRAD

"Pobedograd," Nell read, noticing the suffix. "A city?"

"You're kidding," said Geoffrey.

The tycoon nodded, laughing deeply as they whooshed down the tunnel.

"What does the name mean?" Nell asked.

"Victory City," Maxim said. "Hold on, now!"

The train clattered down the white wormhole, swerving right, left, left, right, and always *down* deeper as the temperature rose. At last, a smudge of light at the end of the tunnel resolved into a subway station floating in the black void: "Here we are." Maxim opened a hand at the window as the subway car emerged into a cavern that stretched to their left, containing what seemed to be a train yard. The surreal train depot ahead was crowned with a rococo entablature inlaid with Cyrillic white letters a yard tall: SEKTOP 7.

"Sector Seven?" Geoffrey asked.

Maxim nodded. "Yes, Dr. Binswanger. The city is divided into seven sectors."

Brass streetlamps highlighted the white marble platform like a rectangular layer of cloud suspended in the solid darkness.

The car stopped at a right angle to the station's platform. They detrained onto a lower landing to the right of the car, and Nell felt the temperature rise into the high 60s. They walked north, as far as they could tell, toward the station, and smelled engine exhaust thick in the air.

Coming out from behind the subway car, they saw a droning portable generator the size of a truck trailer parked on the tracks to the left of the station's platform. Electrical cables ran from the generator to a conduit under the platform, into which much larger cables from the tunnel also fed. Geoffrey's eyes followed the blue rails of the train tracks in front of the station, which headed west as they converged in total darkness.

"You're probably wondering where the tracks go, Geoffrey?" Maxim observed. "Some say workers breached a pocket of poison gas while digging that tunnel. Two hundred men were sealed inside to die. Their ghosts still haunt Pobedograd, or so the locals say." Maxim gave them a sardonic glance. "Others believe it goes all the way to Moscow."

Maxim climbed stairs to the platform and greeted the men there, who looked like bodyguards and brandished automatic weapons. The billionaire led them all into the station house through its doorless entryway. A steel beam supported the high, pitched ceiling inside. The far wall framed a great window of thick leaded glass reinforced with wire mesh. Steel shutters fixed against the ceiling were obviously designed to swing down and seal the window like a blast shield. Geoffrey and Nell could hardly believe the view through the window.

Coming out of the void, a skyline of a city gleamed, trimmed with colored lights reflecting in a subterranean river, a miniature Hong Kong under a sky of solid rock. The far bank of the river was lined with three-story apartments, restaurants, and nightclubs, some still under construction. Behind them, wedge-shaped city blocks of taller buildings with Gothic, classical, deco, and modernist façades, rooftops, and pinnacles radiated from a towering star-shaped building thirty-five stories tall at the center, which reached up to the ceiling of the vast chamber. The central tower was fused to one of two natural columns of rock that buttressed the capacious cavern. Colorful neon lights covered the tower's angular walls like a Las Vegas hotel. A five-pointed Soviet star extended long points across the limestone ceiling from the tower's crown, shedding a soft glow that plated the city with a silver luster like permanent moonlight. Nell and Geoffrey looked at Maxim with wide eyes.

"*This* is my city," the oligarch said. "The last place on Earth that is still free." He looked at his guests, and he smiled. "What happens in Pobedograd, stays in Pobedograd."

Geoffrey noted Maxim's dark eyes burning as he

surveyed his subterranean metropolis. "You built this, Maxim?"

"I bought this, Geoffrey. For $382,772 from the Kaziristani government." The magnate laughed. "Soviets built it. Or more precisely, their slaves did. One of those slaves, buried somewhere down here, was my grandfather." Maxim waved, and one man activated a switch beside what appeared to be a large door to the right of the window. Geoffrey noticed SEKTOP 6 stenciled in faded red letters on the door as it slid sideways into the wall to reveal steps leading down to two Mercedes limousines parked at the curb in front of the station.

Maxim and Galia got into the lead limo, waving in Geoffrey and Nell, who sat across from them. Maxim's bodyguards got into the limo behind them.

"You said there are species that you need us to identify," Nell said. "Is this where they come from?"

"We will get to work soon enough, Doctor." Maxim knocked on the partition behind him, and the car moved forward. "This natural cavern is almost largest ever discovered, I'm pretty sure. Surrounding it are others even bigger! Before Soviets came, the village of Gursk mined salt here for seven centuries. They helped carve this world beneath Mount Kazar. Soon city's power plant will be online, in a few hours now, I believe. Isn't that right, Galia? Then my city will be entirely self-sufficient and will burn as bright as day. Then we will no longer need anything from the surface. It will be a very luxurious resort to live in, don't you agree, Geoffrey?"

"As a last resort, I guess," Geoffrey conceded.

"It's certainly a spectacular place to visit, but I wouldn't want to live here."

To the right of the train station, a string of dim streetlamps arched over a baroque bridge with gilded wreaths carved into the balustrades. As the limos cruised over the bridge, Nell and Geoffrey looked out the left window at the black currents of the river between lampposts wrapped with bronze dolphins. A ghostly waterfall glowed blue in the distance, cascading down the western wall of the cavern. To the right of the bridge, the sparkling river seemed to drop down, flowing deeper into a channel that disappeared under the eastern wall.

"My River Styx!" Maxim proclaimed.

"Wow," Nell whispered.

On the other side of the river, they turned right and then left, heading north along the city's eastern edge. Three-story buildings displaying a dozen European architectural styles flickered past them on either side in their jiggling headlights. Many were lit up and apparently inhabited. Small electric cars zoomed through the city's streets. They passed shops, apartment houses, fire stations, factories, banks, nightclubs, and grocery stores. It was like a museum of architecture, Nell thought as she observed the people on the streets. They were mostly well-dressed adults or construction workers. She noticed no children, though one woman appeared to be pregnant. "How many people live here?"

"Almost five thousand right now," Maxim said. "Mostly workers, but guests have begun to arrive." He activated a special cell phone in the car to check for messages.

Between blocks, Nell and Geoffrey saw spokelike

streets radiating from the central tower's pointed ramparts. At the head of each avenue stood a hulking bronze colossus posed in righteous glory. She recognized Marx, Lenin, Stalin, and other revolutionary heroes. From the star-shaped tower's pinnacle, the five points of the glimmering star stretched over the city's main avenues. Some of the streets were lit only by construction crews and traversed by trucks and forklifts. Other avenues were empty, twilit, and still.

"Pobedograd was originally a giant bomb shelter," Maxim said, turning off his phone. "For Communist Party elite—in case they succeeded in destroying world. I turned it into a playground for rich, and a haven for oppressed—two classes that are often same, eh? But I am only law here. Don't worry, I'm benevolent dictator."

The refined city surpassed anything they had seen on their journey across the impoverished countryside of Kaziristan. *Here,* Geoffrey thought, *under a mountain.*

"Stalin was addicted to underworld," Maxim explained. The hulking magnate's body was outlined in the window of the limousine like the profile of a mountain. His black hair and beard flowed like basalt over his shoulders as he flashed a look at Geoffrey with volcanic eyes. "Koba dug railroads and cities across Soviet Empire. Places where he could plan his disasters, and hide from their consequences. He was Devil, Dr. Binswanger." Maxim looked grimly through the window.

"Koba?" Nell asked.

"You mean Stalin?" Geoffrey asked.

"*Da,*" Maxim grunted.

"You mentioned your grandfather," Geoffrey said.

Maxim nodded. "My grandfather was doctor, like yourself. A physicist. For telling truth, he was sentenced to Belbaltlag so he could help dig White Sea–Baltic Sea Canal, which was very first gulag. Prisoners used pickaxes and shovels to dig one-hundred-forty-mile canal in only twenty months, at cost of twenty-five thousand men—some say one hundred thousand. Nobody really knows." Maxim shrugged and spread the fingers of one hand, shaking his head. "Records are sketchy. The canal was too narrow for ships, however. So it was nothing more than mass grave for criminals, counterrevolutionaries, and enemies of state. My grandfather survived Belbaltlag. One of few. He survived two more gulags, as well, until he arrived here. He was tough man." Maxim looked at Nell. "But here, at Pobedograd, he died, along with seventy-five thousand other men who were building this glorious hiding place for Koba."

"Stalin." Nell nodded softly.

"*Da.*" Maxim sipped from a silver flask, which he offered to Geoffrey and Nell, who politely refused. The oligarch continued, occasionally dropping articles as his cadence stressed certain phrases and words with explosive volume: "My father was *genius,* like my grandfather! Unlike him, however, he did not try to work inside Soviet system. He was entrepreneur in black market, instead. They branded him a gangster, just like me. Gangsters were only ones getting anything done in Russia in those days. Today, still true. The Party did not care. All they cared about was who was breaking law and if they received sufficient bribes to look other way. Our state made us what we had to be in order to survive, Geoffrey. I stepped into my father's shoes at seventeen, after he was murdered by officials who were not bribed enough. Since then, all Russian authorities are my enemies. And I am theirs, since then."

"I see," Nell said with a worried glance at Geoffrey.

Maxim slapped Geoffrey's thigh, grinning in a conspiratorial expression. "You see this city, Geoffrey? It's nothing! The ground of Moscow is hollow with such places. Some were dug centuries ago by Ivan the Terrible. Others are so secret, even Russian government possesses *no record* of their construction!" Maxim laughed heartily, his Russian humor a potent cocktail of despair, outrage, and futility mixed with sly self-mockery. But there was a hidden declaration of war in his laugh, as well. "Under Moscow, Stalin's underground was intended to keep state officials safe. Instead, it became refuge for enemies of state. Even in Stalin's time, a black market of dissidents and geniuses, smugglers and rebels, all marked for murder, took root underground. During the '70s, I, too, was saved, more than once, by hiding in Stalin's catacombs. Many connections I made there helped me carve my slice of Soviet Union when it collapsed. By bribing the right officials and guaranteeing paychecks to oil, gas, and mine workers when Russian state could not, I gained their loyalty and kept power on so people would not freeze. I kept factories, schools, and hospitals from closing when no one else knew what to do. But when Russian government began hunting down so-called oligarchs, to reclaim what they call the 'Party's gold,'

I left, with my family and all of my wealth. That is something Russian government can never forgive, or forget. I own homes on all five continents—twenty-seven estates from Italy to Hawaii, from Manhattan to Hong Kong, from Israel to Costa Rica. I own a fleet of aircrafts, including three DC-10s, an American football team, an Italian basketball team, a French movie studio, and cable news networks in Australia, Eastern Europe, and Brazil. I moved all of my money and all of my family and friends out of Russia so I could not be blackmailed. Many of them live here now. And yet, at any moment, I could be assassinated. Three of my friends, other so-called oligarchs, have been murdered in *broad daylight* in major cities outside Russia. One was killed in downtown Manhattan. Digitalis in his Diet Coke. Another was killed in Argentina. Polonium in his toothpaste." Maxim shrugged. "I am hunted wherever I go. Except here!"

Geoffrey noted the heavy security the billionaire was traveling under and glanced darkly at Nell.

They arrived at a giant steel door guarded by armed men. They read faded red letters stenciled on the steel: SEKTOP 2. Maxim waved out the window, and the guards activated a switch. The door rolled sideways into the wall and revealed a road that proceeded uphill into another part of the city.

The low ceiling over the road resembled the barrel vaulting of a Gothic monastery now. This section of the city seemed to be unoccupied and dark.

"This was a garrison for Stalin's guards," Maxim remarked, waving at the windoow. "It was built as shelter for villagers of Gursk six centuries ago. He sealed all sectors of city with lead-lined doors to protect them from floods, fires, radiation—or revolution." Maxim winked sardonically at Nell.

There was no illumination in this sector except for their cars' headlights. Nell noticed a few rats scurrying across the street in front of the limo.

"Most people born into poverty and oppression deserve it, I think," Maxim inveighed. "The world they are willing to live in is their natural habitat, like crocodiles in mud or rats in sewers."

Nell was startled as Maxim leveled his piercing gaze at both of them.

"And most people born into freedom and prosperity don't deserve it, either—since they did nothing to create it and nothing to preserve it. Indeed, they do a little more each day to tear it down, if only by looking the other way while it crumbles. That is the sad truth, my friends."

"So who are the ones who deserve a better world in your view, Maxim?" Nell asked.

"Those who create it—even as the rest try to tear it down every step of the way." A bitter, world-quaking laugh rocked the hulking man's shoulders. "But you are biologists. Every day you observe the animal kingdom. Surely you have noticed the unsustainable march humanity is on? We are headed back to mud, cannibalizing those who briefly dragged us out." Maxim observed the shocked look on their faces. "Do not worry, Doctors," he said. "I have classed you among those who are deserving. Both of you have courage to fight the status quo. You use your brains, which is to say, you are *honest*. Unlike many of your peers, who sell their opinions to the highest bidder. I have researched your backgrounds and I assure you, when whole world goes to hell, you will always have your place here, if you want it."

"Well," Geoffrey said. "That's good to know."

"I think it would be hard to leave the whole world behind, even for your utopia, Maxim," Nell said. "There is too much good in it."

"It depends, I think, on what you're leaving behind," Maxim said. "There are many here who found the choice quite easy."

They traveled deeper into the medieval sector of the city as the road grew steeper. They slowed and turned abruptly left, still heading uphill. After another few minutes, they arrived at a large steel door marked with red letters:

SEKTOP 1

"Here we are!"

Maxim rolled down the window, waving twice at the waiting guards, who activated a switch. Again, the door rolled sideways into the rock. Both limos pulled into a wide cobblestone courtyard before a glistening golden palace. "Premier Stalin's personal residence," Maxim announced, presenting the baroque façade with a flourish as he noticed his guests' dumbstruck reaction. "Just in time for cocktails."

"Cocktails?" Geoffrey stammered. "It's breakfast time, isn't it?"

"In Pobedograd, day is night," said Maxim.

9:00 P.M. MAXIM TIME

Geoffrey and Nell emerged from Maxim's armored limousine eagerly, and both of them gasped before the resplendent mansion that erupted like a fantasy inside the domed cavern. They noticed a forest of yellow stalactites dripping from the ceiling as they climbed the curving steps to the palace entrance that was framed by a polished marble portico and onyx pillars with gold-leafed capitals.

At the top of the stairs, Nell looked up to see an enormous crystal chandelier suspended under a golden umbrella dome over the foyer. The chandelier illuminated a polished floor of inlaid stone with spiraling geometric designs. To each side, curving stairways carpeted in crimson swept up to the second story.

Maxim stopped to have a word with one of his men in the foyer. "She does not want any guards inside," Geoffrey overheard him tell Galia Sokolof. There was a brief argument between them, and Maxim waved off Galia and the rest of his men. Then Maxim motioned for Nell and Geoffrey to follow him up the crimson stairway on the left.

At the top, he led them between two banks of doors and turned left up a short stairway to a door on the right—another submarine hatch with a dog wheel in the center. Maxim pushed a button. The wheel turned as someone on the other side opened the door inward.

"Please, my friends," said Maxim. "Let me show you my conservatory."

They stepped through the hatch into a rectangular room that was indeed the size of an English manor's conservatory, with a high corbeled ceiling from which three gold-and-crystal chandeliers hung spaced from right to left. In the far left corner of the chamber was a glass tube in which a wrought iron stairway corkscrewed through the floor and ceiling. The back wall of the room seemed to be hewn into the solid bedrock of Mount Kazar, but most of the clawed rock face was covered by luxuriant red velvet curtains. The other three walls were lined with book-laden shelves and mahogany paneling displaying gold-framed paintings that seemed to be forgotten masterpieces. To the right of the door was a great oaken desk, and on the wall behind it was an array of video monitors displaying various parts of Maxim's city.

The room's parquet floor was scattered with silk Persian rugs, and in the center of the room, directly in front of them, was a long banquet table pointing toward them, where four seated dinner guests now rose to greet them.

"Hey, man!" said a moonfaced man with a ponytail. "Oh, my God! Is that you, Nell?"

"Otto?" Nell asked, amazed.

The man ran and hugged her.

"Geoffrey, let me introduce you to Otto Inman," she said. "He was on Henders Island in the NASA lab before you got there."

"Yeah, before it was totally destroyed," Otto said, reaching out to shake Geoffrey's hand. "I didn't figure on Henders Island when I designed it."

"Nice to meet you." Geoffrey shook his hand.

A stocky Asian man with graying hair approached them, and Otto introduced him. "This is Katsuyuki Fujima," he said, uncertain whether he had gotten the name right.

"Yes, perfect." The man nodded at Otto. "Very nice to meet you. I am a biologist from Nagoya University, Japan." He reached out to shake Nell's hand.

"He was on Henders Island, too, briefly," Otto said. "He helped collect specimens on the last day we were there."

"One big happy reunion," Geoffrey said with a puzzled glance at Nell.

Nell arched her eyebrows. "Interesting."

"Yes," Katsuyuki agreed.

A thin, pale, black-haired man with coal black eyes approached them. "Hello! I am Dimitri Lagunov." The slender Russian wore a thin black goatee and glasses. "I am the only biologist here who was not on Henders Island, it seems. It is very good to meet you both. This is Klaus Reiner."

A tall, blond German man wearing spectacles and a business suit without a tie greeted them. "Hello. I'm just an electrical engineer," he said. "Working on the power plant." He shrugged.

Geoffrey and Nell shook his hand.

Maxim strode to a leather armchair at the head of the table, its back to the red velvet curtain. "Please, everyone, sit down!" His basso profundo voice compelled them like a force of nature, and everyone took a seat at his end of the table to either side.

"So are you now going to say, 'I'm sure you are all wondering why I brought you here'?" Nell asked, giggling. "Because that would really be funny right now, Maxim."

The anxiety of the others at the table crumbled into nervous laughter.

Maxim smiled. "Something like that. You seem to have made introductions already." He nodded at the train of waiters who entered the hatch door bearing trays of food and champagne. "Let me welcome you all as guests. I thank each of you for answering my invitation."

With fresh flutes of champagne, his guests obliged him in a toast.

"I wonder if any of you can identify what you are now being served," Maxim said as the waiters placed a dish before them.

Quite obviously, it was a serving of seared mushrooms—so the stakes increased as each scrutinized the variety presented on the plates. All sampled the fungi, which had a meaty flavor drizzled with a tart pomegranate sauce.

"*Armillaria,*" Nell volunteered. "Honey mushrooms?"

"Ah! Our botanist, the newlywed Nell Binswanger, is correct! Very good!" Maxim raised his large hand to signal one of his men, who dimmed the chandeliers in the room.

As the room darkened, everyone gasped to see the mushrooms on their plates, on their forks and in their mouths glowing green, blue, orange, and purple. Maxim's chest quaked as he laughed. "Explain to them, please, Nell."

She recovered from the surprise. "*Armillaria* is a bioluminescent mushroom," she said. "The mushrooms are the fruiting bodies of one of the longest-living fungi. One single organism can spread over three square miles and live for thousands of years. They produce fox fire, which is bioluminescent and grows on rotting logs. In olden days, Scandinavians used them to mark paths through the forest during the long northern nights."

"Very good." Maxim purred like a panther. "She is very good, Geoffrey."

"But this isn't fox fire," Nell protested. "Fox fire is blue or green. This is more like . . . *rainbowfire*."

"That is an excellent name for it, Nell!" Maxim approved.

"Is it edible?" Otto asked, triggering laughs around the table.

"Oh, yes!" Maxim relished a bite of the lightly seared mushrooms, which glowed orange and pink on his fork; then he sipped some champagne. "And quite delicious." Maxim raised his left arm.

Some of his men now carried forward three tall boxlike objects covered in black cloth and set them in a row on the far side of the banquet table. "I would like you all to tell me everything you know about what I show you next."

The men pulled off the shroud from the first box and revealed an acrylic aquarium half-filled with water. Maxim's guests rose and gathered around as they noticed living things inside the aquarium.

"Whoa!" Otto said, laughing. A fluorescent sea spider hunted what looked like swimming snails swishing above it. "No freaking way!" Otto exclaimed.

"Ammonites?" Geoffrey gasped.

The scientists peered with open mouths at the miniature ram's horn coils that jetted through the water like tiny nautiluses.

"They have been extinct for sixty-five million years!" Katsuyuki cried.

"No, Dr. Fujima," said Maxim.

Geoffrey broke into a wide grin. "You found them here?"

"Yes!" said Dimitri.

"Please, tell me about them, Geoffrey," Maxim said.

Waiters served them another round of hors d'oeuvres: ammonite escargot.

"There was a time when they ruled the seas, reaching ten feet across," Geoffrey said. "The Roman historian, Pliny the Elder, named them after examining their fossils near Pompeii and noted their resemblance to the ram horns worn by the Egyptian god Amon. You know, the one King Tut was named after? But this is impossible. . . ."

"Amen," said Otto.

"Don't laugh," Nell said. "But we probably adopted that word from the tradition of invoking Amon in prayers."

Maxim laughed. "Go on."

"Some think these creatures may have plowed across the sea's surface like Jet Skis, hunting with heads and arms like armored squid," Geoffrey said.

"Well, they were right, Geoffrey," Maxim said. "I've seen them do it."

"Do you know how huge a discovery this is?" Katsuyuki said, his hands shaking. "It's a miracle!" Otto gave him a high five.

"How do they taste?" Maxim asked.

"We're *eating* them?" Nell asked.

"*Oishii!*" Katsuyuki nodded, elated. "Delicious."

"Chewy," Otto said, laughing.

"And that's a sea spider," Geoffrey said, pointing at the multicolored eight-legged creature that reached its impossibly long, folding arms out to the racing ammonites. "One of the strangest crustaceans. This one's really colorful! They seem to be a branch that split off from all other arthropods about half a billion years ago . . ."

"Some think they actually *are* arachnids—before they evolved for land," Otto said.

"That's debatable, Doctor," said Katsuyuki, admiring the specimen.

"It's still a cool theory," Otto said. "What's in this one?"

An attendant pulled the shroud from the next tank, which was dry. Inside, yellow and orange animals that glowed circled round and round on the bottom.

"Gammarids?" Geoffrey suggested, looking into the dry aquarium.

"Yes," agreed Dimitri. "Some kind of amphipod, like gammarids, we think. We call them gammies."

"But adapted for land?" Geoffrey said. "With only eight legs?"

"Look at the spikes on their backs," Nell said. "They look like aetosaurs!"

"What are aetosaurs, Nell?" Maxim asked, leaning back in his chair and watching the scientists as waiters served another round of appetizers and replenished their champagne.

"One of my favorite dinosaurs, with spikes on its back pointing to each side."

"It's thought that gammarids may have evolved in Lake Baikal or the Caspian Sea, which isn't so far from here, I think," Otto said.

Dimitri smiled. "Lake Baikal is rather far from here, Dr. Inman. But you are right, the gammarids there have similar spikes on their armor."

"They're also known as *killer shrimp*," said Otto. "They're a big concern at Berlin University. They've been migrating from the Caspian Sea across Europe through the Danube and wreaking havoc. They've even been turning up in England and

Scotland recently. But no one has ever recorded a land-based species! And with only four pairs of legs?"

"They must have undergone an independent Hox gene mutation, like early arthropods, when they crawled on land four hundred million years ago and became hexapods," Geoffrey said.

"Hexapods?" Maxim asked.

"Bugs," Geoffrey clarified. "With only six legs."

"But why are they glowing?" Nell wondered. "They seem to be blind. No eyes, at all! See?"

"They move like tiger beetles!" Katsuyuki exclaimed with an eight-year-old's delight. "So fast! But why in a circle, around and around?"

"We've noticed they move like that sometimes," Dimitri acknowledged, shrugging.

"Wait a minute . . . army ants," Nell murmured.

"Huh?" the others asked.

"Army ants are blind, so they follow scent trails laid down by other ants' abdominal glands. If an ant travels in a spiral, others following it can get trapped in death circles, with thousands of them turning like hurricanes until they die of starvation."

"No way," Otto said. "I've never heard of that."

"But why do the gammies glow if they're blind? Why do any of these species? I don't get it."

"They eat . . . what did you call it? Rainbowfire," Maxim said.

"We think the bioluminescence in the fungus either grows on them or continues to glow once ingested," Dimitri said.

"They must stick out like Christmas lights to predators," Nell said, puzzling. "Maybe that's why they're covered with spikes. . . ."

"How long would adaptations like these take to evolve?" asked Katsuyuki, shaking his head.

"Well, Lake Baikal is the oldest freshwater lake on Earth." Dimitri shrugged. "It lies hundreds of kilometers east of the Urals."

"How old is it?" asked Nell.

"Some say fifty million years."

"It might be a clue." Nell looked at Geoffrey.

"The Caspian Sea is a lot closer," Geoffrey said. "And the Aral Sea. And in any event, I don't think any of them are old enough. We're looking at things that must have origins dating back to the great age of marine mollusks, which ended around the time of the dinosaurs sixty-five million years ago. This is a region with major tectonic activity, which made these mountains. What I don't understand is how could a cave system this size last for so long?"

"The Urals are the oldest mountain range on Earth, Dr. Binswanger. They are two hundred fifty, maybe three hundred million years old," said Dimitri.

"Ah! Who knows when these specimens were trapped underground and begun diverging, then?" Otto said.

Nell whispered in Geoffrey's ear: "This is much better than Kauai, sweetheart."

He nodded and speared a gammarid tail, dipping it in cocktail sauce as she clinked her flute of champagne against his.

The attendant pulled the shroud from the third tank.

The German electrical engineer, Klaus Reiner, who had watched and listened in silent awe as the scientists described the species presented to them at this extraordinary banquet, now spoke up. "What in hell are these?" he said, pointing at glowing bubbles bobbing up and down inside the dry tank.

The others were silent.

Maxim laughed softly.

"We have no idea," Dimitri confessed, "what these are."

Small creatures like Christmas tree ornaments glowed pink and orange with four fins that made them spin or glide as they floated up and down.

"How are they doing that?" asked Otto.

"They look like Dumbo octopuses!" Nell said. "Are they filled with gas?"

A light like an ignited match flared inside one of the small bell-like creatures as it rose inside the tank.

"Bombardier beetles!" exclaimed the German.

The scientists turned to him.

"Sorry. I did a paper on them as an undergraduate. . . ."

"I thought you were an electrical engineer," Nell said.

"I was studying biochemical energy systems for a while."

"Explain, please, Dr. Reiner," Maxim said.

"Bombardier beetles mix hydrogen peroxide and hydroquinone generated in separate glands to create an explosive chemical reaction, like a rocket engine. It generates enough heat to boil water. These things might be using a similar process to inflate a bladder with hot gas."

"Like sky lanterns," Katsuyuki said.

"Hot air balloons!" Nell said.

Maxim blew a plume of cigar smoke straight up. "Excellent."

Geoffrey shook his head, staggered by the implications. "We've got water, land, and air organisms? How elaborate is this ecosystem?"

"Let me show you." Maxim nodded at one of his men, and the man pulled a golden sash that parted the red velvet curtains at his back, revealing a great oval window encircled by a wide bronze frame embedded in the solid rock.

Everyone rushed to the window before the curtains had completely opened, and Maxim swiveled in his leather chair to gaze with them through the thick pane of glass that stretched twenty feet high and forty feet wide. The polished window was dark except for glowing colors and shapes that slowly began to emerge. "Ladies and gentlemen," Maxim said, "May I present Pandemonium."

9:55 P.M.

Slowly, their eyes made out the outlines of another world on the other side of the window.

A vast lake, splotched with swirling patches of color, channeled into the distance through a corridor angling slightly to the right as far as the eye could see. Hundreds of feet above was a vaulted ceiling with iridescent paisley patterns overlapping over the rock.

The faint light of the chandeliers lit up the area closest to the window. As suspended forms moved closer in the dark, they took on real shape; as they moved away, they dissolved into spectral ciphers. Multitudes of phosphorescent creatures swirled in glowing storms and spiral galaxies receding to the vanishing point in the colossal cavern.

Geoffrey scanned the surface of a lake below. He saw creatures snaking over the water, visibly breaking into pieces and rejoining as they swam like the centipede Maxim had shown them. Bioluminous hordes of gammarids darted over glowing patches on the lake's surface.

All the scientists were pressed against the window, cupping their hands to both sides of their heads as they peered through the thick glass. Nell looked up at the cavern's ceiling, which was coated with a shaggy pelt of stalactites. An island of stalagmites the size of buildings soared from the center of the lake with columns reaching all the way to the ceiling at its highest point, six hundred feet above. And every spire was dusted with rainbow-fire.

Purple globes the size of beach balls dangled red tentacles like levitating Portuguese man-of-wars. A faintly illuminated organism like a Macy's Thanksgiving Day parade float moved languidly over the lake in the distance, extending long feathery plumes at one end that fanned cyclones of orange and pink bubbles into its whale-sized mouth.

Nell sighed, holding on to Geoffrey. "What in the hell are we looking at?"

Maxim pointed to a plaque centered on the bottom frame of the window.

имени Ленина

"'Hell's Window,'" Maxim translated. "That's just what Stalin thought he was looking at as he sat in this very chair. I imagine he felt right at home. As for me, I call it Pandemonium." He spoke in Russian to one of his men to the right of the window, who nodded as he pulled down a heavy switch.

The chandeliers dimmed to a flicker, and a rack of locomotive headlamps mounted inside the cavern ignited above the window and flooded the chasm with beams of light. The patches on the lake's surface now appeared to be gray masses like shingled lily pads over which yellow and orange gammarids scrambled. Along the shore, more of the amphipods flowed in herds, ranging from the size of mice to hippos. More poured down over the window from above and across its lower ledge.

Overcoming their initial shock, the scientists began exclaiming all at once, each reacting to something else as they pointed in different directions.

One of the yellow and pink striped blimps drifted toward them under the spiked ceiling. Spiraling feathers recoiled one by one from the air as they snagged swarms of orange and pink balls like the specimens in the tank on the table before them.

"Fuck me!" Otto laughed, delirious as he hung on the window like a boy at the monkey enclosure.

"Sky whales," Nell breathed.

"Good!" Maxim approved.

"Could it be some kind of medusae or mollusk?" Geoffrey wondered, gripping Nell's hand. He realized, as did the rest of the scientists, that not only hundreds of millions of years but also a truly vast environment would be required to produce such a variety of life and all these complex interrelationships.

"The gammies are all over the ceiling, too!" Otto pointed up at the cavern's vault, which was overrun by amphipods grazing on the stalactites.

"Look at that nearest herd, crossing the lake," said Dimitri. "The ones at the perimeter have *mandibles.*"

"Maybe it's another antlike adaptation," Nell said. "Some gammies might be specialized to defend the colony."

"Maybe they're predators, stalking the herd," Katsuyuki said.

"That layer on the lake looks like the bacteria–fungus mats in the Movile cave in Romania," Nell said. "It grows chemosynthetically and is the base of the food chain for thirty-three endemic species."

"Interesting," Maxim said.

"Everything seems to eat the rainbowfire on the walls and ceiling, too," added Geoffrey.

"And everything glows," Katsuyuki said. "Maybe there is a connection!"

"I don't know," Nell said. "Digestive enzymes would pretty quickly denature the luciferase that makes the fungus glow. . . ."

"Most things down here are probably transparent," Geoffrey said. "So their food would glow at least partway down even if the luciferase were hydrolyzed by digestive enzymes."

"Maybe," she considered. "Or maybe the organisms are simply coated by glowing spores."

"Both, I think," said Dimitri. "And they must produce their own bioluminescence, as well."

"Are we going to glow now, too?" asked Otto.

Everyone laughed nervously.

"You already are, I think!" Maxim smiled in satisfaction as he watched the enraptured scientists admiring his world.

A white twenty-foot-long segmented animal swam in a side-to-side motion among the gray patches. It disarticulated into forty smaller animals that raided the grazing amphipods on a fungal mat. The pieces reassembled and snaked through the gammarid herd to *ooh*s and *ah*s from the gallery. One of the mandible-bearing gammarids at the perimeter of the herd crawled over the others with long legs, chasing the centipede.

"They *are* guards," Nell whispered. "The big ones are soldier gammies."

The soldier gammarid seized a segment of the animal, and the other segments scattered, jumping back into the water.

"Huh! The centipedes sacrifice one bit to save the rest," Geoffrey said.

"Like a lizard giving up its tail," Otto said.

The segments reconnected in the water as they swam off.

"See ya later, aggregator," Otto said.

"*Perfect,* Dr. Inman." Maxim stamped his hand on the arm of his chair. "That is what we will call them! Aggregators!"

Geoffrey saw a band of white encrusting the shoreline below. "Is this . . . salt water?"

"Yes." Dimitri nodded.

"How *big* is Pandemonium?" Nell asked.

The others turned to Maxim.

"It goes for sixty miles in that direction," Maxim said, pointing.

"We used a high-powered laser surveyor to find out," Dimitri said. "We think that's how long the cavern is. It may be longer."

"Dear God," Reiner said.

Nell noticed a battery of light beams that penetrated the lake below the surface. "Hey!" She pushed herself away from the glass and pointed at the spiral staircase in the far corner of the room. "Can we go downstairs? Is there another window down there?"

Otto looked up and saw another phalanx of light beams above, which illuminated a pair of cables that seemed to span the lake toward the island. "Can we go *upstairs*?"

"Can we go into Pandemonium?" Katsuyuki asked.

"It's not a good idea right now," Maxim replied, with a deep laugh.

"Papa!" A peal of laughter like a fanfare announced a small girl crowned with tousled golden hair as she bolted into the conservatory, charging past the scientists.

Maxim swiveled as he saw her coming and absorbed the blow as she launched into his lap. The big man grunted and hugged her. "Hello, Sasha! Everyone: let me introduce my daughter."

"Hello to all of you scientists!" She waved. "Did you see the cherry puffs? And the Legopedes? Ha!" Sasha contorted in a snaking motion sticking her tongue out.

Maxim grinned indulgently as she shook hands with each of his guests. "Sasha has names for everything in Pandemonium," he explained. "Some of them are pretty good."

Sasha clasped Nell's hand. "Nice to meet you. What's your name?"

"I'm Nell, Sasha. And this is my husband, Geoffrey."

Maxim extinguished the lights in Pandemonium. "I think that is all for tonight."

The others groaned in protest.

"I am sorry. But it takes huge amount of energy to keep burning these lights," said Maxim. "Tomorrow, you shall begin cataloging and categorizing the animals of Pandemonium. In addition to being a functioning city, I envision Pobedograd as a working museum and laboratory, where scientists can study and preserve its natural wonders for all time. But tonight, please enjoy any of our three riverfront nightclubs where, if you choose to gamble, you'll find each of you has a thousand dollars credit. We will cut you off before you lose too much! There are three wonderful restaurants, too. Cars are waiting in front of the palace to take you to your accommodations. Please enjoy! But don't stay out too late. We will pick you up at nine A.M. tomorrow morning to start work."

10:35 P.M.

Several limousines were waiting for them in front of the golden palace.

As Otto climbed into one of the cars, he called Nell and Geoffrey. "We'll be meeting at Volya later. That's a restaurant, if you're interested!"

"Sounds good!" Nell said. "Maybe we'll meet you there."

The cars shuttled them back to Sector Six, where

the city lights sparkled in the permanent night. Along the riverfront they passed nightclubs spilling raucous partiers into the street and a rooftop establishment their drivers recommended for first-class service, atmosphere, food, and even some civilized gambling. Geoffrey and Nell noticed the blue neon sign that read VOLYA on the side of the building, but they requested they be taken to their accommodations first.

At the west end, they passed a row of newly refurbished apartments. The last one turned out to be their "bridal cottage." The ornate polished brownstone was located closest to the waterfall and seemed to have been carved out of the living rock of the cave's west wall.

The driver of their car pulled their luggage from the trunk and then hauled it upstairs from the street. He opened the front door with a plastic key card and showed them into their luxury apartment. Inside the door was a swank art nouveau entry. Upstairs the driver showed them a living room with plush white carpets and floor-to-ceiling windows overlooking the city.

On the far side, a gray leather couch U'd around a glass coffee table mounted on a fossil ammonite. A gas-fueled fire flickered in a fireplace faced with rock bearing foot-long trilobites. The floor-to-ceiling picture window framed the luminous blue waterfall cascading down the western wall. Lit candles and fresh-cut flowers decorated the suite.

The driver showed them to their bedroom to the right and deposited their luggage. The walls of the high-ceilinged room were paneled with slabs of rock embedded with crinoid fossils like lotus flowers in an Egyptian frieze. The gleaming bed was spread with copper-colored silk and banked high with gold silk pillows. Tucked deep into one of the pillows was a box of chocolate truffles. On top of the polished stone headboard was a magnum of champagne on ice surrounded by tropical flowers. In one lonely crystal vase on the headboard stood the pink rose Geoffrey had picked for Nell in front of Brick Dorm at Woods Hole, a whole world ago.

Nell and Geoffrey both offered the man a tip, but he refused graciously and handed them a card with a number to call for assistance or room service. He informed them that the refrigerator in the kitchen downstairs was fully stocked.

Nell saw the phone beside the bed. "Can we call out?"

"Oh, no." The man shook his head, gesturing around them. "Too deep."

It was only after the driver closed the door downstairs that they squeezed each other in disbelief and totally geeked out.

11:22 P.M.

Nell rested her head on his chest, gazing out the window at the blue cascade. They both lay sprawled in the silken sheets, sunk deep into the Swedish mattress. "A completely new world," she said.

"Even more complex than Henders Island," he said.

"If not as old."

"Much bigger, though."

"But not as dangerous," she said, stretching luxuriously. "I love it!"

"Species that evolved in subterranean conditions could never compete aboveground," Geoffrey confirmed. "So there's no risk of them taking over, I should think."

"It's the opposite of Henders Island: an alien ecosystem that is fragile instead of deadly."

"Most are," he reminded her. "We need to remember that, honey." He squeezed her arm gently. "Henders Island was the exception, not the rule."

"You're right. I know. This is definitely helping me get over my post–Henders Island stress disorder, I think."

"Good."

"Hey, I'm hungry. Let's go to that restaurant."

"Yeah?"

"And gamble the night away." She grinned, eyes wide.

"Good Lord! All right . . ."

11:58 P.M.

Maxim sat on a large crescent-shaped black leather couch in the dark before the wedge-shaped windows of his penthouse. From the top floor of the Star Tower, he presided over the city as the construction crews worked around the clock below. And he waited.

The magnificent lighting fixture carved into the cavern's ceiling glowed like a glass nebula poured into the shape of a five-pointed star. Its five opalescent points flickered like lightning in clouds or a gigantic burned-out fluorescent bulb on the verge of igniting. He was waiting for the dawn.

Sasha burst into the room, startling him as she leaped over the back of the couch onto the cushion beside him. "What are you looking at, Papa?" she asked in English. His precocious daughter spoke Russian, English, and French perfectly.

She was a genius, like her father and grandfather, he realized, with some wariness. "Go to sleep, child! You should be in bed. It's almost midnight!"

"It's never night here," Sasha said. "And it's never day, either, Papa."

"Tomorrow, it will be," he said.

His daughter frowned under her mop of blond hair and squinted at him skeptically. "Where's Alexei?" she asked.

"Your brother will be here, very soon."

"Papa?"

"Yes?"

"Thanks for kicking the guards out of the palace. I don't like them. They look at me funny."

"Who?"

"All of them."

"Have they ever done anything to you, *malishka*?"

"No. But I do not like their guns!"

"They're here to protect you. But from now on, they will stay in front of the palace. They will still have to use bathrooms, though. OK?"

"OK, Papa. Papa?"

"Yes?"

"They won't hurt anybody, will they?"

"Who?"

"The guards. I mean, they won't . . . The scientists will be all right, won't they?"

"Of course, *malishka*."

"Promise?"

"Yes."

"Good!"

"Why do you ask?"

"I just miss the other ones. They were nice."

"I told you, Sasha, they had to leave. They had to go back home. That's all."

"OK."

"Now, *bedtime*!" he roared comically with a monster growl as he waved his arms.

She hugged her mountainous father around the neck and kissed him on his furry cheek before jumping away and running toward the tram dock on the far side of the penthouse. "*Bonsoir*, Papa!"

Her voice receded around the central column of natural stone that supported the Star Tower. When he heard the motors engage, he knew that she had made it to the tram car and was on her way back to the palace. The tram rode a cable from the Star Tower in the center of the city to a private passageway through the north wall of Sector One. Stalin had escape routes from all his escape routes. He had anticipated every means of egress.

Maxim sipped a tumbler of Scotch and water, leaning back on the curving leather couch, tortured by the waiting. Then, at last, like an explosion, the phone rang, and he snagged it like a panther. "What's happening?"

"Sorry, Max," came Galia's voice. It was the only voice that always told him the truth, no matter how dangerous. It seemed grim now, already. "The men you sent to start the power plant . . . are dead. Including Klaus Reiner."

Maxim exhaled, deflating on the couch.

"Thirteen men, Maxim. That's twenty-two so far, in Sector Four alone. Five more in the rest of the city . . ."

"They are *sabotaging me, Galia*!" Maxim bellowed.

"The team was attacked, Maxim! We don't know by what, but it wasn't men and it wasn't sabotage. The workers are demanding to be let go of their contracts. They say they've seen ghosts. They say Sector Four is haunted. They refuse to go in there again!"

"Chush' sobach'ya!" Maxim cursed. "Double their bonuses, Galia."

"It won't work this time."

"If they discover I'm here," Maxim yelled, "they will cut off our power, Galia! It could happen at any time. We must get the power plant *online*!"

"Maxim!" Galia cried, and paused. "I understand. But we need those scientists to tell us what is happening in Sector Four right now or we may never get the power turned on," he implored. "You have to tell them the truth. You have to tell them why they're really here!"

"It's too soon," Maxim said, gazing through the window. "Maybe it's a breach. From Pandemonium . . ."

"You know what has happened," Galia reproached him.

"They did this to me! The fucking KGB!"

"No! You brought this on yourself."

Maxim scoffed. "They set me up!"

Galia sighed. "If they did, you fell for it. You must face it now, my friend! I have more bad news. Your dearest friend, Akiva—"

"What?" Maxim roared, jolting upright and holding the phone like a gun to his head. "No! . . ."

"Akiva was killed yesterday. Shot down in the streets of Majorca. He and his son, Visali."

Maxim fell back as though shot through the heart. "I told him to come here," he sobbed, clenching his teeth.

"This is their reply to you. Don't you see?"

"They can go to *hell*!"

"You can't bargain with them. They have your son, Maxim! *They have Alexei.* He will be next!"

Maxim's seventeen-year-old son had disappeared eleven days ago while hiking in the Himalayas. Russian newspapers had quoted anonymous officials who speculated that Maxim Dragolovich had many enemies, and if he wanted to see his son again, he should turn himself in and face justice in Russia. Though it had been delivered by television and newsprint, it was not a subtle ransom note. His friend Akiva had published Maxim's "response" to them in his own newspaper last week, quoting Maxim's declaration that Russia would reap what it had sown if his son was not returned to him unharmed.

"Maxim," Galia coaxed.

"No one can leave," Maxim whispered. "Guard every entrance. Send this message, through one of Akiva's newspapers," he growled quietly like a dormant volcano, alarming Galia now. "If they touch my son, vengeance for their fifty million murders will rise up across Russia and swallow them all. No one, and nothing, will be spared."

"Chief, I can't—"

"Tell them!"

"Boss . . ."

"Tell them to check their fucking mail!"

MARCH 17

3:32 P.M. PACIFIC STANDARD TIME

Four hendros and three humans watched the news with the volume muted.

On the seventy-two-inch screen in Hender's living room, a red chyron flashed in the lower corner: KREMLIN FIRE! Onscreen a fire blazed out of control over the white façade of a stately building by the banks of the Moskva River. Black smoke and red flames poured from hundreds of windows as cameras in helicopters panned the scene.

Kuzu pointed. "Fire on building," he grumbled.

"Building on fire," Andy Beasley corrected absently.

"Huh?" Kuzu recoiled. He didn't like English; it was stupidly inflexible.

"Yes," the other sels said between mouthfuls of popcorn, correcting Kuzu. "Building on fire."

Kuzu pursed his lips, his bristling fur flushing purple.

"Turn it up," Joe said.

A hendro snagged the remote with one hand and raised the volume:

". . . the iconic building, one of eighteen in the Kremlin complex, now seems to be a total loss."

"I must say, it seems almost impossible that such a building could perish."

"Do you believe foul play was involved in this, Dr. Aaronson?"

"Who can say, but a building as important to the operation of the Russian state—well, it's simply inconceivable that in this day and age such a structure could be totally destroyed by fire. At the very least, it's a grave embarrassment for the Russian government. I think we simply must allow the possibility of some kind of deliberate action."

"Do you suspect terrorists might be involved?"

"As I said, I don't think we can rule anything out at this time."

"Thank you, sir. Noted Kremlinologist and author, Dr. Mitchell Aaronson. We now move to our Moscow correspondent, Amy Schuster. Amy?"

"Wow," muttered Andy. "That sucks!"

"Yeah," Bo grumbled, frowning.

Officially, the isolated base that was the hendros' undisclosed location had been out of use for decades. In fact, it had steadily hosted top secret research programs right up to the present day. Visited daily by unlogged flights ferrying unlisted employees to and from Las Vegas, this dry lake bed in the Nevada highlands was encircled by high-tech surveillance devices that could detect approaches and departures of any living thing larger than a rabbit for miles around. Almost inaccessible due to its geography alone, this godforsaken spot was centered in a sunbroiled wasteland larger than Connecticut. Moreover, "Area 51," as it was designated, had been credited with too many tall tales for anyone to believe the hendros were here, which made it the perfect place to hide them.

One of the base's giant hangars had served as home for the sels before their large habitat was erected near an airstrip along the northern edge of the lake bed. The stadium-sized Mylar tent they now lived in was inflated with cooled air and resembled a Jiffy Pop popcorn package. To ufologists who spied it through telescopes sizzling on the desert flat it looked like the mother ship itself, which military intelligence had concluded would evoke the most advantageously hysterical response. Those who worked there dubbed it "the Zoo"—some because of their disdain for its inhabitants and some because of their respect for them.

"Hey! Call Hender so we can start the movie," Bo said.

Joe nodded and reached for the intercom.

3:34 P.M.

The 1st Darkness

Clouds came before the waves came, 142,221,201 years ago. The waves tore one of the nine petals of our land, which I will call Henderica for humans, into the poison sea. Only songs speak for those lost sels, written down in the Books long after they were all gone.

Read from tablets copied from poems based on legends, sung, remembered, written, and repeated through a dozen darknesses, our history is now stored in tunnels deep in the sinking fragment of our world. The Books are there, but no one can retrieve them for a hundred years, since the humans dropped their bomb.

It was my job, passed down from forever, to copy each chain of pages before they crumbled. It took me 3,000 years. And I remember every word.

Hender read over the first entry of his book, making corrections with three hands clicking the keyboard simultaneously on his MacBook Pro. He could speak and write more than two hundred sel languages, most of which were now long dead. Yet, after mastering all those archaic languages, in all their quirks and mutations, English was still a daunting challenge for him.

Sels were solitary souls. They usually had children when they were tens of thousands of years old, so language had become a tool more for thinking than for communicating. For the last seventeen thousand years, Hender had been the only interlocutor among them, as each spoke a different language. They had paid him a yearly tribute in case they needed him to translate some rare interaction or dispute between them. At times, one of them had found an ancient artifact with writing that they had brought to him to translate.

To humans, Hender spoke English shockingly well after only six months. He was, the humans quickly realized, a linguistic savant. He seemed to have learned some French, a little Italian, German, and even Russian and Japanese during this same time. He continuously taught the other sels English, since they had decided they needed a common language, something they had never had before, in order to communicate with humans and each other in their new and disturbing circumstances.

Hender signed his entry *Shenuday Shueenair.* It was the nearest phonetic spelling of his short name. He didn't mind being called Hender, as Andy had named him. He liked it, actually. And he didn't mind being referred to as *he* or *she* or *hendro,* either. Humans used all those names, and many others, to refer to the sels, even though sels were hermaphrodites. He had suggested that humans use *sel,* which was simple enough to say and ancient enough to have a connection to the languages of all five sels, each of whom was the last of an ancient tribe.

Hender was used to many names that meant the same thing. When the *things* that words named were changed, however, they became lies, he realized now. If a sel lied to another on Henders Island, it could mean instant death. Lies were murder in the world he came from. All this had been troubling him lately.

Hender scanned the crude imitation of his treno tree around him that was made of concrete, rebar, and gunite. Under the Mylar sky, humans had re-created five scaled-down treno trees like the ones they had lived in on Henders Island. The sels were bewildered with gratitude by the strange gesture. But they were beginning to wonder whether humans had liberated them or imprisoned them, instead. They were not allowed to leave, though the humans kept telling them it was for their own good and that it was temporary—a concept that was difficult for them to understand, especially as the days marched by.

A beam of sun swept through the oculus of blue sky in the center of the silver dome. The gold shaft of light poured through Hender's window over the translucent fur on the back of four of his hands that framed fossils he had collected from his island, which he had laid out on his desk next to his computer. Nell, Geoffrey, and Andy had helped him rescue the fossils while they were escaping from the island. Illuminated by the sun, the fragments of Henders Island were "museum-quality replicas" of the originals, Andy told him. The humans were keeping the "real ones" for study. The ones they returned to him seemed exactly the same, but they were made of something else. They were like food made of stone, or stones made of food. Everything in his world was being replaced with something else that humans called by the same name.

Most of the sels' possessions had never been returned to them. Andy, who was the first person they had met on Henders Island and who was now one of their full-time companions, explained to Hender that their things were "pilfered" somewhere along their journey from Henders Island and that some had been sold for huge prices on the "black market" and on online auction sites before the "authorities" were able to stop it.

The voice of Joe, one of the two navy officers assigned to the sels, buzzed through Hender's intercom. *"It's showtime in three minutes, Hender!"*

Hender closed his MacBook. "OK, Joe." He descended from his room, his six hands doubling as feet. His legs rolled like a pianist's hand down the winding stairs until he emerged into a replica of a B-29 fuselage—a little larger than the real one that had pierced his tree house over half a century ago on Henders Island. The others were waiting for him.

Hender scanned the magazine pages and product packages he had stuck to his walls and ceiling, on which he had plastered the garbage he had collected on his beach while studying humans from afar, to remind him of his home. He felt disoriented, his arms reaching out like buttresses to steady himself.

"Come on, Hender!" Bo sat with the other sels on his long red sofa in front of Hender's giant HDTV.

Andy and Joe fussed at a kitchen counter behind the sofa. "Popcorn's done!" Joe announced, taking a large bowl out of the microwave. "What did Steven Spielberg call the shark in *Jaws?*"

"Bruce," said Bo from the sofa.

"Damn, too easy." Joe regretted wasting his turn. Joe and Bo were pop-culture trivia rivals who were locked in perpetual combat. They had lots of time on their hands in the "Hendro-Dome," as they called it, after being indefinitely assigned to this duty ever since contact with the sels on Oahu. In addition to their other duties, they had become emergency handymen and assistants, as well as security, keeping people out and, perhaps, the hendros in. With the desolation and heavy security around the base, their duty wasn't terribly pressing. The sels had no desire to leave their air-conditioned dome to cross the simmering desert, and nobody could possibly reach them here.

After the sels' intense objections, supervising officials had agreed not to subject them to a rotating staff. Hender had explained to the humans that sels needed to meet and know each person individually and that they were intimidated by groups and by strangers. Moreover, the sels were not used to having people leave them. *Ever*. Until death, that is, which was a very rare and traumatic event in their experience.

Though they were largely independent and non-social, they valued the few individuals in each other's presence to an extreme degree. The absence of Nell and Geoffrey while on their honeymoon had been explained to them many times, but still it filled them with dread that they could be gone for two whole weeks.

Andy served them a platter of barbecued spiger brochettes that he had cooked in a George Foreman Grill. "Eat up! We've only got a few hundred pounds of frozen spiger steaks left, so savor the flavor."

Hender smelled the roasted spiger meat with a melancholy pleasure. This meat had been made available to the sels to brighten their mood on special occasions, carved from three spigers killed, sawed to pieces, and dipped in vats of liquid nitrogen before being transported off the island only hours before its destruction. Airlifted to the freezers on board the USS *Philippines Sea,* where most euthanized specimens had been taken for later study, a ton of the meat had found its way into the larders of their kitchen at the base.

Hender smiled at the humans' gesture. They did not realize that, except for Kuzu, sels rarely ate spigers, any more than humans ate lions. But it was a nice gesture—and an exotic delicacy that all the sels enjoyed. Their usual diet now consisted of shrimp, mantis shrimp, crab, peanut butter, cashews, chickpeas, pill bugs, chicken liver, and a continually broadening diet of copper-rich human foods that were deemed safe through testing and tasting by the sels.

"Did you read chapter nine after the changes Nell and Geoffrey made, Hender?" Andy asked. The three humans had been working with him on a *Field Guide to Henders Island.*

"Not yet, Andy," Hender said, standing still in the doorway.

"We don't understand how disk-ants became nants, symbiants, and arthropalms. A little more on that would be awesome."

"Symbiants aren't disk-ants." Hender sighed, his fur color dimming. The "symbiants" that Andy referred to were, in fact, microscopic relatives of disk-ants, the latter being a particularly terrible species from Henders Island. But the symbiants were quite different, beneficial organisms that for millions of years had lived in the fur of sels and other large animals like an exterior immune system fending off the island's myriad predators. This immune system had been stripped away when they were showered with salt water at Pearl Harbor. As a result of losing their symbiants, the sels now required high-powered showerheads to cleanse their fine spinelike fur and exfoliate their skin. And still they suffered side effects, including fatigue and depression as their skin's ability to absorb oxygen was compromised.

"Why don't we start the movie?" Hender said.

"Finally!" said Bo from the couch.

Joe presented a giant bowl of popcorn, and as fifteen sel hands simultaneously grabbed handfuls with their two opposable thumbs, the popcorn disappeared except for one popped kernel. Andy ate the last kernel and Joe got out a few more packages of popcorn.

"Go ahead, Bo," Joe said.

Bo started the movie as Joe put more popcorn in the microwave.

"Come on, Hender," Andy said from the couch.

Hender nodded, watching the titles appear on the wide television screen. The 3-D HDTV was like a window into a different world. The sels, with their eyes that filtered polarized light, did not need to wear the glasses the humans wore to see the images in three dimensions:

A Zero-Leeds Production
ALMOST EARTH:
HENDERS ISLAND

A clip of Cynthea Leeds, the tall, statuesque neurotic who had produced the reality show that first encountered Henders Island, appeared: she was speaking frantically on the prow of the show's ship, the *Trident*. She was one of those who surrounded the sels in a human shield as the navy's ships closed in. Hender remembered the event more vividly than the video on the screen and resented how the video changed things from his memory, chopping up moments and rearranging them. Words appeared on the screen as Cynthea shouted them: "These are the amazing people of Henders Island!" She had said those words, he remembered, on that day. It was fascinating to him the way humans substituted movies for truth and made things happen after they had really happened.

"Here it comes," piccoloed Durlee-Ettle Mai, who was the green and yellow hendro. Her name sounded like a clarinet riff. The humans called her Mai, and she insisted on being called *she*. Mai giggled on the sofa. It was a sound like an alternating buzz and whistle that communicated her amusement across species very effectively. She hunched over the coffee table as she took apart a wristwatch and put it back together while watching the documentary with her other eye and snacking on honey-dipped spiger nuggets rolled in pepper.

Kuzu buzzed deeply. "Your move, Bo." The large sel's fur coat was splattered black, purple, and gold, like a Rorschach test over his muscular frame. Three chessboards were on the coffee table in front of him. Kuzu enjoyed chess, having learned it from Bo, and now carried on three games: with Hender, an inattentive Andy, and the humiliated Bo, who wished he had never taught the sel how to play the game.

Hender watched the TV screen:

"*. . . here are the people of Henders Island. They were saved because humanity recognized one of its own that day, despite a barrier of species that seemed to separate us forever. This is not only the story of how we rescued them. It is the story of how they may have rescued us.*"

"Oh, brother!" Andy blew a raspberry. He pushed back his long kinky blond hair, and laughed. Cynthea's cutthroat showmanship had grated on him from the beginning when they were filming *SeaLife*. She had singled out Andy to be the show's comic relief from the start, which he found out after viewing episodes since returning from the expedition. He resented her greatly for this. On the other hand, since the reality show had been the reason he reached Henders Island, Andy was grateful to her for casting him. The hendros had become the only family he had, and the only people on Earth who really cared about him, other than Nell and Geoffrey.

The hendros clapped wildly, a human custom Andy regretted they had adopted, since only five sels had thirty hands to contribute to every ovation.

Footage of Kuzu, taken a few months ago by Zero Monroe, one of *SeaLife*'s cameramen, now appeared on the large screen. Kuzu's full name appeared in a chyron:

KUZU-THROPINSALUSUVORRATI-
GROPANINTHIZKOLEVOLIZIM-STAL

The camera zoomed in on the hulking sel.

"His full name is too long to pronounce: his occupation was hunter and inventor on Henders Island. He crafted traps and weapons used by sels on Henders Island for millions of years to catch their food. . . . He is Kuzu, and he is over ninety thousand years old. Brilliant and brooding, this brawny sel spends his time learning English along with his fellow sels so that they can persuade humans, someday, to set his people free."

"There ya go!" Bo said. "Not bad, eh, Kuzu?" Bo tried to give Kuzu a high five.

But the large sel looked intently at the screen with one eye as he reached out with two unfolding arms. "Bishop takes pawn, checkmate; queen takes knight." Kuzu exchanged pieces on Andy's and Bo's chessboards. He loved playing Andy, who lost with great melodrama.

"Oh, *crap*!" Andy shriveled. "I'm *never* playing this *goddamned game* again!"

Kuzu honked with pleasure.

"Oh, jeez," Bo groaned as his own predicament dawned on him.

Hender scooped three handfuls of Joe's fresh batch of popcorn and finally strode forward. "Red pawn takes knight," he piped softly. "Check, Kuzu."

He climbed over the back of the sofa to sit between Kuzu and Andy.

Kuzu's fur flashed yellow sparks as he twisted his head and glared at Hender's pawn standing where his knight had stood. Kuzu won at chess 80 percent of the time—except when he played Hender, who won 50 percent of the time. Hender hated chess 100 percent of the time.

Nid pointed at the TV screen as Cynthea's voice intoned: *"This is Moodaydle Nid, the orange sel, a musician. He recently released a single of a traditional melody passed down through his family for six million years."*

They heard a clip of the song that sounded like echoes of wind.

"Nid is 16,511 years old."

"Wooo-hooo!" Nid warbled.

The hendros applauded to see Plesh, the artist among them, wave paintbrushes at the camera, followed by Mai, the doctor, who worked in the lab with the human scientists testing foods for sel allergies.

"All of the sels have become rich overnight with deals to use their images for product endorsements around the world. But they have few ways to spend their newfound wealth, since they cannot leave the place where they have been hidden."

"When leave, Andy?" Mai said irritably.

"When go?" Nid pressed.

"*Why not now?*" Kuzu growled, vibrating the air as he moved his queen. "Checkmate, Bo."

"Damn!" Bo said, stung by Kuzu's board-traversing gambit. "I never should have taught you this fricking game, Kuzu. You *like* it too much."

As the documentary came to a close, Cynthea urged viewers to write to their representatives and petition for the sels' freedom. Then she pitched a sel plush toy, some of the proceeds from which would go to a nonprofit organization called Save the Sels.

"Oh, my God," Andy choked. "Sell the sels is more like it!"

Hender reached out to move his rook: "Checkmate, Kuzu," he said softly.

The birdsong doorbell Hender had purchased from the Hammacher Schlemmer catalog trilled a lark call as Kuzu glared at Hender.

Joe and Bo opened the door a crack. After a moment, Bo called, "Uh, some folks are here with some news for us. Should I let them in?"

"How many?" Hender asked.

"Two."

Hender looked at the others and, after some haggling, waved them in.

A man and a woman in dark-blue suits entered the room, visibly trying to suppress their bulging eyes as they saw the sels. The usual condescending friendliness they got from visiting officials was noticeably absent this time, however. These visitors cut straight to the point.

"I'm Special Agent Jane Wright, and this is Special Agent Mike Kalajian, of the Central Intelligence Agency," said a sharp-eyed, short-haired woman. "It's a great honor to meet you—the greatest honor in my life, actually. I think I speak for Agent Kalajian, as well. We have very good news for you," Agent Wright said.

"Well," Agent Kalajian said. "Hender, you have officially been invited on a trip to London. And we really think that it's a good idea for you to go."

The two agents stared in wonder at the five hendros. For their part, the hendros gave them credit for not fainting, which a lot of humans did upon meeting them.

"Go on," Hender said.

Agent Wright reeled to hear him answer her. She gulped and continued. "You will be representing all of the sels, Hender."

"Representing?" Hender asked. "What does that word mean again?"

"Um," said Jane Wright, glancing at her partner. "It means that you will be able to speak for the other sels to human leaders, who speak for humans."

"Hender will speak for us?" Nid said.

"Yes," Agent Kalajian said.

"How?" Mai complained, confused.

"Hate represent!" Kuzu rumbled, crossing four arms, his fur flushing purple, red, and yellow streaks.

The large brow wedges over Hender's eyes, which were actually ears, pointed down between his eyes, an expression Andy recognized as distress.

"Why not all go?" Kuzu's voice exploded in the room, taking everyone aback.

Jane looked at her colleague in fear, then at Andy. "Humans are being careful, Kuzu," she said softly.

"Will you come with me, Andy?" Hender asked.

"Well—sure, Hender." Andy looked at the agents. "Right?"

Agent Kalajian looked at his partner and nodded. "Absolutely!"

"Why not *us*?" Kuzu's rumbling baritone rattled their bones. Four of the large sel's formidable arms opened twelve feet as he spread twenty fingers in the air.

Jane Wright somehow squeezed out her reply: "Because humans are afraid of you."

"One step at a time," Andy said calmly. "OK, Kuzu?"

The warrior sel regarded Andy with one eye as he glared at Hender with his other. "They think we are spigers, Shueenair,"

"We have to show we are not," Hender said.

The two sels shared a challenging look that ended in a stalemate.

The other sels asked Hender questions in their own languages mixed with English, and Hender summoned them now to the nose of the fake B-29 to confer.

"They're going stir-crazy here, man!" Andy whispered.

"Yeah," Joe agreed.

"So is this some kind of audition now?" Andy glared at the government agents. "Hender is to be displayed to everybody so they can decide whether or not to grant him some rights?"

"In a way." Agent Wright nodded frankly. "It's not an inaccurate way to put it."

"Well, that's pretty shitty," Bo said, frowning.

"Look," Andy said, "Bo, Joe, and I pulled off a miracle getting them out of their homes at the same time to watch this video. The only reason they did it was that we promised them there would be news about getting out of here."

"We know," Agent Kalajian said. "And that's why we came to deliver the news in person. They will get to leave, eventually, I think. But we think it's a good idea for Hender to start breaking the ice first."

"They're developing obsessive behavioral routines like animals in a zoo," Andy said. He pointed at the coffee table. "Mai's taken apart and put together that wristwatch seven times. Kuzu and Nid are hooked on chess and video games. We have to do something or they'll go nuts in here. Not to mention the rest of us."

"I know, Dr. Beasley," Jane Wright said. "We've been instructed to let you know that Geoffrey also obtained permission to give the sels unrestricted Internet access, if that's any consolation."

Andy's eyes popped wide. Then he pumped his fist, jumping up. "Awesome! Why didn't you say so?"

Agent Wright looked at her partner, puzzled.

"Oh, my God, you can't imagine how big that is! They ask me questions night and day, and if I get an answer wrong . . . Google and Wikipedia are going to save my life! Someone else can be wrong now. Hey, you guys!" Andy shouted. "You have Internet!"

The sels flamed colors as they heard the news at the nose of the fake aircraft. None of them even waved good-bye as they rowed six, four, or two of their legs out the door in single file and shot over the rope bridges slung between their tree houses so that they could access the Internet through their personal computers. Even Hender hurried upstairs to his office without comment, as if he were racing the others.

The humans looked at one another. Bo shook his head. "They'll thank us later."

"I wonder what they'll think of porn," Joe said.

"Yuck," said Jane Wright. "Yikes."

"Yep." Andy nodded. "That's probably what they'll think . . . ."

"We'll never see them again now," Bo said.

"OK, guys," Kalajian said. "There's another reason why we're here."

"It's better that the hendros aren't here to hear it," Jane Wright said.

"Nell and Geoffrey Binswanger never made it to their honeymoon destination. They haven't been seen or heard from since the night before they missed their flight."

"What?" cried Andy.

"What happened to them?" asked Bo.

"We don't know."

"I thought you were watching them!" Joe said.

"They gave the Secret Service the slip at Woods Hole." Wright shrugged.

"We heard from Nell the night before their trip to Hawaii," Andy said. "She talked to all of us! Nothing seemed wrong . . . ."

The two agents looked at each other. "That was after we lost contact," Kalajian said.

"There's more," Wright said. "Two other scientists who were on Henders Island before it was sterilized have also been reported missing in the last few days. We're not sure if there is a connection."

"Please treat that information as confidential," Kalajian said.

"And let us know immediately if you hear from either of them," said Wright.

"What are you going to do?" Andy asked.

The agents shared a dark look.

"We're monitoring the situation," Wright said. "We'll let you know as soon as we find anything out."

"They might just be dodging everyone for their honeymoon," Agent Kalajian said. "We just have to wait until we have more information."

Andy glanced at Bo and Joe.

"Some diplomatic advisors will contact you about Hender's trip to London," Wright said.

"Yeah," Andy said. "Thank you."

"Can he be ready to leave in two days?"

"Huh?" Andy asked.

"Cowboy up, Andy," Bo said.

"Yeah, you've got to do it, man," Joe said. "So we can all get the hell out of here."

Andy sighed. "I'll talk to Hender."

"Good. Here's my information." Wright handed Andy her card. "Let us know if you need anything or hear anything from Nell or Geoffrey."

"OK, will do," Bo said.

The agents left, and they all looked at one another. "Why would the CIA—?" began Bo.

"I know," Joe said. "It's weird. What the hell's going on?"

7:13 P.M.

Hender Google Image–searched the word *crowd*. He rolled the scroll wheel of his mouse with his middle finger through image after image of human hordes filling stadiums, city squares, fields, malls, freeways, subways, streets, beaches, and even a desert where thousands of humans watched a towering structure shaped like a human burning.

Hender had met hundreds of people in the last months, but only one or two at a time, and each only briefly, never getting to know any of them well.

The hendros considered every person, whether hendro or human, to be *waku*. The word meant "jungle" in a language so ancient that all the sels still used it. The word also referred to any relationship with an intelligent being, which, like a jungle, was full of danger before it was carefully mapped. Meeting more than one person at a time was a harrowing concept. Large groups were simply unthinkable to them.

As Hender scanned images of outdoor concerts, political rallies, religious pilgrimages, and sporting events teeming with masses of humanity, he strained to control his breathing and cool the colors burning in his rising fur.

MARCH 18

8:17 A.M. MAXIM TIME

Nell closed her eyes as she felt the three glorious showerheads douse her body with jets of hot water. The last two days had been spent peering through Stalin's window into Pandemonium. She was in heaven peering into hell, where each discovery was a revelation.

As she watched the suds spiral down her leg now, her soapy eyes and groggy sense memory suddenly formed the image of a Henders Island disk-ant emerging from the drain next to her big toe. She screamed and jumped two feet against the shower stall as the vision rattled her nervous system like an electric shock.

She shook, naked in the corner of the stall, as she looked down dumbly at the drain, wiping the soap from her eyes as nothing but foam circled the drain. Geoffrey opened the shower door and rushed in, embracing her with his clothes on under the water. He looked at the drain where she pointed and saw nothing, stroking her head. "It's OK!"

She tried to breathe. "I thought I saw a disk-ant. Coming out of the drain!" She sobbed.

"It's OK!" he repeated. "We're not on Henders Island. It's OK!"

She nodded. "OK," she breathed, feeling calmer in his arms. "Damn. I'm sorry!"

"No problem . . ."

"Geoffrey?"

"Yes?"

"We still need to make a call outside to let people know where we are."

"You're right. I'll remind Maxim first thing. It's been easy to forget the past couple days."

"I know, but people will start to worry. We need to do it right away."

"I'll take care of it."

"Thanks." She hugged him, closing her eyes.

8:59 A.M.

Maxim himself waited for them this morning at the curb in front of their honeymoon cottage. He greeted them beside two limousines, one black and one white, offering Nell a bouquet of a dozen fresh roses.

"Nice!" She smelled them. "They're fresh?"

"Grown right here in Pobedograd," Maxim said.

"Really? I'll set them on the stoop for later. Thank you!"

Geoffrey noticed that the air was quite smoggy this morning, having accumulated the exhaust of hundreds of vehicles and generators. Despite Maxim's guarantee that the power plant would be on, the city was no brighter than the "night" before. "Another day in paradise, eh?" Geoffrey said, gently ribbing the tycoon as he waved the air.

"Power will soon be on," Maxim grumbled, rankled by the dig. But he soon recovered his joviality as he reached into his jacket. "I neglected to give you your payments. For you, my dear, and for you." Maxim handed them both envelopes.

"Not *really* two million dollars?" Nell said.

"Each." Maxim nodded. "As promised."

"Wow!" Geoffrey whispered.

"Thank you, Maxim," Nell said.

"It's nothing. Especially after taxes."

"Maxim, before I forget again," Geoffrey said. "We need to make calls outside to let people know we're OK."

"Of course!" Maxim laughed. "With so much excitement, it simply slipped my mind. You may both make as many calls as you like back at the conservatory. But I need both of you this morning, if you don't mind a slight delay. I was hoping you will come with me to activate the power plant, Geoffrey. As well as bringing day to night, and starting the city's much-needed ventilation system, the power plant will charge a whole fleet of electric cars, which will finally clear up our smog problem."

Maxim's daughter, Sasha, jumped out of the white limo dressed all in white, matching her cheerful dog. "I hope so, Papa!" she shouted, running toward him. She jumped up to kiss his beard as he bent down. "Because this place *stinks*! Don't you think so, Nell?"

"I hope you don't mind," Maxim said. "But I told Sasha she could go along with you on a tour of the farm. I would very much appreciate your opinion, as a botanist, Nell."

Nell nodded, glancing at Geoffrey. "Sounds interesting!"

"Don't worry about Geoffrey. We will get him back to Hell's Window by lunchtime," Maxim said. "Then you may make as many phone calls as you wish."

"Promise?" Nell said.

"Yes."

Sasha tugged her arm. "Come on, Nell!"

Nell kissed Geoffrey as they parted.

9:03 A.M.

Nell peered into the back of the white limousine, which was upholstered in lavender leather and rhinestones. Wearing a matching collar, Sasha's happy, snow-white Samoyed barked noisily in the doorway, batting the air with his tail.

"Shush, Ivan!" Sasha shouted. "Don't worry, he's a big baby." She nudged the dog aside and waved Nell into the oval of plush seats.

Nell climbed into Sasha's world as the chauffeur shut the door behind them. She admired the little girl's glacier-blue eyes, which were wide and expectant, exerting an irresistible gravity much like her father's. The white limo charged west as Maxim's black limo pulled a U-turn and headed east along the riverfront.

9:05 A.M.

The friendly dog sat between Nell and the formidable czarina, who inserted a CD of pop songs sung by kids, clicking ahead to her favorite track. "I think you'll like the garden, Nell!" she yelled over the sugary music blaring out of the speakers. "Botanists study plants, right?"

"Yes," Nell said. "Right."

The young girl had a confident and more capable air than her ten years implied. If she was bored giving another tour to a guest, she was handling it quite graciously. There was something else in her demeanor, though, too, Nell thought: a sadness or a maturity, Nell couldn't quite decide which. Either way, Nell was surprised to find herself liking this little princess.

"You'll love Dennis," Sasha said to Nell. "He reminds me of a pear. But he's really nice! I call him 'Veggie-Man.' Not because he grows vegetables but because he *is* a vegetable!" She giggled. "He's *made* of vegetables, I think. Right, Ivan?"

Ivan barked once and smiled next to her, hanging a sly tongue out to one side and panting breath that smelled like smoked salmon.

As the limousine cruised around a curve in the road, they headed north along the cavern's western wall. On the right they passed spoked avenues that glimpsed the giant tower in the city's center and the bronze colossi at the end of each street. "That's the Star Tower, down Lenin Boulevard," Sasha said, pointing up one of the streets. "My dad lives there, on the top floor."

Nell spotted Lenin himself pointing like a setter at the base of the tower.

"That's him," Sasha noted, nodding. "There's a *ton* of statues of him, all over the place. My dad melted a lot of them down to make other statues."

"How long have you been here, Sasha?"

"Two *months*!" groaned the girl, squirming with agony. Nell seemed to have struck a nerve. "But we won't be here forever." Sasha sighed with melodramatic worldliness. "Right?"

"Right." Nell nodded, smiling. "Where's your mom?"

"Dead." Sasha shrugged. "She died when I was a baby. I get bounced around a lot."

"Do you get outside sometimes?"

"No." Sasha seemed to have a lot to say but frowned instead. "I hope Papa turns the power on. How do you like his city? It's haunted, you know."

They came to a gate in the western wall with a steel door marked SEKTOP 5. Sasha rolled down the window, confessing to her in a whisper: "I hate the guards! But they hate me, too, so it's OK." She reached out an arm and flipped them off. The guards opened the door and dryly waved them through.

They entered another gigantic natural cave. The void stretched left and right through the rock, nearly as large as the main cavern, in a long oval that sloped north. The floor of the chamber was covered by rows of tall three-tiered benches, some of which were draped with plastic sheets to make pitched greenhouses. Some carried hydroponic plant beds, but the vast majority carried dark rows of huge glass flasks. Only a small portion of these benches was illuminated with grow lights, spreading to the north and south of a large circular clearing where the limo now stopped.

At the edge of the clearing sat a dilapidated Soviet-era LiAZ bus the size of a Winnebago whose rubber tires were cracked and peeling off its wheels. Nell saw that it was illuminated and occupied. The derelict bus had apparently been retrofitted into some kind of field lab.

As she climbed out of the white limo with Sasha, Nell observed an enormous lighting fixture hanging from the ceiling. Four hundred feet above them, it gleamed like a crystalline structure, an aurora borealis shifting inside the dense lattice of beams.

A friendly-looking man in a lab coat that stretched over his potbelly greeted them now as he stepped out of the big Soviet bus. "Sasha and Ivan!" he called. He gave an awkward wave as he stooped to greet the excited Samoyed that nearly knocked him over.

"Papa wants you to show Nell your garden, Dennis," Sasha said. "She's a botanist!"

"Yes! Thank you, Sasha. I've been expecting you, Doctor. Welcome." He wiped his dog-licked hand on his coat and reached it out to her. "Dennis Appleton. I'm the man in charge of the farm. It's not a garden, Sasha," he chided.

Sasha smirked. "Whatever."

Nell clasped his damp hand, smiling. "Nice to meet you. I'm Nell Duckworth—um, Binswanger," she corrected herself. "Sorry—just got married. Old habit."

"Will you keep both names?"

"Well . . ." She shrugged. "We're thinking about it."

Dennis nodded. "Changing names is a conundrum I'm glad men don't usually have to face." He shook her hand graciously. "But a rose is a rose."

"Thank you," Nell said.

"You're welcome. I am Pobedograd's agricultural engineer. I graduated from the University of Nebraska and was born in Iowa, believe it or not. I never thought I'd end up here." Dennis Appleton laughed good-naturedly. "It's nice to have some company from home. Well, it's not much of a farm right now, I must admit. We're waiting for the power to be turned on." Dennis pointed a baby-carrot-shaped finger straight up. "When the lights are turned on, we should be able to harvest oxygen and enough food to feed the entire city. Let me show you what we've been able to do so far with the limited energy that we have. To the south are all of our greenhouses. We have rows and rows of tomatoes, herbs, greens, onions, shallots, and lots of flowers, which are all quite edible, too, by the way."

"I guess this is where my roses came from?" Nell asked.

"Yes! Maxim insists we grow our own," Dennis said. "Please, come with me."

He led them to the north edge of the broad clearing. Nell, Sasha, and Ivan followed him between two lit rows of plant beds. "Fresh flowers, carrots, tomatoes, onions, potatoes, strawberries, and herbs are already being grown here for the restaurants and guests. The rest of our vegetables are still brought in, but that will change soon."

On one side, the plant beds were replaced by glass vats on benches stacked three high. The jars must have held two hundred gallons each and were half-filled with bubbling green liquid like horror-movie lab props.

"Growing algae?" Nell guessed.

"Yes. Exactly! It's a very good source of nutrients and oxygen. All of these jars and growing benches are original to the city. Apparently, they were preparing to cultivate algae here back in the

1950s, which was a pretty advanced notion back then."

Dennis smiled, and Nell noticed that his teeth looked like white corn kernels. His pale turnip-colored face was crowned by corn silk–blond hair around a pale melonlike bald spot. Nell giggled involuntarily, unable to shake Sasha's characterization of him as the "Veggie-Man."

"We're also growing areca palms, reed palms, English ivy, peace lilies, various ferns, and weeping figs," he said.

"Why those species?" Nell wondered.

"They're low light and have high rates of photosynthesis. And they're all good air purifiers that counteract off-gassed chemicals in the city's atmosphere. We will plant them throughout the city when the power comes on."

"This sector does seem a little fresher than the others." Nell breathed appreciatively. "How many scientists have come here?"

"Well," Dennis Appleton looked a little reticent. "I have a small crew of horticulturists. But you and the others are some of the first outside scientists Maxim has invited. The rest of us had to agree to live here for the rest of our lives just for the chance to work here."

"No! You're kidding?" Nell said.

"No, no, I'm not kidding, sort of," Dennis said, blushing like a russet potato. "We have a good deal here, actually. When they finally get the power on, it will be much better. You guys weren't brought in with the same security agreements the rest of us had to sign off on, were you?"

"I don't think so," Nell said.

"That's because Papa needs your help, Nell," Sasha said. The young girl nodded ominously.

"We're just consultants," Nell confirmed. "Maxim said we could leave in a few weeks, at most. But you *are* kidding, right?"

"Oh, of course, I'm *exaggerating*. He lets us out sometimes." Dennis chuckled.

Nell noted a strange intensity in Sasha's eyes as they reached the end of the illuminated rows. They proceeded past the edge of the light into the darkness. High up on the west wall of the cavern, a multicolored starburst like a cracked windshield stretching hundreds of feet. Its branching fractures glowed colors like a batik scratched in black wax. "Is this chamber next to—?" Nell began.

"Pandemonium?" Appleton asked. "Yes. At least along the upper half of the western wall. I know what you're thinking: that there must be a breach." He pointed a dainty finger at the glowing cracks. "Apparently the hyphae are penetrating through microscopic cracks and fissures in the rocks."

"What are *hyphae*?" Sasha asked.

"The main part of a fungus's body," Nell said, concerned.

"Oh."

"Kind of like the roots and stems," Appleton said.

"Whatever." Sasha shrugged.

"However, as far as we can tell," Dennis said, "that wall's at least eighty feet thick, even at its narrowest point. And no fungus was present here before we brought in a sample from Pandemonium. Speaking of . . ." Nell saw that the shelves to each side carried beds of glowing fungus: fleshy, lacy rinds like tripe ridged with mushroom caps glowed in six colors that were separated into squares. "We grew all of this from one sample scooped from Pandemonium," Dennis said. "It divided itself by color as it spread to each bed."

"Rainbowfire," Nell murmured, delighted to see it up close.

"That's a good name, Nell," Sasha said.

Dennis nodded. "Very apt."

"What does it feed on?" Nell asked.

"In each bed there is a different kind of organic matter. Each color of fungus seems to colonize a different fertilizer. Either that or different nutrients cause them to change color the way hydrangeas turn blue or pink depending on the pH of the soil." Dennis shrugged. "We're not sure."

"So why is it growing in the cracks on the wall, then? It must be eating something organic, right?"

"Yes. We think that a cave-in in Pandemonium may have impacted that wall long ago and caused those fractures. Over many millennia, organic material infiltrated through the cracks. The pattern on the wall did not show up until we brought samples of—'rainbowfire,' as you call it—from Pandemonium into the farm. So we think the spores, which fly everywhere, must have taken root in the nutrients inside the cracks."

"Yuck!" Sasha covered her mouth. "Spores are flying everywhere?" She choked, coughing.

Nell laughed. "Don't worry, honey. If it hasn't killed everyone already, it's probably OK."

Ivan lifted his leg, and a lower flat of orange rainbowfire turned blue where the canine squirted a yellow stream of urine.

Sasha squealed with laughter. "Ivan!"

"It's OK," Dennis said. "That's actually quite interesting."

He and Nell both stooped to look at the color change.

Sasha rolled her eyes. "You guys are *weird*!"

"We kind of hope the spores will spread to other sectors," Dennis said. "At least they would provide some light there. Until the power is turned on, of course."

"Where did you get the sample of rainbowfire?" Nell asked.

"We scraped it from the landing of the gondola."

"Gondola? The gondola that goes across Pandemonium?" Nell turned to him, grinning excitedly.

"Yes."

"Have you ridden on it?" Nell asked, an eager spark igniting in her eyes. "Does it go to the island in the middle of the lake?"

"No, I haven't ridden it." Dennis wiped his glasses. "I really don't think it's still working."

"There's a tram that goes from Papa's tower to the palace," Sasha bragged. "That's what I use to visit him. It's really fun, Nell!"

"That does sound like fun, Sasha. So, how do you combat mildew down here?" Nell asked.

"*Grrr!* If you two are going to talk about *mildew,* can you give me some carrots to feed Ivan, Dennis?"

"OK, Sasha," Dennis said. "Come this way."

He led them back to the carrot beds.

8:58 A.M.

Maxim shouted: "*Sector Three, Boris!*" and rapped on the tinted glass behind him.

"Khorosho!" replied his driver.

Maxim tapped his knees, facing Geoffrey. "How is your honeymoon, my friend?"

Geoffrey grinned. "Fantastic. You're a madman, Maxim. I can't wait to get back to Hell's Window. Nell thinks there must be another window downstairs, *underwater*?"

Maxim laughed. "I promise you there is much more to see. In due time! This morning we are on verge of starting Pobedograd's heart. Without power, this city will die. When plant is on, day will replace night. We will no longer be dependent on surface for power. I appreciate your company this morning, Geoffrey. Tell me. You were on Henders Island, I believe?"

"Yes." Geoffrey nodded. "I survived Henders Island."

"What would you say was best strategy for surviving there, eh?"

Geoffrey shrugged at the random question. "Leaving," he said.

Maxim raised a wry eyebrow. "What else?"

Geoffrey found the question odd, but not unusual. "Well, hendros got around by killing large animals to draw predators into feeding frenzies. It seemed to work. It saved my life once, in fact."

"Ah. Very interesting. A metaphor for civilization, I think."

"Perhaps. Also, many animals on the island sprayed warning pheromones when they detected salt water, an adaptation to life on a shrinking landmass surrounded by ocean. Salt water acts like a tranquilizer on the copper-based metabolism of Henders organisms, paralyzing and killing them, since they could not hypo-osmoregulate. Spraying salt water on the organisms caused them to spray a warning pheromone, which turned out to be a rather effective repellent."

Maxim nodded with great interest. "That is very strange."

"No. Not really. Crows rile up ants to get them to attack and spray formic acid on their feathers, which is an effective repellent for parasites."

"Really?"

"I watched one crow sit for ten minutes with its wings extended over an ant trail." Geoffrey laughed. "Crows are smart."

Maxim grinned. "I see I got the right man for this job." He laughed and slapped Geoffrey's knee. "I like you, Geoffrey. You have passion for your work. That is good!"

They passed work details along the streets, and Geoffrey noticed all the men stopped and stared with blank eyes at the limo as it quickly passed. The expression on the men's faces chilled Geoffrey as the car turned onto the street they had taken when they first arrived, which proceeded north at the eastern edge of the city.

"Pobedograd will be paradise," Maxim said in a forceful voice that was one part dreamer and one part gangster, Geoffrey thought as the mogul continued. "We have natural hot springs, riverfront penthouses, casinos, nightclubs, theaters, spas, swimming pools, art galleries—we even have a unique ecosystem for scientists to study, eh, Geoffrey? Timeshares and property are available to all those who help make my dream come true. You are certainly among those. In case of worldwide catastrophe—which seems more likely every day—such refuge will be valuable. Don't you agree? The population of this city is a cross section of best world has to offer. People of every profession are represented." Maxim considered, and grinned. "Except for politicians. They can go to hell, instead. There is no room for them here. We don't need their laws."

"Many of the world's biggest crooks could afford a ticket to Pobedograd, I guess," Geoffrey speculated. "And probably wouldn't mind a place like this to hide from the law."

Maxim frowned. "Do not worry, Geoffrey. I am businessman. I must have principles to stay in business, unlike politicians. And you should know that heroes are often branded criminals by villains."

"And you are the judge of who is who here. Am I right?"

"Yes. Here, I am."

"I see. Well, in the event of disaster, it's good to know there's a place we can come to live in a dictatorship," Geoffrey mused, challenging the oligarch with a wry look.

Maxim seemed to enjoy his friendly jab. "As I said, Geoffrey, I'm a *benevolent* dictator. Laissez-faire!"

"Yes, but money wouldn't be worth much down here in the event of a global catastrophe," Geoffrey said, probing.

"You are right, again. I accept only *value* as payment, in goods or services, along with lifelong commitment to Pobedograd's security. When we are self-sufficient, people will be able to survive here for generations without ever leaving."

Geoffrey concealed his surprise at the statement. "Well. I would hope leaving is always an option."

"Of course." Maxim grinned. "So do I. But why would anyone want to, I wonder?"

"They justified the Iron Curtain that way, didn't they?"

"A curtain can be a shield, too, Geoffrey, when it's made of iron."

They stopped before the northern gate marked SECTOR TWO. Guards activated the steel door, and the heavy barrier rolled aside.

The limo entered the desolate medieval labyrinth of Sector Two, which seemed to be a grid of streets around square blocks of two-story buildings with crude façades carved into bands of limestone and salt. A hundred yards in, they turned right, and sixty feet later, they stopped before another steel door painted with tall red letters: SEKTOP 3. Two guards rose from their chairs and activated the door.

They passed through a short tunnel that opened on a three-story building on the north side of a short street that dead-ended 150 feet straight ahead at another guarded door that read SEKTOP 4 in giant letters.

A black SUV idled in front of the building as their limo pulled up and stopped behind it. Geoffrey noticed that the windows in the second story of the building were lit. Over the entrance, an entablature read:

ОБСЕРВАТОРИА ИМЕНИ ЛЕНИНА

No Latin lettering this time. According to Geoffrey's faint memory of the Cyrillic alphabet, the first word might be "observatory." But that made no sense under a mountain. "What is this building?" he asked.

"Hospital," Maxim said as he rolled down the window.

Geoffrey smelled the gasoline exhaust waft through the crack; this place was worse than Hong Kong, he thought.

Maxim pushed his head out of the window and yelled, *"Let's go!"*

The black Suburban abruptly pulled out in front of them.

The steel door at the end of the street slid open as two guards stepped aside.

Maxim rolled up the window as his armored limo took off behind the SUV, and Geoffrey noticed the sentries quickly close the gate behind them as they accelerated.

9:07 A.M.

"Ivan hasn't eaten anything but carrots today, but he needs to go doody. I'm taking him for a walk down Compost Alley."

"OK! That's Ivan's personal dog run," Dennis explained. "We compost everything here, of course."

"When you're done talking about *irrigation*, we'll be over there." Sasha rolled her eyes. She motioned Ivan to follow her and disappeared with the dog under a shelf of algae flasks.

"Wow," Nell said. "She's something."

"She certainly is." Dennis nodded and looked at his watch. He frowned, sighing.

"What's the matter?"

"The initiation of our power supply seems to

have been postponed. Once again . . . . I had hoped the lights would be on for our tour today," he apologized. "Most of the projects we are working on will require a strong light source, of course. . . ." Dennis looked up at the dimly lit lighting structure hanging from the high ceiling. "They must be having more trouble."

"*Nell!*" Sasha called. "*Come here!*" Her voice echoed across the rows.

Dennis shrugged. "You might as well go with her. There's not much more to see at the moment."

"Well, it was nice meeting you, Dennis. See you around." Nell shook his hand and ducked under the lower bench of algae jugs. "Where are you?" she called from the next row over.

"Over here!" Sasha's voice sang like an opera singer.

"OK." Nell stooped and crawled under the lower shelf of another row of bottles.

"One more!" Sasha shouted, and Nell climbed under the next row. As she came out from under, Sasha kissed her on the forehead and Ivan licked her face. "Ha ha ha!"

Nell laughed as she climbed to her feet and dusted off. "There you are!"

"Come on!" Sasha ran, leading Ivan and Nell with a lavender flashlight she had taken out of her purse and pointed north into the dark.

"Where are we going?" Nell asked.

"A secret passage!"

"Where does it lead?"

"The palace, of course! Crummy old Stalin wanted to have lots of food for himself, so he built a secret passage to the farm!"

"Oh. Wow!"

Sasha and Ivan took Nell through the dark, led more by Ivan's nose than by Sasha's flashlight, and they finally arrived at the northwest corner of Sector Five. The young girl, her white clothes now smudged with dirt like her snow-white dog, opened a small panel in the rock face, revealing a hatch wheel. She jumped up as she cranked it down, twice. A door popped out, disguised to look like part of the natural wall. Sasha and Ivan wedged it open to a tunnel, which coursed to the left and right.

"The palace is this way!" Sasha whispered as Ivan took off to the right.

Nell followed her through the door, and Sasha pulled it closed. Then they ran after Ivan.

"Where does the other direction go?" Nell asked.

"To your honeymoon suite!" Sasha laughed. "That's where Stalin took his sweeties!" she shouted over her shoulder. "I think it goes to the railroad in Sector Seven, too. So he could make his getaway back to Moscow!"

Nell tried to catch up with the precocious princess through the barrel-vaulted corridor that headed steeply uphill. "Have you gone down there?" Nell panted. "Back the other way?"

"No," Sasha said. "I tried to go down there once, but I saw a ghost! A *really scary ghost*. Ivan tried to bite it."

Nell sweated in the warm, stuffy air as she followed Sasha up the stifling passage, with a few glances over her shoulder at the deep dark behind them.

They finally reached a wall with a hatch, which

opened into a room with a red velvet curtain similar to the one in the conservatory, but only a third of the size.

Sasha closed the door behind them, breathing dramatically. "I'm pooped!" she whispered.

Nell saw a glass-tubed spiral stairway in the far left corner, like the one in the conservatory. Most of this room appeared to be used for storage, with crates of canned and dry foods and stacks of bottled water.

"Can you open these curtains?" Nell said.

"Yes. You're going to love it, Nell!" Sasha ran to the right side of the curtain and jumped up, giving a golden sash a full pull downward and laughing in delight as Nell ran to look through the opening crack.

Nell exhaled and could barely catch her breath as the ten-foot-wide window revealed an underwater world brimming with luminous creatures darting, swirling, and bobbing on the other side of the glass.

Sasha overheard shouts nearby and she ran down a hallway to the right of the window. Ivan ran ahead of her and sniffed at the hatch at the end of the hallway, which was slightly open. Sasha peered through at the palace foyer and shushed Ivan, perking her ear at the opening. She overheard the guards talking there:

"Find Nell Binswanger. Take her to Sector Three immediately, but don't alarm her," said a voice in Russian. "Tell her that her husband requested her presence."

"Yes, sir!"

Sasha didn't breathe as she slowly pulled the door closed and turned the crank wheel to lock it.

Then she ran back to Nell with Ivan. "Stay here, Nell!" she whispered as she ran past her and up the spiral stairway with Ivan.

Nell hardly heard her, gaping through the portal at a sea that might have existed 300 million years ago, but no: almost every underwater species she saw was new, unprecedented, revolutionary. Horned chitons slid over the glass, hunted by fluorescent sea spiders as thousands of ammonites jetted in schools chasing blue squids. A star-shaped giant opened its monstrous arms on the bottom of the lake.

Sasha raised an eye over the edge of the second floor, peering into the empty conservatory. A buffet table had been laid out with breakfast to the right of the great window. Ivan whimpered as he smelled sausages and bacon. But the rest of the scientists were not there.

9:32 A.M.

As Nell's eyes adjusted to the darkness, she could see the giant starfish on the lake bottom open and a plume of particles erupt from its center. Out of nowhere, glowing schools of neon blue bullet-shaped squids appeared, flashing red light as they fed on the plume of food.

9:33 A.M.

Sasha let Ivan follow her into the conservatory, running to her father's desk. Ivan sat, restrained, in front of the breakfast buffet in whimpering reverence as Sasha scanned the bank of video monitors on the wall behind her father's chair. She spotted the one showing the lab in Sector Three. All the scientists she had met two days ago were there except for Nell and Geoffrey. "No," she whispered, and tears streaked her crumpled face. She could see that they were arguing and angry. The men in front of them were guards, and they were pointing their guns at the scientists.

"Sasha!" came a loud voice.

She jumped, and Ivan barked, leaving his place before the altar of food to stand by her side.

Galia pushed in the hatch to the conservatory and glared at her. "Have you seen Nell Binswanger?" he asked.

"Who?"

"Dr. Binswanger?"

"Oh. Yeah. Her." Sasha shrugged. "Why?"

"She needs to catch a shuttle, right away."

Sasha turned away from him. "She's in the farm. Talking about fertilizer, I think." She went to the banquet table and loaded food onto a plate. "Ivan's hungry," she said. She put another plate down on top of the thick pile of food. Then she looked casually at the cadaverous associate of her father, smirking. "And screw you, Galia, by the way."

Galia blushed, adding a little color to his gray face. "Sasha—"

"Toodles!" She waved and Ivan barked goodbye as they both ran and jumped down the spiral stairs.

9:35 A.M.

Nell turned to exclaim in awe as Sasha motioned silence to her and ran past her.

Adrenaline tightened Nell's body as she saw the terrified expression on Sasha's face.

"Come on!" the girl whispered, motioning Nell to follow her as she hurried down the hallway toward the foyer. "I know where to hide you!"

"What's going on?" Nell whispered.

Someone's feet started pounding down the spiral stairs behind them. "Galia!" Sasha whispered.

Halfway down the hall, Sasha pushed on a narrow panel of inlaid stone on the left side and it slid inward, revealing a tight passage. Ivan wiggled through first, and Sasha motioned Nell to follow him. Nell squeezed into the crevice, and Sasha slipped in behind her.

9:36 A.M.

Galia jumped down the spiral stairs two at a time and entered the storage room. He noticed the curtains on the window had been opened, and he touched the fog that was still on the glass from Nell's breath.

Galia pounced down the corridor, following a hunch—which led nowhere. He grimaced. Where could she have gone this time?

9:37 A.M.

"You seem to be in a hurry," Geoffrey said.

"We are in a cave, Geoffrey," Maxim explained calmly as the two cars raced through the void. "Much of our power and all of our oxygen comes from the surface, but we cannot rely on those sources forever. Exhaust from gasoline-powered generators and vehicles is filling Pobedograd with smog, as you have noticed. We need clean energy. We are now *one button* away from creating it. And not a moment too soon." Maxim smiled.

Geoffrey nodded. "Well, what kind of power are we talking about? Nuclear?"

"No! Pobedograd's engineers built a dry steam geothermal generator for the city, but never activated it. The largest dry steam project in whole world is located north of San Francisco," Maxim said. "It was built in 1960 and is most successful alternative energy project in world history. Pobedograd's dry steam plant was built two years before that, and it is completely self-sustaining."

"Ah, well done," Geoffrey said. "How does it work?"

"Soviet engineers discovered a huge reservoir of steam in sandstone layer under Mount Kazar which is heated by six-mile-wide lake of magma," Maxim said. "Using this geothermal energy the dry steam power plant they designed will feed electricity and heat to the city and, at the same time, pump water from river to injection wells, replenishing steam reservoir indefinitely."

"Incredible!"

"All we must do now, Geoffrey, is detonate caps at the bottom of the well. The steam that rises will drive the power plant's turbines. Only *one button* needs to be pushed to set the plant into perpetual motion." Maxim's casual smile failed to mask his apparent frustration.

As he spoke, the car squealed right and hurtled down a narrow road behind the speeding SUV. A long dark warehouse streamed by them on their right. On the left, a steep plane of rock like the polished side of a great pyramid sloped from the edge of the road.

"Well, what are you waiting for?" Geoffrey asked.

The warehouse ended, and a rock wall rimmed the road on the right straight up to the roof, 450 feet above them.

"I mean, if that's all it takes to turn the power on," Geoffrey said, "why haven't you done it already?"

They continued a few hundred yards before they finally stopped at the foot of stairs carved straight up the gleaming slope of rock on the left side of the road.

"We are not waiting any longer, Geoffrey," Maxim said. "We're here. The power plant is up these stairs. Are you ready?"

Five men got out of the SUV in front of them, pointing machine guns in every direction. "Come on, move fast," Maxim said. "As fast as you ever did on Henders Island!"

Maxim opened the door. Geoffrey got out behind him and noticed that the air was at least fifteen degrees warmer in this part of the city.

"What?" Geoffrey did a double take as the five guards ran up the stairway with Maxim lunging three steps at a time behind them. Alarmed by their frantic haste, Geoffrey sprang up the stairs after them, wondering why they were in such a hurry.

He looked around intently, but there did not seem to be any imminent danger. Perhaps they were afraid of some invisible gas, Geoffrey hypothesized, though the warm air seemed fresh compared to the other sectors.

As Geoffrey pumped his legs up the stone steps behind the others, he was reminded of the pyramid in Palenque he had climbed as a boy. He was impressed by the stamina of the billionaire in front of him as his own lungs bellowed and sweat poured down his face. Then Geoffrey saw a large building that resembled the bridge of a battleship at the top of the polished slope to their left. Dim light swirled in the long windows of the building, which he guessed must be the power plant Maxim had referred to.

Half the distance to the building, the stairs ended at a small terrace. The guards' flashlights illuminated a heavy ten-foot-wide steel hatch to their right. It was set in a rock face that reached ninety feet up to the cavern's ceiling, which was bearded with stalactites.

"OK," whispered Maxim to his men, reaching his arms out to them. He had bounded up the stairs without a pause for nearly a hundred yards. He was a powerhouse of a man, Geoffrey realized as he caught his breath. Maxim pressed close, addressing them like a quarterback in a huddle. "Geoffrey, I want you to identify any animals you see."

Geoffrey nodded. "OK."

"Be ready for anything!" Maxim stressed.

A guard who was even bigger than Maxim, a giant, opened the huge door. The other four went in first. Maxim pushed Geoffrey in as the giant guard shoved the heavy door closed behind them.

They stood on a metal landing inside a tall cylinder faceted with purple crystals. The crystals shimmered on the walls hundreds of feet into the dark above them like a gigantic geode. The air felt sauna hot and dry inside the vertical chamber.

A phalanx of seven massive aluminum pipes rose from the bottomless shadow below. Fifty feet above, the enormous steam culverts elbowed together into a tunnel cut through the glittering wall of the crystal chimney.

A short flight of steel stairs before them joined a catwalk that ringed the column of dry steam pipes. On the far side, Geoffrey could see a stairway zigzagging from the catwalk up the wall to a corridor on the left, which presumably led to the power plant. The men's flashlights illuminated electrical conduits running up the side of the huge steam ducts. Thick cords had been patched into the conduits, joining a cable plugged into a heavy-duty yellow switch that lay on the catwalk connected to a car battery between the reaching arms of two men who were obviously dead.

Geoffrey's eyes followed the guard's jerking flashlights over the catwalk and saw that at least a dozen corpses were strewn across it. The empty drape of their clothing outlined skeletons. Their hands were chalk drawings of bone dust. They wore the same bulletproof vests and black uniforms worn by Maxim's other guards, who jabbed their weapons everywhere now as they peered into the shadows.

"When did those men die?" Geoffrey asked.

Maxim raised a finger and whispered back. "Three nights ago."

Geoffrey's blood froze. "What is going on?"

Maxim yelled, "*Now!* Punch that fucking button!"

One of the guards darted down the metal stairs

and tripped over one of the bodies lying there, falling noisily onto the catwalk that circled the steam ducts. The racket echoed up and down the shaft around them.

Geoffrey glanced up into the towering well above. Like pixie dust shaken off the walls, a phosphorescent storm swirled and descended like a living funnel cloud gathering. He hit his host's broad arm and pointed. "Look!"

"What is it?" Maxim said.

"I don't know. But it's coming!"

Maxim roared, *"Hurry!"*

Geoffrey saw the horde of glowing green creatures swirling down the shaft flare brighter at the sound of Maxim's voice. A distinctive hum grew, a wheezing, ringing buzz that paralyzed him; it was a sound he could never forget. He tried to convince himself he could only be imagining it.

The guard untangled himself from an electrical cable looped around his foot as the other guards yelled at him.

They all heard the screaming swarm descending.

"Keep going!" Maxim shouted.

The man dived for the switch on the catwalk below. On the other side of the switch, glowing creatures emerged from the hairy skull of one of the corpses and shot straight into the man's eyes and mouth.

The men above heard his gurgling scream as it was cut short.

Geoffrey recognized the milky flow pouring down the walls as tiny Frisbees launched out of it at the convulsing man on the catwalk and the man reached out his arms toward the detonator, his hands falling inches short.

"No!" Maxim yelled, and he started down the steps, but Geoffrey and his chief guard pulled him with enough strength to hold him back as the horde closed in. Two guards began opening the hatch behind them.

Geoffrey pushed Maxim through the hatch and leaped after him as the guards closed it behind them.

Even through the steel door, they could hear the wheezing drone that filled the well inside. The hulking guard stood with his back to the sealed hatch, talking through his walkie-talkie while directing the others to get Maxim back to the car.

"No!" Maxim shouted, and he dived at the door again as his four guards restrained him.

"You can't go in there, chief!" said the guard who stood against the hatch.

With his mind still scrambled by what he had just witnessed, Geoffrey thought he could see a strange luminescence behind the guard standing before the hatch. As he reasoned that it must be a trick of light, perhaps emanating from the guard's flashlight, a glowing replica of the door peeled away, arching over the guard. "Watch out!" Geoffrey shouted.

The guard looked up and screamed as a luminous creature wrapped around his back and shoulders like a cape.

"Get it off me!" the giant man wailed, trying to move, but the animal stuck to his back like taffy, gluing him against the door.

They all backed away and Maxim pointed at Geoffrey. "Tell me what it is, damn it!"

Geoffrey yelled, "I don't know!"

The screaming guard heaved back and forth, stuck

to the door as a white blob like the head of an enormous slug enveloped his face and its translucent flesh turned crimson.

The other guards opened fire with their machine guns, riddling the man's body until he crumpled forward, peeling away from the hatch. His back was cloaked by a glistening mass. Then suddenly, his headless torso rose and in place of his head was a pale, amorphous lump with huge black eyes. His arms reached toward them.

"Jesus—!" Geoffrey gasped.

The guards fired dozens of rounds at it, filling the cave with cacophonous echoes until the apparition finally fell again.

Geoffrey waved them off and crept forward to look at what was left.

"Tell me what it is!" Maxim shouted.

"It's got suction cups on the bottom," Geoffrey said, shaking his head, incredulous. "I think it's a freaking octopus. . . ." He looked at Maxim in astonishment.

"It's not from Henders Island?" Maxim asked.

Geoffrey looked at him. "What?"

"How did it do that to him?" asked one guard.

"It possessed him," answered another. "Like a devil!"

"It *is* the Devil," said another.

"Shut up, you idiots!" Maxim ordered. "Geoffrey?"

Geoffrey looked down at the squirming flesh that was ruptured by exit wounds on the man's back and limbs. The mollusk's mass had seemed to grab hold of the man's arms and legs like an external musculature and, with beaklike suction cups, vise-gripped his bones at the hips, knees, ankles, shoulders, elbows, and wrists. "It's using him like a puppet," Geoffrey muttered in awe.

The giant muscle contracted on the guard's back, and the dead man's arms and legs jerked into a crouching position before them as Geoffrey jumped back with the others. The mollusk's amorphous head looked at them with glistening black eyes, foaming red blood from its loose mouth.

"Look!" Another guard pointed at the wall beside them.

Three more ovals the size of men slid down the rock face toward them, blending into the rock as they moved.

"More!" Geoffrey said.

The distant sound of breaking glass echoed in the cavern.

The guards turned and bolted down the stairs toward the cars waiting below as Geoffrey pushed Maxim after them.

As they descended, Geoffrey saw a green swarm below flooding over the road toward the vehicles. Up the street, he could see it pouring like a firefall out of a window in the warehouse. He knew, as he looked at the cloud of creatures and heard their whining buzz, that nothing he had seen in Pandemonium glowed this particular shade of green. And there was nothing else that made this sound. Geoffrey heard slaps behind him on the stairs and glanced over his shoulder.

The ghostly octopus was actually using the guard's body to stumble and lunge down the stairs behind them now.

The green cloud of bugs on the road ahead split

about eighty yards to their right, one half flying up over the smooth slope toward the dimly lit windows of the power plant, the other heading straight for the cars below.

"What are *those*?" The guard in front of Maxim pointed at shimmering creatures springing in thirty-foot leaps ahead of the swarm rushing down the road.

"Rats," Geoffrey hissed, dumbfounded.

"They don't look like rats!" another guard said.

"*Henders* rats," Geoffrey muttered.

As they headed toward the bottom of the stairs, he realized the guards ahead of them would make it to the limo in time to avoid the wave of predators, but he and Maxim would not.

Maxim looked over his shoulder and saw the shambling ghost-octopus picking up speed as it perfected its method of locomoting, pulling itself forward with the guard's arms and using his torso like a gruesome sled as it accelerated down the stairs behind Geoffrey. Ten yards from the street, the man-puppet pounced and Maxim pushed Geoffrey down.

"Duck!" the Russian growled, and he crouched with Geoffrey against the stairs as the ghost sailed over them, shooting white tendrils from its head that stuck on the nearest guard's back like gooey ropes. The flying chimera reeled the tendrils in, soaring over their heads and into the guard's back, knocking him into the guard ahead.

All three rolled together down the stairs, landing in a balled heap beside Maxim's limo.

"Wait!" Maxim whispered. He held Geoffrey back, watching.

Maxim's men writhed below as the swarm arrived and struck into them on the street below.

"You said this worked on Henders Island," Maxim said. "You were right, my friend!"

Geoffrey watched as the screaming men were bombarded by the voracious wave of glowing creatures. The mollusk manipulating the headless guard peeled off from his body as it was attacked, and it shot thick goo-ropes through the strange locusts that descended upon it. Animals the size of giant rats launched down the road and dived into the pile. Columns of white bugs streamed down the road, *rolling* toward the writhing heap with wide, long legs like shock absorbers, and flung themselves into the frenzy like discuses.

Maxim waved. "Come on!"

Geoffrey vomited as he saw him jump to the left side of the stairs and slide down the smooth surface, braking with his feet. In another instant, Geoffrey was following him, his heart pounding like an engine. The feeding animals raised an unholy din as they feasted on the street zooming toward them.

Maxim hit the street by the limo with Geoffrey landing right behind him. They darted away from the slaughter, around the front of the car, and opened the door on the far side, jumping in and slamming the door behind them.

"Go, Boris!"

The driver gunned the limo backwards over the pile of bodies. Then they pealed down the street, looking through the rearview mirror as glowing bugs splattered on the rear window. Illuminated by the headlights, two bodies ensnarled in the glue-ropes were still stuck to the vehicle. The creatures that had been heading for the feeding frenzy now turned and chased them in the other direction as they dragged the men's corpses.

"Turn off the lights!" Geoffrey yelled. "And for God's sake, don't slow down!"

Maxim translated to Boris, who immediately complied.

The swarm chasing them only gathered. "Try to shake that off of us!" Geoffrey shouted. "We're leading them on!"

Maxim fired a translation in real time at Boris, who wheelbarrowed down the road in reverse, swerving from side to side as he tried to tear away the grisly lure.

The stampede followed them, thinning as clusters stopped to feed on cast-off pieces of their bait and the road kill crushed under their run-flat tires. As they approached the warehouse where they had issued, a flow of creatures came at them from the front as well, spilling over the skyroof, until they finally reached the source and passed under the shattered window through which the cataract of creatures had sprung.

"They're breeding in that warehouse," Geoffrey said. "These things look like . . . God damn it, *tell* me I'm imagining things, Maxim!"

"You are imagining things," Maxim repeated with shameful obedience.

Backing around the corner, the driver spun the limo, its tires chirping over the cobblestones, and he shifted into forward, accelerating down the final stretch.

"Have them close the hatch as soon as we get through," Geoffrey said.

Maxim looked dazed.

"Maxim!" Geoffrey shouted angrily.

"Get us through, Boris!" Maxim pushed a button on his phone. "I will call ahead."

"I need to see!" the driver shouted, switching on the headlights.

The road ahead was clear, but in the rearview mirror, Geoffrey saw that they were still dragging a stringer of body parts. A flying wedge of predators followed it. Farther back, a group of much larger animals appeared, moving over the others in giant leaps. "Get that off us!" Geoffrey screamed. "We're still dragging bait! Get it the fuck *off us*, Boris!"

The driver fishtailed the limo, and the rear tires finally tore away the sticky ropes. Geoffrey watched the horde descend on the train of carnage as it dropped behind them on the road. The limo squealed around the last corner and charged through the opened gate just as the guards were closing it.

Boris pulled the limo to a screeching stop in front of the hospital.

Miraculously, nothing appeared to have made it through the gate.

"Garage, Boris!" Maxim ordered, banging twice on the partition.

"Yes, boss."

The car flew around the corner of the hospital to the right onto a side road. They turned right again down a driveway to the building's basement. The driver pressed a remote attached to the visor, and a steel garage door opened. They drove in, and the driver closed the door behind them.

"What in the fucking fuck is going on?" Geoffrey yelled.

"Come with me, Geoffrey," Maxim said grimly, opening the door.

"OK, but you tell me! What the hell is happening!" Geoffrey knew he didn't want to know.

"*Please,*" Maxim said, stepping out.

Geoffrey climbed out tentatively as Boris ran up a stairway. Maxim followed, waving at Geoffrey to follow.

They mounted three flights of stairs to a hatch.

Waiting at the top of the stairs, Galia Sokolof greeted them and whispered in Maxim's ear.

"Please, Geoffrey." Maxim pointed to the hatch, his expression desolate but absolute. "In there, you will find answers. I need you to share everything that you know with your colleagues now. I'm sure you know how great the danger is and how urgent. I will join you, shortly."

Galia opened the steel door solemnly and invited Geoffrey in, with an unequivocal nod. Geoffrey noticed all the other scientists inside, terror contorting their faces. He went inside as Galia closed the steel door behind him.

10:07 A.M.

Geoffrey found himself in a brightly lit room with rows of lab counters crammed with scientific instruments both archaic and modern, microscopes and laptops, notepads and iPads, baby bottles and juice boxes. The entire right wall of the long room was dominated by a window. In front of the window stood Otto Inman, Katsuyuki Fujima, and Dimitri Lagunov. Two armed guards escorted Geoffrey into the room and positioned themselves against the wall opposite the window.

Otto turned around and saw Geoffrey first. "Oh, my God, dude," he moaned. The round face of the ponytailed scientist was ashen, his eyes hollow. "It *happened.*"

Geoffrey approached the window, which looked onto a rectangular room the size of a tennis court. Three illuminated chandeliers hung over explosions of green and purple splattered on the floor. On the other side of the glass Geoffrey saw a camera moving on a horizontal track that ran above the window. Apparently it could be slid from side to side and rotated up and down on a pivoting arm.

"Watch out!" Dimitri shouted as Katsuyuki rotated the camera down.

Dimitri stopped the camera just before it crashed into the glass.

Otto looked at Geoffrey with baleful, hollow eyes. "We're fucked," he said. "And that psycho isn't going to let us go."

"Please, please!" Dimitri said. "We need your help, Dr. Binswanger." He clasped Geoffrey's hand in his own ice-cold hands, which Geoffrey noticed were shaking.

Geoffrey stared back into his eyes and let go of his hands as he spoke words that only came out in a whisper. "How could you?"

"I am the one who requested your help, Dr. Binswanger. I never dreamed that we could actually get you, of course." His eyes apologized with sudden tears, though his face was blank. "Maxim is very persuasive."

"Tell me what is going on," Geoffrey demanded, closing his eyes.

Dimitri smiled weakly. "This is the maternity ward of Pobedograd." The scientist swept a thin hand across the window nervously. "Relatives could view their babies here after delivery—that was the idea. I decided to use it as an observation chamber."

"For what?" Geoffrey took a few more steps toward the window. On the floor inside the "maternity ward," he noted color splatters made up of thousands of tiny protruding fins. Each fin had three straight edges, and none was larger than a playing card. Together they formed three rosettes of petals tilting like solar panels to catch the light of three chandeliers above them. Each circle of geometric scales was tinted green in the center surrounded by rings of yellow and red and finally purple at the edges. "Oh, God," Geoffrey breathed, recognizing the growth's characteristics. As he moved closer, he saw a stream of fast-moving white bugs branching down the other side of the glass, rolling with disk-shaped bodies.

Otto nodded at him. "Disk-ants."

"From Henders Island," Katsuyuki said.

Geoffrey stumbled, dizzy as he leaned against a lab counter behind him. He saw the flying creatures looping through the air around the chandeliers inside the maternity ward. One landed on the window and tried to drill into the glass with its yellow abdomen. "Drill-worms," he sighed.

Katsuyuki nodded.

The dissolved remains of what looked like two people were sprawled on the left side of the maternity ward. Their outlines formed natural reeflike blooms of clover, purple hives, and budding Henders "trees." It was not a dream, a nightmare, or a posttraumatic flashback, Geoffrey realized. It was the last thing he wanted or ever believed he would see again.

A wave of nausea overcame him as he turned away, and the chill of shock spread over his body. He saw a five-gallon glass water container on the lab counter in front of him. Inside, Henders wasps, drill-worms, and resting disk-ants suddenly jumped and pressed against the glass at him. A steel ring was fixed to the mouth of the bottle on top. A length of glass tube reached up to another valve. Three extensions of retreating air locks had been added.

"We're trying to see what poison works on them," Dimitri explained. "So far we haven't found one. Please, Dr. Binswanger. Help us."

"You brought Henders organisms here." Geoffrey grabbed Dimitri by the shoulders. "Why?" His head was spinning as he broke out in a cold sweat and a molten rage simultaneously.

"Please, Doctor!" Dimitri said. "Are you feeling all right?"

Geoffrey looked at the armed guards in the room behind them, who were pointing their guns at them, and he lowered his head. "So," he said. "A WMD lab?"

"What?"

"Is that what this is? These species!" Geoffrey sneered. "Was Maxim hoping to sell them to the highest bidder?" he screamed. "Or was he planning to use them himself? Do you think this is like selling off plutonium or old missile parts? This isn't a dirty bomb! This isn't a suitcase nuke! This is the end of the world, you goddamned fool! It's ten times more dangerous than ten times the world's WMDs!"

"He's right," Otto said.

"Yes." Katsuyuki nodded.

"Help us!" Dimitri said. "We think that it breached this containment chamber."

"You think? I just got back from the power plant!" Geoffrey shouted. "This stuff just ate five men, and at least a dozen more only a few days ago! It breached the containment chamber, all right, and it's *breeding* in Sector Four!"

Dimitri bowed his head. "Forgive me."

"That's above my pay grade!"

Otto shook his head. "We're fucked."

9:19 A.M.

"Newspapers are confirming that Alexei has been kidnapped." Galia said coldly, "They are now saying that the kidnappers will cut off one hand unless you comply immediately with their ransom, Maxim."

Maxim combed his fingers through his long black hair, spreading it back from his widow's peak. The Russian magnate was strangely composed as he replied: "I will activate power plant. We will exterminate these pests. Tell those murderers they have seven days to release my son before what happened to Kremlin happens across all eleven time zones of former Soviet Union."

"Maxim!"

"They will use those seven days to try and bargain with me, so that they can locate and attack us. But they will be too late. We will be secure and impenetrable by then, Galia. No one can leave now." Maxim reached for the hatch to the lab. "Do what I ask or I will have you killed."

Galia's eyes teared as he no longer recognized his friend. "Do you not see what is happening to you?"

"Shut up!"

"You have become him!"

"Don't you ever—!" Maxim sputtered. "I do what I must do, Galia! They will kill Alexei anyway, even if they have not already. They are *liars,* Galia! They are *barbarians*! Never forget that! They will give in only if they are overpowered and defeated. That is Alexei's only chance! That is our only chance. Where is Nell Binswanger?"

"We have not been able to locate her."

"Find her now! And bring her here."

9:20 P.M.

Dimitri clutched Geoffrey's arm urgently. "Doctor, *please*," he said. "We have no wish to destroy the world. You *must* tell us how we can control them."

Geoffrey laughed tragically, glancing at Otto hopelessly. "They can't be *controlled*. Where did you get them? Why?"

"Maxim has access to exclusive dealers. . . ."

"The island was sterilized with a nuclear bomb," Geoffrey scoffed. "That should have been enough! Are there more?"

"No," Dimitri said. "Only one sample was available."

Otto shook his head, nauseated. "That's all it will take."

"Where did they come from?" Geoffrey pressed.

"I think I know," Katsuyuki said. "It may be why

I was invited here. A small colony of Henders organisms was recently discovered on an uninhabited island north of Japan." The scientist shook his head sorrowfully. "We don't know exactly how they got there but apparently some species from Henders Island had colonized the island. We thought that we eradicated them in time. But before authorities discovered the infestation, somebody must have collected some specimens."

"How?" Geoffrey asked.

"A crab fisher retrieved a sample," Dimitri said. "Two of his men died trying to collect it. All of this came from one sealed metal suitcase."

"Did they sterilize the island?" Geoffrey asked.

"Yes," Katsuyuki assured him. "I was on the team sent ashore to make sure. It caused an international incident, which you may remember. The Japanese government claimed they had used the island for war games: target practice."

"Oh, yeah," Otto said. "I remember seeing that on the news. Russia was super pissed off."

"How did you sterilize it?" Geoffrey asked.

"Poison gas and a bombardment of incendiary devices."

Geoffrey was only slightly reassured.

"It worked," Katsuyuki confirmed. "After the third try, that is. Don't worry, nothing will live on that island for a million years. Unfortunately, we didn't get there fast enough." Katsuyuki looked at Dimitri.

"These species use a variety of reproductive strategies," Dimitri said. He sounded like a scientist and not at all like a terrorist, Geoffrey thought cynically. "Some seem to have life cycles that allow cloned procreation at different stages of development. This and other reproductive processes seem to be why so many life-forms emerged from such a small sample."

"You still haven't said why," Geoffrey said. "Why did you bring them here? What kind of monster would say yes to jeopardizing the human race and every species of life on Earth as we know it?"

The hatch swung in and Maxim entered. He pushed the door closed behind him and turned to the scientists silently.

"Maxim, what have you done?" Geoffrey demanded. "Do you have any idea how dangerous these species are?"

"That is why you are here," Maxim said. "I want you to make that repellent you described."

"So that you can turn the power on down here?" Geoffrey asked. "If you pump perpetual heat, light, and humidity into this petri dish, you'll be feeding the hell that will end the human race and everything else on the face of the Earth!"

"The power plant must be activated before we seal off Sectors Three and Four," Maxim said. "When we have power, Dr. Binswanger, we will be able to fumigate those sectors with poison and eradicate these animals. Without independent power, we will be trapped down here in the dark. The city will die, and it will be only a matter of time before they escape to the surface and do everything that you claim. There is no choice. Tell me what you need, and I will provide it."

"Where's my wife?" Geoffrey said. "You promised me she could call outside."

"All of that's over now, Doctor," Maxim said. "Your wife will be joining you shortly. And you will stay here as long as it takes."

"Then it was all lies," Geoffrey said. "All of your promises."

"They can still be true, Geoffrey. But if you fail, we will die together here. That is a promise I cannot break."

"Why? Why did you do it? Tell me that at least!"

Maxim spoke to his armed men instead and left them.

Dimitri glanced at the armed guards and whispered. "Pobedograd is only one of a whole network of subterranean cities and bases that Stalin connected by underground railroads from Metro-Two."

"What's Metro-Two?" Otto asked.

"A famous Soviet subway system under Moscow that is not supposed to exist," Dimitri said.

"You mean the train tunnel in Sector Seven . . . goes all the way to Moscow?" Geoffrey asked, glancing at the others.

"Maybe," Dimitri said. "Theoretically. And from there, it may go to cities all across Eastern Europe. During Stalin's reign, every satellite of the Soviet Union had underground shelters."

"What in God's name for?" Geoffrey asked.

"He was a deeply paranoid man," Dimitri said. "I think he may have actually wanted the world to end. So that he could move into this city where he could finally be in complete control."

Geoffrey looked at Dimitri. "If even *one* Henders organism reaches the surface—"

"I know," said Dimitri.

"—through a train tunnel or a storm drain or a sewer or a ventilation shaft or a freaking crack in the sidewalk of East Berlin," moaned Otto.

"If it happens, we are done, we're dinner, we're dinosaurs," said Geoffrey. "This little containment facility is already leaking like a sieve. And I don't know if the nants have dug through the plumbing or the ventilation systems or electrical conduits or the insulation of the wiring that stretches all the way to the power plant; but they *have* breached Sector Four, and it's only a matter of time before they breach the rest of the city."

"What's your advice?" Katsuyuki asked.

"What's my advice?" Geoffrey asked. "The only chance we've got is to throw a nuke in this place, slam the door, and run like hell."

9:18 A.M.

Sasha and Ivan ran through a low tunnel that wormed through solid rock.

"*Nobody* knows about this place!" Sasha bragged, giggling electrically as her voice echoed. "It's my *super-secret* bedroom." Her flashlight flickered. "I need new batteries for my flashlight," she grumbled, smacking it against her leg as they came to a patch in the tunnel where the walls, floor, and ceiling were oddly translucent in the darting glints of Sasha's torch. She stopped. "OK! Are you ready?" Sasha jumped up and did an excited fist pump. "It's so cool." Ivan barked, eyeing the plate filled with sausages that Sasha was carrying in one of her hands. "Ivan!" She pushed him away and dramatically pressed on the left wall.

Nell was startled to see a small square sink around her little hand and then pop out, swinging open. Inside the depression was a little knob. Sasha reached in and turned the knob, pushing in a door that swung inward.

Inside was an invisible room.

Nell wouldn't have thought it was a room at all except for the bed in the middle of the floor. The entire chamber was carved into a vast, flawless extrusion of crystal.

A little over ten feet wide and thirty-five feet long, the crystal box extended into the Pandemonium sea, twenty feet beneath its surface. Sasha had thrown a lavender rug on the crystal floor before the bed, but otherwise the floor and walls were decorated only by churning and darting undersea creatures.

Ivan rocketed into the room first, and Sasha followed. They both ran across the transparent floor fearlessly and jumped onto the bed. "Come on, Nell!"

"OK." Nell stepped into the room as a drift of pink hydras and blue squids darted under her feet.

"This'll be *your* room now," Sasha said. "I hope you like sausage. These are really for her, Ivan! Sorry. At least until I can get you some better food. Oh, and here's some carrots I got from Dennis. One for Ivan, such a good dog!"

Ivan snapped his jaws over the extended carrot like a tiger shark.

"There's actually a bathroom, too, over here,"

Sasha said. "You just go plop down a hole into the water and you can watch the beasties eat it! I'll bring you more toilet paper. They eat the toilet paper, too."

Nell sat on the bed, looking up at the silhouettes of alien creatures locomoting through the water above. She had to close her eyes and process it for a moment. "Your father doesn't know about this place?"

"No! There's lots of things he doesn't know about."

"Doesn't he care where you are? Where you sleep?"

"He's busy all the time. I haven't stayed with him very much. Only the last two months, actually. And when I was a baby, but I don't even remember that! He's so guilty, he lets me do whatever I want."

"I see . . . . Well, what's going on, Sasha?"

"You really want me to tell you?"

"Yes!"

"Well. There were two nice scientists named Mike and Nancy, like you and Geoffrey. They were here before you got here. They were my friends. The thing is, I can see everything that's happening from Papa's desk. You know, on the monitors. When he's not there, of course. When he was in the lab, where Geoffrey is now . . ." Sasha frowned suddenly as instant tears filled her eyes. She pressed her lips together, trying to hold in some sudden grief. "I saw what happened," Sasha whispered. "They went into the room where the beasties are. They were going to look at something. I saw them through the window as they went in. And something bit them. And Papa told them . . ." Sasha bowed her head. She was silent for a moment. "He told the guards to shut the door!" she shouted. "He didn't let them out!"

Nell stroked her head.

"I don't trust Papa since then!"

"I see. Where is Geoffrey? Do you know?"

"He's in the lab, too, now!"

"Where is the lab?"

"On the other side of the city, where Mike and Nancy were. I don't want you to go there, Nell!"

"But your papa said Geoffrey will be back in a little while now."

"No. I don't think so! Papa's guards won't let him go. I saw them pointing guns at the other scientists there!"

Nell gazed into the alien sea all around her. "Then what can we do?"

8:18 A.M.

"Come on, Doctor." Dimitri cranked open a door in the wall opposite the viewing chamber. "Let me show you our quarters, since we'll all be staying here for a while."

Geoffrey followed Dimitri through the hatch into a long room with boarded windows and two rows of beds.

"Choose any bed. Fresh linens are stacked over there. We have a bathroom with running water and plenty of canned food. This part of the hospital was meant to be a delivery and recovery room, but it is our dormitory now."

Geoffrey dropped onto the nearest bed, holding his head in his hands.

"If it's any consolation," Dimitri whispered. "I think they can't find your wife."

MARCH 19

9:33 A.M. PACIFIC TIME

As the government jet zoomed down the runway across Groom Lake, Hender waved good-bye at the silver dome below. He cupped his eye as he gripped his armrests with three other hands, and one of his fingers accidentally pushed the button that reclined his seat.

He exclaimed musically in a rising scale as the plane lifted off the airstrip.

"Get that!"

Cynthea Leeds whispered to Zero Monroe, who was capturing the moment on film. "Are you getting that?"

Zero opened one eye at her. "Yes, darlin'," he said dryly.

Cynthea and her chief cameraman, Zero, who was now her business partner and boyfriend, met while documenting their journey to Henders Island. They were here at the invitation of Hender, who was unaware of how lucrative an exclusive he had given them. All that mattered to Hender was that he was surrounded by humans he knew. Now, as he was about to "fly" to an island called "England" to meet more humans than he could ever imagine, he was even more grateful to have the company of humans he knew.

Hender watched the plane's shadow shrink over the scoured desert mountains below. "I hope we don't drop!" he shouted. Hender's fur bristled with effervescent colors as he looked out the window.

Andy laughed. "It's OK, Hender. This is normal," he reassured him. "Humans do this all the time."

"Humans are crazy."

The first time Hender flew in a plane was inside the cargo hold of a military aircraft from Pearl Harbor directly to Nevada. None of the sels had understood what was happening during that flight, since there had been no windows. It was terrifying, but it would have probably been more terrifying if they had known they were soaring through the air.

As the G-V now pierced a cloud under the stratosphere, the windows turned white and Hender looked around from his seat at Andy and Cynthea, whose seats were in front of his.

Andy smiled back at him. "It's OK, Hender. This is normal, too."

"So cool!" Hender said. "Can I watch a movie?"

"Absolutely," Andy said. "And I'm sure we can make popcorn, too."

"Good!"

"Push the buttons on the arm of your chair." Andy showed him.

Hender pulled up a menu on the screen above him that showed movie selections. "Ooh, *Jurassic Park*!"

Andy reclined his chair and stretched back. "Well, Hender's happy," he remarked to Cynthea, who sat beside him.

"He'll knock 'em dead," Cynthea said. "Can you imagine what this must be like for him?"

"I think so," Andy said. "Maybe a little."

"Maybe that's why they like you so much," Cynthea said.

Andy was rankled by Cynthea's probing. "Maybe so!"

Zero pointed the camera back at them and Cynthea winked, which Zero always hated. "I'm not here, honey, remember?"

She winked again. "I know!"

Hender flipped through the new *SkyMall* magazine. He used the in-flight phone and his credit card information to order a few more things. Then he watched two movies simultaneously—*Beverly Hills Chihuahua* and, on his MacBook, a Buster Keaton movie.

He couldn't understand what humans meant by "black-and-white" movies. Hender saw lots of colors in them. He loved Buster Keaton movies because he thought, at first, that Buster Keaton was Zero Monroe. When Hender found out Buster Keaton had died decades ago at the age of seventy-one, he was shocked by the news. That such a young creature could reach legendary status amazed him. That he could die so young and still leave such a legacy astounded him. That so wonderful a creature could perish so soon troubled him. That his spirit could still live on on television amazed him. What brief and yet immortal animals were his human friends.

Hender pondered the differences between humans and sels as he looked at Zero with one eye and Buster Keaton with the other. Humans lived such a short time, and there were such a staggering number of them, that sometimes they could look quite similar to one another, he realized. He marveled at how many humans there were, and how much each of them did in so very little time. Hender waved with five hands at Zero, who videoed him from his seat.

"Hi, Hender," Zero said. "Just pretend I'm not here."

"OK, Zero!" He waved at Cynthea instead.

Cynthea laughed. "Hello, Hender!"

12:31 P.M. ZULU TIME

After the long flight, they deplaned directly into a waiting motorcade of armored limousines.

Hundreds had gathered behind rope lines to wave, yell, and clap as cameras flashed. Hender, Andy, and Cynthea moved past quickly, as Zero filmed them, when Hender stood high on his two bottom legs and stretched them almost their full five-foot height as he looked out over the crowd and clapped four hands above the people. A great shock went through the crowd, and they answered with a wild cheer.

Hender descended and climbed ahead of the others into a hulking Rolls-Royce Phantom, which left ahead of a thirty-five-car motorcade that moved together off Heathrow's tarmac like a black millipede.

Hender looked out the window at miles of roads,

bridges, and buildings of every variety in every direction as far as his eyes could see.

Such giant, permanent spaces these short-lived humans created for themselves, he thought. The secret of human progress was that they teamed up and worked together with common cause over generations. It excited and terrified him, for it reminded him of disk-ants or drill-worms that worked together to build hives many times their size—unlike sels, who lived long, solitary lives.

Blinking cars charged in front of and behind them as they snaked through the city named London. The motorcade sped over precleared roads, which were all lined with crowds of waving people, some of them thrusting curious signs at them along the way.

The streets were like the corridors inside the jungle of Henders Island, with lampposts and power lines substituting for the trees and vines. Unlike the tunnels at home, however, traffic here moved in both directions sometimes, he noticed.

Hender's probing hands bumped a button, rolling down the tinted window. A certain percentage of those lining the street for a glimpse of him fainted as he stretched out and waved back.

"Hender, let's roll that back up, OK?" Andy said urgently.

"Yes, Andy. Sorry!"

"No problem. Most humans are nice. But there are some wackos, too."

"Oh, yes. I understand."

1:41 P.M.

Amidst an electrical storm of camera flashes from banks of paparazzi twenty paces to either side of the hotel entrance, Hender, Andy, and Cynthea charged from the limousine with Zero filming the moment.

An entourage of Secret Service, MI5 agents, diplomatic ministers, and attachés—who had already disgorged from the motorcade—surrounded them in a flying wedge as they entered the Dorchester Hotel.

Hender took video shots with his phone, uploading the clips to his YouTube and Flickr accounts and putting links on his Facebook page and Twitter feed simultaneously. As soon as they got Internet access, Hender had taken advantage of every way to contact the greatest number of humans possible, and they had responded.

Hender, Andy, and Cynthea went directly to an elevator that took them to one of two floors that had been reserved. They were quickly shown to their connecting suites, which were secret and decided by a coin toss moments before their arrival for security purposes. Andy and Cynthea were scheduled for fittings at 2:35 P.M. for a tuxedo and a formal gown. At 4 P.M. they were to attend a series of press meetings in a heavily guarded still-to-be-determined suite somewhere inside the hotel.

Cynthea, Zero, Andy, and Hender entered Hender's suite and were dazzled beyond their wildest expectations. Hender cartwheeled onto the blue bed and, as he bounced under its flowing canopy, he shouted, "Beautiful!"

"Wow," Cynthea agreed.

"I'll have to travel with you more often, Hender," Andy agreed, too.

Silk wallpaper and brocaded window dressings out of a magazine or a painting appointed the opulent suite. The adjoining room, they soon found, was even more lavish, decorated red and orange with flowing curtains of gold. "OK, this is our room," Cynthea said to Zero. "Andy, you'll have to take the suite on the other side. Sorry! Hender, do you mind if we shut the door so Zero and I can have some privacy?"

"Just knock if you need something, OK?" Zero said.

"Don't worry, Zero. I saw porno on the Internet. I was going to ask if I could shut the door." Hender smiled wide at him. "OK?"

Andy laughed. "I'll be across the hall in the Imperial Suite, Hender."

"OK, Andy! Sweet dreams!"

They all said good night, and Hender closed his door.

3:59 P.M.

Sitting behind a table in the press suite, Hender, Andy, and Cynthea faced journalists from newspapers, magazines, television networks, and webzines from around the world. They had each been cleared by heavy screening and given five minutes to ask him questions.

Hender was ably backed up by Andy and Cynthea, who were seated at his side as the feed from the press conference was broadcast around the world. Commentators remarked that not since man had landed on the moon had such a global sensation monopolized all human communications in such a simultaneous event. Hender treated it as practice for the event scheduled for tonight: a formal gala in his honor at the London Natural History Museum.

There might never have been a more desirable party to attend in London. Hender was told that *everyone* would be there.

8:47 P.M.

Hender took a long shower with six showerheads in his amazing bathroom. He was able to blast the water pressure to get between the tendrils of his fur, which, after drying off with his four blow-dryers, left him refreshed and agreeable for the night's festivities as his skin breathed freely again, enriching his blood with oxygen. Without their symbiants, a thorough shower was the only way sels could exfoliate.

Andy smelled the pleasant copper penny and cilantro odor exuding from his sel friend and knew that Hender was nervous as they neared their destination. Hender's fur began displaying fireworks of anticipation as they arrived, and he squeezed Andy's hand with one of his hands.

The small motorcade that had conveyed them from the hotel came to a stop near the cascade of steps in front of a vast and beautiful building carved in stone. It reminded Hender of the cliff of Henders Island, though it was artfully sculpted into windows, pillars, and arches. With three hands, the sel nervously fingered the invitation he had received in a gold-lined envelope, spindling the paper in three directions as he climbed to the entrance of the "museum."

Flanked by dozens of guards in dark suits, Hender

moved nimbly up the steps on four legs like a centaur between Cynthea and Andy, his fur sparkling bursts of color as he held up his rumpled invitation with one of his upper hands.

"How do you feel, Hender?" Andy asked.

"Awesome." Hender shivered.

They passed under the arched doorway that was like a cave entrance between two towers of rock, and Hender pulled back as he saw inside: the place was filled with humans, on the ground below and along a giant stone ramp to a ledge above where more of them were crowded and looking down at him all around. They all wore "tuxedos" like Andy's that were nearly all the same or else they wore gowns as varied as flowers in the humans' gardens. Females wore the gowns.

In the center of the room, Hender suddenly noticed a huge creature with a soaring neck, and he reached four arms back to protect Andy and Cynthea. The humans around him gasped as he disappeared, using his light-sensitive fur to hide himself.

"That's a skeleton," Andy said, realizing that the bones of the *Diplodocus* arching like a roller coaster inside the museum's foyer had startled the sel. "It's a fossil of an animal that died millions of years ago!"

"A fossil? That's a fossil?" Hender withdrew his arms and folded them as he reappeared, staring in awe at the sauropod skeleton.

The people all turned to him like petals of Henders clover turning toward the sun. One person called for everyone's silence, and Hender was formally introduced by an important human, to deafening applause that lasted five full minutes, much to Hender's amazement.

At Andy's suggestion, Hender waved four arms above his head in greeting, to an even louder ovation.

The crowd quickly quieted when a microphone was handed to Hender.

"Speak into it," Andy urged him. "Like a microphone. Say hello!"

"Hello, everyone."

A swoon swept over all who heard his voice speak English. Then there was a profound and sustained moment of applause that rocked the building like an earthquake.

"Thank you!" Hender finally said, overcome by the thunderous response. "You are amazing! This place is great. I love my hotel room! Congratulations! Let's party! OK?"

Everything he said exhorted more applause as a massive cheer swelled to a global roar through the cameras that broadcast the event to the world, live.

A series of people introduced themselves and posed for pictures with him in front of the giant sauropod skeleton while clasping one of his hands. The great nature documentarian, Sir Nigel Holscomb, who had narrowly survived Henders Island, introduced himself to Hender then, and when he noticed Hender had a BlackBerry, he insisted, to a round of cheers, that they exchange tweets, which Hender happily did, bestowing forty-five million followers on him in an hour.

A bewhiskered and bespectacled man who Cynthea claimed was a noted scientist came forward now and called Hender's attention to a display case containing hendro artifacts.

"Oh, cool!" Hender said. He noticed replicas of some of Kuzu's weapons, which were made from human flotsam fused with native materials.

"I was admiring sel craftwork," said the gray-haired man. "You sels are quite ingenious!"

"I am not all sels and all sels are not me. My friend, Kuzu, made these."

"Ah . . . Of course."

Hender met a woman who seemed to be wearing flowing gold. He flushed striped waves of purple and pink on his fur coat to see what the reflection would look like on her gown. "I love your clothes," he said.

She nodded, awestruck. "Thank you!"

"You must miss your island," said one guest, a movie star quite well known to Cynthea and Andy.

"You have never been there," Hender replied, triggering a round of laughter. He shrugged. "This is much better. Much safer."

Hender was captivated by the setting for the party, which featured a collection of amazing things. As a collector himself, his attention was taken away from one point of interest to another as he wandered up the stairs to the next level of the museum. Cynthea, Andy, and Zero struggled to stay close as he drew a growing train of humans with him. A couple of eminent scientists managed to keep up, along with a huffing and puffing Sir Nigel.

Hender ran up to the museum's wall. "Oooh! What's up here? This is nice!" He pointed at a light sconce between exhibits.

"Yes," said one man. "That is one of our better inventions."

"You invented it?"

"Oh, no, no."

"Why do you say *our,* then?"

"Well, you're right, Hender. Thomas Edison invented the lightbulb."

"I like Thomas Edison."

"Yes, Hender."

Hender smelled food now and moved forward on four feet, gracefully parting the guests as he found a table where shrimp and other hors d'oeuvres were spread over a bank of ice. "Yum!" he said, feeling his hunger. He attacked the shrimp and deviled eggs with four hands. As he reached for another prawn, Hender noticed marks on the wrist of a very old human. He pointed with one iridescent finger. "Color!"

"Tattoo."

"Numbers?"

"Yes."

Hender noticed the man was bald and had a white goatee. Human hair changed color, too, he thought, but only over a long period of time. "Why?"

"It was given to me when I was a child." The man's eyes seemed very wet. "When I was a prisoner."

"Prisoner?" Hender asked.

"Yes. Because my people, my tribe, were different, they put us in a place where we could not escape, a prison, so they could kill us."

"Oh. I'm a prisoner, too." Hender held the man's hand.

Another man chimed in. "Yes, Hender, I'm afraid we are capable of awful things."

"*You* did this?" Hender drew back, afraid.

"No, no!" said the man. "Other humans did. A long time ago. Not me."

"Oh." Hender was relieved, the color returning to his coat. "Don't say *we*!"

"OK, Hender."

"A lot of humans say *we* too much," Hender said.

11:02 P.M.

Hender waved good-bye to the gathering at the entrance of the museum, his coat turning magenta, and the crowds gave him a deafening send-off after an evening that was already being breathlessly reported as a triumph around the world.

On the ride back to the hotel in the motorcade, Hender opened some of the small gifts he had been given, which had been cleared through the security people who intercepted them. He now had a handsome gold magnifying glass, a fantastic pen encrusted with jewels that dazzled his eyes, and a beautiful lighter for creating fire with a click of the finger, an invention Hender regarded as miraculous. On Henders Island, he had collected some disposable plastic lighters on the beach below his house, and Kuzu had figured out how to strike sparks with them; but none of these devices had ever made a flame by themselves.

It started to rain. Hender rolled down the window and smelled the scents that were as varied, noxious, sweet, and pungent as the scents of his native island. Their Phantom rushed through the night as the rain made the endless streets and cars and buildings glisten. The enormous car deposited Hender and his entourage in front of the hotel, where shoulder-to-shoulder police held back the bursting crowd.

Andy noticed that the packed onlookers seemed unruly. As Hender stood waving among the sea of people, they converged on him with dangerous pressure. Despite Andy's apprehension, Hender was at ease now, waving four hands and rising on two legs over the police line, which incited an eruption of applause and cheers. To the horror of those guarding him, Hender contracted and disappeared, rising on the other side of the barrier. Amid an explosion of flashing cameras, he reappeared in vivid color and shook the people's hands four at a time, deciding that he liked humans very much.

A tall man with a shaved, tattooed head shoved his way through the others in front of Hender. Hender noticed that three of the bald man's upper teeth were made of gold. Rushing behind, his bodyguards saw the man raise one muscular arm. A butcher knife flashed in his pale fist. "Piss off, ya grotty devil!" he screamed, and he leaped at the sel, the blade flashing as he plunged it down at Hender's chest.

Before any of the bodyguards could intervene, Hender moved four hands in a blur of motions, removing the knife from the yob's hand with two hands and slamming him on his back on the sidewalk with two more, pinning him with five hands. Red waves of light rippled across Hender's fur as blood pooled under the groaning man's head on the pavement.

The crowd clapped but then backed away, stunned at the lethal display Hender had unleashed on his attacker. Dozens of phones and cameras had recorded the assault from every angle.

Immediately, Hender was surrounded by uniformed humans, who shouted as they gently put themselves between him and his assailant and quickly extricated him from the crowd. Hender gave the police the man's knife as they cuffed and carried the man away on a stretcher.

Hender's security detail rushed him into the hotel, and Andy trotted along with him. "Awesome kung fu, Hender," Zero said.

"Yeah, good work, man!" Andy said.

"Thank you, Andy. I'm sorry I hurt the man."

"It's OK, Hender," Cynthea said.

"He was trying to kill you!" Andy said angrily.

"I hope nobody's mad."

"He was an asshole," Zero growled.

As they entered a private elevator, Andy gave Cynthea and Zero a worried look.

"I want to sleep now, guys," Hender said. "For four hours. OK?"

"OK," Andy said.

"See you in a while, Hender. You were great tonight!" Cynthea said. "Don't worry!"

"Thank you, Cynthea." As he stood inside his door, his fur washed out and grayed suddenly. "Good night." Hender closed the door to his room softly.

Andy's cell phone rang. "Yes? Oh. Really. That's a shame. I see. No, thanks, I think it sucks, but, yeah . . . because it sucks! It wasn't his fault! Right, bye." He looked devastated.

"What?" Zero asked.

"They canceled the audience with the Queen tomorrow."

"Why?" Zero asked.

"Security reasons."

"Oh, shit!" Cynthea said.

"What did they say?" asked Zero.

"They said it would be better to postpone the Royal visit until further review."

"Give me that schmuck's phone number, Andy," Cynthea said.

Andy shook his head. "It's no use, Cynthea. They've made up their minds."

11:59 P.M.

Nestled in the blue whirlpool of blankets on his giant bed, Hender worked quietly on the next bit of his book, working off his nervousness so he could go to sleep:

The 2nd Darkness

According to the Books, 64,985,121 years ago. There were only eight petals on Henderica, and eight tribes, which kept to themselves when they weren't fighting before the second darkness came.

There were over a million sels then, and they built great things like humans do today. Some dreamed of things that could carry them across the poison sea. But when the waves came they carried two petals and two tribes away as the sky turned black.

Sels found the tunnels made by treno trees, whose roots had lived and died and melted away. The tunnels twisted hundreds of miles under the ground. While all other plants died above, the warring tribes came together to save the trenos. For four years, the six tribes fed the trees underground. And they wrote the first Books, to remember.

All of your "dinosaurs" died then. I'm glad. I don't think I would have met humans if they had lived. But maybe I would have met something else, instead.

MARCH 20

11:31 A.M. MAXIM TIME

Geoffrey came out of their dorm after a fitful sleep. He saw that the others were peering through the window of the maternity ward excitedly.

"Trees," Dimitri said. "They must be trees! But they're *moving*. . . ."

"They're *Henders* trees," Otto said.

"They're animals," Katsuyuki explained.

"They only look like trees," Geoffrey said as he approached them and looked through the glass. A miniature jungle had sprung up over the last week and formed tunnels five feet tall through which ravenous jet streams of Henders bugs and even rats now circulated. A variety of the pseudo-palms retracted lines of glistening bait-eggs that dangled from their fronds.

Geoffrey looked at Katsuyuki wearily. "How did these species get to an island off Japan, Katsuyuki?" he asked. "Did you ever figure that out?"

"We think they came from a jar in a raft that washed ashore."

"A raft?" Geoffrey wondered suddenly. "Thatcher?"

"Yes, actually!" Katsuyuki exclaimed. "We found Thatcher Redmond in the raft."

"Alive?"

"No! Very dead."

"A bug jar from Hender's house must have been in the Zodiac," Geoffrey muttered. "Oh, Christ! We used jars of glowing animals to signal the boat that rescued us. We must have left one in the raft! But Hender's jars didn't have rats in them . . . . Where did they come from?"

"You call those rats?" Dimitri said. "They have eight legs and—and two sets of eyes—"

"Yes, and they have two brains," Geoffrey conceded. "They're mammal-like arthropods that evolved in isolation on Henders Island. We just called them rats. What I don't understand is how they got off the island."

"All of this came from one suitcase of specimens," insisted Dimitri.

"Do you have any photographic record of what was in that suitcase?"

"Yes, of course." Dimitri called up a gallery of images on a laptop.

Geoffrey took over from him and scrolled through the images. One photo showed two brown lumps that looked like dates. He paused on them and zoomed in.

"What?" Katsuyuki said.

"Resting eggs?" Geoffrey muttered. He looked up at Katsuyuki. "Like the kind copepods and daphnia lay during periods of stress to make clones?"

"Yes." Katsuyuki nodded. "A very effective survival mechanism. You think Henders rats might use resting eggs, too?"

"I wouldn't be surprised. Maybe Hender put them in his light jars as a food supply for the bugs. I wish he were here so I could ask him. If those things *are* resting eggs and they hatched into clones and mated, they would have exchanged millions of sex cells by now. Both would be assembly lines of baby rats, as would all of their offspring."

"But how could those 'trees' get here?" Dimitri asked.

"They're related to disk-ants." Geoffrey peered through the clear spots as he moved along the window. "A certain percentage of disk-ants latch on to the ground and metamorphose into about six or seven varieties of animal that superficially resemble palm trees."

"How long was this island isolated?" Dimitri muttered in amazement.

"More than half a billion years, three supercontinents ago," Otto said.

"Hey!" Geoffrey spotted something as he reached the center of the window and looked down. The others gathered round and looked where he pointed.

Hundreds of eight-legged Henders "rats" were speeding through tunnels between the trees. They seemed to be converging on a spot four feet from the window, where they delivered regurgitated food to a single rat that had grown to the size of a German shepherd.

"Oh, no," Otto whispered.

"Does that camera work?" Geoffrey pointed at the camera mounted on a track inside the chamber above the window.

"Yes." Dimitri pointed out the control toggle at the end of a conduit hanging down from a hole drilled above the window.

"You drilled through the wall there?" Geoffrey asked as he reached up to toggle the camera down.

"Yes. But we filled the holes with cement," said Dimitri.

Geoffrey shook his head grimly as he rotated the camera down.

Dimitri grabbed his wrist and stopped him. "Careful, my friend! We don't want to break the window."

Geoffrey agreed. "You do it, then."

Geoffrey observed as the Russian used the controls to toggle the heavy camera housing that was mounted on a thick steel arm. The camera slid along the track at the top of the window inside the chamber. When the camera reached them, Geoffrey said, "Point it down at that thing and let's get a look at it."

The image of a large squirming animal surrounded by the rats became visible on a screen mounted over the window and on various laptops on the lab counters. Unmistakable stripes of iridescent colors radiated over its bony frill. Sizzling stripes of pink and orange zigzagged on its furry back. It drummed its limbs in spasms, staying in place. "That," Geoffrey sighed, "is a spiger."

Katsuyuki frowned. "How?"

"We never figured out where spigers come from. But that's one right there. The rats must be able to develop into them. But, why?" Geoffrey pressed his mind for some evolutionary pressure that could explain it. "Why would rats turn into spigers?"

"Maybe they're breeding their own food," Otto said.

"Like we breed pigs and cows!" Katsuyuki agreed.

Geoffrey nodded. "Perhaps. Spigers had scarcely any big game to hunt except for other spigers. So maybe the rats made enough spigers to ensure spiger-on-spiger kills, which would provide the rats with a feast, as well."

"Why wouldn't both spigers be eaten in the feeding frenzy?" Otto wondered.

"Yes, how could they survive?" Katsuyuki asked.

"The larger animals on Henders Island were protected by armies of symbiants," Geoffrey said. "We've been learning about them from the hendros. We call them 'symbiants' since they seem to have been related to disk-ants. They fed on anything that attacked their host, even knitting together to protect wounds. But if a wound was too severe, the symbiants seemed to sense it and abandoned the sinking ship, sometimes even turning on their host. When symbiants turn and are ready to migrate to viable new hosts, other animals can sense it and attack their dying host. As a consequence, only the losers in a spiger fight would have been attacked, unless both spigers were mortally wounded. Healthy spigers could gorge themselves to their heart's content right alongside the rats and not be touched, and inherit a lot of their prey's symbiants simultaneously."

"So rats grow their own beef," Katsuyuki said.

"And butchers, too," Geoffrey said. "These cows are both."

"It's like vultures breeding wildebeest and lions," Otto wondered, his mouth opening in shock. "But how do the rats *make* them?"

“Like bees, maybe,” Dimitri said.

“Of course,” Katsuyuki said. “Bees feed royal jelly to larvae to turn them into queens.”

Geoffrey nodded. “Right. They could be regurgitating food with some enzyme or hormone. Or they could be like locusts. Environmental pressures trigger a dormant genetic expression that changes grasshoppers into locusts. We used to think they were different species.”

“Christ, can you imagine?” Otto said. “If these things got loose above, they’d be creating locusts the size of SUVs.”

Dimitri looked at Geoffrey, betraying fear now for the first time. “So how do we kill this stuff, Geoffrey?”

“Henders life is already eating through the walls,” Geoffrey said. “That lichenlike stuff growing on everything in there uses sulfuric acid to dissolve rock. It’s what carved Henders Island into a giant bowl. We called it clover. And you may have clovores in there, too, creatures that eat the clover with acid. Any number of Henders species could penetrate structural weaknesses down here. Nano-ants probably chewed through the electrical insulation. Clover may have followed and widened the holes. That may be how Sector Four was breached. Who knows? However they did it, they’re spreading—fast. Is this place contained? The whole place, I mean? Is there any way this stuff can reach the surface, Dimitri, other than the railroad tunnel in Sector Seven?”

“The city is sealed, do not worry,” Dimitri said. “The air pumps in all the ventilation shafts are built with elaborate filters, more elaborate than the ventilation system of Cheyenne Mountain, which was built four years after Pobedograd. These filtration systems were engineered to block radiation, poison gas . . . nothing larger than a microbe could ever reach the surface through them, I assure you. And Sector Seven is always sealed off from the rest of the city."

"Not always." Geoffrey frowned. "We came through it when we arrived. If one wasp or ant had gotten through and made it to that tunnel."

"Unless those filters are made out of diamonds," Otto said, "then it's just a matter of time before Henders life eats through them, too. They'll only slow it down. It's got millions of years now."

"And now Maxim wants us to make some repellent so he can turn the power on down here. It's madness," Geoffrey said.

"Why would that make any difference?" Dimitri asked.

"Look through the window," Geoffrey said. "With just those chandeliers, Henders clover has already covered every surface that is directly illuminated. That's the base of the food chain. These species would quickly exhaust the supply of oxygen down here. But with light, the clover will photosynthesize and produce oxygen. Every species will carry scales of Henders clover and distribute it wherever they go. As dangerous as this ecosystem is, the planet may not be threatened yet, since there is limited light, oxygen, and food down here. But if we turn the power plant on, there will be light. We'd be pouring gasoline on a fire."

"He's right, man," Otto said. "You don't understand the reproductive capacity of these things in optimal conditions. Their offspring are already producing offspring before they're even born!"

"OK, OK!" Dimitri said, touching his forehead with trembling fingers. "But it sounds like we should make some repellent, no matter what."

"I've thought about it," Geoffrey said. "And you're right." He looked around the room, spotting the four hatches—one that led to their dorm, another to the garage downstairs, another to the stairs in front of the hospital. He pointed to the last one in the wall to the left of the window. "Where does that hatch go?"

"We don't open that one," Dimitri said.

"Why not?"

"It's an antechamber to the nursery—a storage room—which we used as a sort of air lock for a while, till things got out of hand."

"Till those two died, you mean?" Geoffrey pointed at the dissolved remains inside the chamber, their outlines obscured under growth.

"Yes." Dimitri closed his eyes. "They died after going through the door on the other side of that room. They closed the door behind them, thankfully, but we haven't gone back in since."

Geoffrey considered the situation. "All right. First we have to find out if the ante-room was compromised."

"How?" Katsuyuki asked.

"Get me a stethoscope and a piece of meat." He looked at the guards.

"We can communicate directly with Maxim through the Undernet." Dimitri pulled a laptop on the nearest counter.

"The Undernet?" Otto asked.

"It's a wireless network of relays and transponders that isn't connected to the outside world, unfortunately," Dimitri said.

Geoffrey watched Dimitri's fingers as he logged in to the underground web, but they moved too fast for him to catch his password.

2:19 P.M.

The crystal room around Nell was like a gigantic eye that peered into the world of lucid nightmares tumbling in fluid darkness around her. Two days had passed, according to Nell's watch, which she had set for Maxim's upside-down time zone shortly after arriving.

Nell felt naked in the glass room that protruded into the Pandemonium Sea, where she saw countless creatures as she reclined on the lavender bed, suspended in a euphoria of wonder and fear. A three-foot-wide Spanish dancer nudibranch, its surface outlined by pinlights of purple and gold, flapped like a magic carpet above her. Blue squids shaped like artillery shells chased one another in single file, flashing as they careened around the room. Limpets rasped their radulae against the surface of the crystal walls like Zamboni machines grinding away the strange algaelike growth before it could accumulate.

Nell rolled onto her stomach. In the murky distance through the crystal wall, she saw radiating red and orange arms, each twenty feet long, rising together from the bottom of the lake.

She spotted a light switch next to the window and turned it on, and two dozen beams of light pierced the water in a semicircle outside the invisible room. A new palette of colors emerged from the darkness. The Spanish dancers were now orange, yellow, and red; the gammies were now yellow, red, and white; and the giant arms rising from the lake bottom fifty feet away were reticulated white, purple, and orange.

She now saw that the eight arms bristled with lacy white stalks, each a yard long and releasing a stream of organisms delaminating like budding medusae. Some of the juveniles swam away solo while others linked together and stroked their legs in a pulsing wave. A cloud of multicolored chunks of particulate matter billowed up in the water from the mouth of the mega-medusa. As the plume rose, a squadron of squids converged in a swirling frenzy to feed on the bits of matter. Nell noticed that the young medusae that had broken off from the mega-medusa now did an extraordinary thing: The free-swimming solitary ones latched on to those that had linked together in chains and began dragging them through the feeding animals. As the chains came in contact, the squids and other creatures were instantly paralyzed and sank into the waiting mouth of the mega-medusa.

Perhaps the monster was more like a giant Cassiopeia, Nell thought now—a rare jellyfish that lived upside down attached to the sea bottom. Whatever it was, she had never seen a species whose young hunted food for it so that the adult could concentrate on reproduction—except for ant or termite colonies. "What do you think, Ivan?" she whispered, rubbing the dog's head. Ivan barked. "I agree," she said.

Just then she heard someone clanking on the door outside. Men's voices yelled. The door began to open. Ivan looked at her. She mouthed barking, and he started barking immediately, to her astonished gratitude. She heard men yelling loudly in Russian as the door began to push in.

Nell remembered that Sasha had recorded a message in case the guards found her. Nell scrambled to the CD player and pressed START. Then she dashed around the corner to the bathroom as Sasha's message played: "Get out of here! I'll tell Papa! Don't you *dare* come closer! Oh, my God, *I hate you*! Ivan's going to eat you! *Go away!* I'm *naked*!" Then Sasha screamed long and loud on her recording.

The door closed decisively as Nell hunkered down. She crept back into the room and switched off the lights, crawling under the covers of the bed and trying to hide somehow in the fishbowl of Sasha's secret room.

2:24 P.M.

Maxim sat in the conservatory, scanning the views of security cameras arrayed on the wall behind his desk.

Sasha suddenly banged on her father's desk, startling him. "Papa!"

A moment after, three guards marched through the main hatch to report to Maxim. Their mouths froze open, amazed to see that Sasha had gotten there before them.

Sasha identified the look in their eyes and immediately screamed. "*There* they are! These are the ones who keep harassing me, Papa!"

They visibly shrank in front of Maxim's desk as he swiveled toward them in his chair.

"I've found a nice room for me and Ivan, and these pervs tried to barge in on me *again* just now! Didn't you? Why can't I get any *privacy around here*!" she screamed.

"Now, now, *shinka*!" He glared at the men. "What have you to say about this?"

"Um, we did find a passageway to the room Sasha was in, Chief, and we thought we should check it out. We didn't know she was inside!"

"You're Peeping Toms!" Sasha shouted, pointing at each of them. "They totally heard me and they barged in anyway. Didn't you?"

"All right, what about this, damn it?" Maxim demanded.

"We did not mean to intrude on her, Chief. We were looking for Nell Binswanger."

"We're very sorry, Miss Dragolovich!"

"I was *naked*! Just like the *last time* you barged in on me!"

"We closed the door as soon as we heard her, Chief!"

Maxim glared at the men with ominous fury.

Sasha ran around his desk and kissed him. "Bye, *Papochka*!" Then she trotted to the spiral stairs and waved at the guards before flipping them off and leaving them to fend for themselves.

"I can't believe she got here before us, Chief," said one of the confused men. "We came straight here. . . ."

"She's explored more of this palace than anyone," Maxim fired back in Russian. "Find Nell Binswanger instead of spying on my *naked daughter*!

You are to leave Sasha alone, do you *hear me*? How many times must I tell you! Can you *manage that*?"

"Yes, sir."

"Thanks, Chief!"

"What if—?"

"What?" Maxim snapped.

"A ghost may have gotten her."

"They seem to be everywhere in the city, Chief."

"She might have wandered off by herself and—"

"*Get out!* Find her! Before I feed you to a ghost!"

4:45 P.M.

The scientists in the maternity ward cranked the latch of the door to the storage room and pulled it open a crack.

Geoffrey dumped a can of Vienna sausages into the room, and they slammed the hatch shut.

Otto listened to the door with a stethoscope, noticing his cloven right thumb, the nail deformed after a Henders rat hatchling had split it down the middle on Henders Island. He placed the head of the scope to different parts of the door and closed his eyes as he osculated.

"What if Henders animals don't like the salt in the Vienna sausages?" Dimitri said.

"Yeah, there's a lot of sodium in those things," Katsuyuki agreed.

"For that matter, why do they like to eat us?" Otto said. "We've got salt in our blood, sweat, and tears, just like the ocean."

"It's a myth that we have the same amount of salt in us as the ocean," Geoffrey said. "Seawater has three and a half times the concentration of salt that we have in our blood. We might have the same amount of salt in our blood as the ocean did when our ancestors crawled out on land. But now there is enough of a difference in seawater to trigger a warning signal in these things and not enough in our blood to keep us off the menu. They probably have about as much salt in their blood as we do. They just can't slough off excess salt, so when they're exposed to saltwater the magnesium buildup anesthetizes and kills them. Hear anything, Otto?"

"Nope. Nothing."

"OK, so next, a visual test." Geoffrey turned. "Anyone have a camera with a flash?"

Katsuyuki produced a small camera from his shirt pocket.

Geoffrey charged the flash, and when they opened the door, Geoffrey stuck the camera in, pointed it at the floor, set off the flash, and pulled his hand in as they slammed the door. They saw the picture of all seven Vienna sausages lying unmolested on the white tile floor of the storage room. "The room's clear," Geoffrey said.

"What makes you so sure?" Dimitri asked.

"We're sure," Otto said.

"Let's rig a way to open the far hatch, let in some Henders critters, and then close the door, all from here," Geoffrey said. "Then we'll set up saltwater sprayers to collect their repellent."

"Hey!" Dimitri noticed a security camera view on his laptop sitting on the nearest lab counter: two limousines were arriving in front of the hospital. Maxim and his entourage got out and rushed up the stairs from the street.

"Great," Otto said.

Maxim entered through the far hatch. "Have you figured it out, Geoffrey?" Maxim asked.

Geoffrey turned to him. "We will need saltwater, Maxim."

"We have our own ocean," Maxim replied. "What else?"

Geoffrey held his eyes. "Got any ice chests? Big ones? Fifteen of them would be good. And something we can spray water with."

"Throw in duct tape, rope, and string. And some plastic bags and cable ties," Otto said. As a former NASA systems engineer, Otto considered these items essential prototyping materials.

"And cheesecloth," Geoffrey said.

"E-mail a list to me," Maxim said to Dimitri. "I'm very glad to see you're making progress, Geoffrey. Very good!"

"Where's my wife, Maxim?" Geoffrey said.

Irritation returned to Maxim's face. "We will bring her to you soon. If you do not complete this task, it won't matter, Geoffrey."

"God damn it, where is she, you son of a bitch!" Geoffrey glared at him. "Are you trying to blackmail me? Where is she?"

Maxim looked at him, a startled look in his eyes, which surprised Geoffrey. "Carry on, Dr. Binswanger," he said gravely. "I only meant that all of us are in danger if you fail. Your wife has managed to get herself lost in Pobedograd. I cannot guarantee her safety. Only you can do that, by doing what you can to stop these creatures."

"Why did you bring them here?"

"For insurance."

"To use as weapons?"

"When your enemy has very big weapons, you need them, too."

"You can't *aim* these weapons, Maxim! Not at a country or even a continent. They will destroy everything, everywhere, if they ever get out! What were you planning to do with them?"

"If they ever tried to attack this city, they would trigger their own destruction."

"Who is *they*, Maxim?"

Maxim leaned forward, his ice-blue eyes piercing Geoffrey. "The human race."

After a brief word with Dimitri in Russian, he departed. As he passed, his two armed guards replanted their feet against the wall behind them.

4:49 P.M.

Only when Sasha brought food in and called her name did Nell come out of hiding. "Thank you, Sasha," she sighed. "I think Ivan saved me! He's a very smart dog."

"Of course," Sasha said. "Dogs are as smart as their owners."

"You may be right." Nell smiled. "Interesting theory."

"I brought you chocolate cake. But you have to give me a bite. Here is your dinner, madam," Sasha handed her a plate of piled food with a dramatic flourish. "I even brought you a fork." She handed her a silver fork and then ran, dive-bombing the lavender bed.

"Thank you," Nell said. Through the floor and walls behind Sasha, she saw the mega-medusa's arms now opening on the lake bottom.

Nell sat with her on the edge of the bed, absently nibbling on a couple of eclectic forkfuls of food, finding herself eating a green bean, chocolate cake, and chicken simultaneously and not minding it. She was famished. Ivan whimpered in front of her, sitting as still as one of the Queen's guards.

Sasha scooped a piece of chocolate cake with two fingers and ate it gluttonously in front of the frozen Samoyed. "You shush, Ivan! I'll have to take him for a walk in the farm, again."

Ivan barked and Sasha laughed.

"Sasha," Nell began.

"I got you two bottles of water." Sasha pulled the small chilled bottles from her purse.

"Thank you." Nell reached for one and took a grateful swig. "You said Geoffrey's in a lab with the other scientists on the other side of the city. Right? Can you communicate with them?"

"Hmm. Maybe." Sasha lay back and Ivan leaped onto the bed next to her, licking her face. "We could use the Undernet. Right, Ivan?" She squealed as she pushed off the dog.

"The Undernet?" Nell asked.

8:01 P.M.

Maxim looked into Pandemonium through the oval window embedded in the wall of the small room fifty feet above the conservatory. On the other side of the thick glass was the steel gondola deck, which had been cantilevered from the cave wall. The surface of the subterranean sea was eighty feet below.

On the deck, six men in hazmat suits reeled up buckets of salt water beside the large gray gondola, which looked like two airplane noses fused together and suspended by thick cables reaching out into the gloom.

The men pulled up plastic jugs dipped in the lake and strung on ropes. One man capped and stacked the filled jugs on the landing. In the darkness above, flocks of pink and orange bubbles rose to join a mass like a sunlit cloud near the high ceiling.

"Hey, Chief, it looks like a crowd of gammies are coming," came a voice across an intercom speaker.

"Start moving the water in before they get here," Maxim said. He opened the hatch and waved at them. "Come on, come on!"

Maxim slid the plastic jugs one after another across the floor as one man passed them through the hatch.

Two orbs dangling crimson streamers like the tentacles of Portuguese man-of-wars drifted down toward the men on the landing. "Chief!"

Galia reached the top of the spiral stairs and saw Maxim pulling jugs in through the open hatch. Galia looked through the window to the right of the hatch and saw two floating man-of-wars release a shower of red embers over two men on the gondola deck. He heard them scream as the flaring embers burned through their suits and the paralyzing nematocysts touched their skin with circuit-blowing agony.

Even as both men fell over the rail into the lake, Maxim yelled, "*Keep going!* They are gone! Keep going, damn it!"

"Maxim!" Galia hissed.

Maxim turned, his eyes glinting at him like knifepoints, before he turned back to the men on the landing. "*Come on, come on!*"

The other men hauled in their last jugs of water and began capping them with fumbling hands. Then, from all directions, a tide of gammarids brimmed over the landing like beagle-sized army ants. They tore into the men's suits and climbed over their bodies, covering them up to their heads.

Maxim grabbed the last bucket and shut the hatch on them. He cranked the wheel and gave Galia a look as bloody as his murder. They heard the dying shrieks fade away on the intercom. "Get some men to carry this water, Galia," he said, turning off the intercom with his fist.

"Maxim—"

"*NOW*, Galia!" Maxim screamed.

9:20 P.M.

Twenty 2.5-gallon jugs filled with saltwater were carried into the lab by five of Maxim's men. They also delivered ten large blue Igloo ice chests and two backpack agricultural sprayers that had come from the farm.

Otto inspected these last items. The sprayers shot through a nozzle at the end of a lance to cover a wide area while a pump on the other side of the red backpack tanks was operated by the other arm. "Yeah, these should work."

Maxim came through the hatch from the garage downstairs and approached Geoffrey. "So, you have all you need, yes?"

"To each according to their need," Geoffrey sneered.

"And from each according to their ability," Maxim replied fiercely.

"You said you were a capitalist," Geoffrey said.

"Don't underestimate how serious I can be, Dr. Binswanger, when I must be. This is an emergency. And in emergencies the rules change."

"That's what every dictator says," said Geoffrey.

Maxim reached down and grabbed Katsuyuki's neck with his giant left hand and produced a handgun with his right. He placed the barrel of the gun on Katsuyuki's forehead. "Next time I will pull trigger, yes?"

The biologist fell to the ground, making choking sounds.

"*Now get it done!*" Maxim turned and left the room, closing the hatch to the garage behind him.

"He's out of his fucking mind," Otto said.

3:19 A.M. BRAZILIA TIME

Hender, Andy, Cynthea, and Zero flew twenty-nine thousand feet over the Atlantic Ocean.

The humans slept as Hender quietly typed an entry on his laptop to soothe his worries, translating more fragments of the sels' past from memory.

The 5th Darkness

Before the fifth darkness came, 29,498,517 years ago, one tribe had united and forced all other sels to follow Alok, their angry god.

But the giant waves tore off the last petal of Henderica—the place where the tribe of Alok had lived, and all its leaders were swallowed by the poison sea—all except for one. All of Kuzu's tribe descended from him.

12:01 A.M. PACIFIC STANDARD TIME

Kuzu reviewed YouTube videos of Hender neutralizing his attacker in the human city of London, approving of his technique. But the hulking sel was increasingly angered by what humans were saying about Hender on the Internet.

Some humans continued to protest the sels' imprisonment, and suggested their rights according to the "Geneva Conventions" and the "Constitution" were being violated. But others protested that sels were not people at all and that they were not protected by any law of man, and they used Hender's act of self-defense as evidence that sels were dangerous.

"These beasts were not meant to live with us!" shouted one human on YouTube. "Their island was sinking until we interfered. They don't belong on this planet with us. They are an abomination against God!" Kuzu's fur boiled reds and purples as he journeyed through the Internet, a mounting rage banking in his mind.

9:53 P.M. MAXIM TIME

Hardly speaking to one another, the four scientists connected nozzles made from pinpricked latex gloves with surgical tubing attached to the drains of ice chests set on the top shelves of the storage room.

Working side by side, they clamped the tubes with old Soviet-style paper clips Maxim's men had supplied. They used duct tape to patch garbage bags together, draping them down each side of the room to catch the water and drain it into six ice chests placed on the floor.

They carefully cranked open the lock of the far hatch and tied one rope to the top of the dog wheel on the door, hooking the rope around a pilaster of the shelves to the right of the hatch so that when they pulled on the rope, it would turn the dog wheel enough to unlatch and open it. Then they tied another rope to the center of the wheel to pull the door open wider.

All the paper clips constricting water flow to the gloves were tied to strings taped to a tug-line leading back to the door with the other ropes. Ropes were also tied to the handles of all six ice chests on the floor. They soaked the ends of the tug-line and ropes in trays of saltwater.

"OK," Geoffrey said.

"All we need is some bait," Otto said.

They turned to Maxim's guards.

10:38 P.M.

Maxim's men arrived, carrying an entire side of beef.

They laid it in the center of the floor inside the antechamber between the ice chests and then departed.

"Well, that should do it," Geoffrey said.

The two guards holding pistols behind the four scientists watched, fascinated.

Geoffrey and Otto pulled the outer door of the storage room three-quarters shut.

Otto pointed a webcam around the door, and they watched the video feed on a laptop that Dimitri held. Gripping all the tethers they had rigged, Geoffrey yanked the rope that pulled the far hatch open a crack.

Sparks swirled into the room through the far hatch on the monitor.

"Shut it," Dimitri said.

"Shhh!" Geoffrey put his hand on Dimitri's mouth as another burst of glowing bugs flew into the room. He waited just long enough to suggest he was suicidal before yanking the tug-line and the eight surgical gloves inflated with saltwater, spraying through hundreds of pinholes. "OK," Geoffrey whispered.

Geoffrey and Otto pulled the rope strung around the shelf post and swung the far hatch closed. They gave the line another hard tug, cranking the wheel just enough to latch it. Then they dropped all the other lines inside the room and pulled the near hatch closed.

Just before the door shut, Geoffrey caught a whiff of the Henders warning pheromone, which smelled vaguely like cilantro. . . . "Good going, guys! I think we got it," he said.

They waited.

The men used the time to douse themselves with saltwater.

Inside the storage room, the saltwater continued to spray from the glove-nozzles. Otto put the stethoscope to the door. "Pleasure to work with you, MacGyver." He nodded at Geoffrey. "The room's buzzing, man!"

"OK, let's fill those insecticide sprayers with saltwater and get ready to open the door. Saltwater's not the best repellent, but it's the next best thing.

Maybe we can get the guards to put their guns down and help us, eh, Dimitri?"

Dimitri nodded and spoke to them in rapid Russian.

11:20 P.M.

At last, after a few rehearsals, they opened the hatch.

Geoffrey reached through the crack and took hold of the rope tied to the handle of the nearest ice chest. He and Otto pulled hard on the rope. The guards furiously sprayed salt water through the gap as the chest slid toward the door.

Otto watched the laptop feed coming from the webcam Katsuyuki pointed around the corner. "So far, so good," Otto said. "They're staying back!"

As they widened the door, Geoffrey splashed the water inside the ice chest over the doorway. "Pull it up!"

They dragged the ice chest up and over the hatchway, and the others clapped the cover on it as Geoffrey and Otto closed the door.

"We did it," Dimitri sighed.

After hoisting the ice chest onto a lab counter, they filled plastic water jugs with repellent through the drain, which they filtered through cheesecloth. They emptied the backpack sprayers and refilled them with the repellent-infused mixture.

They proceeded to spray this mixture through the hatch as they opened it to retrieve the other five ice chests.

It worked perfectly until, as they were pulling

the last one through, a seven-inch Henders wasp made it through the door, defying the repellent.

"Get it!" Geoffrey yelled, slamming the door shut.

"Kill that freakin' thing now!" Otto moaned.

It landed on the stomach of the guard next to Geoffrey. Geoffrey punched the guard as hard as he could. The man doubled over, but the five-winged, ten-clawed bug was crushed and fell into the ice chest, bursting a cloud of blue blood.

The other guard grabbed Geoffrey angrily.

"He just saved his life!" Otto shouted.

Dimitri spoke rapidly to them in Russian and the guard backed off.

As they looked into the last ice chest, they were startled to see a number of Henders specimens caught in the water, moving very slowly under the surface. Ants, wasps, and drill-worms sprayed repellent as they died, producing an oily rainbow sheen on the water's surface.

They filled the rest of the 2.5-gallon jugs from the ice chests, and Geoffrey labeled them with a black felt-tip, when a phone rang. Dimitri answered on the landline phone next to his laptop on the lab counter. "How soon will you be ready?" Dimitri relayed.

Geoffrey sat on a lab stool, exhausted, looking at Otto and Katsuyuki. "Tell him it's ready."

Dimitri relayed the news. "Maxim is very pleased with the progress you have made, Geoffrey."

Geoffrey nodded. "Awesome."

Dimitri hung up. "It looks like we'll be testing your repellent tomorrow. That is, four hours from now."

"Testing it?" Geoffrey got off the stool, putting his hands on his hips. "What?"

"The power plant," Dimitri said.

"OK, we have to think about this," Geoffrey said.

"Let's get some sleep," said Dimitri. He motioned toward their dormitory with his eyes, and they all got the message. They went to their quarters, away from the guards.

11:58 P.M.

"We can't let him turn the power on down here," Geoffrey whispered.

"Agreed," Otto said.

"Yes!" Katsuyuki said.

"Hey," Otto said to Dimitri. "Are you with us?"

"Maxim is insane," Dimitri agreed. "If I must choose between him or the world, then of course I'm with you." Dimitri jerked as he noticed something on his laptop, which he had brought in and set next to him on his bed. Dimitri called Geoffrey over. "Look." He pointed to an e-mail he had just received from Maxim's address:

> Hey guys. I'm here in the palace with Sasha.
> Can we help?!
>
> BTW, WE CAN SEE YOU RIGHT NOW!
>
> Wife

"She's alive!" Geoffrey shouted.

"They must see us through that camera!" Otto pointed at a camera mounted over the hatch.

"They must be in Maxim's office," Dimitri said.

They all waved at the camera frantically.

11:59 P.M.

Sasha and Nell looked at a screen behind Maxim's desk in the conservatory and saw the men waving.

Sasha had shown Nell how the hatch to this room could be locked from the inside, as could all the doors radiating out from this room throughout the city. No one could enter now as they accessed the Undernet.

"Wait—look!" Nell indicated Maxim's e-mail box as a reply arrived.

How are you? – Husby

"We should go. I'll erase these messages so Papa doesn't see them."

"Wait! Here comes another."

Are you safe?

"Type *yes*, Sasha!"

"OK." Sasha sent the reply.

"They're replying!"

I'll try to come and get you. Don't come to us. Bye.
(It's bad.)

OK, BYE, Nell typed, and sent.

Sasha deleted the messages and emptied the trash. "Come on. We better go."

Nell looked back at the monitor on the wall as Geoffrey waved to her.

"Papa comes here sometimes. But not after two A.M., usually. We'll come back then. OK, Nell?"

"OK . . ."

MARCH 21

2:28 A.M. MAXIM TIME

Maxim sat in the middle of the thirty-foot crescent of his couch atop the Star Tower, gazing through the glass walls of his penthouse apartment at his subterranean utopia. Life went on below. For the moment, at least, the power lines from the surface had not been cut off. In a few hours now, it would not matter.

The phone rang on the couch beside him. "Yes?" he asked, his thick voice cracking.

"My friend . . . ," Galia said. "News from above."

"Just tell me what you have to say, damn it."

"I can't—"

"*No!* Tell me!"

"Alexei is dead, Maxim."

"Don't say it. . . . Damn you!"

"Maxim," Galia implored.

Maxim exhaled his soul as he turned off the phone.

Galia knew then what he must do. He headed for Sector Seven. He was the only one, other than

Maxim, with the authority to make the guards let him pass.

2:35 A.M.

Sasha waved Nell on up the winding stairway to the conservatory, which was now dark and empty. The curtain had been drawn over Hell's Window. They both ran to the wall behind Maxim's desk on the far side of the room.

Nell and Sasha saw a screen on the wall showing Geoffrey, Otto, Katsuyuki, and Dimitri. They were standing in an observation room of some sort, looking through a wide window.

"Wait a minute . . ." Nell looked closer at the HD screen. "Can you zoom this view closer and see what they're looking at through that window, Sasha?"

"Of course!" Sasha clicked the mouse and the camera zoomed in. "You want to see the monsters from Henders Island, right?"

"Yes—what?" Nell turned pale as she looked down at her. "Why did you say that, honey?"

"The creepy-crawlies that Papa bought."

Nell fell back in Maxim's chair, the air sucked out of her lungs.

"What's the matter?" Sasha said.

"What . . . are you talking about?"

Sasha zoomed in on the view of the window in the lab. "Papa's monsters. That's what they're looking at."

"Henders—" Nell couldn't speak as the image expanded on the screen.

Sasha shrugged. "Papa said you're an expert on Henders Island. That's why he brought you here."

Ivan jumped on the arm of the chair and licked Nell's face.

"Are you OK, Nell?"

2:35 A.M.

The hatch door from the garage burst open and Maxim stepped through, followed by four armed guards. The billionaire strode forward and pointed at Geoffrey, his arm like a rifle. "Get repellent ready. We are starting power right now, Geoffrey. You!" He pointed at Katsuyuki. "Help my men take that downstairs." He pointed at the five-gallon water bottle on the lab counter, which was filled with live Henders specimens. They had been testing various poisons on the specimens, which had not seemed to be affected by any of the toxic substances they had tried.

"Why?" Katsuyuki asked. "What are you going to do with them?"

Maxim pointed his pistol at Katsuyuki's head and fired the gun.

The scientist fell to the ground, dead, as the others staggered back in horror.

"You!" Maxim pointed the gun at Otto. "Do it!"

Geoffrey glanced at Otto.

"Maxim!" Dimitri hissed. *"Do not trust them!"*

Maxim wheeled and pointed the gun at Dimitri in blind rage before he had processed what Dimitri had said.

Geoffrey reached up and toggled the controls of the camera outside the window.

"Watch out!" Dimitri shouted, pushing Maxim away.

The heavy camera swung down and shattered the glass.

Geoffrey grabbed a scalpel and slashed open one of the plastic jugs of repellent. He pulled Otto's arm and dumped the repellent out of the jug over both their heads as bugs and rats gushed into the room through the window.

The flood of creatures avoided them as the other men screamed, instantly attracting orgies of feeding predators. Geoffrey grabbed another jug, and Otto snagged one of the backpack sprayers as they both ran toward the door to the garage, ducking behind the 2.5-gallon jugs stacked on the lab counters.

Maxim's men dragged him through the hatch into the dormitory as he fired his gun at the two scientists, but the bullets struck the water jugs as Geoffrey and Otto slipped through the door and slammed it closed behind them.

As they cranked the wheel, Geoffrey and Otto felt someone on the other side of the door twisting it in the other direction. Geoffrey and Otto heard shouting, and they both bore down, bracing themselves against the wall. They could hear a whine of Henders animals whirring like a jet engine on the other side of the hatch as the pressure resisting them weakened and finally stopped. They turned and plunged down the stairs to the garage.

"Where are we going?" Otto asked.

"Maxim's car!"

2:38 A.M.

Nell and Sasha saw Maxim point his gun at Katsuyuki. They saw the scientist fall and Sasha screamed.

Then they saw the window shatter silently. Geoffrey and Otto ran out of the camera's frame to the right. Dimitri and Maxim ran to the left with two of his bodyguards as Maxim fired his gun again. The guards shoved Maxim off the screen as strange animals flew through the broken window. Sasha saw her father and his guards appear in the screen below, inside the room where they had first spotted Geoffrey and the other scientists. A guard sealed the hatch behind them.

On the screen above, the rest of Maxim's men who had failed to get out of the way of the rushing horde were swarmed. A spiger as big as a deer jumped through the window and spiked the chest of one of the men. The man beside him screamed and was instantly covered by a mass of flying bugs and disk-ants.

In a screen to the right, they saw two more guards running down a flight of stairs, chased by the glowing bugs flowing through the open hatch behind them. In the next screen over, they saw the guards run down the stairs in front of the building to an SUV parked at the curb. Nell and Sasha watched the deluge of animals spread over the screens on the wall. "Oh, no!" Nell shouted, desperately searching the screens for any sign of Geoffrey.

"Papa!" Sasha screamed.

2:39 A.M.

Geoffrey and Otto leaped into Maxim's limo in the garage. With trembling fingers, Geoffrey pushed the remote door opener on the visor. The door began to open and Geoffrey pressed the gas pedal, launching the limo in reverse and scraping the still-rising door.

The heavy car's tires screeched as he mashed the brakes, shifting, then tearing forward.

"We gotta get to the train station in Sector Seven!" Otto said.

"No. We can't let anything get to Sector Seven. Not even us! We gotta get to the palace!" Geoffrey shouted. He turned right and approached the gate to Sector Two.

"Tinted windows," Otto said as they approached the guards. "That's handy."

Geoffrey nodded, adrenaline racing through his bloodstream as he approached the gate. "This is Maxim's limo, so they might let us through," he said, his voice distant as his rushing pulse pounded in his ears.

"What if they don't?"

Geoffrey noticed a machine gun resting on the seat next to him, and he pulled it closer with a shaking hand.

The two guards jumped up from chairs and operated a control panel. The gate began to open and they waved them through.

"Awesome," whispered Otto.

The guards on the outside of the gate also waved them along, but as the gate started rolling shut behind them, Geoffrey saw one of the guards on the other side grab his neck and fall just before it closed.

Geoffrey turned right and stepped on the gas, pushing the heavily armored car up the road as fast as it could go. "This is the way to the palace, right?"

"Yeah, I think so," Otto said. "My God, Maxim killed him." He shuddered and looked at Geoffrey. "He shot Katsuyuki! What are we going to do, man?"

"Make sure that sprayer's ready," Geoffrey said. "Something might be chasing us. If we get through the door to the palace, we can't afford to let anything get in with us."

"How will *we* get in, man? There must be guards with fucking guns outside the gate and they won't just wave us through this time!"

"This is Maxim's limo," Geoffrey said. "It can probably take a direct hit from a nuke. And Stalin's palace is the most secure place in the city."

"Shit, this is hairy, man, I don't know!"

"It's all we've got. Get ready!" Geoffrey hit the brakes and skidded around a corner to the left, pushing the gas up the last length of tunnel.

2:40 A.M.

Sasha and Nell spotted the limousine racing toward the palace on ever closer cameras. Sasha cried, tears streaking her face. "What about Papa?"

"He's OK," Nell said. "He's safe, Sasha. We've got to let them through the gate, all right?"

Sasha tapped the keys on her father's keyboard. "We have to rescue Papa!"

"We will! But you've got to open the gate! Geoffrey will die if he can't get through!"

"I can open the door," Sasha said.

"Great, honey. Thank you!"

Sasha sniffled. "The guards inside will kill him, though."

"They will?"

"Yes."

Nell thought. "Can we call Geoffrey and warn him, honey?"

"*Uuuh*—hey, yeah." Sasha clicked on some prompts and they heard a phone blurting on the computer's speakers. "Good thinking, Nell."

2:40 A.M.

Geoffrey followed his headlights up the long tunnel, its walls honeycombed with the doors and windows of medieval dwellings carved out for the villagers of Gursk to inhabit in the event of invasion. He did not see anything following them in the dark through the rearview mirror. "Answer the phone, Otto."

"Phone?" Otto asked.

Geoffrey pointed at the ringing phone on the dashboard. "Answer it!"

Otto grabbed it. "Yeah?"

"Geoffrey, the guards will kill you," Nell said.

"Nell?" Otto said.

"Oh, Otto—is Geoffrey with you?"

"Yeah, he's driving."

Nell sighed. "Listen. We'll open the gate for you. But the guards will kill you when you come through the door. OK?"

"Um, OK. Nell says she can open the gate but the guards will kill us."

"How many guards are there?" asked Geoffrey.

2:40 A.M.

Nell heard his question. "How many guards are there, Sasha?"

"Two outside the gate and two on the stairs. I kicked the others out of the palace."

"Is that all?"

"I think so. . . . There might be more. I don't know," Sasha sighed, waiting with two fingers poised over the keyboard.

2:40 A.M.

"Two at the gate and two on the stairs, maybe more," Otto relayed.

"Where are Nell and Sasha?" Geoffrey said.

2:41 A.M.

Nell heard him and answered, "We're in Maxim's conservatory. Can you lock the gate from the inside, Sasha, after they get through?"

"All the doors lock from the inside around the palace so Stalin could keep everybody out. I can change the entry code so nobody can come in. Want me to?"

"Yes! Good!"

2:41 A.M.

"They're in Maxim's conservatory," Otto said. "They can lock the gate."

"Get the sprayer ready in case anything is chasing us. And hand me that machine gun. See if you can figure out how to take the safety off without shooting me, OK? Let's see if we can get through without a fight first."

"Right." Otto shrank down under the dash as Geoffrey approached the guards before the steel door marked SEKTOP 1 in tall red letters. He whispered in the phone: "We're at the gate now."

The two guards strode forward leisurely with Kalashnikovs. Apparently they had not been warned yet by the others. The man who approached the driver's side waved to lower the window.

Geoffrey rolled down the window ten inches and stuck his hand out, waving twice as he imitated what he had seen Maxim do. He raised the window again. That's when he realized his mistake. Maxim had waved from the backseat, of course. He had waved from the driver's seat.

The man knocked on the window hard as the other guard lifted a walkie-talkie from his belt.

2:42 A.M.

"Come on, Sasha," Nell said.

"*Um,* I'm trying to figure it out!" Sasha yelled. "Wait!"

"We don't have time, honey."

"I know, I know!"

2:42 A.M.

The guard proceeded to the window behind Geoffrey and knocked on the window.

"Shit," whispered Geoffrey.

"Uh," Otto whispered into the phone. "We're fucked. . . ."

The other guard moved in front of the limousine and pointed his weapon at them.

Geoffrey reached for the machine gun, hoping the glass was truly one-way.

"Watch *this*!" Otto heard Sasha shout in the phone.

The gate behind the men started sliding open, surprising the guards. The men shrugged and stepped aside as Geoffrey surged forward through the opening gate. They must have assumed it was OK since the gates could only be controlled remotely by Maxim or Galia. The men answered their walkie-talkies as Sasha was closing the gate behind the limo. Geoffrey noticed them suddenly wave their arms as the doorway narrowed. They shouted at them to stop. In the rearview mirror, Geoffrey saw them point and fire their machine guns through the closing crack, scarring the bulletproof rear window as the door slid into the rock wall and sealed them off.

2:43 A.M.

"Lock the gate, Sasha!" Nell shouted.

"OK, OK! I'm trying! There it is. I need Papa's password."

"Do you know it?"

"Sure." She typed out the letters with one finger as she said them aloud. "*A-L-E-X-A-N-D-E-R-G-R-eight*. That's after my brother, Alexei," she said. "Wait, where's the eight again?"

Nell saw the men outside the gate running toward the switch to open it. "Hurry, honey!"

"There it is!" She poked a dimpled finger.

2:43 A.M.

One guard ran down the steps in front of the palace as he fired a Kalashnikov across the courtyard at them. The bullets raked the windshield.

"Ram him!" Otto shouted.

As the bullets sprayed in front of his face, adrenaline exploded through Geoffrey's body and tears streamed from his eyes as he steered the heavy vehicle toward the guard, whose body slammed with grisly smacks into the hood, windshield, and roof, each sound impacting on Geoffrey's soul.

2:43 A.M.

"Got it!" Sasha squealed. "It's locked."

"So they can't open it?"

"*Duh. Yeah!*" Sasha said.

"Awesome, Sasha. Good job!" Nell hugged her, hiding Sasha's eyes from what she saw Geoffrey doing on the screen.

2:43 A.M.

Flooring the gas pedal of the monster limo up the cascade of steps, Geoffrey spotted another guard rushing down the stairs and firing a high caliber handgun right at Geoffrey that cracked spiderwebs into the windshield. The sparks of the rounds blinded Geoffrey for a moment.

"Kill him!" shouted Otto.

Geoffrey accelerated, ducking behind the dash, feeling the slight thud; he pulled his foot off the gas and saw the guard's body fly backwards into a marble pillar, tumbling to the ground. Geoffrey sobbed as he drove past the man's broken body directly into the palace foyer, the tires stamping bloody tracks on the inlaid marble floor.

He stopped and turned off the limo's engine, hanging his head as he gripped the steering wheel, breathing hard and nausea welling in his throat.

"You did good, man." Otto slapped his arm. "You got us through. That was freaking awesome! They were trying to kill us, dude. They *would* have killed us! It's OK. Don't worry about it!"

Geoffrey shook his head. "Man," he breathed. "Is that ever easy for you to say."

"We'd be dead now if you didn't do it!" Tears streamed from Otto's eyes, too, now, in the aftermath.

"It's not a fucking video game," Geoffrey said.

"I know." Otto gripped his shoulder. "OK. Let's just wait here. We'll watch and listen for a while before we do anything. Right? This car is the safest place we can be right now, right?"

"Yeah." Geoffrey nodded. "Are they still on the phone?"

Otto checked the line. "Hello?"

2:45 A.M.

"Hello?" Nell asked. "They're not there, Sash!"

"Yeah, the phone doesn't work inside, because the palace is lined with lead or something."

"How does it reach outside, then?"

"Transponders?" Sasha shrugged dramatically.

"Is there a camera in the foyer?" Nell said.

"I'm looking." Sasha scrolled through galleries of security camera views, looking for the limo.

"God, he's got more cameras than London," Nell muttered. "He must be more paranoid than Stalin!"

"You might be right," Sasha said pensively.

"There—that looks like the riverfront, Sasha." Nell tapped the screen. "And that over there looks like the bridge to Sector Seven. Maybe go back in the other direction?"

"OK . . ."

"Maybe the closer to us the camera is, the closer to the top of the list?" Nell said.

"That makes sense!"

2:50 A.M.

Five minutes passed as Geoffrey and Otto peered out of the limo in all directions through its blackened windows at the domed foyer under the glittering chandelier. Neither of them could see or hear anyone.

"OK," Geoffrey said finally. "Let's try to get to the conservatory."

Otto turned sideways on the seat and strapped the repellent-sprayer on his back. Geoffrey lugged one of the 2.5-gallon jugs of repellent onto his left thigh and slung the shoulder strap of the machine gun over his neck. Holding the gun's grip with his right hand, he kicked open the door. "You're sure the safety's off?"

"I think so."

"All right, let's go."

They both stepped out of the limousine into the foyer. Geoffrey carried the jug and pointed the gun erratically with his right hand as they ventured up the red carpet of the curving staircase on the left.

When they reached the upper level, they saw no

one. They ran between a row of doors, and one of them suddenly opened.

2:50 A.M.

"There they are!" Sasha jumped up and down and put the view on the big screen. "They're right outside!" she yelled.

"Let's open the door!"

"Wait— Oh, no!"

2:50 A.M.

A guard buttoning his jeans emerged from a door on the other side of the hall. He noticed them, and one of his hands fumbled for a pistol strapped under his shoulder.

"Wait!" Geoffrey said. "It's OK! Don't shoot!"

The guard unsnapped his holster and pulled out his gun.

"Wait!" Geoffrey said.

"Shoot him!" Otto yelled.

The guard fired first, the first shot striking Otto in the neck, the second shot striking Geoffrey in the foot as he jumped to the side and fired a barrage of wild bullets that wounded the guard's hand. Geoffrey dropped the jug of water and lunged at the guard, who picked up the gun with his other hand. Geoffrey aimed his machine gun and shouted, "No!" But a mere touch of the trigger blasted three bullets into the guard's face.

Geoffrey retched as the guard fell forward, his head splattering on the stone floor. Geoffrey turned away, limping on his bloody foot, and saw that Otto was lying still. Using the gun as a crutch, he hobbled closer. He could see that Otto was dead from the vacant look in his staring eyes. Geoffrey grabbed the water jug from where he had dropped it and ran to the end of the hall, turning left up the short flight of stairs to Maxim's office, leaving a red trail of footprints.

He pounded on the door. The hatch opened.

"Come on!" Nell said.

He clambered through the hatch and dropped the gun and heavy jug before falling to his knees.

Nell shut the hatch and cranked the wheel, locking it.

Sasha approached Geoffrey, staring at his foot. "You're bleeding!"

Nell embraced him from behind. "Come on! We have to look at that!"

He turned and kissed her as though she could absolve him, knowing she could not. He had watched ten people die in the last few days, some, certainly, because of him.

She stroked his head and saw the blood spatter on his shoulder. "I would never have forgiven you if you had gotten yourself killed," she said. "You did what you had to do." She squeezed his hand in hers.

After they got him to the chair behind Maxim's desk, Nell pulled off his shoe. He noticed the screens on the wall. She pulled the bloody sock off and saw that the bullet had gone through the bone in his foot leading to his small toe. She pulled the lace out of his shoe and tied it around his ankle, cinching it tight.

Geoffrey pointed to one of the screens in which a burning SUV had crashed into the wall across the street from the hospital. Green cyclones swirled over the bodies of two men in the street. They watched a man get out of a limo parked in front of the hospital only to be immediately smothered by wasps and drill-worms gushing out of the door.

Sasha hid her eyes, turning away.

"They're from Henders Island," Geoffrey murmured.

"I know!" Nell said.

"We've got to warn people," he said.

"Sasha, do you know where a first aid kit is?"

"Yes."

"Where?"

"In the bottom drawer of Papa's desk."

Nell pulled it out and saw an antique leather-bound book on top of the first aid kit. She set the book on top of the desk and opened the kit.

Geoffrey saw on the next screen over that the two men still stood guard outside the gate of the hospital sector. He sighed in relief. "Thank God," he said, feeling woozy as he gripped the arms of the chair. "The gate closed in time. We can't open the gate to Sector Three." The screen to the other side showed the dormitory where they had stayed next to the lab. Maxim, Dimitri, and two of his bodyguards were now trapped inside.

Geoffrey saw Maxim pointing at him through the TV screen and realized that Maxim must be able to see them. Then he noticed a webcam over the screens extending toward them. "He sees us!" Geoffrey whispered.

"Papa!" Sasha ran to the computer. "I think he

can hear us, too." She boosted the volume as her father moved closer to the camera, climbing on a bed as his face filled the monitor.

Maxim shouted: *"The whole world will pay for what you did!"*

"Papa!" Sasha cried.

"Sasha!" Maxim's face recoiled.

"You be nice to Geoffrey!"

"We can still make it out of here alive, Maxim," Nell said. "Help us!"

"Why?" Maxim bellowed. "Then they will kill me, and there will never be justice for what they've done!" Maxim gestured behind him to one of his men, who opened a laptop on the bed and kneeled in front of it.

"Maxim!" Geoffrey yelled. "You can't!"

"Let hell rise . . . ."

"Where's Alexei, Papa?" Sasha said.

"Alexei is dead!" Maxim roared in a cruel eruption.

"For God's sake!" Nell said as Sasha fell to the floor, sobbing.

"There is no God!" Maxim laughed hideously. "There is only the Devil! They killed my *son*! They killed my grandfather, my father, my brother, and *millions* more! And there was no justice! There were no charges, no trials, no convictions. As if there were no *crimes*! And they call me a criminal?"

"You condemn the whole human race?" Geoffrey asked. "You would slaughter all the innocents, all the ones you love, to get back at the guilty? You sound like Koba, Maxim."

"They began it! *I will end it.*"

"What about your daughter?" Nell said.

"They will kill her, also. They will hunt her down like the rest! And they will go on and on and on, forever!" Maxim looked down at the laptop his guard now held for him. He typed with one hand. *"But not this time!"*

"Hey!" Sasha jumped up now and pointed at two screens on the wall. "He's opening the gates!"

2:55 A.M.

Dimitri watched the tycoon, who was hunched intently over the laptop at the edge of a bed in the dormitory. Maxim's face contorted with fury as he tapped the keys, scanning security-camera views of his city. One screen showed luminous creatures flying through the opening gate from Sector Four and spigers with fiery coats leaping into the hospital sector. On another, the gate to Sector Three opened and hordes of rats and swarms of Henders insects poured into the garrison sector, overwhelming the two guards there. Another view showed the door to the main city in Sector Six opening. Then Dimitri saw the gate to Sector Seven opening at the train station across the river.

"Maxim, what are you doing?" Dimitri screamed.

Maxim accessed the password screen for each gate and bashed his right hand on the keyboard to set a new password—hihu9-g7890—copying it, confirming it, and closing the window as he moved to the next.

2:55 A.M.

"Stop, Maxim!" Geoffrey implored. "Don't do this!"

"I had hoped to save some souls here, Geoffrey. But that's impossible now. Find a way out if you can. You'll have some years left if you do."

Geoffrey noticed Maxim's daughter beside him, jabbing the keyboard furiously with two fingers. Trying to delay him, he shouted, "You will be worse than everything you hate, worse than Stalin ever was!"

Maxim lashed out at the camera, pointing at him. "You made this happen!"

"You're delusional!" Geoffrey answered as Sasha probed his security system. "Where were you going to take that bottle of Henders specimens?"

Maxim was quiet, shrinking on the screen.

"You were planning to use these species as weapons all along. You were taking that sample to Sector Seven to release them, weren't you? You knew they would migrate through the train tunnel. All the way to Moscow, isn't that right? That is what you were going to do, Maxim! Admit it!"

"The deaths of millions made this place and a thousand others like it," the billionaire muttered.

Nell pointed at a screen that showed the gate to downtown Pobedograd opening as the letters of SEKTOP 6 disappeared into the rock wall. "Oh, my God. Sasha, you have to close that door!"

"I can't close it," Sasha said. "He locked it!"

"The city!" Nell said. "Close the door to Sector Seven, then, Sasha!" she hissed.

"Are you going to sit back and watch everyone inside your city die? What kind of devil are you?

God damn it, shut the gates, Maxim! Now!" Geoffrey shouted.

Tears streamed down Sasha's face as she called up window after window of security clearances until she finally got in to the password authority prompt for Maxim's user ID. Nell watched her type in a new ten-letter password painfully with two fingers, confirming it twice: ILOVESASHA. Then the young girl confirmed it once more before clicking open the gate control interface and closing the gate to Sector Six.

On two screens, Nell, Geoffrey, and Maxim could see the gate to the main city at the northeast corner stop and reverse its motion, as it rolled closed.

"What?" Maxim growled.

"Awesome, girl!" Geoffrey whispered to Sasha.

Dimitri sighed gratefully behind Maxim.

But as the gate narrowed, a truck tried to squeeze through from the city, and halfway through the door, the truck's trailer was caught and pinched like a tube of toothpaste. The truck tires burned on the road as they spun. Two men jumped out of the cab and surveyed the totaled trailer wedged inside the door. In the next instant, both were struck by a glowing wave and they sprawled on the ground, writhing as the attacking creatures swarmed around the truck trailer, flying and slipping through the gaping gate into the city.

2:56 A.M.

Dimitri wept as he saw the door to the city jammed open. A spiger the size of a hippo vaulted onto the truck cab and wriggled through the crack on top of the squeezed trailer.

Maxim switched to another view that showed the spiger pulling itself with spiked arms on top of the truck trailer as flying and leaping creatures burst into Sector Six.

Dimitri bowed his head into his hands, unable to watch.

2:56 A.M.

Geoffrey saw that the large door in the train station's façade was now wide open. "Sasha, you've got to seal Sector Seven!"

"Close that door, honey," Nell urged her softly.

"There's still time," Geoffrey said. "But hurry!"

"I'm trying!" Sasha sobbed as she navigated the door's controls.

"What are you doing?" Maxim roared through the speakers, glaring at them through the screen on the wall.

"Shut up, Papa! Shut up!" Sasha shouted as she finally activated the gate and locked in a new password. It rolled out of the wall, sealing the train station as the red letters on the door emerged: SEKTOP 7.

2:56 A.M.

Maxim called up another screen, this one showing the front of the train station across the river. Its large steel door was now sealed.

"Thank God, Maxim," Dimitri breathed.

Maxim punched keys with his fingers. The gate control now asked for his password. They must have hijacked his own user ID and changed the door codes. Who could do that? "Sasha!" he shouted. He typed in his password again and it was rejected.

"Thank God, Maxim," Dimitri said again.

Maxim swung at Dimitri, knocking him onto the bed behind him. He tried passwords now that she might have used: IVAN, SASHA, ALEXANDRA, ALEXEI, ILOVEIVAN. . . . Finally, the security system locked him out and he smashed his fist onto the keys.

Dimitri almost fainted in relief as he watched the hulking back of the madman, who threw the laptop on the floor and sobbed, seizing his head in his giant hands.

The other two men, Maxim's elite bodyguards, glanced at Dimitri from across the room and one of them ran to Maxim now. "What you need, Chief?"

Maxim was unresponsive as the other guard approached and picked the laptop up off the floor. "We'll need this, Chief," he said softly.

"The room is secure," said the first guard. "We have plenty of food and water to last awhile here, and even a lavatory."

The second guard looked harshly at Dimitri. "What happens if we lose power?"

"An emergency generator downstairs will kick in," Dimitri said. "After that, we're down to batteries and that bicycle generator in the corner." He pointed.

"How long do we have air?"

"Each room has separate air ducts, and the filters should hold them back," Dimitri said.

"All right." The guard patted Maxim's shoulder. "Get some sleep, Chief. You've been up too long. We need you to be sharp. OK?"

Maxim fell sideways on the bed and curled into a fetal position.

Outside the boarded windows, they heard what sounded like a haunted house of shrieks, cackles, and whining hums.

"Let's turn off some of these lights," Dimitri said. "They're attracted to light and sound."

2:57 A.M.

Sasha's ice-blue eyes melted tears as she looked at her father crumpled on the bed. "Papa," Sasha cried. "Why don't you know the password?"

The room around her father darkened by degrees as the men turned off the lights.

"He's OK, Sasha," Nell reassured her. "Can you shut the gates to Sector Three and Four?"

"No! He changed the codes for them before I could get there," Sasha cried.

"He should be safe till we can help him," Geoffrey said.

A stream of howling creatures poured out of Sector Four and flooded past the hospital into the garrison sector, gushing into downtown Pobedograd. Nell hugged the little girl, hiding her eyes from the screens arrayed on the wall as, one by one, they turned into a horror show.

A night-shift construction crew in the center of the city was besieged and chased down the street by cat-sized animals that sprang in thirty-foot leaps. In the center of the city, thirty-five stories up, workers installing windows and lights on the Star Tower were welding, showering comet tails of sparks down the face of the building. Then squadrons of flying creatures, attracted by the light, arrived and attacked, and the workers' bodies fell from the scaffolding.

Feeding frenzies clumped, like ants around sugar cubes, in the streets as a new kind of traffic began coursing through the streets and people ran in terror on screen after screen.

"Geoffrey," Nell whispered. She looked at him hopelessly.

He shook his head.

They saw a view from a camera on a lamppost looking east along the riverfront. Groups of people stampeded down the steps in front of the restaurant where they had eaten on their first night in Pobedograd. Some of the patrons fell down, while others ran ahead toward the screen. Three young spigers the size of mastiffs launched behind them off their catapult tails, raising their spiked arms.

"God!" Geoffrey whispered.

Sasha recognized Dennis Appleton, who made it closest to the camera before a horse-sized spiger bit him in half with vertical jaws.

Sasha tried to look, but Nell blocked her view. "No, sweetie!" Sasha pushed her head against Nell's stomach, sobbing.

They watched helplessly as the city was inundated by a carnivorous tsunami. The mayhem spread, a premonition of what would engulf the globe if any of these species reached the surface.

"What about the farm? Can anyone get to the farm in Sector Five?"

Geoffrey touched the screen that displayed the steel door marked SEKTOP 5. There was no motion on the street outside the gate.

"Can we warn the people in the city, Sasha, so they can try to get to the farm?" Nell asked.

Then a glowing green speck streaked by the farm's door on the screen.

"Damn!" Geoffrey said as a dozen more shapes like large dragonflies passed the door from the right. A few stopped, hovering, their bodies hanging straight down like glow sticks. "They've already made it to the other side of the city. . . ."

Fear pressed down on them like the mountain above as they realized their predicament. Geoffrey gripped Nell's hand. "We're safe here, for now," he insisted.

"There's food and water downstairs," Nell said, nodding and hiding her tears from Sasha. "Is there any way to communicate with the outside world, Sasha?"

"No!" she yelled angrily.

"Come on, let's fix your foot, Geoffrey. It looks like there's morphine, antibiotics, and even a sewing kit in here. Sasha, can you help me? Geoffrey needs our help. OK?"

Sasha pulled away from Nell and wiped her eyes. "OK, OK!"

Nell noticed a large lavender envelope on Maxim's desk. "To Sasha from Uncle Galia, with love," she read. "Have you seen this, Sasha?"

"Huh?" Sasha said, reading it. "I *hate* Galia!"

"Open it."

She tore open the envelope and pulled out a card. She read aloud, "I will come back for you, Uncle Galia."

Sasha threw it down on the floor.

Geoffrey and Nell looked at each other. Nell

took the card and saw the date written on the card: it was today's date. "That's good news, honey," Nell said.

"He left without us!" Sasha cried. "And he's *not* even my uncle!"

MARCH 26

2:37 P.M. PACIFIC STANDARD TIME

Kuzu had not left his computer for hours. After venturing again into the World Wide Web, he was even more traumatized as he peeled back layer after layer of the humans' boundless inhumanity. He scrolled through an endless catalog of images of murder, massacres, jihads, wars, and genocides down through ages of human history that left him dazed with pity, fear, rage, and disgust. They even killed their *gods,* Kuzu thought.

Indeed, in their short time on Earth, humans had discarded the vast majority of their gods. Kuzu came to realize that humans were like everything on Henders Island—except for the sels. They survived the violence and carnage they unleashed only because their rapid birthrate continuously replaced them.

Kuzu reviewed the video of Hender fighting the human who attacked him, reading the latest comments left by humans, many of whom called Hender dangerous for simply defending himself.

Kuzu brooded as long-still depths stirred in his mind. The other sels were probably playing online video games with humans now. Two of them had become *World of Warcraft* celebrities. His fellow sels did not seem to mind the death in human games: they thought they were funny. They had not seen what he had seen. They had been corrupted by their gifts of games and toys.

Meanwhile, the other sels convened a secret meeting in Hender's house to discuss their concerns about Kuzu, who had increasingly shut himself in, appearing more erratic each time he emerged. Normally, they would never have paid any heed to what another sel chose to do. This time, they had no choice.

6:30 P.M.

Kuzu arrived and noticed the others were already there at Hender's home, which roused his suspicions.

Andy waved him over. "They should be here any minute, Kuzu."

Hender observed Andy's tension and the paleness of his skin. Andy had lost weight and had rarely spoken for the last week. When Hender tried to console him, Andy only smiled weakly and tried to console Hender instead. "What's the matter, Andy?" Hender asked him now.

"Well." Andy bowed his head. "We still haven't gotten any news about Nell and Geoffrey. And nobody knows where they are."

"Oh!" Hender said, clasping four hands together. "Are they OK?"

"We don't really know," Andy said. "They called us here to give us some news."

The sels gasped, clicked, whistled, and growled.

Hender's birdsong doorbell rang, and they all swiveled heads toward the door. Joe and Bo opened the door a crack. Hender waved them in with two outstretched arms. Special agents Jane Wright and Mike Kalajian entered the room. Both of them waved jovially as they came in.

"It is a great honor to see all of you again," Jane Wright said.

"Just tell us," Hender said.

"Where are Nell and Geoffrey?" Nid asked.

Agent Kalajian cleared his throat. "I hope that you will all listen to me closely because what I am about to tell you could not be more important to both humans and hendros. We have received information from a reliable source that Nell and Geoffrey were abducted and taken to what is apparently a salt mine located in a mountainous region of Kaziristan. Everything I am about to tell you from this point forward must never leave the people in this room."

"We need a solemn vow from all of you to never divulge what I am about to say," Agent Wright said.

There was silence.

"Yeah, that's not going to happen," Andy informed them. "Hendros never leap before they look. They won't promise anything in advance. Just cut to the chase. They'll decide afterwards if they agree with you or not. OK?"

"Um, OK." Jane looked at Mike and nodded. "If you understand *after* we've told you why it is important not to talk about it, will you promise to keep it secret?"

"You're confusing them now," Bo said, shaking his head.

Joe nodded. "Me, too."

"OK."

Andy noted how readily she had conceded, and it made him even more anxious. "What's going on?"

Mike Kalajian went first. "We know now that the Russian oligarch, Maxim Dragolovich, is trapped inside an underground installation in Kaziristan, where he has been manufacturing weapons of mass destruction. The WMDs he has been manufacturing are species from Henders Island."

"What?" Andy asked, his mouth falling open.

"They are contained within the facility, but the species have apparently gotten loose, and Nell and Geoffrey are trapped inside, as well," Jane Wright said.

Kuzu sat forward, both eyes extended. The hendros had understood varying degrees of what had just been said, but what they did understand put them on full alert, their fur bristling and flushing colors.

Wright sat on the edge of a chair and looked at Hender. "There was practically no way to trace where your friends were for quite some time," she said. "We were about to rule their disappearance a homicide, since no ransom demands had surfaced."

"What is homicide?" Hender said.

"When humans kill humans," Kuzu said.

"Yes," said Kalajian.

The sels all gasped in horror.

"A few days ago, a man named Galia Sokolof walked through the front door of CIA Headquarters in Virginia," said Kalajian.

"Galia Sokolof is Maxim Dragolovich's right-hand man," Wright said. "He is the only man who managed to escape from the underground facility before it was sealed off and overrun by specimens from Henders Island."

"Wait . . . what?" Andy shook his head in confusion.

"You may have seen the news about a fire in the Kremlin," Wright said. "That fire was deliberately set by the government of Russia because Maxim Dragolovich managed to deliver a box of cigars to one of its offices. One cigar tube contained disk-ants."

"The only way to contain them was to burn the entire building to the ground," said Kalajian.

"Holy shit!" Andy said.

"Yeah," Kalajian agreed.

The hendros glanced at one another silently.

"Go on," Andy said.

"According to Galia Sokolof, the city was built around a salt mine by Stalin in the 1950s. It was purchased by Maxim Dragolovich ten years ago," Kalajian said.

"Apparently, he kidnapped Nell and Geoffrey and at least two other scientists who had been on Henders Island. They went missing around the same time," Jane said.

"What can we do?" Hender asked.

"We are sending in a special-ops team to rescue them and make sure that the facility is sterilized and sealed off," Jane said.

"Good idea," Andy said.

"We would very much appreciate the guidance and assistance of one of the sels when we put our team in," said Agent Kalajian. "We are dealing with Henders organisms. If they get out . . ." He shrugged. "I think you know what that would mean, Andy."

Andy nodded.

"We're asking for volunteers," said Wright, looking at each of the sels. "It is urgent that we get your help. No special-ops team on Earth has ever dealt with this kind of threat."

"Will you help us?"

Hender's fur flushed deep blue. "Humans saved us," he said. "I will go."

"Then I will go, too," Andy said.

"Thank you, Andy."

"I go, too," Kuzu rumbled.

"Excellent!" Kalajian said.

"Fantastic," said Wright. "We need to leave tonight."

Hender raised four hands. "Wait." He looked at Kuzu with one eye. "We will do this only if you guarantee our freedom to leave here when we are done."

Kuzu nodded. His voice registered a deep bass vibration and hissed like a cement mixer: "Good, Shenuday!"

The other sels watched nervously as Hender and Kuzu blackmailed the humans.

"We will have to check on that," said Jane Wright.

"We need to make some phone calls," Kalajian said, and they stepped away to confer.

Andy gave them a fist pump. "Right on!"

8:11 P.M.

After prolonged discussions on their cell phones, the two agents returned.

"Yes, yes. We will agree to that," Kalajian confirmed.

"At least as far as it applies to U.S. territory," Wright said.

"What about the rest of the world?" Andy asked.

"That will take longer," Kalajian said, sneaking a look at Andy.

"But, considering the value of your help," Jane said, "I don't think we'll have any difficulty obtaining that small debt of gratitude from other governments."

"Provided you succeed, of course," Kalajian said.

Hender glanced at Kuzu, who laughed quietly as he admired Hender's diplomacy. "My weapons."

"Weapons?" Kalajian looked confused.

"Kuzu's weapons are in the London Natural History Museum," said Hender, his brows lowered in a *V* over his eyes. "I saw them there."

"We'll get them." Kalajian confirmed it with his partner, and she punched in a number, speaking into her phone. "You need to be ready to leave in five hours," he said. "We'll pick up Kuzu's weapons at our first stop. Good enough?"

Kuzu nodded.

Hender squeezed Andy's hand. "Thank you for coming, Andy."

"Sure," Andy said. "We better pack."

Hender could see that Andy was afraid, and he reached out and touched Andy's arm with three hands. "I will protect you, Andy."

11:16 P.M.

Tapping another channel of memory, Hender typed into his laptop with three hands:

The 7th Darkness

10,000,003 years ago came a darkness that lasted two years. Some sels saw a star fall and smash into the sea before the waves came and covered most of Henderica except for the highest mountains, killing all but a few sels from each of the five tribes, who went underground again.

The creed of Alok took hold of Kuzu's ancestors, and they tried to kill the sels who would not follow them, deciding that they had brought the darkness by not believing in Alok.

The 8th Darkness

6,598,718 years ago, as Henderica continued to fall into the poison sea, the 8th Darkness came. For 200 days, the tribes went underground, again, but this time they built walls inside the tunnels to protect themselves from each other.

MARCH 28

6:42 P.M. CENTRAL EUROPEAN TIME

The phone shattered Standish Harrington's tranquillity as he sat on the balcony of his Swiss chalet, watching the sunset purpling the waters of Lake Geneva. He watched a Jet Skier draw a chalk-line across the mirrored surface, sipping sherry and smelling the bratwursts his girlfriend was grilling.

Standish was a happily retired investment banker at the ripe old age of forty-seven. He was indebted to several politicians, who had provided him with a platinum parachute to bail out of his own financial *Hindenburg*. But the parachute had come with a lot of strings attached. One of them was attached to the phone, whenever it might ring, for the rest of his life. He noted the number of the incoming call and picked it up, waving off his girlfriend, who walked away, annoyed. "Yes?" he answered.

Someone proceeded to give him the names and numbers of two men who might be susceptible to a financial incentive for accepting a certain assignment.

The task was to make sure that neither of the hendros joining a certain dangerous expedition survived.

Standish poured himself another drink and gazed across the darkening lake.

MARCH 30

10:27 A.M. CENTRAL EUROPE TIME

Hender, Kuzu, and Andy were belted into seats against the wall of the C-130 Hercules transport plane as it took off from the Zürich–Dübendorf military airfield. Around them sat ten others comprising the rescue team that had been assembled.

Much to the humans' surprise, Kuzu turned "invisible," his fur projecting the wall behind him, as the aircraft raced down the runway and took off. When the plane was airborne, and they were all finally allowed to unbuckle and move about inside the transport plane, Kuzu finally reappeared, freaking them all out.

"Nice trick," said a large man seated next to Kuzu who had fine blond stubble on his head.

Captain Craigon Ferrell, a former American Army Ranger and now a Delta Force operator, gave a sudden two-fingered whistle beside Kuzu. The soldier's angular face was all business. His crew-cut hair was jet-black. "Listen up!"

The black T-shirt over Ferrell's chiseled chest sported a dragon brandishing samurai swords. A black and red tattoo on one of his biceps showed an eagle gripping two bloody daggers, and there was a skull-and-crossed-machine-guns patch on his cap. "As you know, we are entering an underground facility that has been identified as a WMD lab. An outbreak of dangerous biologicals has occurred inside the facility. Our first objective is to set explosives in a railway tunnel to stop the outbreak from spreading to points unknown. These exceptional units have joined us for the mission." He extended a hand presenting the hendros.

"*Mmm,*" Kuzu buzzed like a subwoofer.

Ferrell flashed a nervous smile at the sel and looked at Andy. "Do you need to translate for them, Dr. Beasley?"

"Understand," Kuzu said.

"Me, too," Hender said.

"They understand." Andy nodded. "If Kuzu can't, Hender can translate. Please continue."

Ferrell had seen a lot of things during his life in the service, but it took all his focus and training to overcome the shock and awe of being in the presence of alien beings that appeared to have something like human intelligence. And yet they were said to have evolved on Earth; indeed, they were said to have lived longer on Earth than humans. "Our secondary goal," he said, "is to locate and rescue Nell and Geoffrey Binswanger and capture or kill Maxim Dragolovich, the terrorist who funded the construction of this place and who might still be trapped inside this city."

"Whoa, wait—*city*?" exclaimed the large man

sitting next to Kuzu as he set up a miniature chessboard on his cannon-sized thigh. Jackson Conway Pierce was a six-foot-five Alabama farm boy with a 171 IQ, a black-ops officer for the United States military with a very dry sense of humor. "Nobody said anything about a city." He gestured to Kuzu. "Chess?"

Kuzu looked at the big man. "Yes."

"Well," Ferrell said. "It's a city. Is that clarified enough for you?"

"Yeah," Jackson said. "Go on."

"The city was called Pobedograd in Stalin's time. It was built in the years before his death and purchased by Russian bazillionaire Maxim Dragolovich about ten years ago. It would be a lot easier, of course, to just place a tactical nuke down there and call it a day. But we have targets to rescue and targets to kill or capture, if possible."

Andy's heart plunged. Finding Nell and Geoffrey alive seemed to be a conflicting and secondary objective of the mission.

Ferrell continued with mechanical efficiency. "The government of Kaziristan has buckled under considerable pressure by both the U.S. and Russian governments to let us send in this team. The Kaziristanis claim they have no knowledge of this facility, at all. They also claim they have sealed off all known ventilation shafts and entrances to it, so you do the math. The Russians have provided us with a map of the city in exchange for letting these three comrades join our team. Let me introduce them to everybody. This here is Spetsnaz *stariki* Commander, Dima Volkov, Russian special forces."

A light-haired, green-eyed man with a sharp,

devilish grin, Dima waved at the others cheerfully. "The only reason we decided to let you Yanks come along was because you brought hendros. *Zdrastvooy-tyeh!*" he laughed.

"*Spasiba,*" Hender replied.

Dima's tanned face blanched. "You speak Russian?"

Hender smiled. "Russian is fun to speak, *da*?"

Dima looked at his Russian comrade in shock.

Ferrell pointed at the huge commando who was relacing his boots beside Dima. "Spetsnaz Alfa team leader, Tusya Kovalovich."

"A small hand for the big man." Jackson nodded.

Andy clapped, then stopped, cringing in embarrassment. Jackson winked at him. "Did you say his name was Sonuvabitch?" Jackson said. The big American cupped his ear with his broad right hand as he set up the last couple of chess pieces on his magnetic board with his left hand.

Ferrel cleared his throat. "Ladies and gentlemen, former Army Ranger, Delta weapons specialist and all-around asshole, Jackson Pierce."

"Did you say Jackoff?" Tusya cupped one hand behind his ear and gripped Jackson's hand with the other in a crushing handshake. "Pleased to meet you!"

"OK," Jackson chuckled. "Let go now, Sonuvabitch!"

Tusya let the big man's bloodless hand go. "*Da,* Jackoff!"

Dima snickered.

Ferrell's jet-blue eyes burned under charcoal eyebrows as he pointed at a large man sitting across from Kuzu. "That California redwood sitting in the corner is Teddy 'Bear' Jenkins."

The big man with cropped black and silver hair nodded his scarred head, irritated.

"Bear's a former Army Ranger who's now a Delta Force sniper and sapper," Ferrell said, referring to a clipboard. "And one-half Blackfoot Indian."

"Even though he was one of the ones who screwed up at Tora Bora, we brought him along, anyway, mostly for his charming personality. Right, Bear?" Jackson laughed.

"Fuck your mother's ear," Bear growled. The mountain-faced man, who had been tuning a crossbow on his lap, extended a hand to Tusya, who immediately regretted taking it as Bear vised his grip. "Nice to meet you." Tusya felt the bones in his hand grind together as Bear grinned.

"OK!" Tusya yelled, conceding.

Kuzu watched as Bear finally let Tusya's hand go.

"Thank you, Bear." Jackson winked at the wounded Russian.

Kuzu admired Bear's weapon, stretching his neck as he peered at it with both eyes.

"OK, General Ferrell," Jackson sneered, "since you seem to be Mr. Voice and have a pipeline to SOCOM, why don't you narrate exactly what's going on in this movie?" Jackson looked down at Kuzu's latest rapid-fire move, perturbed. He enjoyed chess, but he did not enjoy getting his ass beaten like an omelet in less than four minutes by this genius spider crab.

"Let's look at the map of the city," Andy said.

"Let me introduce you to our expert in Russian excavations." Ferrell held out a hand to a slender black-clad woman who had blended like a shadow into the fuselage. "Anastasia Kurolesova from the

Moscow Geological Institute—or should we call you Doctor?"

The rather beautiful woman with short black hair smiled sardonically. "Call me Nastia." She leaned forward as she pulled a large blueprint out of a leather tube at her feet.

"Nastia is an honorary member of the Diggers Russian Underground club, I believe," Ferrell said. "She's helped map hundreds of miles of passageways in Metro-Two under Moscow—isn't that right, Doctor?"

"Of course not," she smirked. "Metro-Two does not exist. In any event, mapping it would be illegal. But, I am an expert on Soviet-era engineering projects, especially underground projects. And I'm also a musophobiac."

"What's that?" Jackson said.

"I am terrified of rats," she said.

"Then why would you devote your life to studying sewers?" Bear asked.

"Exactly." Nastia gave a faintly ironic smile as she whipped a rolled sheet of paper open on the floor of the plane between them. Her caviar-black eyes glittered with excitement as she admired the faded blueprint. "I obtained this plan of the city from Kremlin archives two days ago and was only allowed to bring a copy because of the dire circumstances. The Diggers have been requesting maps such as this for over twenty-five years, and we were always told they don't exist because, of course, none of these places exist. So, I suppose that means this is the only underground city that exists, since this is the only map that exists." She deadpanned them with 90-proof Russian sarcasm. "Stalin called it

Pobedograd—'Victory City.' Construction went on from 1950 to 1959 before it was abandoned, shortly after Stalin's death."

They gathered around the blueprint. Kuzu and Hender immediately began memorizing it like a gameboard or like a jungle, tracing walls, passages, and escape routes.

Nastia waved her hand over the large circular cavern at the center. "Sector Six is the main chamber of Pobedograd. It has a central tower thirty-five stories tall that was built for party officials. The streets radiating from the tower were to be lined with workshops, supply depots, factories, fire stations, and even restaurants and taverns. Along the river at the south end of the city are apartments and a bridge crossing the river to a train station at the southeast corner. In the northwest corner is Sector One, Stalin's palace." Her hand motioned over the blueprint as she continued. "South of the palace is Sector Five, a farm, and to the east of the palace, in Sector Two, was a garrison for Stalin's guards. Further east is Sector Three, a hospital and medical laboratory, and east of this—" Nastia pointed her red-nailed index finger at the upper right corner of the map. "—warehouses and a self-sustaining power plant."

"A power plant?" Jackson whistled.

"What kind?" Ferrell said. "Nuclear?"

"No," Nastia said. "It's quite funny. In the 1960s, the Soviets built over one hundred thirty-five robot lighthouses along the Arctic coast of Russia. The long polar night makes navigating those waters extremely dangerous. No one today knows how many or exactly where all of those lighthouses are, but since it was impossible for crews to maintain them in such remote locations, it was decided to power them with nuclear reactors that produce strontium-90. Once they were built, the Soviet work crews just threw the switch and left. They were supposed to be fully autonomous, turning on when the Arctic night arrived and turning off when day returned months later, all while radioing signals to passing ships."

"The Russian authorities might not know where all of them are, but scavengers have been dismantling those things and hauling off scrap for years," interjected a small, wiry American with brown hair and wide-set gray eyes around a hawkish nose. He had not spoken until now, and he flung a crumpled juice box between them, dropping it neatly into Dima's duffel bag just as he was zipping it open. He winked at the surprised Russian.

Captain Ferrell looked at a clipboard. "Let me introduce you to Specialist Steve Abrams, formerly with military intelligence. I hope you're as good with a grenade, Specialist."

"I'm better with grenades," Abrams answered. "If I were two inches taller, I'd be at Disney World right now with a shiny new Super Bowl ring. Instead I'm here with you assholes. Lucky for you. Hey, Bear, bet you twenty dollars I can toss this one-dollar bill in your upper pocket."

"You're on, jerk-off."

"You can't move."

"Go ahead, try it, asshole."

Abrams wadded up a dollar bill and tossed it with a perfect parabola, lobbing the balled-up note into the soldier's shirt pocket.

"Damn, dude," Bear said.

Hender and Kuzu were impressed.

"You owe me a double-sawbuck," Abrams said, turning to Nastia. "Terrorists have been trying to plunder those lighthouses for years now, darlin', as well as hundreds of other former Soviet sites powered by those nifty little portable nuclear reactors. You see, the Soviets made over five hundred of those damn things. Over a hundred have never been accounted for."

"Shit." Dima scowled.

"Yes, but finding them and taking them anywhere would probably kill you," said Nastia.

"Yeah, sure. Like that's a deterrent," Abrams said.

"Death is always a deterrent," Nastia said. "Since 1991, with help from America, Russian authorities have been trying to locate all the lighthouses so they can replace their reactors with solar-power sources. It is true that some of the reactors were already missing by the time inspectors got there. In 2001, salvagers apparently tried to strip parts from one of the lighthouses. But the men who took them were never found."

"I rest my case."

Nastia shrugged, unfazed. "You would know better than I, perhaps. But Siberia is not a pleasant place, especially along the Arctic Coast. And carrying a radioactive cargo would not make the journey any easier."

"But even the Soviets wouldn't put a nuclear power plant in an underground city," Andy said. "Would they?"

"Why not?" Abrams said. "Maybe Maxim Dragolovich has been selling strontium-90 on the black market."

"Maybe this Henders Island horror story is just a cover," Jackson concurred. "Maybe they were making a dirty bomb and had an accident down there."

"But why would they bring in scientists who had visited Henders Island?" Ferrell asked.

"It completes the illusion," Abrams said.

"Supposedly, the power plant of Pobedograd is geothermal," Nastia said. "A dry-steam generator."

Kuzu pinned Jackson's king.

"Aw!" Jackson groaned.

"Checkmate, Jackson," Kuzù said.

"Let's play," Abrams said, taking the board off Jackson's knee and setting it up on a crate in front of Kuzu. "OK?"

"OK, Abrams. Play," Kuzu said.

Abrams winked. "You go first."

Hender pointed at the map on the floor with a long arm. "Where are Nell and Geoffrey?"

"We don't know for sure," Ferrell answered, irked by the well-spoken creature. "We don't even know if they are still alive. The odds aren't good. But according to our source, they might be in the palace." Ferrell pointed at Sector One.

"Where is Maxim?" Kuzu asked.

"Just what I want to know," said Dima.

"He may be trapped here in Sector Three," said Ferrell. "This was the last place Galia Sokolof reported him going. Which brings us to our special guests, Dr. Andrew Beasley, Hender, and Kuzu." Ferrell nodded at each of them in turn. "The hendros are the only ones with any experience in this theater. They survived for thousands of years among these critters. They're here to tell us what we're up against. And what they tell us may well be the difference between life and death down there, so let's all pay attention."

"Don't leave anything out," Bear said.

Kuzu looked back at him, leaning forward with one iridescent eye that had three stacked pupils. "You survive, maybe," he said, and his lips spread into a foot-wide smile over three wide upper and lower teeth.

Andy fished his cell phone out of his vest pocket. "Can you take a picture of that map, Hender?"

"OK, Andy." Hender took the camera and unfolded his two-elbowed arm six feet as he took a picture of the map from directly above it. He handed the camera back to Andy.

"Wow," Jackson approved.

"Send that image to me, too," Abrams said, echoed by the rest.

"Sneakernet, not wireless," Ferrell said.

"Yeah, let's not bounce that image off a satellite," Abrams agreed.

"I'll pass around a memory card," Andy said, setting his phone on a crate in the middle of the floor. Then he clicked on the projector function and beamed an image from a slideshow he had prepared on a canvas tarp blocking the forward cargo in the C-130.

"What are we looking at here?" Abrams asked.

"Help us, Obi-Wan Kenobi," Jackson snickered.

"Pay attention, Jackson," Hender admonished.

The ranger's gum fell out of his mouth.

"Yeah," Andy said. "Pay attention."

The first image Andy projected was a still photo of rolling wheel-like bugs. "Disk-ants are small, but they might be the deadliest life we found on the island," said the biologist. "Their backs are covered with spirals of babies whose backs are covered with spirals of babies, and so on, down to the size of nano-ants, or 'nants,' as we call them. They roll on their edge, moving much faster than normal ants, and when they strike, the nants unload from their backs and melt flesh right off their prey's bones. They can crawl on either side, as well, and hurl themselves through the air like Frisbees."

"Frisbees?" Dima asked.

"Like Chinese throwing stars," Andy said.

Hender nodded at the blond-haired Russian soldier. "They're very bad."

Dima nodded, chilled. *"Da."*

"Each disk-ant is really a whole colony," Andy continued. "But they travel in packs." Andy clicked to a shot of three many-legged creatures in midleap, their spiked arms splayed and their round heads gashed with fang-filled smiles. "These are Henders rats: fast-breeding opportunists that eat anything alive. The average Henders rat can leap twenty feet."

"They don't look like rats," Ferrell muttered.

"They're not," Andy said. "They're bioluminescent, nocturnal, and diurnal mammal-like descendants of crustaceans with stripes that flash colors on their heads to confuse prey and predators."

"It wouldn't confuse me," Abrams said. "Or my machine gun."

Bear laughed. "I hear that, brother."

"Don't run straight," Kuzu said as he moved his knight to counter Abrams's bishop.

"Ah," Ferrell noted. "Good tip from Kuzu, everybody."

"Zigzag." Hender nodded.

Andy clicked to the next image of a strange growth covering what looked like a log. With oddly geometric edges, the lichenlike growth was colored green, orange, yellow, red, purple, and white. "This is Henders clover. It's not dangerous, but everything eats it and it eats everything. Plus it photosynthesizes and makes oxygen. It uses sulfuric acid to eat through just about anything."

"Run on green," Kuzu said. "Better."

"Huh?" Abrams said.

"It's better to run on green clover," Hender agreed. "Purple will melt your feet."

"Gotcha! Thank you." Jackson looked at the others.

"Go on," Bear said grimly.

Andy clicked to the next image: a six-legged beast launching off a thick tail with vertical jaws and giant spiked arms.

"*Chërt!*" Dima cursed.

"What the hell is that thing?" Jackson said.

"A spiger," Tusya chided. "Where have you been, in a cave?"

The others laughed.

"Yes, that's a spiger," Andy said. "They grow as big as a pickup truck and can jump thirty-five feet or more and swallow a man whole. I don't see how they could have gotten live spigers here, but you should see it, just in case. This snapshot was taken by a *National Geographic* photographer on the machine gun turret of a Humvee in which the famous naturalist Sir Nigel Holscomb rode across Henders Island. The spiger chasing them was roughly the size of the vehicle it's chasing in the photo."

"OK, so spigers just kill you," observed Jackson.

"Yeah," said Andy. "Pretty much."

"Looks like a big damn target for an incendiary grenade to me," Abrams said, throwing a wadded-up Nicorette package at the projected image and hitting the spiger's mouth dead center.

Kuzu leaned down and whispered into Abrams's ear chillingly: "You might live, too."

"OK," Ferrell said. "What else?"

Andy put the next image up. Curving "tree" trunks bent together like whale ribs along a twisting jungle corridor. "They look like trees," the biologist said, "but they're animals. Some of them shoot poisonous bloodsucking darts, others have jaws for bark, and most hang sticky eggs like bait for passing predators."

"Welcome to the jungle," Jackson grunted, popping his last square of Nicorette gum.

"What else?" Bear said.

Andy clicked to an image of two flying bugs, one with five wings over ten opposing praying mantis-like claws and a fanged abdomen. "That's a Henders wasp. They have a brain at both ends, eat with their butts, and inject larvae through a needlelike ovipositor at the same time. Their larvae bore through flesh, seeking out the electrical signals of nerves in order to immobilize their prey with pain."

"Jesus H. Christ," Bear said.

Andy showed a picture of another buglike species, this one with three wings, three long legs and a drill-bit abdomen. "The drill-worm. Its butt can drill through wood, human flesh, bone, and just about anything else but glass, rock, or steel. Both of these bugs are bioluminescent and highly active, day or night. You don't want to see either of them without something between you and it."

"Shit. I'm starting to think we should just set off a dirty bomb down there and call it a day," said Jackson.

"Me, too," Dima agreed.

"What is your plan?" Andy asked. "Because this stuff is worse than any WMD. These are weapons of *global* destruction. They're self-replicating and absolutely lethal to all life on land. If this stuff gets anywhere near us, we're as good as dead. And if it gets out, it's the end of the world. Everything on Henders Island evolved to kill in an all-predator ecosystem over hundreds of millions of years. It fights everything that doesn't kill it first. It never backs down. It always escalates. Not even a mongoose lasted more than a few minutes on Henders Island."

"Well, we've got a few killing machines of our own," Jackson said, rising.

"Like what?" Nastia said. She looked pale and terrified by Andy's slideshow.

"Let's take a look," Jackson said. "Ferrell, why don't you give me a hand?"

Ferrell and Jackson pulled up the tarp on which Andy had projected his images and revealed a number of large flats stacked with high-tech equipment.

Jackson tapped each item with reverence through plastic wrapping as he ran down their inventory: "AA-12 fully automatic combat shotguns with detachable thirty-two-round polymer drum magazines, each with a forty-meter range. Based on what we're hearing, I'm definitely packing one of these puppies. Right here we have a crate of M84 flash-bangs, which produce a one-million-candlelight flash and a 180-decibel bang. Yell 'fire in the hole' when you throw one and make sure to cover your ears and eyes. Right here we have M7A2 riot-control tear gas grenades and AN-M14 thermite incendiaries that burn at four thousand degrees Fahrenheit, the temperature on the surface of the sun. They burn underwater, too. And these right here are some good old-fashioned M67 fragmentation grenades. Plus an assortment of even nastier stink bombs with assorted internationally banned contents."

Andy pointed to a humanoid erector set that looked like a collapsed Transformer in the center of the flat. "What's that?"

"That, my friend, is the latest Sarcos Raytheon XOS Exoskeleton," Jackson said.

"No shit?" Bear grunted.

Kuzu was distracted by Abrams's sacrificing his queen as the small, wiry human stood up to get a closer look at the battle gear.

"Who's going to be the Terminator?" Tusya said.

"I am," Abrams said. "I'm the reason it's here, actually. And I'm the only one trained to use it."

"Well, then, Iron Man, tell us what it can do," Ferrell said.

"It comes with full body-armor like something out of *Star Wars,* too." Abrams winked at Kuzu, leaving his queen in danger as he approached the mountain of equipment. "When suited up in this thing, a man can lift two hundred pounds with each arm, punch through brick walls, and run at twelve miles per hour for ninety minutes before changing batteries. *Heh, heh*. It's more fun than a new Rush album."

Kuzu took Abrams's queen.

"Well, well," Abrams said, bending down to take Kuzu's knight with a pawn that was now one move from queening.

Kuzu's fur flushed violet. Abrams had disguised offense inside a seemingly reckless defense, Kuzu noted, learning from him.

"Well, you won't be the only robot down there," Jackson said, resting his hand on some cylindrical shapes under the shrink-wrap. "These babies right here are Dalek combat robots, flying Crock-Pots with four landing legs. They can hover or cruise at twenty miles an hour, automatically turn around corners, and feed back reconnaissance. And we've got the latest crawling bugs, too. These little knights in shining armor are Talon SWORDS, robot rovers with M249 SAW machine guns, which fire a thousand rounds per minute. They can climb stairs, travel over sand, snow, water, and debris while transmitting video back in color, black-and-white, infrared, or night vision. Best of all, we've trained these hounds to heel and follow us wherever we go." Jackson walked around to the other side of the swaddled flat of equipment. He raised his arm in a flourish. "Last, but not least, we brought the Big Dog." He patted the plastic-covered shape. "The latest quadrupedal all-terrain cargo robot. Wait'll you see her." Jackson lifted what looked like a video game controller hanging from a cord around his neck. "All these bots follow this dog whistle, which also signals commands."

"I want a dog whistle," Abrams said.

Dima nodded. "Me, too."

"All right, that can be arranged," Jackson said. "But I'm the alpha dog."

"There's an alpha dog override function I'll show you how to use on your own dog whistles," Ferrell said.

"But only if the alpha dog says it's OK," Jackson said.

"Or dies," Ferrell said.

"That's good," Tusya said.

"That brings us to body armor," Jackson said. "We've got the best in the world, Dragon Skin. It's made of laminated silicon-carbide ceramic and titanium matrices overlapping like dragon scales covered with Kevlar. We all have full suits that cover wrists and necks, with helmets whose exterior microphones transmit sound to the ears and whose radios transmit our voices to each other. Our helmets also have rearview visor display. Since we'll mostly be communicating with our helmet radios, we have to remember to keep them switched on, folks. We have a large supply of oxygen canisters on hand in case the gas in the cave becomes unbreathable. These species may be more evolved for battle than we are, but we've got technology, folks. I guarantee they've never come up against what we're bringing to the fight."

"We want Russian body armor," Dima said.

"Kirasa!" Tusya insisted.

"Boys, I know you're proud of your country," said Jackson. "And I'll give you a lot of credit for that. But compared to what we've got here, Kirasa armor is crap. No offense."

Dima spit.

"We'll do it your way this time," Tusya said.

Kuzu marveled at the amazing devices the humans had made to compensate for their physical frailty.

"Checkmate, my friend," said Abrams.

Kuzu looked down. The human had trapped his king with a second queened pawn. The hendro nodded, impressed. "Thank you, Abrams."

Abrams marked the creature's dignified defeat warily.

Nastia sat beside Andy. "What are you doing here?" she asked the skinny biologist whose shaggy blond hair and thick glasses marked him as a civilian.

Andy frowned, already asking himself the same thing. "I'm here with the hendros. I'm the first human they ever met. And my friends, Nell and Geoffrey, are trapped inside."

"I think you're crazy," she said.

"What are you doing here?"

She laughed. "I'm an expert in underground Soviet installations. And, also . . . Well, my grandfather died in this city. Trofim Lysenko sent a letter to my grandmother. He told her he had met my grandfather, who was a mining engineer, inside a great city under a mountain. I think this is the place he was talking about."

"You're crazier than I am."

"You're probably right."

"*The* Trofim Lysenko?" Andy asked.

"Yes. He also said that there were monsters inside the city," Nastia said.

"Like what?"

"Well . . . he said that my grandfather was attacked by a ghost."

"Oh," Andy shrugged. "Ghosts I can handle."

Kuzu retrieved his bow from below his seat as he examined his weapon.

Bear noticed him and brought his bow over to

compare with Kuzu's, which was a three-armed bow, made to be loaded with a fourth arm. With all his might, Bear could only half bend it. Kuzu was pleased to find that Bear's arrows could equally work with his bow, and especially pleased when Bear offered him a dozen of the aluminum shafts.

Hender approached Kuzu and spoke to him in his own language. "*Do you still think humans mean us harm?*"

Kuzu replied, "*They want to kill off everything else from our world.*"

"*They? There is no 'they,' Kuzu,*" Hender said in a buzzing rebuke. "*Remember? There is only one. And one. And one. No 'they!'* "

Kuzu let loose a long, rumbling laugh, his chest compressing like bagpipes. "That *is how you win, Shenuday,*" he said. "*I learn from you.*"

"*This is not chess, Kuzu,*" Hender said.

"*Oh, yes, it is.*"

9:11 P.M.

They arrived in the town of Gursk by helicopter, landing on a children's football field in the pouring rain.

Three waiting cars conveyed them to a small hotel, where they had twenty minutes to deposit their luggage and freshen up. The sels occupied the room adjoining Nastia and Andy's room. Andy overheard them arguing, in Kuzu's language mixed with English. They had been given a room together, which was a mistake and one that the small hotel seemed unable to rectify despite Andy's efforts.

Twenty minutes later, the sels and humans met

downstairs in a private dining room, where they were joined by Kaziristani officials and a man who introduced himself as Galia Sokolof. He was the man who would be their guide into the city.

"How could your government allow terrorists to take over this facility?" Andy asked the officials tactlessly.

Galia answered, to the consternation of the Kaziristanis. "The government of Kaziristan sold the city of Pobedograd to Maxim Dragolovich for 380,000 American dollars in the year 2001 in a perfectly legal transaction. He is not a terrorist."

"We sold salvaging license to company whose stated intent was to scrap city for steel," snapped one of the officials, butting out his cigarette in an ashtray on the table and shooting a look at Galia.

"I won't argue," Galia said, closing his eyes and waving a hand.

"Well, it sounds like a bargain for a whole city," Andy said.

"It's not unusual," Nastia said. "Many of these underground facilities from the Cold War have been sold for bargain basement prices by local authorities. Nobody has much use for them. In Moscow, the underground is so extensive and secret that some people even live there, in places the government does not even know about. An entire subculture of people are devoted to exploring and mapping these places," she said. "Of course, I am not involved with such individuals."

"Of course," said Dima. "That would be illegal."

The Kaziristani official continued. "There is only one way left into the mine. We have already sealed all other entrances with explosives and concrete, including all the city's ventilation shafts on Mount Kazar."

"Are you sure?" Andy asked.

"We are sure. And we were going to seal off the last entrance, too, before we got word that we must let your team in. We will do so, but with these conditions: You are to set timed explosives in the train tunnel heading west from the city. No one seems to know how far that tunnel goes. And you will have eight hours from the time you enter to complete your mission before we seal the entrance. Is that understood?"

The Russians looked at one another across the table and the Americans looked at one another, as well.

"All right," Jackson said, raising his warm beer and taking a swig. "So I guess we're done?"

"All right," Ferrell agreed. "Thank you for the hospitality, and I guess we should all get some sleep. We'll meet here at 0500. Sweet dreams."

"Don't let the bedbugs bite." Bear grinned at Kuzu.

MARCH 31

5:49 P.M. MAXIM TIME

Geoffrey, Nell, and Sasha looked through Hell's Window together, sitting in chairs in front of the banquet table, which they had turned parallel to the long portal. Each night they all took an hour after dinner to observe the world of Pandemonium, a necessary distraction from the mountain of terror pressing down on them as they waited for help that might never come.

Nell had opened the leather-bound book she had found in Stalin's desk, ruffling its marbled edges. As she leafed through the pages, penned in Cyrillic script, she thought it might be a journal of some kind, with many illustrations that looked like the animals of Pandemonium. On the inside cover of the antique book she now noticed a name and a date: *Трохим Денисович Лисенко, 1958.* "Geoffrey . . ."

"Yes?"

"What do you think of this?" She showed him the name in the book. "Could this be . . . Trofim? . . ."

"Denisovich . . . Lysenko?" Geoffrey completed the name as he looked closer and compared the strange letters to the name of the famous Ukrainian agricultural scientist. "You could be right!"

All biologists, especially plant biologists like Nell, knew the story of Trofim Lysenko, who rose in the Soviet Union on his unorthodox theories of acquired inheritance before falling when those ideas proved disastrous for Soviet farming. His star had already dimmed by the late 1950s, Nell remembered. "Maybe Stalin sent him here when he fell out of favor."

Geoffrey scanned the sketches that recorded fantastic species, some of which they had seen today, each looking like something imagined by Jules Verne. "If it is Lysenko's journal, then he must have been here."

"Look at his drawings, Sasha," Nell marveled. On the first page was a cross-hatched pen-and-ink drawing of an oval window with curtains to either side.

Sasha pointed at the drawing. "That's this window!"

"Yes," Nell said.

The book's pages were filled with sketches of species they had not yet seen or even imagined.

"Wow, honey," Nell suddenly realized. "Look at all the underwater species he's cataloged here."

A fuchsia and orange sphere of six-inch tongues rolled over Hell's Window above and Sasha shouted. "Hey, you guys! Here comes the *sushi wagon*!"

They both looked up. "Sushi wagon?" Geoffrey asked.

"It's a sushi bar on *wheels*! Everything loves the

sushi wagon," she said. "I was wondering when one would show up. Watch!"

The buoy-sized ball rolled down the window like the sticky toys children throw at walls; and when it reached the bottom of the window, gammarids and even aggregators leaped out of nowhere to tear off the sashimi-like tongues of flesh covering the globe's surface.

"It's like a giant *Volvox*," said Geoffrey, shifting his bound foot that continued to throb with pain. The large ball rolled along the window's ledge with its vividly hued tongues. "Maybe it's a colony of creatures that fuse together into these spheres." Animals were attacking it from all directions.

"Everything's ripping off pieces of it. How does it survive?" Nell wondered.

"Don't worry," Sasha said. "That's how the sushi wagon makes babies. Dimitri told me that one out of a hundred pieces of sushi has eggs inside that hatch in the stomachs of the animals that eat them. They turn into new sushi balls and burst out!"

"Wow," Geoffrey said. "Now that's bad sushi."

Nell pointed at a milky slug or flatworm that was the size of a throw rug, which glided over the top edge of the window. She rose and examined its ventral surface as it shimmied over the glass. "I think I've seen one of those before."

Geoffrey noticed there were ten *S*-ing rows of suction cups extending around the giant flatworm's head. "I've definitely seen one of those before," he said, and he hobbled to his feet and stood closer to the window. "It's some kind of land octopus. . . ."

"It's a ghost!" Sasha cried, clutching Nell's arm.

"No," said Nell.

"Look," Geoffrey countered, pointing at the suction cups.

"Amphipods and mollusks," Nell said.

"Both ancient groups of animals," Geoffrey agreed.

"It makes sense," Nell said. "They must have been isolated for hundreds of millions of years to diverge this radically."

"But how could this place have existed so long?" Geoffrey shook his head. "That's what puzzles me."

"Henders Island existed longer," Nell reminded him. "Back to the pre-Cambrian. One tiny fragment that made it through."

"Dimitri said the Urals are the oldest mountain range on Earth," Geoffrey recalled as the opalescent creature rippled rows of suction cups like a kaleidoscopic caterpillar moving down the glass. The creature turned, moving parallel with the bottom of the window, and about three feet from the edge, it stopped. Peeling its lower edge from the glass, the ghostly mollusk lifted the right side of its body outward.

"What is it doing?" Nell breathed.

They watched anxiously.

One of the gammies flitted past on the window ledge beneath it and, with shocking quickness, the creature slapped down and pressed the kicking amphipod against the window.

"Whoa!" Nell said.

What happened next was like a diabolical miracle: the amorphous mollusk stretched down over each jerking leg of the pinned gammarid. Suction cups on its underside clamped into each joint of the gammy's legs with some kind of beaks.

"They have suckers like colossal squids!" Geoffrey exclaimed.

"They're more like *jaws,*" Nell whispered.

After each joint of the animal was vised by the suction clamps, the terrestrial octopus moved its head into position and crunched the amphipod's neck with knifelike blades that sawed through its nerve cord. All at once, the gammy's legs went limp.

"Dear God," Geoffrey muttered.

The paralyzed creature's legs suddenly pointed forward and then backwards across the window, flexing in unison as the mollusk seemed to be testing its control of the animal's body like a puppeteer.

"What?" Nell gasped, looking at Geoffrey.

The octopus rolled off the glass, now in full possession of its prey, and grabbed hold of the window ledge with the gammarid's long legs. The flesh of the octopus changed color before their eyes, matching the amphipod's checkered yellow-orange-and-white pattern.

"Did that just happen?" Nell asked.

Geoffrey nodded. "It's like some sort of mimic octopus," he said.

"What's a mimic octopus?" Sasha asked.

"The mimic octopus," he explained, "can fake the shape, color, and motions of more than a dozen creatures. It can make itself look and even move like a lionfish, a flounder, a sea snake, a mantis shrimp, and even brittle stars—animals from completely different branches of life. This animal might be some kind of cousin or crazy uncle of the mimic octopus."

Nell felt a deep, primal fear as she watched the ghoulish animal move the carcass of the gammarid, testing its control. "That thing attached itself to the gammy like an external muscular system!"

Geoffrey nodded. He stared at the creature, remembering what one of them had done to the guard outside the power plant. He didn't want to tell them what he had seen, and he didn't want to scare Sasha. "Octopuses are incredibly smart," he said.

"An octopus predicted the winner of the World Cup!" Sasha said.

"That's right." Geoffrey laughed.

"I hate them!" Sasha said, wrinkling her nose.

"There's a species of fungus that turns ants into zombies," Nell said as she stared at the ghost octopus moving the gammy's limbs in jerky motions now, mimicking the other gammies. "The fungus actually makes the ants cut leaves for the fungus to feed on, all through a strange kind of mind control."

"Really?" Geoffrey asked. He squeezed her hand. "That's why I married you."

A group of gammies leaped past the window now, and the ghostly octopus followed them with its gammy body, joining the herd.

"Is it a parasite?" Geoffrey wondered.

"Maybe it hunts gammarids like a wolf in sheep's clothing," Nell said.

"Does it kill its prey or just ride it like a bicycle while it's paralyzed?"

"Or does it do *both*—and trade gammy bodies for new ones when it's through, like a predatory hermit crab?"

"Maybe it lays eggs inside the gammy?"

"Why?" she asked.

"It could be the only place its offspring won't get

eaten by other gammies, at least until they gestate. Maybe it moves among them while its eggs hatch and eat the gammarid's insides, and when the offspring are big enough, they come out to catch a ride of their own. It could be something entirely new, honey."

"Well," Nell allowed, "most animals on Earth have many parasites that live in and on their bodies. Nearly a thousand species live only inside the human mouth."

"Yuck!" said Sasha.

"Bacteria, viruses, fungi, and single-celled microbes outnumber cells in the human body by ten to one, and there are ten trillion cells in the human body. We're all walking ecosystems."

"But I've never seen this kind of relationship before. Yes, each of us is an ecosystem that makes up one superindividual," agreed Geoffrey. "But have you *ever* seen a parasite that climbed on board and turned its vegetarian host into a hunting machine?" Geoffrey asked.

"Yes," Nell said. "We turned horses into hunters and engines of war."

"Oh." He nodded. "Right."

"That's why you married me."

"Uh-huh."

"You guys!" Sasha shouted, rolling her eyes. "You make me sick when you do that! Look!"

A giant gammarid the size of a lion scrabbled on six long legs over an outcrop ten yards below the window.

"A soldier gammy!" Geoffrey whispered.

"It's like the monster in my apartment in New York when I was an undergraduate," Nell said.

"Huh?" Sasha wondered.

"I killed a roach that big with a butcher knife one night, I swear."

"Oh, Nell," Sasha said. "That's not true!"

The soldier gammarid flexed giant mandibles and was covered with spikes pointing laterally in each direction. It was surrounded by much smaller specimens with smaller mandibles that scrabbled underneath it. Then Geoffrey noticed the rippling muscles on the soldier's back. "It's a ghost!"

The possessed gammarid suddenly attacked the smaller amphipods around it with its zombie legs and mandibles, controlled by the mollusk on its back, which fed them into the gammy's mouth.

"Well, that answers it," Nell said. "They're predators that probably lay eggs inside their prey and feed the brood when it hatches inside the exoskeleton."

"Parasite-predators," Geoffrey said.

"Parators?" Nell suggested. "Parasites that parrot their prey."

"Perfect." Geoffrey nodded.

"You guys like naming things, too!" Sasha said. "I still call them ghosts."

"That's actually a really good name, Sasha," Nell said. "Ghost octopus." She shuddered. "You were right. This place is haunted."

With a violent flash of light, they were left in sudden, silent darkness before the glowing creatures of Pandemonium.

Sasha screamed.

"The power went out!" Nell whispered.

Geoffrey looked around, waiting.

After a beat, they heard an engine kick-start and

chug somewhere below. The lights came back on, at less than half strength.

"The emergency generator," Geoffrey said.

6:04 A.M.

Maxim continued to key in passwords Sasha may have used to access the door controls. He could try only five before he was locked out and had to wait half an hour before trying again.

The stuffy dormitory was strewn with empty cans of tuna and pineapple, their subsistence for these last days. They had kept watch through the city's cameras, surveying the city and the train station for any sign of entry by humans.

Suddenly, the lights went out.

"Chief!" shouted one of his guards.

"They cut off our power," said Dimitri.

A generator kicked on, throbbing distantly through the floors below, and the lights came back on.

"They're here," Maxim said, grimly.

6:05 A.M.

Nastia spoke through her headset to the others inside the noisy helicopter as they approached Mount Kazar.

"Cold War American complexes like Mount Weather and NORAD's Cheyenne Mountain are dwarfed by the projects of the former Soviet Union," Nastia explained to Ferrell and Jackson, who stood with her behind the cockpit. "Five percent of the population in each republic of the USSR was provided with subsurface accommodations in the event of disaster, though few such facilities were ever finished or adequately supplied." She fired off factoids nervously as they choppered up the snow-patched slopes.

"Hey, let me guess. Did you write a book about this?" Jackson said.

Nastia turned to him seriously and then laughed. "Yes. It's called *The Underground History of Planet Earth*."

"I'll be sure to buy it at Barnes and Noble, ma'am." He winked. "I must say, you're very pretty for a bookworm. No offense, there, Dima."

Dima had, in fact, tensed as Jackson flirted with Nastia. He tensed more as Nastia noticed it now.

"You're very smart for a soldier," she replied wryly. "No offense."

"I know," Jackson replied.

"All right, we're touching down, folks," Ferrell announced sharply.

The olive drab CH-47 Chinook set down like a locust on a field beside a knoll on Mount Kazar's foothills. The government official sitting up front pointed to a hatch that resembled a closed eyelid. A cracked concrete ramp led down to the rusty hatch.

"That's the entrance you will use to get into the city," said the Kaziristani official in the helicopter. "We cut off power a few minutes ago."

"It's a large elevator," shouted Galia, "which drops down to the main subway line into the city!"

"Does it work without power?" Abrams asked.

"The cable powering the elevator is still live," said the official. "We will open this door only once more, if you make it back here before eight hours. After eight hours, we are sealing this exit with concrete. We are taking a chance we don't want to take right now by leaving this entrance open. You understand? Many are wondering why we are letting you do this. But we need to make sure the train tunnel is sealed. If you are not back in eight hours, you will not be able to get out. Ever."

"Yes, sir, we understand," Jackson said. "Just be ready to open it any time *before* eight hours. Right?"

"Of course. But the clock starts as soon as you go in."

Jackson pursed his lips and looked at Abrams. "We got it. And also please remember we're doing you a favor. We'll seal that tunnel. And you won't ever have to thank us, whether we make it back or not."

The Kaziristani heard him. "Yes. And you will still have eight hours. No more. And I promise, whether you make it back or not, I will thank you, if you seal that tunnel."

6:31 A.M.

The men unloaded their gear from three helicopters onto the foothills of Mount Kazar, which were dusted with yellow and blue wildflowers.

The soldiers inspected and loaded their weapons and stowed additional ammunition, battery packs, and other equipment on the Big Dog, which Jackson now activated outside the mine entrance.

The robot sprang to uncanny life as it balanced on four mammalian legs. The others continued to load parcels onto the robot's back as it reacted to each payload like a pack mule, shifting its four feet as it absorbed the weight and maintained its balance.

"This thing is freaking me out," Bear said.

"Isn't it awesome?" Jackson said.

The Big Dog could, in fact, carry a half-*ton* payload. It was, for all its futuristic strangeness, part of a long and established lineage of mechanical mules employed by the army since World War II.

Ferrell helped Andy get into his Dragon Skin body armor on the slope of Mount Kazar. Jackson helped the Russians and Galia get zipped up, as well. Abrams snapped himself into armor that resembled a medieval knight crossed with a comic book superhero. He then climbed into the exoskeleton and buckled himself in, rising to eight feet as he walked to the entrance of the mine.

Andy watched him move in the XOS, with effortless grace and balance that reacted precisely to the motions of his own body. Abrams winked at Andy as he ran around in a quick circle on the grass with ease despite the weight of the machine. The robotic muscles made only a whisper of noise inside the hydraulic actuators. He helped load the last heavy boxes of ammo, explosives, and batteries onto the mule, each arm lifting two hundred pounds with only ten pounds of pressure.

"God almighty." Jackson almost drooled. "That thing rocks."

The Kaziristani officials looked at each other with wide eyes.

Kuzu pursed his lips, glancing at Hender. "Humans," he muttered.

Ferrell produced a plastic jug. "This is a synthesized version of a pheromone that Henders animals spray as a warning signal." Ferrell tipped some onto his hand and rubbed it over himself. "It's supposed to be a good repellent." He offered it to Hender and Kuzu, who smelled it and declined.

The others now poured some from the jug and splashed it over their armored bodies.

"All right, everybody. We've got eight hours. Let's not waste any of it. The first stop is the train tunnel. We set our explosives and move on. Hender and Kuzu, if we meet up with any critters down there, don't be shy about giving us advice on how to fight them. OK?"

"How to *fight* them?" Kuzu asked, and he seemed to laugh as his crest resonated with a deep snorting sound.

"Kill the big one," Hender said, "and run."

They all looked at one another, wondering if Hender was joking.

"They'll turn on the biggest animal that goes down," Andy said. "Otherwise, they'll probably keep attacking." The scientist tried to breathe calmly in and out through his helmet's air filter. "Also, keep changing directions, never travel in a straight line, and don't ever stop."

"All right. Good advice," Ferrell said. "Is everyone's helmet mike working? Everyone can hear each other? Bear?"

"Affirmative."

"Abrams?"

"Check."

"Dima?"

"*Da.*"

"Tusya?"

"Yes."

"Jackson?"

"Loud and clear."

"Nastia?"

"What am I doing here?"

"Andy?"

"Yes!"

"Galia?"

"I hear you."

"Can you hendros hear us?"

"Yes!" they both answered.

"OK. Good. We don't want the speaker volume to be too loud. Everyone set it on three and turn up the microphone ears to nine," Ferrell said. "And turn your rearview display on."

"Yeah, we definitely need to know what's coming at us from both directions," Andy said. "Many Henders species have two brains and two sets of eyes."

"I can't process that much data very effectively," Abrams said. "I've only got one brain."

"Together we have a lot of brains. Shout out if you see anything approaching according to the hands on a clock. Six o'clock for something behind us, twelve o'clock for something in front. Everyone put the rearview on your visor display now. Let's open the door!" said Ferrell.

Men stood ready with flamethrowers as the Kaziristanis tried to crank the huge wheel on the hatch, but it was stuck.

"Move aside," Abrams said as he gripped the wheel with two metal hands and easily turned the dog wheel in a steady squeaking rotation "hand" over "hand." Then he pulled open the wide door that was big enough for a semi truck to drive through.

Inside, the light of the headless mule revealed a tunnel to another door.

"A double hatch," Jackson said.

"They were afraid of radiation," Galia said.

"These doors are probably lead-lined," said Nastia.

"Yes," Galia said.

"Good," Ferrell said. "Come on."

The mechanical mule followed Jackson in, and the others followed. The men outside shut the door behind them and cranked the wheel closed.

Ferrell instructed everyone to start the stopwatch function on their watches at eight hours. They counted down together, and on his mark the seconds began dissolving the zeros.

07:59:58

Abrams slid open the second door, which opened to a huge elevator. They filed in and Galia pointed out the actuator. Ferrell depressed the switch, and the lift sank into the earth.

07:58:02

They reached the bottom and pushed open the wide doors. They found themselves in a barrel-vaulted subway tunnel running north, according to their wrist compasses, which were the only global positioning devices they would have from now on. They turned left and proceeded north down the tunnel.

After a quarter mile they came to a bronze plaque on the wall that Nastia translated with a dry flourish:

ALL HAIL OUR VALOROUS 1,609 FALLEN COMRADES WHO GAVE THEIR LIVES TO THE GLORIOUS SOVIET STATE TO BUILD THIS CITY UNDER ORDER OF PREMIER JOSEPH STALIN.

"That's a lie," Nastia said. "Seventy thousand men died constructing this city, at least."

Hender was amazed.

Kuzu silently scanned everything around them in the dark as they walked, an arrow nocked in his three-handed bow.

"According to official records, the city was abandoned when Stalin died," Nastia said, glancing at Dima and Kuzu.

"The locals believe the workers left because they struck Hell," Galia said. "They believe the ghosts of the men who died here still haunt the city."

"What do you believe?" she asked.

"I have seen worse things than ghosts down here."

"Do you believe in ghosts, Nastia?" Abrams asked as he gracefully pranced along in the XOS suit next to the subway track.

"No," said the geologist, looking around as she imagined her grandfather being taken down this tunnel.

"How far are we from the station, Galia?" Ferrell asked.

"It's not far now. Around the next bend, we should see it."

As they came around a slight bend, the headlight of the mule illuminated a small building with a pillar-lined platform. In front of the station was an abandoned subway car. Railroad tracks headed west, to their left, disappearing into a lightless void.

To the right of the station was a steel gate large enough for trucks to pass.

"From inside that station, you can see across a river to the city," said Galia.

"All right. Let's take a look," said Ferrell.

They climbed onto the marble platform and entered the subway station through a doorless arch, the mule gamely following up the steps behind them, along with their two tank-treaded Talons. Through the reinforced windows, they could see mostly pitch-blackness; but when they turned off the robots' lights and their flashlights, they could see glowing clouds swarming in the distance, outlining the negative shapes of buildings and a central tower that touched the capacious cavern's ceiling.

"My God," Nastia said. "That chamber must be larger than the Big Room in the Carlsbad Caverns of New Mexico, maybe bigger than the Sarawak Chamber in Borneo . . ."

Hender looked through the window and recognized what he saw across the river. "Very bad."

"Yeah, what's that glowing stuff out there?" Jackson said.

"Henders species are equally active at night," Andy said, recognizing them even from this distance by their color. "And many of them are bioluminescent. Those glowing clouds are swarms."

"He did it," muttered Galia.

"Damn," Abrams said.

Some of the green lights had linked together in spirals like floating nucleotides, twinkling over the black river. "Those long chains are Henders wasps," Andy said. "They link together when mating."

"Awesome, they're mating," Jackson said.

"Talk about an assembly line," Abrams said.

"Yeah," Andy said.

"Very bad," said Hender.

"Sector Six is breached," Galia said, and he hunched over in grief. "There were five thousand people living there."

"God Almighty," Ferrell muttered.

"Hender, can you get us through there?" Abrams asked.

"No."

"OK. So what should we do?" Andy said.

"We'll need to find another route," Galia said.

A swarm of light that looked like a giant phantom soared over the bridge toward the station.

"This station is sealed, right?" Dima asked.

"Yes," Galia said. "But we should pull down these shutters." He pointed at the blast doors hooked against the ceiling. "The shields are lined with lead and should be too heavy for anything to push open when they're lowered."

"Get her done, man," Jackson said.

Since they had the highest reach, the hendros and Abrams reached up. Unfolding their lower legs, the hendros stretched out their arms to unlatch the metal shutters from the ceiling. All three of the steel panels swung down on low-geared hinging mechanisms, booming softly against the window frames.

"There're no locks on those?" Jackson said.

"They're very heavy," Galia said. "Nothing will get through."

"Let's go," Ferrell said. "The first thing we gotta do is seal the tunnel."

"Stalin often had secret ways to enter and exit,"

Nastia said. "There may be a secret passage to the train tunnel from the palace."

"You are quite right," Galia said. "There are many secret routes. Nobody knows them all."

"OK," Jackson said. "Keep an eye out for one along the way."

07:35:27

In the dark conservatory, lit only by the luminescent creatures in the window, Nell noticed movement on the monitor that showed the train station in Sector Seven. "Honey!" she yelled.

07:35:28

Geoffrey gazed through the window upstairs at the steel gondola that was caked with rainbow fire like the encrusted hull of a boat. The gondola had a 1950s sleek and rounded shape pointing in both directions. It hung from cables dusted with rainbow-fire that were strung over the lake to a towering stalagmite on the jagged island in the lake. No doubt Stalin had planned this as another escape route, but had he carried it to completion? He must have exposed hundreds of people to fatal danger in order to build it. The state of the gondola did not look promising. A large, antique diesel engine on the landing apparently pulled the cable car over the lake. Had Maxim refurbished it? Canisters of fuel stacked in front of it looked new.

Suddenly, he realized Nell was calling him, and Geoffrey hopped down the spiral stairs. Just before the bottom, he slipped, crashing on the floor knee-first. "Ow, *fuck*!" he groaned, just as Sasha arrived from downstairs with Ivan.

"Dear, be careful," Nell said. "Use the cane!"

"Yes," he agreed, propping himself up with Stalin's cane.

"Someone's in Sector Seven!" Nell's pulse raced as a number of people entered in heavy armor, wearing helmets and carrying weapons. A quadrupedal robot trotted behind the people into the station like a reindeer loaded with packs. The bizarre bot moved with surprising animality though it appeared to lack a head. Then, to her amazement, she saw Hender and Kuzu enter the frame of the screen. "Honey!" she yelled.

"I see them!" he said, as he limped over.

"Wow!" Sasha said. "Are those *hendros*?"

"Yeah, Sasha!" Geoffrey said. "The good guys. There's Hender!"

"Kuzu, too," Nell said.

"Unbelievable!"

She switched on the microphone inside the train station and turned up the sound on the monitor. They heard a snippet of English: "*. . . train tunnel.*"

"Can we talk to them, Sasha?"

"There's no intercom to the train station."

Nell looked at Geoffrey urgently. "I have to get to them."

"You're not going," he said.

"Can you walk that far?"

Geoffrey knew she was right.

"It's now or never," she said. "You know I have to."

"Then we should go with you," Sasha said. "I

told you, the tunnel's haunted, Nell. It's loaded with ghosts!"

"I'll go with you," Geoffrey said. "I can make a splint or something."

"There's no time. And it's just as important that you stay here, with Sasha," she said. "You have to watch the security cameras. There's a camera at the end of Stalin's escape route over his private train platform, right, Sasha?"

"Yes." Sasha nodded. "Papa put a camera there. But what about the ghosts?" She grabbed Nell's hand.

Nell called up the camera view on the monitor. "There it is. OK. They have to pass that way."

"Nell, it's crazy, damn it!" Geoffrey frowned.

"Keep watch from here. I'll come back to get you. If they got in, they can get us out, Geoffrey! But that hatch is probably locked from the inside like all the rest. Somebody has to let them in."

"It's true," said Sasha sadly.

Geoffrey shook his head.

"There's no choice!" Nell said. She grabbed the jug of repellent and started splashing it over herself. "Help me. Please."

07:34:02

Downstairs, Geoffrey doused Nell with the jug of repellent he had brought from the lab one last time. She taped a flashlight to the muzzle of the machine gun. The weapon still seemed to have a lot of ammunition. "Sweetheart," he said, his throat tightening. "You better come back." He hugged her and squeezed her to him.

"I know," she whispered. "Take care of Sasha." Then she kissed Sasha. "Take care of Geoffrey."

"OK. He needs a lot of help! You smell funny."

Nell and Geoffrey twisted the hatch wheel and opened the door to Stalin's secret passage, which headed due south. She kissed him hard before she pulled away and shone her Maglite down the barrel-arched corridor stretching downhill in front of her.

"Go fast!" Sasha called.

"I will," she promised, and she started running, disappearing into the gloom.

Geoffrey pushed the door closed behind her. "Come on, Sasha," he said. "Let's go upstairs and help her from the computer, if we can." He limped toward the spiral stairs as a school of pink bullet-squids rocketed past the underwater window.

Sasha darted ahead of him and pulled on his arm as he lumbered up behind her in agony. "Oh, forget it! I'm running upstairs to check on Nell!"

"Great." Geoffrey winced as he grunted in pain each time he pushed off his foot.

07:20:18

The insertion team jogged west over the train yard. The Big Dog trotted beside them, and both Talon robot ROVs rolled fifteen yards ahead, shining their floodlights and transmitting video feeds. The dog whistles around their necks enabled Abrams, Dima, and alpha dog Jackson to control the ROVs as they moved forward into the wall of blackness.

"Let's go a klick down this rail line and set the explosives," Ferrell said.

"Sounds good," Abrams said.

"Look for a door in the north wall," Nastia said. "Stalin may have had a private connection to the train somewhere along this line."

"That would be nice," Bear said.

"I think you may be right," Galia said. "It would have been to a direct line out of here."

"Keep an eye out for it," Ferrell said.

"Yeah, we'll need some other way into the city or this will be a short mission," Jackson said.

"Stalin planned to build a ten-kilometer tunnel under the Nevelsky Strait to connect mainland Russia to Sakhalin Island," Nastia said, chattering anxiously as they crossed the train yard.

"Yeah?" said Abrams. He was willing to hear anyone other than by-the-book Ferrell right now.

"Yes," Nastia said. "Twenty-seven thousand prisoners were sent into the tunnel, but they were too ill-equipped to complete it after thousands of men died trying. Only when Stalin died was the project abandoned, halfway under the Nevelsky Strait."

"What nice stories you tell," Dima said with a laugh as he glanced at her.

She shrugged. "They're my specialty."

The train yard narrowed to one wide-gauge track and one narrow-gauge track that dipped downhill into a tunnel. The white ceiling was arched with a lining of dingy tiles. Abrams sent Talon-1 about thirty yards ahead and Talon-2 on the other side of the tracks some distance behind them with its night vision camera aimed backwards. They all monitored the rear bot's display on the visor of their helmet as they moved steadily deeper into the tunnel.

"In 1947," Nastia continued, if only to fill the senseless void, "Stalin ordered work on the Death Railway of Abkhazia in northern Siberia. It started and ended in the middle of nowhere and cost forty million rubles. It also cost the slave labor of three hundred fifty thousand, and the lives of at least a hundred thousand more. It was never intended to be used. It was built to kill the men who built it. It stretches six hundred kilometers through frozen tundra and forests and can be reached only by helicopter. But that is nothing compared to the White Sea–Baltic Sea Canal, or the gold mines of Kolyma. . . ."

"OK," Bear said. "Enough."

"Yeah, you're freaking me out now," Andy agreed.

"Sorry. Someone else talk, then," she said. "Please!"

"How about some silence?" Abrams suggested.

"That'll freak me out more," Andy said.

"Me, too," Hender said.

They pushed on in uncomfortable silence as nobody could think of anything to say. They hurried due west inside a bubble of light as the tunnel felt like an esophagus swallowing them. The hiss of Abrams's exosuit, the whizz of the ROV motors, and the buzz of the Big Dog's servos were magnified inside the tunnel.

Kuzu nudged Hender with an elbow, turning an eye toward him as they each glided on four legs over the ground beside the humans. "*Watch them closely, Shenuday,*" he said softly in his own language.

As they pressed into a seemingly endless darkness, the ROV in front of them carved away the stubborn shadow with its headlights.

"How about another gulag story, Nastia?" Jackson cracked.

"Stay focused, people!" Ferrell snapped. "Let's not get sloppy."

"No worries, Capitan," Abrams drawled.

Nastia noticed a large cement block to the right of the tracks. Above it was a steel hatch in the tunnel wall. "There." She pointed. "I told you! That door isn't in the city plan. That must be it!"

"Yes." Galia nodded. "I think you're right. . . ."

"If we could get through that door, would it lead to the palace?" Abrams asked.

"Yes," Galia said. "Probably."

Tusya and Dima climbed onto the landing and tried to crank open the dog wheel on the hatch. "No good," reported Dima.

"Let me try." Abrams jumped to the top of the landing in the exosuit and gripped the wheel on the door with his bionic arms. The pneumatic muscles quaked as he wheeled the crank, but he couldn't budge the wheel. "No way. It's jammed solid."

"It probably opens only from the inside," Galia said. "Most of the gates that lead to the palace lock from the inside."

"We'll have to try to blow it open or melt through it with incendiaries," Jackson said.

"That'll be a hell of a job," Tusya said dubiously, glancing at Dima.

"Come on," Ferrell said. "We've got a job to do first."

"Yes, sir," Dima said, jumping down from the ledge. Abrams jumped down after him, his heavy suit buzzing as it absorbed the landing.

They moved on another fifty yards up the tunnel.

07:20:09

Sasha and Geoffrey sat at Maxim's desk as they watched the monitors on the wall. Sasha noticed something on the monitor showing the inside of the train station. "Look!"

One of the heavy blast shields that had been lowered against the window was being pushed inward with erratic thrusts.

Geoffrey switched to the camera over the gate of Sector Seven in front of the station.

A giant rogue spiger leaned against the station's window. With the trebuchet-like force of a mantis shrimp's strike, it smashed its spiked arms through the glass, jolting the steel shutters. "Oh, crap." Geoffrey sighed.

Sasha squealed. "It's a monster!"

"Yes, sweetie, it is."

The view inside the station showed one heavy shutter being wedged as two seven-foot spikes levered it open.

07:16:21

Three minutes in, running at full speed, Nell saw the first ghosts gleaming on the roof and walls ahead. Their flesh caught the light of her flashlight like cat's eyes as she sprinted down the tight corridor, too fast for them to react to her as she passed.

She saw a lot more ahead.

07:16:20

Talon-1's night vision showed a split in the tunnel on the dog whistle's screen.

"There's a fork up ahead," Ferrell said.

They stopped at the fork where the railroad tracks continued to the right with no tracks heading into the tunnel on the left.

"Which way to Moscow, comrade?" Jackson asked Galia.

Galia shook his head, mildly annoyed. "I've never been here before. I know that one tunnel is a dead end, and the other goes on. Only Maxim knows how far it goes. I suspect it goes far enough."

"OK. We've got to check both tunnels," Jackson said. "And we'll set charges in both."

"Right," Ferrell said. "Let's go at least a klick down each branch before we set charges. Let's split up. You guys take the mule and go right. That seems to be the main line. This is probably the dead end. Kuzu, Tusya, and Andy, you come with me. We'll take Talon-1 with us." Ferrell took one of the backpacks filled with explosives off the mule, and Talon-1 followed him. "Set the charges to go off in eight hours, then meet back here!"

"OK," Abrams said. "Let's leave a transponder here so we can communicate by radio."

"Yeah," Jackson said, setting down a cylindrical device that popped antennae out, which rotated as he activated it with a button. There was no way communications could penetrate the solid rock walls down here.

"See you guys." Nastia waved as they followed Jackson into the tunnel on the right with Hender.

"Bye, Hender," Andy said.

"Bye, Andy! Bye, Kuzu!" Hender said as they separated.

Kuzu emitted a rumbling bass frequency like a

tiger's purr beside Andy as they headed into the tunnel to the left, following Ferrell and Tusya behind the robot into total darkness.

07:12:12

Nell spotted a ghost peeling off the ceiling ahead. It hung down before her, shimmering light in its glistening flesh. She fired the gun at it, almost deafening herself as the sharp reports echoed down the tunnel.

The ghost dropped before her as another flipped down behind it, also dangling from the ceiling.

She fired again, jumping over the first ghost and stepping on one of its suction cups, which bit into the heel of her shoe with a *crunch*. She pulled her foot out of her shoe and lurched forward as she shot two more bullets into the ghost in front of her, aiming at its amorphous head as she felt two punches hit her back. She twisted around to see two thick ropes sticking to her shirt that had been shot from an octopus behind her.

She fell on her knees before the molluscan predator as its amorphous head dropped down from above and faced her. It reeled in its gooey cables that were wrapped against her right arm, pinning the gun against her chest, and began attaching suction cups to her shoulders. She convulsed in desperation and jammed the glowing hot muzzle of the weapon with her left hand into the slug's mouth from below, the flashlight illuminating its translucent head. The creature's entire body recoiled, turning white beneath her, and she pulled out of her shirt, wrenching the gun free as she ran down the tunnel.

Ahead of her at least three more ghosts hung from the ceiling to intercept her. The closest curled its snail-head toward her and she aimed the gun between its large black eyes. She fired only once to conserve bullets and her ears as she ran forward, cursing herself for not wearing a bra. In fact, she should have worn multiple layers to slough off the mollusks' sticky webs. Now, they could attach to her bare skin.

07:12:10

Hender accompanied the others down what appeared to be the main train tunnel heading west from the underground city. Talon-2 rolled thirty-five yards ahead of them. After about two hundred yards, the grade leveled off and went downhill.

"Dead end!" Dima said, watching the ROV's camera feed.

The others soon saw the ROV light up a concrete wall ahead. As they approached, they saw a memorial inscribed in the wall. Nastia translated it for them:

MAY THE 109 HEROES OF THE
REVOLUTION WHO DIED HERE
REST IN PEACE.

Jackson smirked. "I hate to think how many *that* translates to in real numbers."

Nastia chuckled dryly. "You're catching on."

"Well, it looks like they did our job for us," Jackson said.

"*Ne gruzís',*" Dima said.

"*Da.*" Nastia nodded.

Abrams radioed the other team: "Hey, guys! We hit a dead end. We're going to head back. We'll rendezvous at the fork. Over?"

07:07:23

"Right, thanks," Ferrell acknowledged, turning off the receiver on his helmet radio. "I guess this is the main line," he said, glancing at the others. He gestured one hand forward, erratically, Kuzu noted. "We'll pick a spot half a klick farther down the tunnel to set the charges. Let's try to find a curve first to shelter us from the blast. All right?" Ferrell looked intently at Kuzu.

Kuzu realized the human must be referring to him. "Yes," he said. "OK, Ferrell."

Tusya looked at Kuzu and then smirked. "All right," he said.

Andy followed alongside Kuzu down the tunnel, which seemed to go straight as an arrow into infinity. Talon-1 rolled fifty yards ahead of them, shining its lights until it came to a jog where the tunnel was slightly misaligned with an opposing tunnel, as though they had met from different directions. Though there were no train tracks in the tunnel they had come through, there were tracks in the tunnel that joined from the other direction, stretching off like laser beams into the darkness.

"This must be it," Tusya said. "This must be the main line!"

Ferrell checked out Talon-1's camera feed on his visor. The rails headed down more steeply up ahead. He stopped and radioed the others, glancing at

Andy and Kuzu. "OK, we're going to set the charges," he said.

"Need any help?" came Jackson's voice on his helmet radio.

"No sweat," Ferrell said. "We'll be done in a bit. Just wanted to reach minimum safe distance so the boom doesn't collapse our egress."

"Roger that," Jackson said. "We should be at the fork in five minutes. See you there."

Andy took off his helmet next to Ferrell, breathing heavily. His scraggly blond hair was damp and drooping with sweat. He looked at Ferrell defiantly. "We should be safe enough here to take our helmets off, I think," he said. "OK? God, I just need to take a breath."

Tusya and Ferrell both followed suit, setting their helmets down as they opened their backpacks and a case filled with sixteen cubes of M183 explosive. They proceeded to set all sixteen charges in an arch spaced over the ceiling and down each wall. Kuzu assisted them with his twelve-foot reach, memorizing each of Ferrell's actions as he selected wires and detonators and connected them to the explosives. Then Kuzu noticed Ferrell set the countdown for twenty minutes.

"Hey," Andy said. "Why'd you set it for only twenty minutes?"

Ferrell casually put a pistol to Tusya's head and pulled the trigger twice, destroying the man's brain.

Kuzu vanished.

"What are you doing?" Andy screamed.

Ferrell turned the gun to Andy.

"Oh, you fucking asshole!"

Ferrell shot two bullets through the marine biologist's forehead. Andy fell to the floor, dead.

Kuzu hissed, invisible, as he clung to the ceiling.

Ferrell wheeled, pointing the gun where Kuzu had been, and he registered surprise as the sel seemed to have disappeared.

Pressed against the arched ceiling, the sel's fur camouflaged him against the tiles. He saw strange creatures clinging to the ceiling nearby and another that peeled off the wall behind Ferrell. The creature hung down like a giant tongue behind the human, shaping itself to the contours of the soldier's body without touching him.

Ferrell looked up and seemed to make out Kuzu on the ceiling. He raised his gun just as the animal closed over his back, arms, legs, and head simultaneously, immobilizing him.

Kuzu looked into Ferrell's eyes as the human shrieked, dropping his weapon as the strange creature overpowered him from behind. The beaklike mouth of the slimy animal clamped into the soldier's neck with scissorlike blades, and the man's scream was cut off as the dog whistle fell from around his neck, its chain severed, bouncing off one of the railroad tracks below. Ferrell's eyes looked back at Kuzu as his face drooped and the transparent creature flushed bloodred on his back.

Kuzu's eyes jerked in different directions. He suddenly noticed other glowing animals stuck to the ceiling around him. He leaped down as jetting ropes just missed him and looked off into the tunnel that stretched miles into the unknown—all the way to one of the humans' cities, they thought, and possibly to many more. He reached down to the detonator, and Kuzu switched off the timer.

Then he grabbed the dog whistle lying between the railroad ties and galloped back on five legs up the tunnel as Talon-1 followed him.

06:52:59

The others waited at the fork. They thought they heard the faint echoes of shouts and gunshots before they reached the branch but could not make radio contact.

"Ferrell, how's it going, copy?" Jackson repeated through his helmet radio, but still no answer. "I repeat, how's it going, man?"

"Look!" Abrams said.

Out of the darkness, a point of light now raced toward them.

"Andy!" yelled Hender, his voice reverberating in the throat of the tunnel like a shrill clarinet.

Hearing nothing back, the others yelled, too. Then they saw Talon-1 approaching. The ROV came within twenty yards of them before they saw Kuzu, emerging behind the robot, alone.

"What happened?" Jackson said. "Where are the others?"

"Animals attacked," said the sel.

"No way," Bear said.

"From Henders Island?" Abrams asked.

Kuzu shook his head.

"Where are the others?" Dima said.

"Where is Andy?" Hender asked.

Kuzu looked at Hender with both of his large eyes. "Dead."

Hender pulled back as if he had been physically struck.

"Bombs all set, Jackson," Kuzu said, eyeing the big soldier with one eye.

"Bullshit!" Bear yelled. "You killed them!"

"What the hell—?" Jackson paused as they saw something hurtling toward them in the tunnel.

A shocking specter shambled out of the shadow into the light. They trained their weapons on the approaching figure, which ran toward them like a glowing dog. As the creature came closer, they caught flashes of Craigon Ferrell's face pointing at them. They saw his body running on all fours, his head raised with open mouth and eyes. His body, gripped by a glowing mass, lunged forward.

"God almighty," Jackson said, backing up.

"A ghost!" Galia cried.

Suddenly, with a smacking sound, Ferrell's head fell forward limply and they could see the slug's head in its place with a pouting, bloody mouth and wide sullen eyes glaring at them.

Dima and Jackson shot a barrage of gunfire at the apparition, which finally crumpled on the floor of the tunnel before them.

Bear examined the remains. "Are you sure this ain't from Henders Island?"

"No," Hender said, shivering. "It's not!"

The others looked at the pulverized carnivore that was still squirming on Ferrell's back, jerking the human's arms and legs randomly.

"It must be some kind of mollusk," Nastia said, her eyes and mouth wide as she crouched to look in morbid curiosity at the flinching flesh of the creature.

"Many in tunnel." Kuzu pointed behind.

"But the charges are set, right, Kuzu?" Jackson said.

"Yes, Jackson," Kuzu said. "Charges are set."

"Damn, one of those ugly bastards is above us right now!" Jackson's flashlight exposed several ghost octopuses converging on the ceiling over them.

"Yes." Kuzu pointed.

"God, let's go, man!" Abrams backed away as the others scattered.

They rushed back up the tunnel toward the station.

As they ran with the mechanical mule loping alongside the tracks, they passed the hatch that they couldn't open earlier. The lights of Talon-1 shone ahead on a huge creature barreling toward them from the direction of the train station, rapidly growing larger and glowing vivid colors. Abrams ignited a magnesium flare and took aim, hurling it forty yards down the tunnel, illuminating the beast in a blaze of light.

"Oh, no," Hender cried.

"Spiger!" Kuzu growled.

Abrams grabbed an incendiary grenade out of a pouch on the trotting mule. He took a few steps and sidearmed the grenade like a quarterback. "Fire in the hole!" he shouted.

The grenade zipped down the tunnel and landed perfectly between the front legs of the animal that was thirty-five yards away. But the spiger launched off its tail so hard, it slid along the tiled ceiling as the grenade ignited behind it at 4,000 degrees Fahrenheit.

The spiger screeched like an air-raid siren as it

landed forty feet in front of them, its elaborate frill pulsating colors like a neon marquee. Its tail curled underneath it as it scuttled away from the heat source, rapidly moving toward them and raising its arms.

Jackson ran to meet the beast, firing two AA-12 automatic shotguns and emptying both magazines of explosive ammo at close range as he shredded the creature's manelike frill.

"No!" Hender said. "They *like* noise. Don't stand still: *Move!*"

The spiger recoiled as bits were blasted off its frill and buckshot pierced its armored back. Jackson stood his ground in front of it, spraying the beast as it raised one of its spiked arms and brought it down in a blinding streak, stabbing the soldier through the faceplate of his helmet through his rib cage and pelvis into the ground. Then the monster lifted the big man's body sideways before its widening vertical jaws.

"Throw another grenade!" Nastia said.

"Not at this range," Dima said. "We'll burn, too!"

"Back up!" Abrams shouted.

Nastia ran in the other direction, weeping hysterically.

As they retreated, Abrams used his dog whistle to send in both Talon robots, which opened fire with their M249 machine guns as they rushed the spiger.

One of the spiger's long spike-arms turned sideways and flicked the Talons up the tunnel toward the group like a couple of corks. Revolving in the air, their machine guns fired in all directions, their rounds ricocheting off the walls. Abrams disabled their guns as the bots clattered past them, rolling for another forty yards.

"*Chyort voz'mi,*" Dima cursed. "I'm hit!"

"Where?" Bear asked.

"The head!"

"You're OK, then," Abrams said. "Must have rung your bell, though."

"Shit," Dima said. "Good helmet."

The spiger continued to pick Jackson's meat off its arm like a shish kebab as Bear and Kuzu advanced, firing their bows simultaneously at the beast. Bear skewered the spiger's head between its eyestalks with an aluminum shaft. Kuzu moved in and struck its second brain between the eyes on its back. The great beast crashed to the ground.

Kuzu strode toward it then and, as the others watched in awe, the sel placed three hands on the dying beast's fur. He turned his head on his elastic neck to look at Hender. "Come on, *Shueenair*!" His commanding voice vibrated Hender's bones.

"What's he doing?" Dima asked.

"Don't go near spiger," Hender warned them.

Kuzu's fur smoldered red as millions of "symbiants" evacuated the fallen predator, pouring into his fur. They attacked like needles at first, but then radiated peacefully, spreading a pleasurable feeling like an itch being scratched over his entire body. Their millions of quick pricks stimulated glands under the hendropod's skin that produced an ameliorating hormone. After feeling naked since the humans had exterminated the exfoliating symbiants so integral to the sels' health, Kuzu finally felt them reestablish themselves on his body and replenish the external immune system that had made it possible to survive in their native ecosystem.

Another two spigers lunged down the tunnel in the distance, a cloud of flying creatures following them.

"The train station is breached!" Abrams shouted.

"No shit!" Bear said.

"The incendiary grenade's still burning on the tracks behind the spiger," Abrams said. "It should keep the rest at bay for the moment, but the heat barrier won't last long."

They were trapped between the Henders predators on one side and no other place to go.

"Throw another grenade at them!" Nastia cried.

"No!" shouted another female voice behind them. "Come this way!"

Thirty-five yards behind them, standing on the cement landing under the hatch they had passed, a shirtless woman waved a flashlight. "This way!" she called.

"Who the Christ are you?" Bear said, awestruck by the vision.

"Nell!" Hender shouted.

"Dr. Binswanger!" Galia hailed her bashfully.

Nell waved her arm angrily. "Come on!"

The sels followed the humans quickly as Nell pulled Nastia up onto the landing first.

Kuzu pulled Hender up, and Hender could feel a sprinkling of symbiants warm his arm like a pleasurable narcotic that spread momentarily on his skin before they jumped back onto Kuzu. Kuzu's voice rumbled softly as he spoke in his own language: *"I must tell you what happened in the tunnel, Shenuday."*

"Yes." Hender nodded.

Nastia looked at Nell. "Is that tunnel safe?"

"Safer than this one," Nell answered.

"What happened to you?" Nastia said.

"I lost my shirt. Let's go!"

"OK," said Nastia.

Dima and Abrams judged that the mule could get through the hatch as Nastia and Nell went through first. Dima jumped on the ledge as Abrams pulled a variety of grenades from the packs on the mule's back and, aided by the XOS suit, pitched the grenades as far as he could in both directions. Then he helped push the mule onto the landing and through the hatch. The mule gave a kick of its hind legs as it got a purchase and trotted through the tunnel behind Dima, Nastia, and Nell.

Before bringing up the rear, Abrams fired five more gas and incendiary grenades up the tunnel and three more in the other direction. Talon-1 came charging back down the tunnel now, and Abrams reached down and lifted it onto the platform. Then he saw one of the spigers, soaring through the air in a mighty leap directly toward him. He pulled Talon-1 inside, but before he could close the hatch the spiger jammed a spike inside the crack.

"Shit!" Abrams cursed, trying to close the door, but even the strength of the XOS suit was outmatched when both the spiger's spikes shoved into the crack to pry it open.

Bear looked through the lurching hatch and glimpsed the giant spiger: its head was bigger than the hatch itself. "Come on! It can't get through anyway! Let's go!"

He stuck a shotgun through the crack and fired,

blowing off one of the beast's eyes, which only seemed to make it wrench the door open wider as it trumpeted like an elephant.

Abrams and Bear ran up the corridor.

"There are ghosts in here!" Nell called back to them as she led them forward through the passageway. "Clinging to the walls. So move *fast*! They're dangerous."

"We know!" said Nastia.

They rushed behind Nell as she ran. "This is one of Stalin's escape routes," she said. "It leads straight to his palace."

"I told you!" Nastia said with relief. Then, to Nell, she said more quietly, "You know you're topless, right?"

"Yes! I know! I'll care about that later, OK?"

Nastia nodded. "Just making sure!"

06:43:22

Geoffrey and Sasha watched through the camera outside Stalin's secret train landing as the battle ensued in the tunnel—but they could see no sign of Nell. When the spigers arrived, Geoffrey felt his hope sink: Sector Seven had been breached.

"Yay!" Sasha said as she saw Nell open the door and step out onto the platform, waving at the others.

"She made it!" Geoffrey whispered.

The others retreated into the passageway and left the train tunnel filled with smoke and fire. "Thank God," he sighed; he had been gripping Sasha's arm the whole time and now apologized to her as he let go.

"You're really strong, Geoffrey," Sasha said, rubbing her arm. "Was Nell wearing a shirt?"

"Um . . . . I don't think so," Geoffrey said, wondering what could have happened.

06:41:08

"Are these 'ghosts' related to ghost slugs?" Nastia asked.

"What are ghost slugs?" Nell asked.

"Carnivorous white slugs discovered in Wales a few years ago that are believed to have evolved in caves."

"No." Nell shook her head and laughed darkly. "You must be a scientist, too."

"Yes," Nastia said.

"They're mollusks, but these things have suction cups. They're land octopuses," Nell said.

"Incredible!" Nastia said. "Are they from Henders Island?"

"No! There weren't any mollusks there!"

Abrams checked his rearview headcam and immediately saw bad news: the spiger had somehow squeezed through the hatch behind them. Elastic diaphragms between three bony rings inside its body enabled the giant invertebrate to inchworm behind them through the tight tunnel, extending its head and snapping its jaws like double doors as it drew closer in four-foot lunges. "Heads up, that frigging thing got through!"

"Damn!" Bear said.

A translucent silhouette of a man reared up in the tunnel ahead.

"A ghost!" Nell warned.

"Oooh!" Hender trilled, disappearing as he reacted to the figure whose flesh effulged prismatic colors in the beams of their flashlights.

Nell stopped next to the tunnel that headed east toward the city.

"Just shoot it and let's keep going!" Nastia said.

"I'm out of bullets!" Nell cried, unnerved and visibly shaking.

Dima fired at the ghost and it folded down, dropping to the ground, revealing a dozen more hanging or standing in the corridor behind it. He kept firing, revealing one after another in an infinite regress.

Nell shone her flashlight up and saw two large ghosts peeling off the ceiling above them. "There!"

Bear glanced behind them as the huffing and puffing spiger pushed toward them up the tunnel. "Come on, man! That thing's coming!"

"This tunnel should go to your honeymoon suite, I think, Nell," Galia said.

Nell looked back at the man who had spoken, wondering who he might be under his helmet. She remembered that Sasha had referred to their suite as Stalin's love nest.

"Come on!" she shouted, and darted right into the smaller tunnel that headed east, the others following.

06:38:02

They emerged through a hatch that opened to a hidden room behind their bridal suite on the second story of their honeymoon cottage. The mule barely squeezed through as it followed them through a second hatch that opened into their bedroom. Dima closed both hatches behind them.

Nell looked at their unmade bed as she grabbed a T-shirt and pulled it on while the others took off their helmets, turning away. "Yeah, this was our room," Nell said, noticing the wilted pink rose on their bedspread. She reached into her bag by the bed and pulled out some banged-up sneakers, pulling the one shoe off her foot and slipping into the new pair. "I took these to go spelunking in Hawaii," she muttered, tying them on with trembling fingers. She looked at the faces that were now revealed around her and noticed Galia Sokolof, Maxim's chief of operations. "Well, hello, Mr. Sokolof." She scowled. "What brings you here?" She rose to confront him.

"I brought them to rescue you, Dr. Binswanger," Galia said, his deep-set eyes full of remorse.

"We came to get you, Nell!" Hender said.

"I've no doubt that you did, Hender." Nell smiled at him, squeezing his hand and kissing his soft-whiskered cheek as he embraced her with four aquamarine arms.

"Where is Sasha?" Galia asked.

"She's at the palace with Geoffrey," Nell said.

"Oh," Galia said in surprise. "Thank God! And the others?"

Nell scowled once more. "You mean Maxim? Everyone in the city is dead now. But Maxim? Well, he may still be alive, I think, Galia, if that's what you're concerned about."

"I tried to stop him."

"Not hard enough!" Nell shouted bitterly.

"All right, now!" Abrams said, raising his bionic arms gently. "There'll be time for that later."

"Come on," Nell said, leading them to the split-level dining/living room of her honeymoon condo, the dining room of which viewed the city and the living room to their right the phosphorescent waterfall.

Abrams powered down the XOS and detached its grips from his armored suit, stepping out of the machine. "Pretty swank honeymoon suite," he quipped.

"Yeah," Nell said.

Kuzu rushed to the window and looked over the city. On the street below, a stream of glowing Henders species flowed, in the same direction, flying, rolling, and leaping past the window from right to left, clockwise around the city.

"We should be safe here," Galia said. "The windows are bulletproof."

"Yeah, sure," Abrams said.

"We better look around and make sure no ghosts are in here, or anything else," Nastia said.

They all inspected the walls and ceiling carefully and finally were convinced the room was clean.

"Turn the light off now," Hender warned with a soft, sing-song voice.

"Hender's right," Nell said.

They doused their lights immediately and gathered behind Kuzu, who was peering through the window at the dark metropolis.

Glowing swarms of bugs and iridescent eight-legged "rats" charged up the street, followed by giant spigers with fluorescing stripes rippling light on their frilled skulls. At several intersections in the distance, they could see spigers clashing and locked in mortal combat, causing grisly pileups like traffic accidents. Henders "trees" had already begun to sprout on the sidewalks, their palmlike branches dangling red and blue fruit over the streets.

"Look, *Shueenair*," Kuzu said.

"Oh," Hender sighed sadly.

"Like home," Kuzu said in his own language.

The first bloom of Henders clover was visibly spreading, encrusting the streets and buildings, intermingled with patches of glowing colors that Nell recognized as rainbowfire. Great glowing patches of rainbowfire had spread across the high ceiling of the cavern, as well.

Nastia noticed the glowing patches with alarm, remembering the phosphorescent splotches on the walls of an abandoned Soviet uranium mine she had explored a few years ago. It was the scariest place she had ever seen, until now. "Is that uranium?" She pointed at the roof of the cavern.

"No!" Nell said. "It's a fungus that grows here. It must like eating clover. . . . They were trying to get it to grow in here, but there was nothing for it to eat before."

"Nell," Hender interjected, clasping her shoulder. "Andy is . . . *gone*!"

Nell was gutted by the news, finding it difficult to believe. "No! What was he doing here?"

"He didn't want us to go without him," Hender said. His fur flickered dark colors as he reached another trembling hand out to her.

Nell gasped as Hender squeezed her hand. "How?" She looked at Galia furiously.

"A ghost got him," Hender said.

Nell bowed her head, gritting her teeth from the blow of grief that punched her.

Abrams peered through the window on the other side of the apartment overlooking the river. To the right, a waterfall of blue light bounded, formed by water that had percolated through the bedrock from the slopes of Mount Kazar from a reservoir of bioluminescent algae that fed the subterranean cascade. Nastia looked with him through the window. "That waterfall looks like the waves back home in San Diego, when the algae are blooming," he said.

"There must be bioluminescent organisms in the water," Nastia said, marveling at the blue cataract.

"It looks like we're safe here for the time being," Bear said. "Let's sit down for a second and get our bearings."

They sat on the leather couches around the glass coffee table that reflected the waterfall in the window. The headless mule twitched behind the couch where Nastia, Bear, and Dima sat. Nell sat across from them, exhausted and grief-stricken, her eyes glazing over as she stared at the strange machine that continuously balanced on four legs like a foal behind the couch across from her. "That thing's a robot, right?"

"Yeah," Nastia said, putting a hand on her shoulder. "It gives me the creeps, too."

"OK." Nell nodded.

Abrams reached into a pack on the side of the mule and fished out a fresh Dragon Skin tunic, tossing it to Nell. "There ya go, Rambo. Put that on."

"Thanks." Nell pulled on the heavy jersey. "A ghost ripped my shirt off."

"You did damn good for a civilian," Abrams said.

"Yeah." Bear nodded. "And you saved our asses."

"*Da.*" Dima smiled. "Thanks."

Abrams pushed several buttons that snapped open his body armor, and he stepped out of it. "OK, we just lost four men. And it looks like we just lost our only known escape route. What's our plan?"

Nastia pulled out the city map and unfolded it on the coffee table between them.

Hender sat on the couch and typed into his phone:

The 14th Darkness

26,439 years ago, a long night came again, and sels came together, peacefully this time, at last. Only five were left.

"Write now?" Kuzu chided Hender as he sat beside him.

"The Books are written to remember, when darkness comes," Hender reminded him, and he finished typing his final entry:

The 15th Darkness

Today, the 15th Darkness came.

Kuzu read it before Hender put the phone back into his belly pack.

Nell pointed at the southwest corner of Sector Six on the blueprint. "We're here, in the main cavern of the city."

"Yes. Where is Maxim Dragolovich?" Dima said.

"Do you want to rescue him," Nell asked. "Or kill him?"

"I want to capture him," Dima said. "And bring him back alive."

Nell laughed, weeping. "So this whole thing is partially *your* fault," she said. "Maxim said the government was persecuting him." She shook her head weakly. "Though I think he was probably insane already, too."

"I don't know anything about that," Dima said.

"He was mad," Galia said sadly. "But they drove him mad."

Nell pointed at the dormitory inside the hospital sector, which was located on the opposite corner of the map from where they were. "Maxim is trapped here on the second floor of this hospital," she said. "He was trying to turn on the electrical plant up here." She pointed to Sector Four. "His men were seconds away from pushing the button and feeding this place with perpetual power. Can you imagine what would have happened if they had succeeded?"

"What, Nell?" Kuzu asked.

"With light and steam and heat down here . . ."

"Yes?" Kuzu's deep voice vibrated the air. Purple sparks flashed in his blackened fur like lightning in a storm cloud.

The others regarded him apprehensively.

"The Henders ecosystem would explode, swiftly multiplying until it found a way to spread to the surface, Kuzu," Nell said. "And kill us all."

"Oh."

"As it is, they have already infested the sectors between Maxim and the power plant," Nell said, pointing. "They're the only thing now that is stopping him, thank God. He's trapped and surrounded."

Galia looked pale, staring inwardly, his shoulders falling. "He was a great man, a great hero. You have no idea."

"He may have been. I'm sure he was," Nell said. "But he might be the greatest villain in human history, Mr. Sokolof."

"They have more blood on their hands than all the villains of the world," Galia scoffed with a ragged grimace of irony.

"You still don't understand, do you?" Nell asked. "If *any* Henders species reaches the surface, not one flower or insect will survive longer than a few more decades on any continent on the face of the Earth. The entire world will look . . . . like this."

"I have bad news," Nastia said. "It is believed, by Russian authorities, that the railway line we just set charges in was completed, after all. It may still connect all the way to Metro-Two in Moscow, and from there may well reach points throughout Eastern Europe. I believe I am authorized to tell you this now, considering our situation. It is a secret that the Russian government did not want to reveal, even to this small group, unless it was absolutely necessary. But now that Sector Seven has been breached, you must know. Unless we detonate charges in the train tunnel immediately—"

"Shit!" Bear said.

"They're set to go off in less than seven hours now," Abrams said.

"Those incendiary grenades have probably burned out, man," Bear said. "Those things can move now! There's nothing stopping them!"

Abrams exchanged the heavy lithium battery pack of the XOS suit with a fresh one. "There's enough poison gas in that tunnel to choke a herd of wildebeests."

"Like what?" Nell asked. "What kind of gas?"

"I threw in a cocktail of everything from tear gas to chlorine to tabun gas."

"Great," Nell said. "Tabun works only on mammals, tear gas probably won't have any effect on Henders organisms, but—chlorine gas, you said? That's good. That should work. But it buys us only a little time before it is dispersed and no longer lethal."

"It's a tunnel. It'll take a while to disperse," Abrams said.

"You guys killed a spiger, too," Nell said. "That's good. That should occupy the predators for a while and keep them from moving on."

"Yes," Hender agreed.

"How can we get to the charges in the train tunnel to set them off sooner?" Dima hissed. "With all that poison gas in the tunnel now?"

"Maybe we can rig explosives to one of our flying bots," Abrams suggested. "And control it remotely from here?"

"Yes! We could use the tunnel we just came through," said Dima. "That spiger left the door open behind us." As he pointed, a sound like a battering ram shook the building, making them all jump out of their seats, coming from the bedroom.

"What is that?" Galia cried.

Abrams and Bear grabbed their guns and the others ran behind them. They opened the door behind the bed and heard a pounding and scraping sound squealing against the dented hatch on the other side.

"Fuck," Abrams said. "That spiger *followed* us!"

A shattering blast hit the door, bending the thick steel.

"No way it can get through," Bear said.

Kuzu laughed deeply. "Spiger's *stuck*!"

Dima looked at Nell. "OK, so there goes any chance of sending an ROV from here."

"Let's get out of here, and close this door, too," Nell said.

They retreated to the living room again, and Nell waved them back to the map on the table. "OK, let's look at this."

"There must be another way," Nastia agreed.

Kuzu sat next to Hender as the others gathered around the table. The large sel felt his energy surging as the symbiants that had migrated off the spiger into his fur now separated and multiplied at a rapid rate, colonizing his body. His skin could breathe again as they exfoliated it. He whispered to Hender in his own language. *"Listen to me, Shueenair. Ferrell killed Andy and the other human. And he tried to kill me, too!"*

Hender replied in Kuzu's tongue. *"You did not kill Andy, did you, Kuzu?"*

"No! I would not kill Andy."

"Are you lying?"

"You only ask that because they have lied to us so many times. They will try to kill us, too. This is their chance. But it is also ours! It need not be the last darkness. If you follow me now, the whole world will be ours."

Nastia suddenly screamed, startling everyone.

Behind the couch where she was sitting, the hooded head of a ghost octopus reared up on the mechanical mule where a real mule's head would have been. Dima used his dog whistle to back the mule away from the couch, but the muscles of the ghost had encased the robot's legs and fought its firing servos for control.

Kuzu seized the opportunity and sprang over the couch, landing on the far side of the mule. With four hands working at blinding speed, he pulled two handfuls of magnesium flares from under the ghost and then, from a compartment in the mule's side, grabbed an explosives pack like the one Ferrell had carried into the train tunnel.

The ghost on the robot's back turned its snail-head toward Kuzu and shot ropes at two of Kuzu's hands, immobilizing them. Without breaking his rhythm, Kuzu used two other hands to pick up a combat knife, unsheathe it, and slice the ghost's ropes. Then he put the knife in another pack and slung it over one shoulder, backing away. He snagged his bow and quiver where he had set them near the stairs and shouted, "Shueenair!"

"No!" Hender replied.

The others watched, confused, as Kuzu's fur flushed red.

"Then die!" Kuzu roared in English.

And the sel sprang down the stairway to the front door.

Bear jumped up and shot the ghost octopus on the mule's back twice in the head with a pistol. It drooped and slid off the side of the robot as Bear followed Dima down the stairs after Kuzu, who was already gone, the front door wide open to the street.

Dima saw Kuzu on the front steps throwing a lit

flare into the road in front of them, and Bear emptied his Glock pistol at the sel; but Kuzu became a shadow in the same instant as he darted up the street to the right, weaving against the flow of creatures.

The flare burned in front of the building and drew emerald swarms down from the tall buildings as Dima and Bear jumped back inside and slammed the door.

"Crazy mother!" Bear said.

Dima groaned as they both ran upstairs. "What in the hell is he doing?"

Nastia watched through the front window with Russian LOMO night-vision binoculars. She barely caught Kuzu galloping on four legs along the side of a building up the street, before she lost him.

"Ferrell tried to kill Kuzu," Hender told Nell. "And he killed Andy, too!"

"What?" Abrams said.

Galia bowed his head. "No," he sighed.

"I can't believe that," said Bear.

"Hender!" Nell said. "Why didn't you tell us before?"

"Kuzu just told me," Hender said.

Nell took one of Hender's shaking hands. "I'm sorry."

"How do we know this one's telling the truth?" Bear asked.

"Hender never lies," Nell said.

"The other one lied!" Bear said.

"Because he thought we were trying to kill him!" Nell said. "Because one of us lied to him!"

"Someone must have gotten to Ferrell," Abrams said. "With a bribe, or blackmail, or something. Jesus!"

"And a threat, too, probably," Galia said.

"I guess you never know who it's going to be," Bear said.

"Sure you can." Dima spit. "The *American*!"

"I'm surprised it wasn't one of you bloody Russians," Galia said.

"Hey, this isn't the time or place," Abrams said. "We're in this together, right? And you're all assholes."

"Kuzu said you're going to kill us," Hender said. "Kuzu said that's why you brought us here. Are you going to kill me?"

They turned to the sel as the colors on his coat muted to blue and black, fading almost invisibly into the couch as they looked at him.

"No, dude, we're *not* gonna kill you," Abrams said, reaching out to shake his hand.

Hender reached out and took it uncertainly.

"Never, Hender!" Nastia said, extending her hand, too.

"Please help us, Hender," Nell said with a reassuring squeeze of his other hand.

"*Da!* We all need each other now." Dima took his fourth hand as he became visible again.

Hender shook the four humans' hands. "Thank you, thank you, thank you, thank you," he said to each.

"So what can we do, then, Nell?" Bear asked. "How do we get out of here?"

Nell pointed back to the map. "If we can get through this part of the city to the farm—less than two hundred yards away—we should be able to make it to the palace from there unharmed."

"Oh, man," Bear said, shaking his head.

"Through that shit?" Abrams asked. "I don't know."

"And from the palace we can send an ROV down the passageway I took to the train tunnel and detonate the explosives to seal it off. We have to try!" Nell said.

"That's crazy," Bear said.

"Do you have a better suggestion?" Dima asked.

"Is that possible?" Nastia asked. "Can you send a robot that far through solid rock by remote control?"

"Yeah," Abrams said. "The Dalek can drop signal boosters along the way. If it can get through the ghosts, it can definitely go the distance."

"But what then?" asked Nastia.

"Well," Nell said. "If we can get to the palace . . . there might be a way we can escape from there."

"How?" Abrams asked.

"By gondola. Through Pandemonium."

Abrams laughed at her dark humor.

"She's not joking," Galia said.

"*Pandemonium?*" Abrams frowned.

"It's another vast chamber that adjoins the palace," Nell said, motioning with her hand off the edge of the table. "That way. It's not on this map, but it's where the ghosts come from. Stalin built a gondola that crosses the giant lake there. It may be our only way out."

"Shit," Bear said. "That's crazy!"

"We tried to fix it," Galia said. He shook his head. "But it would be very, very risky."

"Then it's true," Nastia muttered.

Nell looked at her. "What?"

"There were some cryptic lines I came across by

Trofim Lysenko in a letter to my grandmother. They referred to 'monsters marvelous and fearful to behold in the depths of the Earth.' "

"He was right," Nell said. "We found his journal, I think, in a drawer of Stalin's desk. He may have been sent here to help set up the farm. I'll show you, when we get there."

"You say you fixed the gondola, Mr. Sokolof?" asked Abrams.

"The motor runs. But the pylons . . . one of them has partially collapsed over the lake." He shook his silver-haired head grimly. "And the creatures there pose an even greater danger. We decided it was too risky to give it a trial run." Galia eyed the others now with large, sunken eyes. "What about Maxim, then?"

"I hate to break it to you, friend, but there's no way Maxim Dragolovich is getting out of here," said Abrams. "I mean, I'm sure you'd love to have his head on a flaming pike, but we can't risk it and we don't have time."

"He wants to rescue Maxim Dragolovich," Dima said. "*I* want his head on a flaming pike."

"Oh, sorry," Abrams said. "Either way."

"Hender." Nell turned to the sel. "What do you think? Is there any way we can get to this gate? It leads to the farm, where we should be safe. We just need to go two hundred yards up the street outside. The others have armor. I have this jersey. Can we make it?"

Hender frowned, looking at Nell, and he shook his head. "No. The others will make it, maybe. But you won't make it, Nell."

"We have less than six hours before they seal the

way we came in," Abrams said. "And then flood this place with mustard gas, or whatever they're planning to do."

"We can't go back anyway," Bear scoffed.

"I agree," Nastia said, pushing her bobbed black hair back from her tense brow. "I don't trust them, either. They might not even open that door for us, anyway. They let me know secrets I've been trying to find out for twenty-five years. That alone makes me nervous. They may have lured us all here just to seal the city and exterminate the hendros. And us along with them."

"That's crazy talk," Abrams said. "Someone must have bribed Ferrell. Unless he just went nuts."

"We have to make it to the farm, Hender," Nell said.

Hender bowed his head and closed his large eyes. "Let me think."

The others looked at one another as the sel rose from the couch and sat on the carpet before the fireplace, holding four hands up at them as he folded his three-jointed limbs against himself like an Egyptian scarab. His coat began pulsing pink in slowing waves until his fur turned black that pulsed yellow about once a minute.

Bear whispered: "What's he doing?"

Nell shrugged, having never witnessed this behavior. "I don't know."

05:15:40

Kuzu sprang on four legs, leaping like a Hindu Sagittarius clutching a three-handed bow. He blended into the façades of the buildings as he crossed the city, throwing flares down side streets to create diversions and downing two young spigers with his bow to draw off predators.

The nants on the sel's body now counterattacked insect predators, provoking them to spray warning pheromones that further protected him. Kuzu felt his energy increasing with each stride as oxygen enriched his copper-based blood. The memories and reflexes of his entire life's experience returned to him as he ran and leaped and bounced off walls, swinging from lampposts, flipping, skidding, rolling, cutting, spinning, and sprinting with a practiced, inspired physicality that would seem mystical to all but the most skilled human athletes. Michael Jordan and Magic Johnson practiced moving for twenty years to reach their astonishing level of prowess. Kuzu had practiced for ninety thousand years. What he could do *was* magic to human beings.

He chose the most direct route to the hospital and followed the city's map imprinted in his mind's eye. Memorizing terrain was an essential skill on his native land. As he passed each cross street, Kuzu noted the star-shaped tower in the center of the dark city. Its glowing statues of humans peered over the streets like blind sentinels. The sides of the Star Tower were illuminated by masses of wasps and drill-worms in colorful nurseries whose steady, humming drone filled the air. The skyscraper had been turned into a giant hive, and it pleased Kuzu.

When Kuzu approached the door to Sector Two, he found a crushed truck stuck in the half-closed gate. He jumped onto the vehicle's roof and crawled through the gate, noting that the truck's windshield had been gouged open by spigers. The cab's doors were open, and there was no trace of humans except for their guns and some clothing scattered on the street ahead. He picked up a Kalashnikov and slung it over one of his shoulders.

Then he padded up the street on three legs in the dark, his eyes attuned to the meager light emanating from a side street up ahead on the right. He turned the corner to the open gate of Sector Three just as a horde of brown rats stampeded in the other direction. The large sel stretched and blended against the wall as the squeaking mammals passed him, chased by a wave of glowing Henders rats that launched over their mammalian counterparts, tackling them to the ground.

As the massacre of the mammals ensued, a cloud of bugs arrived, spraying an attack pheromone that signaled a feeding frenzy, and carnage rained from the sky over the screaming rodents.

Kuzu glided on four feet along the south wall and through the gate, sneaking down the street until he jumped onto the roof of a crashed limo and leapfrogged to another, as if between stones in a river.

He launched through the air and landed on the hospital steps, which were illuminated by a dimly burning light in the foyer. He slipped invisibly up them and through the wide-open front door.

Kuzu crept through the lobby and charged up the stairs, using two feet while pulling on the wide stair rails. As he slung himself to the top, wasps whizzed down over his ducking head and under his belly.

The small room at the top got to a hatch, also

open, which led to a room filled with counters, a large broken window on one side. According to the map, Maxim was inside the far door on the left.

Kuzu streaked to the door and cranked the hatch wheel, camouflaging his fur as his symbiants stirred up repellent to fend off the flying predators pouring through the broken window behind him. He sensed someone trying to stop him from opening the wheel on the other side and heard a shout through the steel. He gripped four hands and cranked with all his strength, pushing the door open and throwing two men backwards at the same time.

He fired the Kalashnikov at the two men as he entered, killing them instantly while slamming the hatch closed with his leg. As Kuzu moved into the dark room, a thin man with glasses and a goatee came running toward him. Kuzu flung two of his throwing stars at him, the disks striking him on each side of his neck, dropping him to the floor.

In the far corner, a large man sat on the bed, not moving. He turned his head to stare in Kuzu's direction, his eyes and mouth widening at the sight of him.

05:31:07

As he rose, Maxim saw the dead bodies of Dimitri and his two loyal bodyguards behind the creature that reared over him now with a body blazing purple and red. "Are you the devil?" he murmured in horror.

"You're Maxim?" Kuzu asked.

The large man crumpled to the ground before him, and Kuzu reached out with three hands, gripping

Maxim around the ribs and hoisting him off the floor. Rising to his full nine feet, the sel slammed the tycoon against the corner of the room and looked into his small eyes with eyes that were twenty times larger, with six pupils focused on his soul. Like a volcano, Kuzu's voice erupted: "POWER! NOW!"

The man looked up at him and fainted in his grasp.

Kuzu looked at him, perplexed. He threw Maxim on a bed and leaned over his face. "*Wake up!*" the sel wheezed like a steam whistle, stirring the human to consciousness. The man opened his eyes and looked up at Kuzu, blinking.

Maxim beheld the apparition, remote and delirious, convinced that he was dreaming or even dead as the demon sat down on one of the beds across from him. Like a Satanic chimera, a pagan monster, the being folded all its limbs intricately against its body, and its fur blushed a deep maroon that darkened to black. Mesmerized, Maxim watched Kuzu's body shine a pale silvery light that popped with effervescing colors for an entire hour that seemed outside of time.

Hypnotized by the transforming light effulging from the nightmare sitting before him, Maxim was startled when Kuzu finally moved again. The devil incarnate unfolded his limbs and rose.

"*Down!*" Kuzu's deep voice tolled, tearing open the air with its violence, and Maxim submitted, bowing down; and the great man wept before the terrible demon, accepting its sentence in a delirium of shame and terror.

With four hands, Kuzu rubbed fingers into the

human's hair, face, neck, and shoulders. Maxim shuddered as he smelled a strong scent exuding from the monster's hands. He sobbed as he felt a flush spread like fire under his clothes and across his skin.

Kuzu stepped away from the human and watched. The sel knew that millions of nants were now colonizing the man's body. They poured over him, gripping his skin like microscopic cat's claws, each a shield that would link to another like chain mail to protect the human's soft flesh. The nants continued to spread a thin mesh that would stop only at the moist edge of his eyelids and orifices, where chemical signals would compel them to stop.

Maxim knew then that his soul had been condemned as his body was utterly possessed. He had never believed in hell, or the devil, until now. Now that he was doomed he believed in them with all his soul.

"Safe now, Maxim," Kuzu said perversely. He touched Maxim's head, and the microscopic nants continued to flow from Kuzu's four hands into the human's hair. Maxim was paralyzed with awe at his own damnation as his entire body seemed to burn. "I make nants protect you or kill you. Understand?"

Maxim saw the hendro's grin reveal wide yellow teeth, and he whispered, almost involuntarily: "Yes!"

Kuzu picked up an empty orange-juice bottle and examined it. Then he reached out and touched the screen that showed video feeds from different parts of the city. "Ah. Good!"

Then Kuzu lifted Maxim to his feet, leering

inches from his face with his giant eyes. "Power. NOW!"

04:02:37

Hender sat still for more than an hour, his limbs folded against his body.

He had responded only once, when Nell, twenty minutes into his strange trance, asked if he was OK. Opening one eye, he had said, "I will save you, Nell." Then he closed his eyes again, remaining perfectly still.

The others had watched in astonishment as Hender's fur went black and then burned with pulsating colors until he disappeared and his coat turned dark again, twinkling white points like a midnight sky. They became increasingly worried and frustrated as the time ticked by.

"What on Earth is he doing?" whispered Nastia.

"Is he dead?" Bear wondered.

Then Hender suddenly opened his eyes and rose on two feet. "Kuzu is rescuing Maxim," he announced.

"Jesus," Dima said.

"That smart son of a bitch," Abrams said.

"How does he know?" Bear demanded.

"Why, Hender?" Nell asked.

"Chess," Hender said simply.

"Huh?" Bear said.

"Damn it, Hender, you're right," Abrams said. "It's exactly the right move."

"Yes, Abrams." Hender nodded. "Kuzu will use Maxim to turn the power on. He is the most powerful piece on the board."

Nell bowed her head. "Shit."

Galia bowed his head. "What can we do?"

"The charges in the tunnel will not detonate," Hender said then. He opened both his large trinocular eyes and looked at each of them. "Kuzu lied."

"Fuck!" Dima said.

"I thought hendros never lied," Nell said.

"He learned it from humans. I'm sorry," Hender said. "I did not see his plan until now."

Abrams nodded. "Check-fucking-mate."

"We've got to get to the palace," Nell said.

"You don't even have full body armor, Nell," Abrams said.

"We must try, anyway," Dima said.

"How?" Nastia said.

"Give me four knives," said Hender.

03:01:03

Glowing bugs dive-bombed Maxim as he emerged from the hospital, gashing his head and hands. But his attackers immediately retreated and sprayed a scent that drove off other predators as nants closed over his bleeding wounds.

Kuzu snatched three wasps out of the air and stuffed them inside the empty orange-juice bottle. He shoved Maxim into the front seat of the limo that was parked in front of the hospital. He got in on the other side and closed the door. "*Drive!*"

The wasps and drill-worms buzzing inside the vehicle tried to attack Maxim again, but they were all attacked by nants and sprayed repellent inside the car. Kuzu cracked the window and they flew out. Then he closed the window.

Maxim turned the vehicle toward the gate of Sector 4. His wounds were already being cleaned up by symbiants, which consumed the blood as they knitted a shield over his injuries.

"*Go!*" Kuzu commanded.

Maxim drove the limo through the gate to Sector Four and turned left, heading north toward the power plant.

"*Go fast!*"

Maxim pushed down the pedal, his soul upended as he zoomed into the blackness pierced by their headlights, Henders wasps and drill-worms splattering on the windshield.

"*Go right,*" Kuzu ordered, following the map in his mind.

Maxim turned the wheel with shaking hands.

"*Go faster.*"

They passed the giant warehouse on the right, where a cataract of creatures still poured out of the broken windows. Maxim wept, but a part of him rose up, urging him to crash the car.

"*Stop!*" Kuzu commanded with a voice like an earthquake.

At Kuzu's command, Maxim slammed on the brakes, doubting that he had any free will left inside him now that he was damned. He was either in Hell or hopelessly insane and, in either event, no more than a spectator of his own fate.

Pushed by the beast, he staggered out of the car at the base of the stairs. Then the creature lifted him like a toy and carried him on its back as it ran with a three-legged gallop up the narrow stairway, fending off the flying predators with mantis-like reflexes.

They rose over the polished slope as Kuzu loaded and fired three arrows in rapid succession, twisting with Maxim on his back and downing two spigers that were climbing the stairs behind them. Both of them tumbled and slid down the smooth slope to the street, paralyzed by bull's-eyed shafts that pierced their second brains.

They arrived at the entrance to the geothermal well. Through its door was the one goal Maxim wanted more than any other thing.

He wondered then if this was the shape damnation took.

03:25:04

Hender unsheathed two of the four knives they had given him. Two were combat knives from Dima and Abrams, the other two butcher knives they had found in the kitchen. "Now, wait for me."

Hender glided down the stairs and pushed open the hatch, closing it behind him.

Crowding at the window, they watched the riot of animals that had gathered around the smoldering magnesium flare Kuzu threw in front of the apartment. A feeding frenzy had accumulated after a curious spiger was wounded by the flare, with fatal results. Hender scampered down the brownstone's steps like a shadow and jumped onto a streetlamp while this was happening.

"He's climbing a lamppost," said Abrams, who could see his silhouette clearly through his night vision goggles.

"What's he doing?" Nastia asked, watching through her Russian-issue NV glasses.

Nell shook her head, bewildered. "I can't see a thing."

"He's climbing the lamppost," Abrams said again.

"Why?" Galia fretted. "What's he doing?"

"Don't ask me!" Abrams shrugged.

Hender climbed out on the arm of the streetlamp in front of the apartment, which reached out to the middle of the street. Positioning himself directly over the feeding frenzy that swirled around the flare, Hender seemed to bunch up like a spider, descending on his stretching tail.

"What's he doing now?" Nastia wondered. "You look!" She handed her binoculars to Nell.

Nell looked. "I've never seen this!"

03:23:02

Hender dangled on his elastic tail over a smaller spiger that had jumped on top of the pile below him. With four quick motions, the hendro stabbed both the spiger's brains with knives. Then he clung, invisible, to the spiger's back as he felt its nants abandon their host and adopt Hender as their next host, spreading rapidly across his skin before any other scavengers arrived to ravage the fallen predator.

02:58:12

Kuzu and Maxim opened the steel door to the power plant and stepped inside the giant steam well.

The hulking sel pushed Maxim inside and pulled the door closed behind them, leaving them in almost total darkness as the sweltering heat burned their skin. Kuzu shook up the empty orange-juice bottle, which made the Henders wasps trapped inside glow more brightly. He handed the bottle to Maxim.

Maxim took the glowing jar as Kuzu pushed him forward. Maxim stumbled down the steel stairway, Kuzu close behind, and they reached the catwalk that encircled the massive steam pipes.

Maxim saw the detonator, which was still on the catwalk between the chewed and tattered clothing of two men. The heavy switch was connected to a battery from which led thick cables.

Kuzu noted Maxim's recognition of the switch. He lifted the switch with one long arm and handed it to Maxim.

Maxim looked up at the angry, wedged brows of the beast as it took his hand and pointed his finger like a prod, pressing down on the large red button of the detonator.

Nothing seemed to happen for a moment, and Maxim looked up with a glimmer of hope. Then they felt the deep blast welling up through layers of rock and swaying the catwalk as crystal chunks broke off the walls above them.

Kuzu dodged and deflected the falling crystals, protecting Maxim with his body.

Maxim looked up from under the devil at the vibrating conduits as superheated steam rose through them and fed the waiting turbines in the plant above. A whining hiss grew, rising in pitch, and immediately a hundred lightbulbs glowed in fixtures on the wall of the well around them, some popping as they ignited.

They felt and heard the generators revving in the

plant above as Maxim saw the needles in the glass gauges on the sides of the pipes rising steadily and pushing into the red zone before finally leveling out.

A deep chugging vibrated in the rock then, echoing in the vertical chamber as pumps began drawing water from the distant river into injection wells and belching air pockets. The perpetual-energy source of Pobedograd was priming itself with perfect efficiency, just as it had been designed to do half a century ago.

02:55:02

Geoffrey and Sasha watched different views of the city near the tunnel, searching in vain for Nell and the others when, suddenly, light dawned over Pobedograd on the screens, flooding every sector, every building.

"Look," Geoffrey whispered.

The star on the cavern's ceiling ignited, dawning like a summer sky.

"Papa turned it on!" Sasha shouted.

"Yes, he did," Geoffrey said.

02:55:02

"What is Hender doing?" Dima asked.

"If I had to guess," Nell said, "I'd say he's replenishing his symbiants."

"Huh?" Bear said, peering into the dark.

"Symbiants are microscopic animals that take the place of bacteria and microbes on our own skin, helping to exfoliate the hendros," Nell said. "They also defend them from attack and help heal their wounds. The hendros lost them when they were taken from Henders Island and doused with salt water."

"Wow," Nastia said.

The streetlamp above Hender suddenly flared brightly and exposed him hanging above the maelstrom of hungry carnivores. The light agitated the gorging animals, attracting them to Hender as it grew brighter over him.

"Hey!" Bear yelled. "What's happening?"

"The lights are turning on," Nastia answered, lowering her binoculars.

As they all watched through the window, a sudden dawn illuminated the city as the five-pointed star ignited across the sky 350 feet above. Its five radiating arms infused with golden light that filled the streets below even as streetlights spluttered and flared throughout the city.

The windows in the star-shaped tower lit for one blazing moment above all the buildings before the surge of power blew out thousands of antique bulbs. Clouds of wasps and drill-worms were revealed in the sunlike radiance as they swirled around the building, energized by the blazing rays of light.

The entire city gasped before them, breathing the oxygen that wafted from the instant greening of clover covering almost every surface. Pobedograd sighed, groaning with the ghastly sound of ten thousand radiators filling with steam for the first time and haunting its hundreds of buildings with a hellish chorus as Henders organisms joined in.

"Talk about chess," Abrams said. "Kuzu just queened us."

"He turned the power on!" Nell said.

Neon signs blinked to life across the city, streaking across the Star Tower itself. As they watched, they knew they were seeing a preview of every city on Earth as it was overrun by the explosively prolific hunters of Henders Island.

"*Mautam,*" Nell breathed, staring hopelessly.

"What?" Nastia asked.

Nell shook her head. "Every forty-eight years, bamboo expands across northeastern India and explodes with fruit. The rat population doubles and ravages crops, causing mass starvation. *Mautam,*" she repeated.

"Never heard of it," Bear said.

"You're looking at it," Nell said. "This is Moscow, Berlin, Paris, Mecca, and Mumbai, only a few decades from now, if we don't seal that tunnel. And a few years after that, it will be Lima, Los Angeles, Vancouver, Taiwan, and Tokyo."

As they watched, Hender slid over the lamppost to the sidewalk.

"Somebody has to open the door for him!" Nastia yelled.

Abrams jumped down the stairs. "Tell me when!"

"*Now!*" they all shouted.

Abrams swung open the door as Hender leaped through and slammed it shut.

"Thank you, Abrams!" Hender breathed.

"Sure," Abrams said.

Hender leaped upstairs and Abrams followed.

"OK, Nell," Hender said. "I protect you."

02:49:33

Maxim wavered at the top of the long stairway outside the steam well as he stood beside the six-limbed beast. The long, vaulted corridor outside the power plant lit up as long bars suspended from the ceiling ignited for the first time since they were installed. The steam pumping through the plant was finally powering the city's grid.

Red and purple clover on the slope to each side of the stairs turned green in front of their eyes under the dawning light. Centralized heat and hot water began circulating like blood through the city's veins. As he followed the creature down the stairs, Maxim knew only then the extent to which he had betrayed his species—his world—himself. And he knew there could never be redemption.

02:43:28

Hender gazed at Nell with both his trinocular eyes. "I'm going to put nants on you now," he said with a smile.

"Wait," Nell said. "How do you know you can do that?"

"Because Kuzu turned the lights on," Hender said.

"I don't understand," Nell said.

"Maxim must have helped him," Hender said.

"I don't understand, either," Nastia said.

"He must have done for Maxim what I will do for you," Hender said. "He could not have reached the power plant any other way. Understand?"

"Yes," Abrams said, for the record.

"But how can you pass your nants to me?" Nell asked.

"Because I'm pregnant, Nell. So is Kuzu."

Nell looked at Hender in awe.

"Did I miss something?" Abrams said.

"Fuck!" Bear groaned.

"Sels are hermaphrodites," Nell explained. "They mate once in youth but don't get pregnant until they will it, which can be thousands of years later. Hender! Why now?"

"When I'm pregnant, I can make my nants cover you," Hender said.

Abrams shook his head. "If I ever get out of here, this is gonna be a bestseller."

"Nah," Bear said. "They'll never believe it."

02:47:16

Kuzu followed Maxim down the long stairway, and when they got to the bottom, the sel pushed Maxim through the car door and got in the other side.

"Go back!"

Maxim stepped on the gas, obeying the infernal voice as though it were his own will speaking for him.

02:40:51

Hender rubbed his fingers in Nell's hair and stroked her neck, shoulders, and back with four of his hands, which secreted a mellow scent like wax and vanilla. Nell tried to remain calm as she felt the migration of microscopic animals flowing over her body as Hender rubbed the scent over her skin.

"Whoa," Abrams said softly.

Nell felt the nants mesh together on her ears and right up to the edge of her lips and eyelids, gasping as her heart quickened, squeezing one of Hender's wrists. She knew that each microscopic organism was attaching itself to the others around it, all of which were equipped with a circle of eyes on their backs and transmitting relays to millions of others with identical signals like ripples on water. She focused on regulating her breaths and slowing down her heart to manage the sensation of panic that was overwhelming her.

"How do you feel, Nell?" Nastia asked.

"Warm." She exhaled. "Like I just took a niacin tablet."

"Are you OK, man?" Abrams asked.

"Yes," Nell breathed.

"Good!" Nastia said, reaching out a hand to soothe her.

"Don't touch!" Hender trumpeted, grabbing Nastia's wrist. "Nell can't control them. They will attack you, Nastia. Don't touch!"

Nastia withdrew her hand.

The others watched with growing impatience and incredulity as, for twenty minutes, Hender laid his hands on Nell. They began to suspect Hender's motive for taking so much time when they saw that Nell's skin refracted purple pixels of color at shifting angles as it was coated with microscopic creatures.

"God, what are you doing to her?" Bear asked.

Hender removed his hand from her and stood back. "Nell will be safe," he said.

"What about the rest of us?" Dima muttered.

"You have armor," Hender answered. "Now Nell does."

Nastia was suddenly terrified. "If we go out there, we'll be slaughtered!" She looked at Nell. "It doesn't matter if we have body armor! If one of those spigers comes along . . . Be honest with us, Hender! We can't make it! You know there's no way!"

Hender pointed to the gate on the map spread out on the coffee table. "That is where we are going?"

"Yes!" Nastia said.

"And it is safe inside the farm?" Hender asked.

"Yes." Nell nodded.

"We can make it there, Nastia," Hender said. "The mule—" He pointed. "—send it the other way."

Abrams nodded. "Right. We'll pack that big dead slug on top and light it up with some flares. We'll send it down the street like a Fourth of July barbecue!"

Hender nodded. "Very good, Abrams."

"Then what?" Nastia asked.

"We run like hell in the other direction," Dima said.

"Yes, Dima," said Hender.

"All right," said Abrams. "A two-hundred-yard dash is all we've got."

"Can we duck into buildings along the way?" Dima asked.

"*Nooo!*" Hender's woodwind voice intoned like a bassoon. "Moving is better!"

"Then, how should we do this?" Bear asked.

"We run in groups of two, looking forward and behind," Nell said. "We change direction when the one behind tells us."

"Yes," Hender agreed.

"OK." Abrams started clamping on his armor. "Suit up, fuckers!"

Nell felt a rush as her entire epidermis seemed to itch and be scratched simultaneously, producing an overwhelming euphoria.

"The farm should be lit now," Galia said. "All the sectors should have power from independent turbines in the power plant."

They all looked at Maxim's thin gray-haired assistant for a moment.

"OK," Abrams decided for all of them. "I guess we don't have to worry about flashlights. But let's take them anyway. Anything we need from the mule, I can carry on my back. Anything we don't need, kiss it good-bye."

Nastia covered her face. "Oh, no! This is crazy!"

"What's crazy is a woman who hates rats studying sewers," Dima said gently, putting his arm around her shoulders for a moment of reassurance.

"I know," she agreed, laughing tragically.

"It's OK," Dima urged. "We can do this."

Nastia hugged him. "*Spasiba.*"

"We've all got to watch each other's backs now," Abrams said. "Hender, you look after Nastia and Nell at the rear."

Hender nodded. "OK, Abrams!"

"All right, let's get to work."

01:49:48

The magnesium flare in front of the building finally burned out, and the feeding frenzy that had gathered moved on now with the stream in the direction they were heading.

Since they didn't have helmets, Nell was given a walkie-talkie along with Hender so they could communicate with the others. She clipped hers to her vest as the others suited up. Abrams encased himself in his body armor and climbed into the buzzing exoskeleton.

After embedding flares in the flesh of the ghost octopus, which they had lashed to the back of the mule, they walked the robot downstairs, lit the flares, and sent it out the door.

Dima steered the robot with his dog whistle against the stream of traffic as it hit the street, and the headless machine trotted forward, drawing a vortex of attackers with it.

They opened the door.

"Remember," Hender buzzed. "Keep moving! Change directions! Never stop!"

"OK!" Abrams said. He handed Nell a field shovel. "Not a bad weapon," he said.

"Thanks." She nodded, taking it.

Then he leaped out the door, carrying a terrific load of gear on his bionic back as he bounded down the steps and turned left, jogging up the street. Battered and scarred, Talon-1 charged down the stairs behind him, following.

01:48:08

"Wait!" Geoffrey exclaimed. "What's that?"

Sasha had clicked on a camera view in front of their honeymoon condominium at the west end of the river. Just before she switched to another camera view, Geoffrey had noticed the front door of the apartment opening. She hit BACK.

"There they are, Geoffrey!" Sasha shouted.

"Oh, God," Geoffrey said.

01:48:01

The sound of Henders Island came rushing back to Nell as the unforgettable howling drone filled her ears again. Only now was she grateful that Hender's nants covered her flesh.

Dima waited until Abrams had gone fifteen yards before opening the door and jumping down the stairs. He zigzagged from the sidewalk to the middle of the street and back again in five-second intervals per Hender's direction.

Fifteen paces behind him, Galia and Bear did exactly what Dima did. Bear even threw a chunk of ghost-flesh to each side as he zigged and zagged to throw off pursuers.

Nastia, Nell, and Hender ran behind them, Hender's fur camouflaging them from behind as he smacked leaping rats away with four arms moving in a blur.

Nell felt like raw meat with her bare head exposed. She was sure the animals around her could smell her deep fear. With little else but a microscopic veneer defending her skin, it was inevitable that the first bug would strike her, a drill-worm that gashed her forehead. "Hender!" she shouted as blood trickled into her eyebrow.

"It's OK, Nell!" Hender piped behind her. "Keep running."

Nell smelled the cilantro-like scent of the warning pheromone, which the drill-worm had sprayed after encountering the nants on her forehead. She was struck again, on her back, then again on her arm. This was it, she thought—in another instant, she would be the main course of a feeding frenzy.

But the wasp and drill-worm that struck her both retreated, spraying her with repellent, and the feeding frenzy that she expected never came. The wounds on her arm and forehead seemed to heal even as the blood from the gashes disappeared.

A big Henders rat vaulted through the air past Hender, Nastia, and Nell, who batted it away with the field shovel Abrams had given her.

"Good," Hender said. "Go left!"

Nastia and Nell veered left as the eight-legged "rat" hit the street, only to be tackled by smaller rats and disk-ants as it skidded and rolled across the road in a growing ball of carnage.

Meanwhile, Abrams charged up the sidewalk in a straight line, deliberately drawing the attention of their pursuers. Henders rats and bugs slammed into him, but they did not succeed in denting the shell of his armor or toppling the hydraulic exoskeleton. A pony-sized spiger catapulted off its hind legs and tail, landing behind Abrams and striking his leg with one of its spikes, which sent a shock wave of pain through his calf. With its low center of gravity, the suit absorbed the blow, however, and Abrams wasn't toppled as he turned to fire a fusillade of lead into both brains of the predator. Then he doubled back and kicked the beast to the other side of the road.

Abrams was mauled by a storm of creatures.

"Shit," Dima said.

"Let's get in the game!" Bear said.

"No worries," Abrams said through the radio calmly. "I got it. My leg's a little dinged, though." He turned and charged ahead, swarmed with bugs.

The headless mule, meanwhile, drew off half the

traffic as it piled up behind them and turned back in the other direction and chased it against the flow. It sensed debris on the road and clambered over it, nimble as a mountain goat despite being bombarded by predators. Unable to knock the indomitable machine off course, the attacking creatures were further thwarted and provoked by the flares burning on its back. Henders rats leaped onto the slab of cooking meat and were wriggling wildly as they carved out mouthfuls of octopus flesh with razor-toothed jaws even as babies emerged from their sides to gorge themselves around the burning flares.

The street curved north ahead as Abrams came to the first cross street that radiated from the central tower. One actuator was sticking, and his right leg dragged as a severed hose was bleeding out. He freed his right arm, even as his robotic arm continued to rise, and he flung a flashbang grenade like a quarterback in a high arc about thirty-five yards up the broad avenue, hoping to cause a traffic jam.

The intense flash of the grenade lit up the buildings and a strip of the skyline above. The deafening pop stunned the Henders creatures for a moment before they became even more aggressive and attacked one another.

"OK, guys," Abrams called. "We got a good fight started up here! Now's a good time to get past this street!"

Dima pushed a button on the dog whistle to call the mule back before they lost sight of it behind them. He figured it couldn't distract their pursuers if it was too far away. The robot came around the bend and cantered forward, its metallic body dripping with creatures like a beehive.

A rat struck Nastia's back with spikes that felt like bullets even though they were deflected by her Dragon Skin armor.

Bear ran back and swatted the rat that clung to her back. It grabbed his hand, striking it with a piercing blow. Cursing in pain, Bear flung the animal to the ground in front of him and crushed it under his boot. "*Fuck!*" he yelled, pulling Nastia as he ran ahead.

"Thanks!" Nastia said.

"Don't shout, Nastia," Hender reminded her. Nastia ran ahead behind Bear as Nell followed, and Hender knocked leaping rats and flying wasps out of the air behind them.

Abrams's XOS suit wheezed as he drove forward up the last stretch. He tossed flares to the other side of the street as he had observed Kuzu do, but now, in the daylight, the ploy was less effective, judging by the storm of creatures still pursuing him. He pumped his bionic body forward through the thickening swarm that felt like a hailstorm impacting on his armor now. He noted that the cross street coming up on the right ended at an arch cut into the wall on his left. As he drew closer, he saw large red words stenciled on a door inside the arch:

SEKTOP 5

"We're here!" Abrams said through the radio. He took a beating as a group of rats pummeled him, but his armor held up as he reached the farm's gate.

The entrance to Sector Five faced another avenue that stretched directly to the central tower. A flood of creatures came down this street now like rush hour New York, but they curved in front of Abrams to join the clockwise gyre of predators circling the city. Once more, Abrams freed his throwing arm and fished out an incendiary grenade. He lofted this one forty yards up the avenue, targeting a giant spiger coming down the middle of the road. The grenade ignited as it tumbled like a star through the air. Amazingly, the giant spiger leaped up like a tight end, opening its vertical jaws, and swallowed the blazing grenade, which lit up its head like a jack-o'-lantern as it exploded.

The headless behemoth crashed on the road, sliding forward as its back legs still kicked under its second brain's control.

"Nice catch!" Abrams muttered.

The ensuing feeding frenzy over the giant drew back the flow of creatures for the moment, and all of the predators attacking Abrams departed, sucked into the slaughter. Abrams used his dog whistle to drive Talon-1 after them now, firing its machine gun into the crowd. "Come on, guys!" he shouted as the bullets added to the beasts' buffet.

01:46:03

"Open the door, Sasha."

"I'm trying, Geoffrey! OK?"

"That's good, honey. Just keep trying."

"I am! Jeesh!"

01:45:51

Abrams reached the gate and then called Talon-1 back. "There's a keypad lock! What's the code, damn it!"

Galia yelled, "Punch in 00009999!"

Abrams focused one clumsy, armored finger on punching the keypad next to the gate. But even as he realized he had missed a button halfway through the code, the gate started sliding open, and he and Dima slipped through the crack. Abrams pulled Talon-1 through the door and pressed the button on the controls inside to close it. The controls responded readily and he stopped the lead-lined gate an inch from sealing. "Holler and we'll let you in!" Abrams said, peering through the crack and glancing at Dima. He noticed a giant antique light switch next to the modern door controls.

Nell could hear the herky-jerky buzz of the Big Dog's motors as it rounded the corner behind them. The mechanical mule was now a writhing mass of wasps and drill-worms as it kicked down the road like a colt. A spiger rounded the corner, skidding sideways as it stretched its head forward and swallowed the mule whole in its giant snapping jaws.

After a moment, the gigantic spiger spewed the machine onto the street, where it kept kicking on its side. Then, swiveling its head like a tank turret, the spiger searched for a new target, and its frill pulsed with waving light as it fixed its gaze on Bear.

Hender saw it pull forward with its four front legs and shove off its massive rear legs and tail. As it soared through the air, raising its spiked forearms high, Hender shouted, "Bear, turn left!" and leaped over Nastia and Nell. "Keep moving!" he yelled down at them as he landed on the soaring spiger's back.

The spiger struck the street to the right of Bear, who had just scrambled far enough to the side to avoid being crushed, and Hender stabbed two of its three rear eyes in the same moment that he jumped into the air and then plunged another knife into one of its two front eyes. His legs burned as the spiger's nants engaged in battle with his own and he leaped off the creature's back, hooking his tail on the lamppost overhanging the spiger. "Run, Bear!" he shouted like a steam whistle as he spun round the lamppost in a tightening spiral.

The big man raced toward the left side of the street as Abrams opened the gate for him and shouted, "Hurry!"

Bear jumped through and Abrams closed the gate, leaving only a crack for radio signals.

Hender launched off the lamppost and landed on the back of the half-blinded spiger.

The beast honked and bucked in front of the gate to the farm, trying to scratch him off with slashing legs. Hender gripped its neon-striped back as he reached out two arms to pierce both its remaining eyes, planted a final knife in the center of its posterior brain with the expertise of a matador. Before Hender sprang off the disabled giant, some of its symbiants had already sensed its demise and changed allegiance, leaping into Hender's fur.

Nell sprinted beside Nastia as they made their final run against the western wall. "Another spiger's behind us," Nell said calmly, masking her fear.

Nastia looked back and hyperventilated. "Oh, God." The red spiger came around the corner behind them, even larger than the one it had been hunting. It seemed to spot the wounded giant beside them and locked on. As the hulking invertebrate prepared to spring, rats and swarms gathered around it, ready to share in its spoils.

"It's coming!" Nastia screamed, seeing it on her visor.

"I don't think it sees us yet," Nell said. "It's going after the spiger!"

They were only thirty-five yards from the gate. "Change directions when I say! OK?" Nell said.

"OK," said Nastia.

"Two heads are better than one," Nell said. "Tell me when it's coming!"

Nastia saw the spiger in the rearview window of her visor. "Just go straight," she said as she saw the giant flying toward them. "OK, go right!"

They cut right toward the other sidewalk as the predator landed where they had just been.

"Keep going!" Nell yelled, running at full speed as she crossed in front of the beast that was gathering itself for another leap.

Nell pulled an incendiary grenade Abrams had given her from a pouch on her jersey and found the firing pin by touch as she ran. The spiger leaped diagonally up the street toward them.

"Here it comes!" Nastia screamed.

"Go left!" Nell yelled.

They felt the creature's shadow fall over them as they headed across the intersection toward the gate.

One of the spiger's six-foot-long spiked arms

whipped past Nell so hard, she felt the breeze in its wake as it impaled the street like a pile driver. She almost lost her footing and she triggered the grenade, rolling it under the spiger's body behind her. At the same moment, the spiger stretched its neck down to the left with open jaws.

Nastia screamed as she saw the jaws engulf Nell.

01:45:48

Sasha spotted the two figures running toward the camera that was mounted over the gate to the farm. Geoffrey pointed, gasping. "That's Nell and somebody else!"

Sasha screamed as she saw the spiger leaping behind them.

"Zoom in, Sasha!" Geoffrey said, gripping her arm.

Sasha did so reluctantly, as they saw the dragon swallow Nell.

Sasha covered her eyes, crouching down as Ivan barked. "I hate you!" she cried.

01:45:47

Nell felt the forest of pincers inside the spiger's mouth stab into her back as acidlike digestive enzymes showered the Dragon Skin. The nants on her body burned in battle as the grenade under the spiger's chest ignited, causing the beast to blow ten feet straight up as its jaws opened in shock, spilling Nell onto the road. The creature landed behind her and snapped its jaws involuntarily near her as she jumped to her feet and ran with Nastia.

"How'd you do that?" Nastia breathed.

"Let's go!" Nell said.

01:45:39

"Oh, my God . . . oh, my God!" Geoffrey felt dizzy as he held his head. "She made it."

"She did?" Sasha looked out from between her fingers. "You liar! She *did*! I love you, Geoffrey!"

01:45:39

Nell and Nastia bolted toward the left side of the street, directly toward the gate of the farm now. In the cross street opposite the gate, the stream converged on the spiger Hender had downed and now attacked the spiger Nell had felled, as well. Hender appeared briefly against the wall near the gate. "Here!" he hissed.

As they reached him, Hender wrapped his arms around them to camouflage them against the wall as they moved in front of the door, which Hender pounded with two fists to signal the others.

"Let us in, Abrams!" Nastia shouted.

Abrams opened the door. "Quick!"

A hundred Henders bugs rushed in before he closed the heavy door behind them with a rolling *boom*.

The farm was completely dark, and they were momentarily blinded as they turned toward Abrams.

01:45:37

"Switch to a camera inside the farm, Sasha!"

"Let me find one. . . ."

"Hurry!"

"I am, Geoffrey. I'm hurrying! I'm ALWAYS hurrying!"

01:45:39

As their eyes adjusted, Nell and Nastia staggered back in horror to see the glowing shapes moving over the floor, walls, and ceiling, and rising and falling in the air.

A rock fall had opened a gaping hole in the cavern's ceiling above in the northwest corner. Filling the cavern with psychedelic phantoms, the creatures of Pandemonium had invaded the farm.

Glowing green, the Henders bugs that had gotten through the door flew up amidst the jellyfish-like animals suspended in the air, instantly clashing in battle as the molluscan balloons showered them with stinging cells.

Hender shrieked in fear, grabbing Nell's shoulders as he cringed at the glowing shapes that filled this alien world, chirping and clicking around them.

"Follow me, fast!" Abrams yelled. "The others are in the bus!"

He dashed ahead in the squealing XOS, and they followed as glowing gammies spotted them through the rows of growing benches to either side of the road.

In a circular clearing ahead sat the RV-sized vehicle that had been converted into a field lab for the farm. As the creatures converged behind them, they chased them over the last thirty yards past bullet-riddled bodies of gammies that were already being devoured by other gammies.

Bear opened the door as they arrived and let them in.

Nastia turned and sat down on the steps, holding the door shut with her feet. "No, no, no!" she shrieked, sobbing.

Dima reached out and squeezed her shoulders. "It's OK. You're tough enough for Spetsnaz," he said in Russian.

"No, I'm not! Who's going to keep this door shut?"

"It's locked now. Right, Bear?"

"Yes. Nothing can get in! Relax."

Nastia pulled away from the door, and Dima pulled her to her feet. She turned and sobbed against him for a moment as Dima patted her back, and the others peered grimly through the windows of the bus. Nell saw the giant hole that had opened up in the roof of the chamber to the northwest.

Nastia quickly recovered and pushed away from Dima. She looked out the far windows of the bus and noticed the pile of jagged breakdown that reached fifty feet up the far wall of the cavern. "There was a cave-in?" she said.

"Yes," Nell said.

"I thought you said we'd be safe in here," Bear said to Galia.

"We would have been," Galia said.

"This must have happened in the last few days," Nell said, incredulous.

"Jeezus *Christ,*" Abrams said.

"What the hell is this, Nell?" Nastia asked.

Nell sighed. "This is Pandemonium."

01:47:03

As Sasha found a camera view, they saw Nell and Nastia climbing into the bus, chased by a column of gammies.

"What?" Geoffrey exclaimed, moving his throbbing foot higher.

"Uh-oh," Sasha said.

01:48:29

Abrams shook his head, climbing out of the XOS suit. "OK, what now?"

Nastia pulled out her phone with shaking hands to photograph the multicolored creatures swirling around them in the darkness.

"What are you doing?" Bear asked.

"This is an entirely new ecosystem," she said.

Bear laughed. "We'll probably never make it out of here, and you're taking pictures?"

"That's enough!" Dima said, glaring at Bear.

"The rumors were true," Nastia said. "There are monsters here. They did run into Hell while digging this city." The terror that had possessed her the moment before was momentarily replaced with scholarly satisfaction. "I have studied caves all my life," she said. "There has never been a system of troglobites such as this. How big is the cave system they came from?"

"It stretches a hundred kilometers," Galia said.

"Wonderful!" Nastia whispered.

"You should see the underwater window in the palace," Nell said.

"You mean there are stygobites as well as troglobites?" Nastia laughed nervously.

"Hundreds of terrestrial and aquatic species," Nell said. "Like nothing you've ever imagined."

"OK," Abrams said. "Is everyone all right? I think my fibula's broken. I don't know how that thing did it through this armor, but my calf's fucked up."

"Spigers have a trebuchet-like strike, like the mantis shrimp," Nell said. "A big one could probably shatter that suit like an egg."

"Glad I didn't know that till now," Abrams said.

"Hey, your back's smoking, Nell!" Dima said.

"Better take that off," Nastia said. "She was *inside* the spiger's mouth! You should have seen it."

Nell's tunic seemed to be steaming as she pulled it over her head and discarded it. "Wow—must be digestive juices," she noted. "Thanks."

"You were *inside* its mouth?" Abrams asked, chuckling. "OK, Rambo. You win."

"That's pretty awesome." Bear nodded.

Dima reached out to shake her hand.

Hender grabbed Dima's wrist firmly with one of his hands. "No! Nell can't control the nants. Don't touch her. OK?"

"Oh, yes." Dima nodded. "*Spasiba*."

Nastia noticed the purple sheen on Nell's face and arms, taking a step back.

"How do you feel, Nell?" asked Nastia.

"Like I'm wearing a wetsuit."

Bear pulled his glove off. "That rat bastard cut my finger off right inside my glove."

Nastia's eyes widened as she saw his hand missing his middle finger as Bear pulled his hand out of the bloody glove. She looked at the big man, horrified.

"It's OK. I've got four more." He grinned, laughing.

"Tape that up, Nastia," Abrams said, pulling a bag off the XOS suit and fishing out a first aid kit.

"How?" she protested.

"Spray this on his finger." Abrams handed her a bottle of an antibiotic disinfectant coagulant.

Dima took the bottle from him. "You think she is automatically nurse?" he said.

"I think anybody not doing anything is automatically nurse," Abrams said. "Whatever. You take care of it, Romeo."

Dima sprayed the bloody stump of Bear's finger as the big man gritted his teeth.

Nell noticed Hender's lower legs and hands were stained blue. "Hender, you're bleeding."

"That's blood?" Abrams asked.

"Yes," Nell said. "It's copper-based."

"You OK, Hender?" Nastia asked.

Hender's fur was nearly translucent now, faintly projecting what was behind him as it mimicked invisibility. "Yes." He nodded, bowing his head in exhaustion. The blue bloodstains seemed to fade on Hender's silvery fur as nants scoured each filament clean.

Outside the bus, rows of stacked shelves holding glass jars and flats of soil stretched north and south from the circular clearing. Nell looked through the skylight at the glowing clouds of hovering shapes drifting through the air. Beams of faint light crisscrossed the cavern's roof.

"So this is a farm?" Dima asked.

"Yes," Galia said.

"What do they grow here, mushrooms?" Bear asked.

The sound of scrabbling legs scraped the bus on all sides as dog-sized gammies crawled over the vehicle now.

"Nell!" Nastia pointed at one of the gammarids, which sat in the driver's chair.

"That one's dead," Bear laughed. "We had to kill a few that got in."

Nastia smirked.

"We should move." Abrams squirmed as the mass of gammies crowded around the bus. "I don't like being in the counter of a delicatessen."

"He's right," Bear said. "We better get where we're going, fast."

"Nell and Galia—what's the next move?" Abrams asked. "How the hell are we going to deal with these fricking things now? There're millions of them out there."

"There must be a powerful lighting system above us," Nell said.

"There is," Galia said. "With the power on, it should light the whole farm."

She frowned in thought. "Most of these creatures are tuned to very low light."

"There's a light switch next to the entrance," Abrams said. "A huge switch like something out of Frankenstein's lab."

Galia nodded. "Yes. I believe that switch does turn on the farm's lights."

"So, if we turn it on . . ." Dima looked at Nell. "What?"

"We will blind many of the species," Nell said. "At least temporarily." She looked at the dead gammy sitting in the driver's seat. Its bullet-riddled body was pale under the cabin lights, its back covered with jutting spikes. Its head was smooth, however, with small, sharp mandibles. "But gammies don't have eyes."

"Wow. You're right," Bear said.

"I thought they were herbivores," Nell said, examining the mouthparts. "But apparently they're omnivores."

"Hmm." Abrams looked at the giant bug. "How do they get around without eyes?"

"They're a lot like army ants, which are also blind," Nell said. "They must follow scent trails."

"OK," Abrams said. "Since light won't affect them, what can we do?"

"I think I know," Nell said. "We have one ROV left, don't we?"

"Yeah, Talon-1 is still with us." Abrams nodded.

"Good. Bring the dead gammies over here and give me a field knife," Nell said.

"Why?" Dima asked.

"Some ants use glands to lay down a scent trail—one pheromone acts as a primer and another completes the trail-following scent." Nell sliced open the gammarid's abdomen and pulled open the exoskeleton, probing with the knife. Two long sacs of fluid led to a nozzlelike orifice at the point of the abdomen. "Here! These must be the scent glands." Nell blew away a strand of her hair from her face as she cut around the sacs. "I need a rag, or some cotton. Any in the first aid kit?"

"Yeah." Abrams gave her a wad of cotton from the kit on board.

"We need to rig something on Talon-1 so it can drag a swab behind it."

"OK. But I don't see how we can draw enough of them away to make a difference."

"Cut that other gammy open, Dima, just like I did," Nell said, pointing to another of the creatures lying on the floor. "Can I borrow your gloves?" she asked Nastia. "I'm afraid I'll have to throw them away afterwards, unless you want those things chasing you out there." Nell winked.

"Here," said Nastia. "They're yours."

01:30:07

"What happened?" Geoffrey asked.

"It caved in, Geoffrey," Sasha said. "Yesterday."

"What?" Geoffrey said.

"I had to take Ivan for a walk in the ballroom, instead, yesterday. I didn't tell you 'cause I didn't want you and Nell to be scared."

Geoffrey shook his head.

"Sorry, Geoffrey!"

"It's OK, Sasha." He bowed his head, covering his face with both hands.

01:29:57

Inside the dormitory, Kuzu found the humans and Hender on Maxim's laptop through a security camera: They were inside a large vehicle in a wide clearing. Hender had gotten them somewhere else, somehow. If they made it to the palace, they could reach the train tunnel again through the tunnel Nell had taken and possibly set off the charges. But Kuzu saw that they were trapped now by a multitude of weird animals inside the giant cavern of the farm. He turned to Maxim. "*Where?*" his voice crashed like thunder. "*Tell!*"

Deep inside, Maxim had reconstituted a small piece of himself as he began to calculate a way to beat this devil.

01:28:50

"OK, Talon-1 can run backwards. It can lower the swab attached to the barrel by aiming the gun down," Abrams said. "You wanna drive, Nell? Just look in this screen—it's just like a video game."

"Yeah, I'd be happy to," Nell said. "Let's open the door and send it out."

Abrams and Dima guarded the door as Bear opened it. Nell toggled the ROV forward from the lowest step onto the ground. They closed the door as a few small gammarids got in, but the men squashed them under their boots.

Slowly, in fits and starts at first, Nell drove the ROV around the bus. "How do I lower the swab?"

"Here," Abrams said. "Now?"

"Yes."

He pointed the gun down, and the yardstick taped to the barrel lowered the saturated wad of cotton to the ground.

They watched as Nell drove the Talon to the other side of the bus and then began steering it in a wide circle around the clearing. The fast-moving amphipods began flowing behind the bot as they picked up the scent of the sternal glands.

When Nell had almost completed the circle, she turned the bot into a gradual spiral, ultimately toward the center of the clearing. The gammies emptied off the bus and came from between the rows on either side to follow the powerful scent the bot was dragging. Each time she came around in a clockwise motion, the gammarids filled in an ever-tightening spiral.

"What are you doing?" Nastia asked.

"They're taking the bait, all right," Abrams observed. "That's the damnedest thing I ever saw! Nice driving, by the way."

"Thanks," said Nell, sticking her tongue out as she operated the joystick with her thumb.

Hender was nearly invisible with terror as he stood next to the others in front of the window.

Nell finally reached the center of the clearing with the Talon and shut it down, exhaling a long sigh as her shoulders slumped.

"Awesome job," Abrams said.

Gammarids north and south continued to emerge from the rows of the farm to join the circle, climbing on top of one another into the vortex and piling into a higher and higher mountain as they reached the dead end at the center the spiral.

"OK! That should keep them occupied," Nastia said.

"For how long?" Bear asked, incredulous.

"If they're anything like ants, as long as they live." Nell said. "When army ants get locked into death circles, they keep on going until they starve."

"No shit," Abrams said, laughing as the widening mass of amphipods rotated in front of them, like a glowing galaxy.

"Now what?" Bear asked.

"We turn on the lights and then run to the northwest corner. There's a secret entrance there, not far from the palace," said Nell.

"There is?" asked Galia, surprised.

"Sasha showed it to me," Nell said.

"Right on," Abrams said, climbing into the XOS suit. "Then what?"

"There may be more ghost octopuses in the tunnel," Nell said.

"I hate them." Hender shuddered.

"OK. We'll take care of them when we get there. We should be able to blast our way through. It's not far to the palace."

"Great plan, Nell. Dima, Bear, and I will turn the lights on and be right back," Abrams said. "When we come back this way, you get out and follow us north between those benches. Got it? Suit up. I'll go first," Abrams said.

"No, no," Dima protested. "Bear and I should go first and fire at whatever we see. You can hold our ammo bag."

"That's more like it," Bear said, unloading the eighty-pound bag from his back.

"All right," Abrams said, taking the duffel bag of ammo easily on one robotic forearm. "But let's save some for any ghosts that might be in the tunnel."

Abrams set the arms to steady-carry the load in front of him and freed his own arms to carry an AK-47. "OK, everyone out of the way, I'm coming through." Abrams power-walked toward the bus door, his XOS suit dangling bags and equipment and cradling the ammo packs. Bear and Dima pulled the door open and he jumped out ahead of them.

01:26:12

Kuzu watched the humans inside the bus on Maxim's laptop. He showed the city's map on the screen of his phone to Maxim. "Where?"

As the creature used a common phone, Maxim realized he was not some hallucination or mythological creature. He realized it must be one of the famous hendropods. How or why it was here was a mystery to him. Maxim shivered and felt the nants that coated his flesh rippling as they shifted. His skin felt pleasantly numb, thick, and somehow impervious. Then his captor touched his chest and in an instant turned his shield into a layer of acid that burned his flesh. Maxim quickly indicated Sector 5 on the map.

"Where they go?"

Maxim pointed to Sector One. "The palace," he groaned, too readily.

"*Why?*"

"I don't know!" Maxim sighed in agony, reaching under the mattress of his bed and grasping the loaded Beretta he had hidden there.

Kuzu looked at him quizzically, then extended a hand, exuding the ameliorating pheromone that prevented the nants from devouring the human's flesh. The sel decided that the human was not deceiving him. Kuzu looked back at the screen as three of the humans burst out of the vehicle, running toward the camera.

01:25:59

Bear, Dima, and Abrams ran the fifty-yard dash to the gate.

Down the road behind them rushed gammies like Pac-Mans coming out from between the rows of benches and funneling into the road. But they were not nearly so abundant as they had been before.

As Dima reached the switch beside the gate, a

horse-sized soldier gammarid charged at him from the right. Abrams fired at the animal. Dima, oblivious, jumped the last two yards as smaller gammarids raced down the wall and crawled over his feet. He grabbed the switch with both hands, pulled it down through squealing corrosion, and slammed it against the wall.

Even the humans were blinded by the sudden swell of light that filled the cavern as the lattice glowed white hot above.

Dima kicked the amphipods off his legs as he bolted behind the others. The creatures that had been following them scattered, trampling one another as they sought shelter from the blazing sunlike heat generated by the lights.

01:24:27

Kuzu saw the humans running toward the bus and noticed Hender and the others bursting out of its door to meet them. They all turned north.

01:23:10

They ran in single file up one of the rows. Each row of growing benches was a pyramid of shelves rising eight feet, many of them holding two-hundred-gallon glass flasks designed for growing algae. Nell looked above at the floating carnival of creatures that were crashing blindly into one another in the blazing light. Some of the buoy-sized man-of-wars rose too close to the crisscrossing beams on the ceiling and burst as they were fried by the heat. Thankfully, at least, the avenue they raced down was clear of gammies at the moment.

Nastia looked up, awestruck, as a flock of globular orange butterflies drifted above them, making clicking noises. "What are these things in the air?"

"Mollusks, mostly," Nell said.

"Then why are they *flying*?" she asked.

"They do that here," Nell said.

"I don't like mollusks," Hender grumbled, running ahead of Nell, Nastia, and Galia. Abrams, Bear, and Dima charged in front.

Nastia noticed something coming up behind them in the visor of her helmet. "Nell!"

Nell looked back and saw an aggregator, rippling like a thirty-foot centipede as it chased them. She noticed that every segment of the beast had an eye on each side.

Nastia screamed.

"Shush!" Nell said, realizing all creatures down here must have acute hearing.

"It's moving faster than us!" Nastia yelled. Suddenly, she dived under the row of shelves to the right.

"Nastia!" Nell hissed. She dived under after her, rolling to the other side as six segments broke off the aggregator and followed them.

Hender leaped over the shelves.

Alone behind Abrams and Dima now, Galia saw the many-legged animal behind him. "Something's coming!"

"Shoot it," Abrams said, ahead of them.

Nastia raced down the next row in a panic, and Nell had a hard time catching up to her. Hender landed ahead of Nell, nearly invisible now as fear triggered his camouflage.

Galia turned and emptied the Glock they had given him into the head of the creature. It fell, revealing the next head, which ate the first. The rest of the aggregator kept charging toward Galia over the other segments, and he threw the empty gun at it and ran.

Nell noticed the pieces of the aggregator reassemble as it chased them, rowing legs like a galley's oars. She held the machine gun low to pierce as many of its segments as possible and fired. The three segments in the back broke away and scampered under the shelves on each side. "Keep running!" she said, turning and charging after Hender and Nastia.

Suddenly, Galia screamed from the next row as the lead segment of the aggregator detached and grabbed his pant leg in a bear trap of teeth, slashing his calf through the Dragon Skin armor. He stomped his other foot down on the pale white creature, crushing its outer shell as another leaped forward. Dima fired at it, and it fragmented like a pumpkin as Galia limped forward, his right knee surging with agony with each step.

Dima brought up the rear then. "Keep going, old man," he said. "I can't carry you if you fall." He looked behind them and saw with horror the growing train of the aggregator as more segments joined it. Above, a flock of firebombers, colorless now in the light, drifted over them, their pale tentacles glistening in the artificial sun.

In the next row, behind Nell and Nastia, another long aggregator was forming. And the bulbs of drifting firebombers swooped down, seeming to follow the running people.

Nell fired her gun at the glass flasks lining the shelves behind them. As they exploded, showers of shrapnel spread over the path and blasted into the air.

Seeing what she was doing, Dima followed suit, firing at the giant jars behind them and filling the air with flying blades that pierced the flock of firebombers while covering the ground with slicing shards that stopped the rushing aggregators and gammarids in their tracks.

They reached the northern wall of the farm. "Go left!" Nell shouted, and they all turned west toward the hidden door. Galia's left leg was covered with blood, but the older man hustled to keep up.

They continued laying down a wall of flying glass beside them as they ran, but as they reached the northwest corner, they saw that they could go no farther. A slope of thousands of tons of fallen rock had buried the door.

"We're screwed," Bear said.

"What now?" Abrams said.

A squadron of pale spheres trailing pink tentacles drifted through the breach of Pandemonium above, sinking straight for them.

"More firebombers. Take cover," Nell said. "They drop stinging cells that can paralyze on contact."

"Where the hell can we go?" Nastia yelled.

"Over here!" cried a voice.

"Nell!" squealed another voice, behind them.

They turned and saw a large open door in the north wall. Geoffrey and Sasha frantically waved at them in the door.

"Oh, awesome!" Abrams said, running in the limping exoskeleton behind Bear. "Come on!"

As they all turned back, Nastia, Nell, and Hender reached the door first. Geoffrey reached out to hug Nell as Hender pushed him away. "No, Geoffrey!"

Sasha ran out the door with Ivan at her side, waving the others in. "Come on!" she yelled.

"Sasha," cried Galia as he came behind the others, stumbling. "Dear girl! I'm so happy to see you." As he hobbled toward her, a large firebomber dipped down above him, streaming its tentacles with their payloads of nematocysts. "I told you I would come back," he cried.

"Who are you?" she asked.

Galia pulled off his helmet, and an uncharacteristic smile broke over his grim face. "I'm Galia, dear!"

"I hate you!" Sasha shouted.

"OK." Galia smiled. "I love you, little girl."

Red sparks showered from the tentacles of the sphere, sprinkling over them. Galia saw the firefall and leaped forward, tackling Sasha, and it felt like molten lava was pouring over his neck and head.

"Get *off* me!" she screamed underneath him.

"You're safe, *Sashinka*," Galia whispered. He had landed on his knees and elbows, but now he collapsed with his full weight on top of her. She convulsed under him and screamed even as Abrams reached down with his robot arm and pulled him off, rolling his limp body aside. His eyes were frozen open. "Let's go, honey!" Abrams barked.

She sprang up, crying, and ran through the door.

Dima ran to Galia, shooting down a number of spheres, the bullets breaking stalactites off the high ceiling in the distance. Galloping down the slope of broken rock from the cave-in above was a giant soldier gammarid mounted by a fantastic ghost octopus with a dazzling coat of orange thorns that elaborated on the gammy's design. It raced toward him and sprayed two streamers of goo at them.

"Old man!" Dima shouted, trying to rouse Galia, but then he realized that Galia was dead.

Bear leaped through the door, and Dima jumped after him as a rope of goo caught his ankle. Before they could close the door, Dima was pulled backwards and they saw Galia's body being reeled in by the other rope. They yanked Dima through and the door cut the goo-rope, preventing Dima from Galia's fate.

"What happened to him?" Sasha bawled. "What happened to Uncle Galia?"

"He's gone, sweetie," Abrams said.

"No!" she screamed.

"Sasha," Geoffrey said. "We've got to go now."

Hender was amazed to see the human child. He had never actually met one this close. The golden hair and blue eyes of the miniature human beguiled him, and he reached out and touched her head as his own fur blazed golden, with bubbling rings of blue and pink.

Sasha looked up and her face wiped clean with awe. "Hender?" she asked. All children on Earth had seen his image.

"Yes, Sasha. Let's go, OK?" Hender said.

"OK." Sasha rose from beside Ivan. "Follow me, Hender!"

The others rushed behind Sasha and Ivan as they headed west. They turned north through a tall, arched corridor. At the end, Sasha opened a door into the hallway between the underwater window and the palace foyer.

Turning left, they emerged in the room with the window on their right, its red velvet curtains open and revealing the aquatic half of Pandemonium.

"That's the hatch to the secret passage," Nell said, pointing to the left. "Those stairs lead to the gondola." She pointed to the spiral stairway in the far right corner.

Hender and Nastia stopped before the dark window in awe. Glowing colors and forms surged in schools and waves before them like abstractions in the dark.

"Most are mollusks and arthropods," Geoffrey said, leaning on his cane. "All are new species. I'm Geoffrey Binswanger, Nell's husband." He reached out and clasped Nastia's hand.

Nastia took his hand without taking her eyes off the window. "Nell's husband." She smiled. "You are a lucky man."

"I know." Geoffrey turned on the battery of lights with the switch beside the window, illuminating the lake. "It's saltwater. We think it must be hundreds of millions of years old."

Hender cringed.

"Hender doesn't like saltwater," Nell said, joining them as the soldiers started breaking out their gear behind them. "Saltwater kills species from Henders Island. It's why they never left."

Abrams unbuckled himself from the XOS and started pulling packs off its back as Dima and Bear helped him.

Nastia held out her phone as she recorded video

through the window in reverence. "The Urals were formed when Baltica, Siberia, and Kazakhstania smashed together to form the supercontinent Laurasia," Nastia said. "That a cave system from that time could still exist . . ."

"I know," Geoffrey said. "It's unprecedented."

"No, not unprecedented," Nastia corrected. "The Jenolan Caves in Australia are three hundred forty million years old. But it is remarkably rare."

"Saltwater?" Hender asked.

Nell patted one of his "shoulders" reassuringly.

"Why can you touch Hender and not Geoffrey?" Nastia wondered.

"Yes?" Geoffrey asked. "Why is that?"

"I can control nants," Hender said. "But Nell can't."

"Nell?" Geoffrey gasped.

"I didn't have any body armor, so Hender gave me his."

He looked at her, terrified as he noticed the purple sheen of the nants coating her skin. "Are you OK? Is she safe, Hender?"

"Yes," Hender said.

"I'm OK," Nell said, shaking her head in amazement.

"That's good . . . so you got your symbiants back, Hender?"

"Yes!" Hender said, flushing green and blue with pleasure.

"But why don't they attack Nell?"

"They think she's my child," Hender said. "I'm pregnant, Geoffrey."

Geoffrey opened his mouth. "Oh! Congratulations."

"OK," Hender said.

"Hey," Abrams said. "Why can't we unleash hell on those monsters? I mean, if there's another window upstairs, why couldn't we just blow it up and open the gates? Then they could duke it out down here."

"That's actually not a terrible idea, Abrams," Geoffrey said. "Using one ecosystem against the other—"

"And if we blow the windows down here, too—" Nell suggested.

"Saltwater!" Geoffrey agreed.

"Brilliant," Nastia said. "An Augean stables solution."

"What's that?" Dima asked.

"The Fifth Labor of Hercules," Abrams said, impressed. "King Augeas commanded Hercules to clean out his stables, which he knew was impossible, but Hercules diverted two rivers into the stables and got the job done."

"Right," Nastia said. "That's very good."

"Thanks," Abrams said. "We have enough explosives. If that lake is big enough, we could flood the whole damned city."

"It's big enough," Geoffrey said.

"It probably wouldn't drain more than a few feet and still flood Pobedograd," Nell said. "So long as we plug the drain."

Abrams nodded. "We're working on that right now." He reached up to one of the two snare drum-sized robots strapped onto the rack of the exosuit. He unclipped the ROV and set it on the floor before them on its four legs. "The Dalek combat robot."

"Do you know how to work it?" Bear asked.

"Jackson said the dog whistle operates all of these, didn't he?" Dima said.

"Yeah, it's easy," Abrams said.

"Can that make it through the tunnel with all those ghosts in there?" Bear asked.

"It can go twenty miles per hour, which may be fast enough to get by them."

"How can we transmit radio signals to it through solid rock?" Geoffrey questioned, dubious.

"It drops a trail of remote signal relays—it should have, let's see—" Abrams counted the detachable transponders on board the device. "—five. I should be able to set them to deploy every five hundred yards or so. That should be enough." Abrams raised his eyebrows at them. "Let's wake it up!"

He pressed the select button on the dog whistle, scrolled down to DALEK-1 and pushed START. Two rotors popped out of the unit and whirred in different directions, lifting the bot off the floor. It stopped before hitting the ceiling as though repelled by an invisible cushion and then hovered with a loud, high-pitched whine.

"Let's see if the cameras work!" Dima shouted.

"Yeah, I see you!" Abrams yelled.

"OK, set it down. Maybe we can put a charge on it," Dima said.

"Not one big enough to seal that tunnel," Bear said.

"No. But big enough to detonate the charges already set in the tunnel," Abrams said.

"If they were set," Bear glanced sideways at Hender.

"Kuzu wouldn't lie," Hender said.

"He *did* lie," Abrams said. "He said one of those octopus-things killed the other guys and then later he said Ferrell did it. One of those was a lie, Hender."

"He would not lie to me," Hender said sadly.

"Oh, great," Bear said. "Kuzu is two moves from checkmating the entire human race, man! How do we know this one isn't in on it?"

"I'm not Kuzu," Hender said.

"Presuming he's not," Abrams said, "even if they didn't set the charges, there's a full pack of sixteen charges in that tunnel. If we can reach it and detonate the Dalek next to it, that should do the trick."

"*Da,*" Dima said. "We have to try!"

"We'll set a charge on the Dalek to go off in, say, seven minutes," Abrams said, punching in the number. "That should give me enough time to find the charges in the tunnel and park this thing right there."

"Sounds good," Dima said.

"How can you steer it through the tunnel?" Nastia asked.

"Just like a video game." Abrams pulled the dog whistle from around his neck. "I just point it where I want to go. It's got wall avoidance sensors built in, so it can't crash—theoretically."

"Let's do it," Dima said.

"Hoo-ya," Bear said.

"You guys rig the charges," Nell said. "I'm going upstairs to check out the gondola."

Bear glanced at Nell. "A lot's riding on that gondola, darlin'."

"I know!"

"Dima, why don't you go with her?" Abrams said.

"Yeah, OK." Dima nodded at Nell as she climbed the spiral stairs inside the glass vestibule. He caught up to her as Bear rigged the ROV with explosives.

"We can set some charges in the underwater bedroom as well as this window," Geoffrey said.

"Hey," Sasha objected. "That's my room!"

"We need to, honey," he said.

Sasha frowned.

"Can you show Bear where it is? And leave all the doors open, and open the door to the foyer, too, OK?"

"OK. Come on, Bear. Ivan and I will show you the way."

"Nastia, come here and help me," Abrams said as he revved up the Dalek.

"I'm worried about Kuzu," Hender said.

"Then let's go upstairs," Geoffrey said. "We can check the security monitors there."

01:16:10

Kuzu had located a camera view from inside the room with the underwater window where they had gathered. He had turned up the volume on Maxim's laptop and heard every word they said.

He rose now and tossed the laptop onto the bed. He grabbed his backpack full of explosives. "*Come now!*"

Maxim gripped the pistol he had slipped into his pocket as he went with Kuzu to the limousine.

01:10:10

Nell and Dima reached the gondola deck one hundred feet up.

Dima peered through the window in the granite wall, inspecting the landing of the gondola. The car was a '50s Soviet space-age shape encrusted with rainbowfire except for its windows, which had been kept relatively clean, perhaps by mollusks like those that scraped the underwater window and the walls of Sasha's bedroom.

"That's it," Nell said. "It's driven by a diesel engine. Cans of diesel fuel are stacked next to it—see?"

"Yes. So we have to make sure it's fueled up and prime the engine. It probably hasn't been started in sixty years."

"They started it recently. At least I think so," Nell said as she threw the switch that turned on the bank of floodlights above the window. They illuminated the gondola's dual cables that curved down and then up across the lake to a pylon rising from a nearby island. The vast space beyond the floodlights was aglow with creatures, some of which loomed like pink blimps in the distance to their right. Firebombers flared as they rose and fell in slow motion, streaming vivid pink tails. Orange bubbles flowed in flocks, changing direction in unison. Vividly colored balls rolled down the walls, and hundreds of yellow and orange gammies leaped on their long legs past the window with alarming speed. Hordes of creatures writhed on the gray mats that spread across the surface of the lake, which was filled with glowing shapes like giant flowers and winding snakes.

"What do those words say?" Nell asked, pointing to the sign over the hatch.

"'Hell's Door,'" Dima muttered, looking at her.

"Ah." Nell nodded. "It says 'Hell's Window' downstairs."

"Oh," Dima said. "This gondola—it's supposed to get us across that lake?" He frowned. "And then—where?"

Nell shrugged. "It must be another escape route for Stalin. We think it must lead out of the mountain."

"We hope?" Dima shook his head. "Well, it better."

"It's better than nothing."

Dima gazed out the window at the hellish world there. "I don't know about that."

01:10:10

Abrams and Nastia opened the hatch and he fired in tight circles down the passageway. The rounds scarred the walls, floor, and ceiling as they raked the tunnel. He targeted ghosts as they peeled off in the distance, blasting them to calamari as they dropped to the floor. Leaving nothing to chance, he used all but a few ammo magazines to clear the Dalek's path as Nastia plugged her ears.

Bear returned with Sasha after setting charges on the crystal walls of her bedroom. Sasha immediately ran with Ivan upstairs to get away from the loud noise of the gunfire, and Bear began rigging the underwater window with Semtex.

01:07:34

Hender stepped off the stairs into Stalin's conservatory and ran to look at the video monitors over Maxim's desk.

Geoffrey limped behind him.

"Oh, *nooo*!" Hender quailed.

"What?" Geoffrey panted, hobbling forward with Stalin's cane.

"Where is this one?" Hender pointed at the screen on the wall.

Geoffrey moved closer to look: a limo barreled past the gate of Sector Three. It turned right into Sector Two, heading north—toward the palace. "Oh, no," he agreed.

Hender said, "Kuzu."

"But he can't get through that gate. It's locked. Right, Sasha?"

Sasha was just coming up behind them with Ivan. "Right. Papa never guessed my password. He doesn't know the door code." She folded her arms and glared at the limousine on the monitor.

01:07:19

"Here goes."

Abrams set the bot down in the secret passage and started it with the dog whistle. It hummed like a giant Henders wasp as it levitated. An accelerometer inside the remote transmitted tilt and trajectory commands to the flying bot as Abrams sent it forward. With the Dalek's forward camera, Abrams could see the tunnel on the screen of the dog whistle as it cruised at twenty miles per hour, equally distanced from the ceiling, floor, and walls.

"Amazing!" said Nastia.

"Yeah, it's cool," Abrams said, pursing his lips as he focused.

Bear finished setting three charges on the window. "I set the charges in that girl's room to go off in twenty minutes."

"Good. Set the charges on the window to go off in ten minutes," Abrams said. "I set the charge on the Dalek to go off in nine minutes, but that's more than I'll need."

"Roger. Ten minutes it is."

"Did you open that door to the foyer?"

"Shit, I forgot!" Bear set the timer on the detonator and trotted down the corridor to wheel open the hatch at the end. "Woo!" he yelled back. "Somethin' died out here, man." He came back into the room and looked over Abrams's shoulder. "That's pungent. Hey, I hope that spiger's still stuck in the side tunnel. Remember?"

"I was just thinking about that." Abrams frowned as he started dodging the first ghosts peeling off the walls and ceiling the Dalek passed.

01:05:40

"We need Abrams to go out there and start the engine," Dima said. "Those gammies are too crazy, and he's got the best body armor."

"Maybe we should shut the lights off and turn them on just before we head out to the gondola," Nell said. "That will temporarily blind the aggregators and firebombers, at least."

"But not those freaking gammies," Dima said.

She nodded. "Probably not them."

"I'll get Abrams." Dima jumped down the stairs.

"I'll check the security monitors," said Nell, right behind him.

01:03:04

Abrams accidentally turned the Dalek off as it sped down the passageway, and it came down in a controlled landing. "Damn it!" He restarted it, mashing the button and getting it going again as a ghost dropped down behind it and blew sticky trails that fell just out of the propellers' circumference. "That was close!"

The Dalek dropped a signal relay as Abrams tipped the controls forward, pushing it faster down the stone artery toward the railroad tunnel. Up ahead, he saw the spiger backing out of the side tunnel, one of its hind legs trying to pry it free. Abrams steered the Dalek toward the wall, and the bot's radar sensed the collision and corrected its flight path, curving it perfectly around the spiger's thrashing leg.

"Nice move!" Bear said, shuddering.

Abrams could see the open hatch and piloted the Dalek through, rising in a barrel roll as he dropped another signal relay and veered to the right down the train tunnel.

"Good luck, man!" Bear grabbed another demolition pack and headed upstairs, passing Dima on the way down.

"How is he doing?" Dima asked. "We need him upstairs."

Bear shook his head. "He's busy."

Dima approached Abrams. "How long till you

get there? We need you to get the gondola's motor running."

"OK. I'm in the tunnel now. You wanna do this?" Abrams asked. "My hands are tired."

"It doesn't look too hard."

"Just set it down when you spot the charges in the tunnel. The fork should be coming up ahead. Just remember to go left. Here!" He handed Dima the dog whistle. "Do I need the XOS?"

"Whoa," Dima said as he tilted the Dalek too far and its avoidance system repelled it from the wall.

"You sure you can do it?" Nastia asked.

"*Da*. Can you get up the stairs in that suit?" asked Dima.

"Hell, yes!" Abrams said, strapping in and firing up the exoskeleton. He charged up the stairs, taking them two at a time as they shook and swayed inside the glass vestibule.

Nastia watched Dima steering the bot. "Sasha should do it," she said, cringing. "Kids are good at this sort of thing!"

"Don't worry! I can do it. It's actually kind of easy. . . . *Ahh!*"

01:02:27

Hender saw Bear enter the conservatory from the room below. Abrams passed him in the XOS suit, heading upstairs. Bear immediately started pulling out charges from a demolition pack and spacing them across Hell's Window. "Better get upstairs, you guys," he said. "Abrams is getting the gondola going."

"Kuzu's at the front gate!" Geoffrey said.

"Oh, shit," Bear said, turning.

The others watched the monitor as the sel got out of the limousine with Maxim in front of the gate to Sector 1.

"Papa!" Sasha shouted angrily.

01:02:12

As the Dalek flew down the train tunnel, Dima noticed something glowing in the bot's minimized rearview cam. He maximized the rear view and saw the spiger burst out of the secret passage and bound down the tunnel after the Dalek like a Labrador.

Dima tilted the controls and his whole body forward to pick up the bot's speed in front of the leaping giant, whose one remaining eye was better than two human eyes as it bounded down the tunnel like a dog chasing a squirrel with trinocular vision.

01:01:01

Hender noticed that, outside the gate to Sector One, Kuzu was doing the same thing that Bear was doing. "Kuzu!" He pointed.

Nell saw that the sel was setting explosives on the gate. "He's setting charges."

"How does he know how?" Bear asked.

"He's smart!" Geoffrey said.

"You better go upstairs and help Abrams, Bear," Nell said.

"OK, but you better hurry. You've got six minutes to get your asses up there." Bear set the detonator on the window and ran upstairs.

Nell turned up the volume as Kuzu approached the camera outside the gate. He rose up, his face before the camera, one baleful eye staring into it with three stacked pupils. Then he spoke, in his own language: "*Shueenair Shenuday, come now with me. We will make this world our own. We will be remembered by all sels, forever.*"

"*Let me meet you at the gate,*" Hender responded in Kuzu's language. "*Nell can unlock it. Let us talk, Kuzu.*"

"*Yes. Open. Good idea, brother.*"

Hender gripped Nell's hand, and she felt the symbiants tingle on her skin. "Will you help me, Nell?"

"How?"

"Come with me to talk with Kuzu."

"Sasha, you better go upstairs now, honey," Nell said.

"I'm scared!" Sasha cried. "What about Papa?"

"Sasha," Hender said to her, his fur illuminating lavender and green.

Sasha stared at Hender, mesmerized.

"Go upstairs now, OK? We will help him," Hender said.

Maxim appeared on the screen now behind Kuzu, looking up with huge, tragic eyes into the camera, and Sasha saw him. "You didn't guess the password, Papa!" she shouted, weeping, running to the screen.

Maxim's eyes were kind suddenly, and he smiled, finally seeing it. "I love Sasha," he said. "That's the password, *Sashinka*. Isn't it?"

Tears spilled down her cheeks. "You *guessed* it!" she shouted.

"Go with them, Sasha," Maxim said. "Go with them now, *Sashinka*."

"OK, Papa!"

"Hender and Nell will meet you at the door, Kuzu," Geoffrey said.

"Good," Kuzu said. *"Come now!"*

01:00:44

"All right. I'm going out there and am gonna take a look at that big bad engine." Abrams put his helmet on and cranked the dog wheel. He and Bear pulled the hatch open. As it swung inward, Abrams went through and Bear shut the door behind him. Bear stomped on a gammy.

Through the window on the platform, Bear saw Abrams check the fuel drums. Gammarids flowed like roaches onto the platform around his feet and crawled over him, moving in short, nervous bursts. But they could not bite through the hard-shelled body armor. Abrams lifted the hood on the large diesel engine and scanned it for the fuel intake and carburetor, shaking his head. He reached down into the engine.

Bear saw Abrams give a thumbs-up and jump down. Grabbing a heavy drum of fuel, he uncapped it and tipped it into an intake tube. He emptied it and threw it aside, opening another. He was crawling with bugs, small and monstrously large, as he tipped the drum with the robot arms. With his own arm free, Abrams pulled a pistol from his shoulder harness and fired five times at the platform, killing five gammies for the rest to feed on.

01:00:43

Nell led Hender down the stairs outside the conservatory, leaving the hatch open behind them.

"Dead," Hender said as they smelled decaying flesh.

As they crossed the arcade at the top of the stairs, they passed the corpses of two men.

"Yes, Hender," she said, stifling her nausea as they rushed past the bodies.

They hurried down one of the grand staircases to the foyer. Hender saw the limousine parked at the bottom with two open doors. The smell of death was overpowering. There were more corpses below.

"How die?" Hender asked.

"They were trying to kill Geoffrey."

"Geoffrey *killed* other humans?"

"Yes."

They passed through the palace, past more bodies, to the curving steps that cascaded over the courtyard outside.

"Why did he have to kill them, Nell?" Hender asked.

"To save the people he loves."

"I see, Nell," Hender said with a low, faint voice.

They crossed the courtyard to the gate, and Nell reached out to the touch screen control panel on the left side. Glancing at Hender, she cued the gate open a few feet and then stopped it.

Kuzu and Maxim entered, along with a gust of Henders creatures that streaked through before Nell could close the gate.

The flying bugs, ants, and rats that got through

immediately homed in on the rotting corpses, tearing and drilling into their flesh.

Kuzu stood in front of the gate, and Maxim, seeming small beside the purple and red sel now, crouched meekly at his side.

01:00:42

Dima righted the Dalek and tilted the controls with exaggerated motions to point it forward as he drove the flying bot at increasing speed before the driving spiger. He reached the fork as he saw the glowing form behind him grow closer in thirty-foot lunges. He took the left tunnel at the fork and pushed the bot forward as fast as it could go, while the spiger loomed huge in the image-stabilized rear view display.

Nastia gripped his arm. "It's going to catch you!"

"How much time is left on the timer on that window?"

Nastia ran to the window and looked at the red digital readout. "Two minutes and forty-five seconds!"

"Go upstairs!"

"Will you make it?"

"Go!"

"No!"

00:58:51

"Come now, *Shenuday*!" Kuzu said.

"You can escape with us, Kuzu," Hender said. "We can live with humans. They can live with us!"

"Now you lie, just like them!"

"There are good humans and bad humans! Kuzu!" Hender said. "Just like us."

"Come!" Kuzu's voice gunned like an engine, resonating in the courtyard. "This whole world can be ours. You must see it!"

"They saved our lives," Hender said. "I love them, Kuzu."

"Love humans?" Kuzu spit. "You make me sick!"

"There is no 'sels' or 'humans,' Kuzu," Hender said. "There is only one and one and one. Don't you remember? How we survived?"

"Remember, yes. I remember your kind never believed. That is why we almost died." Kuzu trained both his trinocular eyes on Hender: *"Die then!"*

Hender turned to Nell. "Run!"

Kuzu turned to open the gate, and Hender leaped onto the larger sel's back. Gripping all his limbs with his six hands, Hender tried only to thwart and neutralize his fellow sel as long as he could.

Meanwhile, Maxim stared at them, almost in a trance. Kuzu reached back with his upper arms, twisting Hender's head as he tried to bite into Hender's stretching neck.

Hender fended off his jaws with a hand that lost two fingers as Kuzu's jaws clamped closed.

00:54:58

Dima waved the dog whistle through the air as the spiger snapped its jaws just to the left of the Dalek.

"Good!" Nastia cried, clutching his arm.

Dima looped the bot across the arching ceiling

to the other side, thirty-five seconds from detonation.

He could not yet see the charges the men had set in the tunnel ahead stretching uphill into the endless gloom. As he rolled the bot in another spiral, the spiger leaped again, gaining another ten feet. The next leap would be enough, and he dodged to the right at the last second and then saw the charges wired across the tunnel's ceiling. He killed the power and dropped the ROV just as the vertical jaws of the spiger swallowed the Dalek, and the signal went dead.

Dima stood frozen in dread.

"What happened?" Nastia said. "It didn't work."

Dima bowed his head, muttering a prayer.

A shock wave rumbled through the ground as the secondary explosion confirmed the target was destroyed. Wiping the sweat from his forehead, Dima turned and squeezed Nastia in a crushing embrace. "We did it!"

He carried her toward the spiral stairs with twenty seconds to spare before the charges on the submerged window ignited and saltwater washed around them.

00:54:01

An explosion rumbled in the bowels of Pobedograd.

Kuzu overpowered Hender, driving him into the ground on his belly. His four hands bunched into a single fist to bring down on Hender's head.

Maxim moved closer as they struggled. As Kuzu pummeled Hender's horn with glancing blows, Maxim pulled out his gun. With shaking hands, he pressed the muzzle against Kuzu's body, and he fired three bullets into the beast that had possessed him.

Kuzu twisted as he looked at Maxim, flushing yellow and red as blue blood spurted across his fur. "*No!*" he roared. He grabbed Maxim's hand. "I told you, you would be safe with me!"

"Go to *hell!*" Maxim roared at the monster, condemning himself at the same time. And he knew that he had, in that moment, saved himself, too, somehow.

Another explosion reverberated.

Reeling from his wounds, Kuzu gripped Maxim, and the nants now turned. Maxim's skin burned as his entire body was covered in blood. He screamed as the bones on his wrists appeared before his eyes. With a last effort, he squeezed the gun in his right hand three more times, firing the bullets into Kuzu before they collapsed together on the cobblestones of the courtyard.

Hender ran to Nell, who had waited on the steps for him. Another terrible explosion rolled through the ground beneath them, sending stalactite spears down from the ceiling.

Kuzu crawled toward the gate as he coughed blue blood. And lying on his side, he reached out with one long arm and touched the control panel, opening the gate wide.

A flood of Henders creatures stormed into the courtyard as water swept down the steps of the palace.

"Climb on my back," Nell said, and Hender jumped on as the wave of water flowed around Nell's legs. She carried Hender, who was much lighter than she'd expected, to the foyer and onto the staircase on the left, where Hender jumped off and both rushed up the steps. Two spigers and a column of rats raced behind them, skirting the saltwater pouring into the foyer from the left and lunging up the staircase opposite them. Nell and Hender reached the top first and ran straight back to the open hatch of the conservatory as a riot of gammies gushed out.

Hender grabbed Nell then and leaped through the hatch into the conservatory, reaching out two long arms and grabbing onto the chandelier. He swung to the next one with his long unfolding arms, past the shattered window as the creatures of Pandemonium stormed over the floor below them led by a giant soldier gammarid ridden by a ghost octopus that sprayed its sticky ropes at the spiger charging straight for it.

As the monsters locked in mortal combat, Hender and Nell reached the glass vestibule of the spiral staircase at the far corner. And as all hell broke loose around them, they hurtled up the stairs.

00:52:45

As the vast lake of Pandemonium drained into the palace, roaring down the passageway to the railroad tunnel and flooding through the gate into Sector Two, the burning water came up to Kuzu's chest like acid. He saw a giant gammarid come down the stairs of the palace and spew its webs over the spiked arms of a leaping spiger. Then Kuzu saw the green glow of Henders wasps and drill-worms colliding with swarms of glowing orange orbs and tentacled balls in the air. For a moment, Kuzu was gratified, for he thought surely his world would prevail. And then, to his surprise, Kuzu died.

00:52:02

Nell and Hender reached the gondola station, and looking through the window, they saw the others already inside the swaying tram car as Abrams poured a last drum of fuel into the engine's intake. Abrams waved them in.

Four or five gammarids skittered through the crack as Nell opened the door. Hender jumped, but instinctively reached out with four hands, swatting the squat, spiky creatures to the ground.

Nell turned the battery of bright lights on and off rapidly on the gondola deck. "Come on!"

They leaped through the hatch and crossed the momentarily cleared landing. The others opened the gondola's door quickly to let them in. Below the gondola's landing, they saw a great migration as creatures were funneling through the shattered window below.

Abrams, still on top of the gondola's engine, hooked the battery cables to his last XOS battery and depressed the ignition plunger on the side. He primed, choked, and gunned the great engine until it finally turned over, coughing but running and then clearing its throat like a dragon before roaring to life. The heavy diesel motor had been well designed to run after sitting dormant. Slamming the hood, Abrams jumped down, unstrapped the XOS suit, and ran to the lever that engaged the bull wheel. "Here goes!" he muttered, throwing the latch.

The gondola moved out over the lake as he ran

and jumped through the door as they closed it behind him.

The dangling tram glided down the cable into Pandemonium.

00:51:24

They silently watched the diaphanous apparitions and phantoms glimmering in the dark around them, praying that the tenuous thread from which they hung would not give way. They heard a cacophony of clicking sounds as sonar-sensing creatures avoided colliding with the gondola. Below they could see two fonts of air bubbles roiling the lake near the shore where water swirled down into the underwater breaches.

Abrams sat down on the bench that circled the tram's interior, breathing heavily as he slumped in his stiff suit and petted Ivan. He cracked open the armor over his leg. His calf was swollen and bruised.

"How are you?" Dima asked.

"Hell, Jack Youngblood played the Super Bowl with a broken leg." Abrams grinned and snapped the armor back on. "How much time before our eight hours is up and they drop a nuke in this place?"

Bear looked at his watch. "About fifty minutes."

"It's like fireworks out there," Nastia observed.

"Yeah," Geoffrey said. "Those floating jellyfish shower bioluminescence over the man-of-wars."

"Why?" Nastia asked.

"Maybe to attract larger predators," he said. "Deep-sea organisms do the same thing to turn the table on their enemies."

"Ah!" Nastia gripped the holds on the gondola with white-knuckled hands, shivering.

Dima put his arm around her shoulders.

Abrams looked out of the window behind them. "So far, so good," he said.

Nastia noticed a large, glowing sea serpent swimming on the lake below. It broke into pieces that attacked a large squidlike creature illuminated by blue and green sparkles of light.

"Aggregators," Nell said. "They swim, too."

"Oh! They're dreadful! What are those huge eight-pointed stars?" Nastia asked, pointing at a shape under the water that opened like a giant water lily.

"A mega-medusae," Nell said. "Here." She handed Nastia a leather-bound book from her pack. "Trofim Lysenko's journal. Why don't you take it? He describes dozens of Pandemonium species."

Nastia took the book. "Thank you! So he *was* here! Does he mention my grandfather? Boris Kurolesov?"

Nell smiled. "I don't know. We can't read it."

Nastia held it to her breast and sighed. She looked excitedly back out the window. "What are mega-medusae?"

"They live on the bottom of the lake," Geoffrey said.

"We think it's a medusa that is devoted to producing several kinds of offspring, some of which attack predators lured by the chum it releases from time to time. Her children sting and paralyze meals for her, which sink into her maw," Nell said.

"Nell spotted one that must be thirty-five feet wide," Geoffrey said.

"Incredible!" whispered Nastia, videoing as much as she could now with her phone as the gondola reached its lowest point over the lake and began climbing higher.

Hender looked with wide eyes in all directions, holding on to the gondola with all six hands. The idea of dangling over saltwater was terrifying enough without the water being filled with horrible monsters.

"What's that stuff glowing on the ceiling?" Abrams said.

The entire roof and walls of the cavern, as well as patches on the surface of the lake, glimmered emerald, turquoise, crimson, and green.

"Rainbowfire," Nastia said. "Right, Nell?"

"Yes," Nell said. "We think it's related to fox fire, a glowing fungus that grows on rotting wood in forests. Otherwise known as will-o'-the-wisp or fairy fire. The glow is caused by an oxidizing reaction of luciferase with luciferin that emits light."

"Aristotle was first to describe it, I think," Nastia said, using her night vision glasses to scan the growth that seemed to burn like embers all over the cavern walls. "In Mark Twain's book *Huckleberry Finn,* Huck and Tom use fox fire to light their way while digging a tunnel." She smiled.

"It seems to be the base of the food chain here," Geoffrey said. "That and the patches of growth on the surface of the lake."

"Maybe that's why so many species glow!" Nastia said.

Ivan whined and jumped up, standing over Sasha's lap and barking out the window. Sasha sat next to Hender, resting her head against the shifting patterns of his fur that soothed her sadness. "What are these flying things that look like butterflies?" Sasha asked, pointing a finger at one that had stuck on the window next to her head. It looked like a pink balloon with wide transparent wings around a deflating bladder of flesh. Three fangs gnawed at the glass in its amorphous mouth.

"I call them nudibats, Sash," Nell said. "I think they're some kind of flying nudibranch-like mollusk that uses a heat-producing chemical reaction to fill an air sac and rise like little hot air balloons."

Nastia videoed them with her phone.

"This place is crazy," Bear said. "Where the hell are we going? Does anybody know?"

As he said it, the gondola rocked, jarring them forward and backwards as it passed the first pulley, which hung from a structure fixed to a giant stalagmite on the island. They started sinking lower again on the other side, deeper into the haunted darkness.

"You say this cave is a hundred kilometers long?" Nastia said.

"That's what Maxim said," Geoffrey replied.

"It must follow a vertical fault line, like Son Doong Cave in Vietnam," Nastia said, squeezing Dima's hand with excitement.

Suddenly, a group of what looked like large jellyfish floated up around them. The purple and white balloons were four feet wide and trailing red tentacles covered with deflated orange and pink nudibats.

"Those things bob up and down all the time," Geoffrey said. "When their bladders flare light, they head back up again, sometimes in groups."

Up ahead, they could see a steel tower on the far side of the island. It was bent to one side and seemed on the verge of toppling over into the lake. The tram car dropped another ten feet and bounced, swinging back and forth from the cable.

"That pier up ahead looks pretty sketchy," Abrams said.

"Maxim said one of them was partially collapsed," said Nell.

"Terrific," Bear said.

"Let's bail out some stuff and lighten the load," Abrams suggested.

They started throwing the few packs they had brought with them, keeping only a few pistols and grenades, some rope, duct tape, the first aid kit, a machine gun, batteries, and flashlights. The rest went overboard as explosions of bioluminescence splashed and spread on the water where the gear struck the surface of the lake.

The tower that carried the cable's pulley bent closer to the sea as they climbed closer, and they all gasped. Then, about fifty yards from the tower, they stopped. The tram rocked and pitched as it tried to push forward.

"Something's blocking the cable from passing through the pulley!" Geoffrey said.

"Oh, man. This could strip the gears of the bull-wheel," Abrams said.

"Give me your knife, Bear," Hender said.

Bear gave him his knife, and Hender put it in his belly pack as he opened the door and climbed onto the roof.

"Hey, you're missing two fingers," Bear said.

"That's OK, Bear. I've got twenty-eight more."

They watched as Hender cartwheeled hand-over-hand beneath the cable with all six of his hands.

"Wow!" Dima said.

"I wish I could do that!" Sasha said, and Ivan wagged his tail, barking next to her.

Nastia held Dima's hand as they watched nervously.

Hender's fur turned almost black with terror as he tried to camouflage, knowing that a menagerie of hungry monsters thrived in the saltwater lake below. Hender kept two hands on the cable at all times as the pylon ahead creaked and dipped lower and lower. He reached the pulley on the bent pier that was caked with fungus and pulled out the three knives he had stashed in his belly pack. Mats of growth and crushed ghost-flesh, which must have been riding on the cable, had jammed into the pulley, gumming up the works. He held on to the tower over the pulley with three legs as he cut and loosened the clogged flesh in the wheel with all three knives, his hands moving like a Cuisinart.

"He had an elevator back home," Nell explained, watching anxiously. "It had a pulley, too."

"God, maybe he knows what to do?" Geoffrey wondered.

"Really?" Dima glanced at Nastia with raised eyebrows.

Suddenly, the cable moved and sheared off the debris as the car jolted forward.

"He did it!" Abrams said. "Awesome!"

They cheered inside the lift as it lurched and started moving, lower and lower toward the bent tower.

"Well, where is he?" Nastia asked.

"Maybe he's going to jump on the roof as we pass," Abrams said.

The water was only about sixty feet below them and the gondola was still sinking. Only then did they see the huge ghost octopus that had been riding on the bottom of the gondola as it slid up over the windows.

"Oh, damn it," Abrams said. "Get up there and shoot that thing!"

"I'll go," said Bear.

"Don't shoot us through the roof," Dima said.

"Angle your shots!" Abrams called as Bear climbed through the window to the roof.

"Copy that!" Bear said.

The ghost slid up one side as Bear climbed up the other, and they reached the top at the same time. Bear fired at the ghost, grazing it as it slipped back down, covering the window with its waving rows of suction cups. Bear ducked as they passed under the pylon and Hender jumped from the tower onto the roof in front of him.

They held on as the gondola jostled. The tower and pulley wheel passed over them and the gondola dipped down on the other side to about thirty feet from the surface of the lake. They came within twenty feet before it finally started climbing higher.

"Hi, Bear." Hender waved as the tram car finally lifted from the water. "Thank you!"

Bear pointed his gun at Hender, his face twisted with pain. "Yeah, I'm sorry," he said. "But you were part of the mission."

"What?" Hender said. "Why?"

"I guess humans just aren't ready to share this planet!"

Bear aimed his pistol at the middle of Hender's large forehead.

As a rope of white goo snagged the soldier's outstretched arm, another stuck to the side of his head. Both streams came from the oral papillae of a ghost that now rose up and, with a vigorous pull, reeled in its sticky ropes, tipping the tall soldier on the roof as he fired his weapon into the darkness. As Bear's feet slipped, he plummeted behind the gondola, his heavy weight ripping the ghost off the side of the tram with him. The soldier howled all the way down before he plunged into the lake, still attached to the ghost, directly over the opening maw of a megamedusa, which reached out its eight glowing arms from the bottom as its stinging offspring wrapped glowing chains around them both and paralyzed their mother's food.

Hender climbed down the gondola and cautiously crawled through the partially opened door, his fur drained of color.

"What happened?" Abrams shouted.

Hender was silent, trembling, and he skulked into the corner by Nell, blending into the wall. His eyes were swiveling rapidly at each of them. "Don't kill me," he said with a warbling voice.

"We won't, Hender!" Nell said, squeezing two of his trembling hands.

"Damn!" Abrams frowned. "What the hell happened?"

A shower of green sparks surrounded the gondola as a flock of nudibats passed around them.

"Another fire alarm?" Nastia asked.

"They could have mistaken us for a predator," Geoffrey said.

"What happened, Hender?" Nell said.

"Bear . . . tried to kill me!"

The others looked at one another.

"Shit!" Abrams said. "No offense, but it's a little hard to believe . . . ."

"You fucking Americans," Dima sneered. "It's not too hard to believe."

"OK!" Geoffrey said. "Let's not start that! We won't kill you, Hender. I promise you, we're in this together!" He reached out a hand and took one of Hender's hands.

"*Da,*" said Dima, taking another of his hands.

Sasha took one of his hands then, too. "We love you, Hender!" she shouted.

"Yes!" Nastia said, and she held yet another of his hands as Abrams and Nell took his remaining hands in theirs.

"We're in this together, Hender," Geoffrey said.

"We won't lie to you," Nell said. "Will we?"

"No!" everyone answered.

"OK," Hender's voice quailed.

"Fuck!" yelled Abrams. "Look!"

Dima pointed. "What is *that*?"

They all saw a giant pink and yellow blimp drop down on a collision course toward them as it filled the windows on the right side of the gondola. Feathery fans waved around its mouth as it collected the pink and orange nudibats like a whale filtering krill in its baleen. As the buoyant leviathan closed in, it opened its mouth and swallowed the gondola whole, dragging on it as it moved over the cable toward the next pulley, which hung from long cables attached to the roof of the cavern.

Sasha screamed as the windows were blocked by

the pink and yellow skin that surrounded them like the ribbed insides of a dirigible.

"We can't get past that pulley inside this thing," Geoffrey shouted.

"Look!" Nell said. "Its walls are lined with quilted bladders that must contain hot air to keep it afloat."

"Do we have any concussion grenades?" Dima said.

"If we rupture those gas bladders, it should fall," Geoffrey agreed.

"I saved one, just in case," said Abrams. He pulled one out of a pack on the floor. "Where should I put it, Doc?"

"Up its belly, and aim high!" Geoffrey said.

"Duck!" Abrams pulled down the window and hurled the grenade into the floating whale, a perfect lob that detonated at its apogee, shredding the two large bladders that kept it afloat and shattering two windows of the gondola, as well.

The giant sank like the *Hindenburg,* losing its grip on the gondola as its thin fabric was finally ripped away before they reached the pulley hanging from the ceiling, the last one before the end of the line.

Passing down the other side of the wheel, they could see the far shore as they sank toward the water.

Hender shivered next to Nell, and she stroked his back reassuringly.

As they approached the far shore, they saw the band of salt crystals crusted above the waterline, which had already lowered a few inches as the subterranean sea filled the city of Pobedograd.

The gondola stopped then, and it swung gently back and forth, not moving forward. "What now?" Nastia said.

"The motor may have overheated," Abrams said. "Or run out of fuel."

After another few minutes, it was apparent that they were not going anywhere.

00:17:03

They hung there, rocking, with two windows now gone. They smacked at the nudibats that fluttered in trying to take a nip at them.

They were trapped a hundred feet over the lake and a hundred yards from the shore.

"OK, we've just got to zip-line the rest of the way," Dima said. "We double up that thick nylon rope we kept. Come on," he said. "Abrams, you go first, OK?"

"Forget it."

"Got a better idea?"

Abrams looked at the crude loop of nylon rope in Dima's hands. "The friction on that cable will burn right through that rope," he said.

"Then what do you suggest?" Geoffrey said.

"OK." Abrams broke off the halves of the armor over his arms and legs, except for the shell on his injured calf. Then he duct-taped and roped each half shell over the cable so it could anchor a rope line.

The others looked worried.

"This armor is bulletproof, fireproof, and shatterproof," Abrams said. "And it'll slide down that cable like greased lightning."

"Tie it in a loop so we can sit on it," Dima said.

"I don't want to have to hang by my fingers all the way to the shore."

"OK, that should be easy enough," Abrams said as Geoffrey already started to measure off another length of rope and taped another half-shell of armor to it. Hender joined in, copying him with two more sets of hands.

Abrams tied the ends of the rope together on the first loop. "OK, there you go, Dima. Let's go! We've got about fifteen minutes left, man."

"OK, OK," Dima said, and he took the lines above, sitting on the sling of rope as he pushed forward out of the gondola's window.

They watched him pick up speed until he hit an upswing that slowed him down before he finally dropped onto the stone landing of the gondola station on the jagged shore. He waved, and Nastia cheered as she saw him through her night vision binoculars. "He made it!"

"You're next," said Abrams.

Geoffrey and Hender re-created improvised harnesses in an assembly line.

Nastia sat nervously in the loop of rope and Abrams shoved her out the window. She was stone-silent and still the entire way down the cable until Dima caught her in his arms on the landing.

"How is Ivan going to get there?" Sasha yelled.

"Geoffrey, can you carry him across if we strap him to you?" Abrams asked.

"Absolutely."

"Good, 'cause we're not leaving a dog behind if I can help it." Abrams cast the next rope over the cable and jerked the armor collar over the cable. Then he tied the sling below with a sturdy knot.

"OK, honey," Nell said to Geoffrey as he climbed in.

He reached out to hug her.

"No, Geoffrey!" Hender shouted.

"Right. I can't touch you," she said. "But I'll see you on the other side."

"OK. Bye." Geoffrey embraced the dog as Abrams tied him securely to Geoffrey's chest.

"Ready, buddy?" Geoffrey reassured Ivan.

"You're sure he can't get loose?" Sasha cried, and Ivan barked, thrashing suddenly.

"*Shhh!*" Abrams said to her, holding a finger to his lips. "Don't upset him."

Geoffrey whispered in Ivan's ear, then grabbed the lines, and Abrams gave him a push out the window.

"I'll go next," Hender said, and he jumped out after Geoffrey, without a zip-line, cartwheeling under the cable all the way to the shore.

"Wow!" Sasha shouted.

"Your turn, girl," Abrams said.

"She should go with you," he said to Nell.

"She can't go with me. Remember? Nobody can touch me," Nell said.

"Oh yeah." Abrams slung the last two harnesses over the cable and tied both into loops. "Ladies first," he said.

"No, you go. I'll go last," she said.

"OK, then. Come on, sweetie. We're going for a ride, just like Ivan. I'm going to tie you on to me, but you hang on around my neck, OK?"

"Just do it, Abrams," Sasha said.

"OK, then." Abrams looped the rope to secure Sasha to his chest. "Good workin' with you, Doc. Good luck. Come right behind us now!"

"I will! Get going," Nell said.

"OK. You can close your eyes if you want to, Sasha. Here we go!" Abrams stepped onto the ledge of the window and plunged down the line over the glimmering lake.

"I hate you, Abrams!" Sasha shouted.

The last one in the gondola, Nell gripped the heavy-duty nylon rope and stood on the bobbing edge of the gondola's window. She saw a squadron of man-of-wars drifting toward her as she jumped.

She sped over the lake's surface behind Abrams, and as they crossed over the landing ahead of her, she heard Sasha cry, "I love you, Abrams!"

As Nell rapidly approached the shore, she saw a deep, dark patch of water at the lake's edge where no animals were visible. She let go of the harness, plunging into the briny water.

She swam as fast as she could through the warm water, fueled with adrenaline and moving violently, spinning and kicking forward. At last, she climbed out on the ledge.

She ran up the rocky shore and hoisted herself onto the gondola's concrete landing with the others as Dima and Abrams shot down several man-of-wars that were chasing her. Nell ran to Geoffrey and embraced him, soaking wet. "I had to get them off me," she whispered.

"Oh!" he whispered back, and he squeezed her to him. "That's why I married you."

"Come on, you guys!" Sasha said.

They all ran up a flight of stairs chiseled into the hard limestone that ended at a steel hatch in the cavern's vertical wall. "Beach balls" of various sizes rolled down the wall as they served up sushi to the gammarids.

Hender cranked the hatch's wheel with four trembling arms, and they all pulled, bursting the door open through layers of corrosion and rainbowfire. Inside was a tunnel as dark as midnight that cut through the rock.

Geoffrey pulled the hatch closed and turned the dog wheel behind them as Abrams lit a flashlight and led the way through a twisting tunnel that climbed almost straight up through the mountain's bedrock.

After twenty minutes, they had begun to wonder if they would ever find an end to the spiraling passageway, when they finally spotted what looked like a dead end a hundred feet above them.

Abrams yelled as a door materialized in the light of his dying flashlight.

As they reached the hatch, their excitement grew, and Hender, Geoffrey, and Abrams all grabbed the wheel, pulling it hard, finally turning the handle. They pushed the door until it yielded. And as it opened, a cold gust of fresh air met them, and they saw blue sky.

Squeezing through the gap, they found themselves on the northwest face of Mount Kazar, and they laughed together as they pushed the rock-covered door closed and it blended once more into the mountainside.

Geoffrey gave Nell his sweater as they ran down the slope that was covered with blindingly bright patches of snow. They looked up at the sky, eager to pull that open expanse into their eyes and breathe the crisp air blowing over their faces.

"You probably lost all your natural microbial defenses, too, in that salty water, honey," Geoffrey said, limping on his right leg.

"Guess I'll have to roll in dirty sheets for a night to get them back."

He smiled. "We need a honeymoon."

"I agree, Dr. Binswanger." She took Geoffrey's cell phone out of his sweater pocket and punched in a number. "Hey! It works!"

JUNE 23

2:14 P.M.

The New Light

Just before the last spark went out, a new light came. Now sels are free in a much bigger world. Humans saved us: we saved each other.

Hender took three hands off his keyboard as he got a Skype call. With all three hands overlapping, he could type 180 words per minute without seeming to move his fingers. He clicked his mouse with a fourth hand and opened one window on his computer screen in which was Mai waving at him.

"Happy birthday to your little one, Hender!" Mai was sitting on the roof of her penthouse on the island of Manhattan, where she had become a celebrity.

"Thank you, Mai. Wait, I'm getting another call." Hender clicked open another Skype call and saw Plesh, sitting in his home in Japan, where a giant mountain rose, nearly filling the window behind him.

He was holding up his painting of Andrewshay, Hender's golden child.

"How do you like the painting, Hender?"

"Beautiful!"

Nell entered. Hender rose to greet her.

"Come downstairs, the guests are here," she whispered.

"OK. Plesh and Mai, I have to go!"

"Nid says happy birthday to Andrewshay," Plesh said.

"Nid is in Ireland recording a birthday song for him," Mai said.

"Thank Nid for me. Now, bye."

Hender ended the calls and held still for a moment. He looked out through the flowered jungle at the twinkling blue Pacific as the breeze ruffled his coat. Everything had changed since the verdict of the humans had come in: the sels' symbiants were deemed to be strictly clones that could not mutate into derivative species, so the humans let them keep their nants. And the humans kept their word and set them free.

Hender went down to the kitchen and found Geoffrey, Bo, and Joe, as well as Nastia and Dima, who were now newlyweds. Sasha and her aunt Kyra had come, and Abrams, who had just arrived through the security gate around their well-guarded compound. Sasha, tall for a girl of twelve, smiled brightly and ran to hug Hender.

"You are much bigger now," Hender said, his coat popping with color. He put her down. "I love you, Sasha!" he said, both his guava-sized eyes looking into hers with three pupils.

"I love you, too, Hender." Her face was content,

older, leaner, her glacier-blue eyes showing the hopeful aftermath of a distant nightmare.

"Hi, Pops!" Andrewshay jumped up.

Hender cradled his child in four of his arms. "Happy birthday."

"Did you get that, Zero?" Cynthea Leeds said, as her business partner, cameraman, and boyfriend, Zero Monroe, videoed the party.

Zero turned his head to her, grinning. "Yup."

Nell and Geoffrey's one-year-old son sat on Geoffrey's arm, laughing and waving at Hender with both hands. Both their children were celebrating a birthday, though Andrewshay was only one year old today, having gestated for 21 months. The two families had separate homes on their estate on the garden island of Kauai.

They moved onto the wide redwood deck of Hender's home. The canopy was decorated with crepe paper streamers and multicolored balloons. Ivan was chasing a feral chicken through the trees below, the white dog barking excitedly. Hender loved his secluded home overlooking Hanalei Bay.

He reached down to the fernlike sensitive plant, which Nell called "*Mimosa pudica*," and which grew wild here. Hender had planted some in a pot. Its tiny jade leaves fringed featherlike branches that surrounded little pink flowers. As he touched it, the leaves crumpled closed and pulled away from him, and Hender smiled.

MAP AND ILLUSTRATIONS

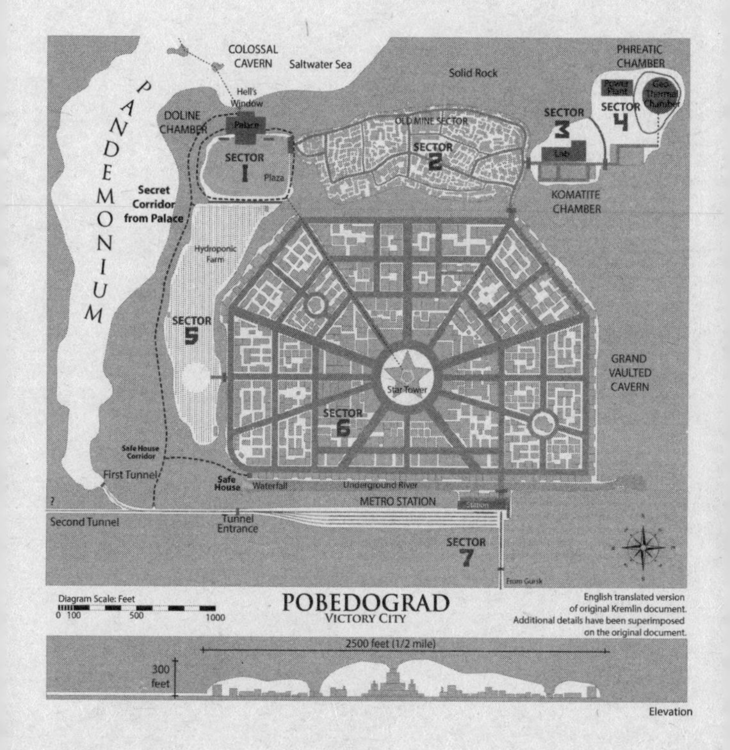
COLOSSAL CAVERN
Saltwater Sea
Solid Rock
PHREATIC CHAMBER
Power Plant
Geo-Thermal Chamber
SECTOR 4
SECTOR 3
Lab
KOMATITE CHAMBER
PANDEMONIUM
Hell's Window
DOLINE CHAMBER
Palace
OLD MINE SECTOR
SECTOR 2
SECTOR 1
Plaza
Secret Corridor from Palace
Hydroponic Farm
SECTOR 5
Star Tower
SECTOR 6
GRAND VAULTED CAVERN
Safe House Corridor
First Tunnel
Safe House
Waterfall
Underground River
METRO STATION
Station
?
Second Tunnel
Tunnel Entrance
SECTOR 7
From Gursk
Diagram Scale: Feet
0 100 500 1000
POBEDOGRAD
VICTORY CITY
English translated version of original Kremlin document. Additional details have been superimposed on the original document.
2500 feet (1/2 mile)
300 feet
Elevation

Journal of Trofim Lysenko, page 29

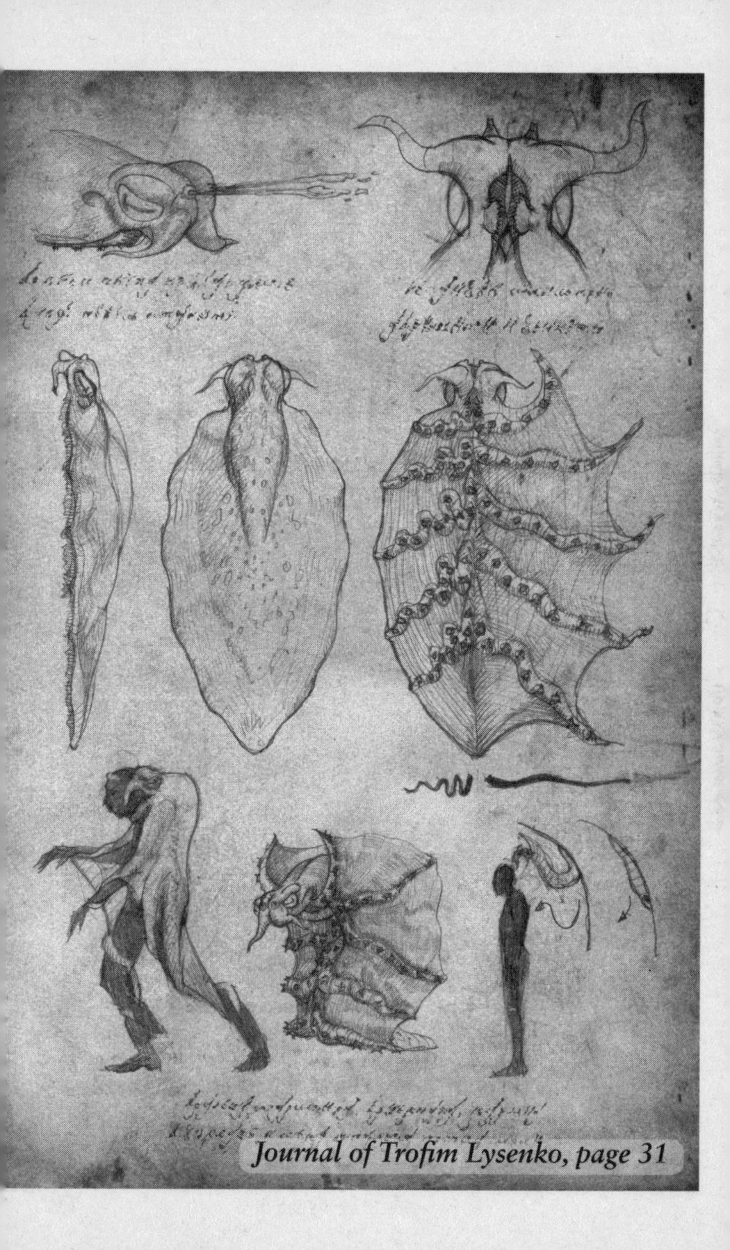

Journal of Trofim Lysenko, page 31

Phylum	Order	Genus	Species
Mollusca	*Cephalopoda*	*Pneumoderma*	*imbrinicendia*

Fire-bomber

Pneumoderma imbrinicendia

These creatures rising and falling, spiraling and swooping in the dark, may seem at first glance to be some kind of jellyfish or Portuguese man-of-war. But they are actually a kind of mollusk, and they do not rise and fall through water but through *air*.

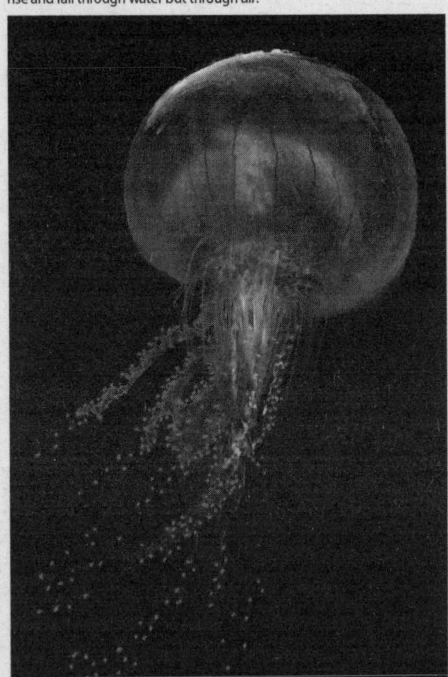

Reigning Death
The "fire-bomber" rains down venomous bioluminescent cells similar to a jellyfish's nematocysts. Mingled with its eggs, the cells paralyze prey and provide food and shelter for the mollusk's young. The fire-bomber is, in a real sense, at the top of the food chain in Pandemonium—unless it glides into the path of a hungry *blimp-whale*.

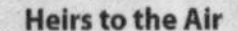

Heirs to the Air
Like Christmas tree lights, the fire-bomber juveniles emerge from the carcasses of prey to begin their lives, rising as their bladders inflate with air heated by a chemical reaction.

Length / Weight	Reproduction	Diet
up to 3m / 0.1 kg to 1 kg	*egg bearing*	*carnivorous*

Population	Habitat
2% fauna mass	*Aerial, occasionally marine water surface*

Pandemonium

Our Alien Subterranean World

From blimp-whales devouring flocks of butterfly-like nudibranchs to living ammonites jetting through the dark sea, many of the creatures in Pandemonium's ecosystem are from the mollusk family, one of the core groups of animals that arose during the Cambrian. Dangerous fire-bombers float and glide like airborne Portuguese man-of-wars in the 60-mile long cavern, using chemical reactions to generate heat that causes bladders inside them to inflate with hot gas like Chinese lanterns. The fire-bombers shower their prey with stinging cells called nematocysts that paralyze on contact. Meanwhile, under the Pandemonium sea, squid and Spanish dancers dodge the mega-medusae anchored to the bottom, whose offspring link together in deadly chains to snare a meal.

Primitive arthropods also abound in Pandemonium, from the rare sea spider, which is literally in a class by itself, to swarms of micro-to-mega gammarids grazing on the fungus glowing on the walls and on the surface of the subterranean sea. Thought to be distant relatives of scorpions, Pandemonium sea spiders hunt limpets in the vast underground waters much like their relatives in oceans around the world.

Vicious Collaborators
Equally adapted to land and water, the fearsome "aggregator" (*Brevilithobius congalineas*) is unlike anything on Earth. This bizarre species of centipede swims and crawls in train but separates into equally voracious segments to attack prey en masse.

Psychedelic Swarms
Like this gammarid (*Magnagammarus grexiformis*), many of the creatures in Pandemonium are bioluminescent, perhaps owing to rainbow fire, the light-emitting fungus that covers most surfaces and is the base of the food chain. Animals that ingest the fungus often glow, too. Since this light is available, many animals have highly sensitive eyes in addition to using echo-location, long limbs and antennae to sense their world.

Base of the Food Chain
(Mycena pobedogradensis)
Pandemonium's walls are covered by "rainbow fire", a bioluminescent fungus related to *Armillaria*, commonly known as honey mushrooms or "foxfire." This family of fungi is among the most extraordinary organisms to inhabit our planet. A single individual has been known to cover areas as large as three square miles beneath the ground and may live thousands of years, in addition to sprouting mushrooms that glow in the dark.

Nudibats
(Pterodoris ypsimorphis)
Nudibats are little pink and orange bubbles, which share a trick with bombardier beetles: they mix hydrogen peroxide and hydroquinone to create heat. The heat turns the tiny mollusks into hot air balloons that rise and fall in swarms scouring the air for rainbow fire spores.

When threatened by grazing fire-bombers, nudibats release bioluminescent cells to draw larger predators, such as blimp-whales *(Polyneumocystus magnadevorus)*, to scare off their attackers.

Sushi Wagons
(Sphaeractinapoikia troglodytica)
These colorful spheres of glowing tongue-like feet roll over walls like sticky beach balls. Each tender foot is like a bite of sashimi for predators. However, one out of a hundred of these snacks is filled with embryos that hatch inside unlucky diners, growing into new bait balls that emerge after devouring their host, rolling on to serve more hungry customers. Is each bait ball a colony of separate individuals like a giant *Volvox*, or is the entire bait ball a single large individual? Among scientists, the debate has not been settled.

Disk-Ant Life Cycle

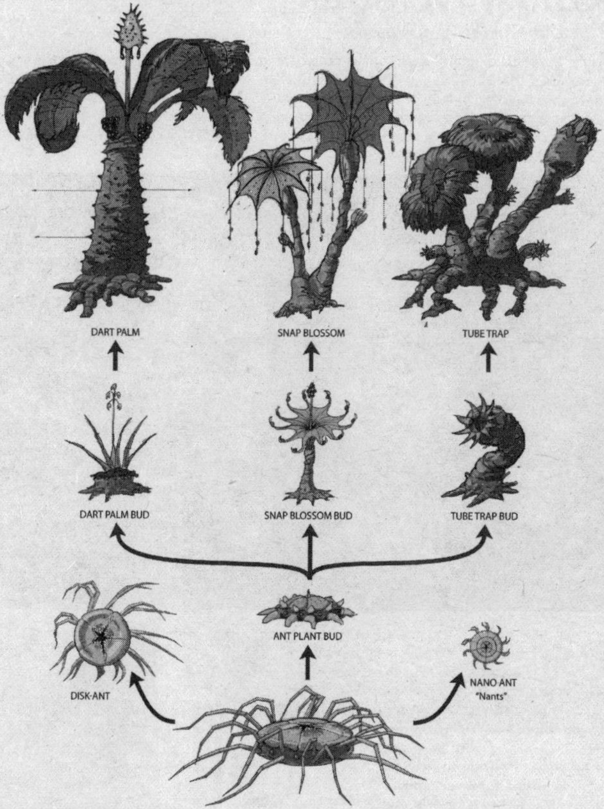

DART PALM
SNAP BLOSSOM
TUBE TRAP
DART PALM BUD
SNAP BLOSSOM BUD
TUBE TRAP BUD
ANT PLANT BUD
DISK-ANT
NANO-ANT "Nants"

From animal to plant?

Rotaformica hendersii, or the Henders "disk-ant," is an unlikely seed. But it grows into the variety of "trees" comprising the jungle of Henders Island. A certain ratio of disk-ant juveniles develop into ant plant buds, taking root and expanding, some growing 40 feet tall. But these trees are animals, and while some photosynthesize, all are carnivorous. Under the palm-like fronds of their jaws garlands of berry-like eggs entice their prey. Some of these eggs will later sprout into clones of the specific kind of tree they fell from. Disk-ants are a virtual rolling ecosystem in a very small package.

Phylum	Order	Genus	Species
Mollusca	*Cephalopoda*	*Fantasmatuethis*	*pandemonii*

Ghost Octopus

Fantasmatuethis pandemonii

As the top predator in the Pandemonium ecosystem, the ghost octopus has perfected the arts of camouflage, shape-shifting and mimicry. This creature has the unique ability to literally puppet other animals, using its ten webbed arms, each equipped with nerve-sensing clamping suckers. Ranging in size from a few centimeters to over 3 meters, this adaptable predator can spray ropes of binding goo, like modern-day velvet worms, to snare its wide variety of prey. They inject their eggs, wasp-like, into the bodies of gammarids.

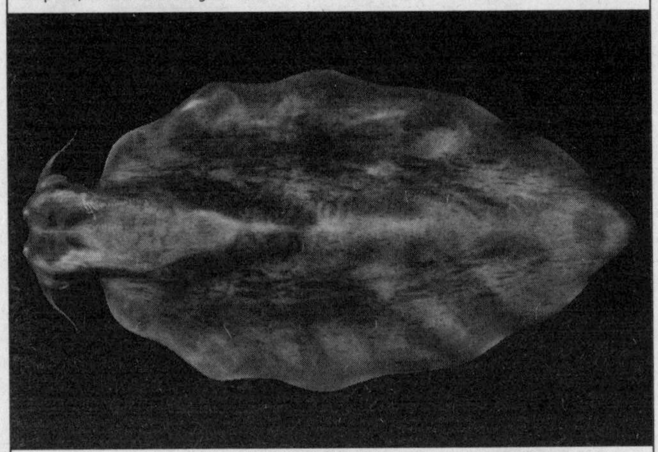

Puppet Master

A master of disguise, the ghost octopus can seamlessly mimic almost any surface. What's more, this frightening creature practically *becomes* its prey. After moving with surprising speed to launch its attack and overpower its victim, the ghost clamps down on key skeletal joints. Using its own amorphous muscular structure to replace the muscles of the animal it has commandeered, the mollusk manipulates its body like a marionette.

A ghost gains control of a human exhibiting extreme adaptability. (From *The Sketchbooks of Trofym Lysenko.)*

Length / Weight	Reproduction	Diet
5 cm/0.2 kg to 3.5m/80 kg	*egg bearing*	*carnivorous*

Population	Habitat
approx. 3% fauna mass	*Terrestrial*

"HENDER"
Shenuday Saylenair Shueenair
(Based on a photographic portrait for *Link Magazine*)

"KUZU"
Thropinsalusuvorrati-Gropaninthizkolevolizim-Sta
(Based on a posed portrait by Plesh)

The Ages of Henderica: Earth History & Extinction Events

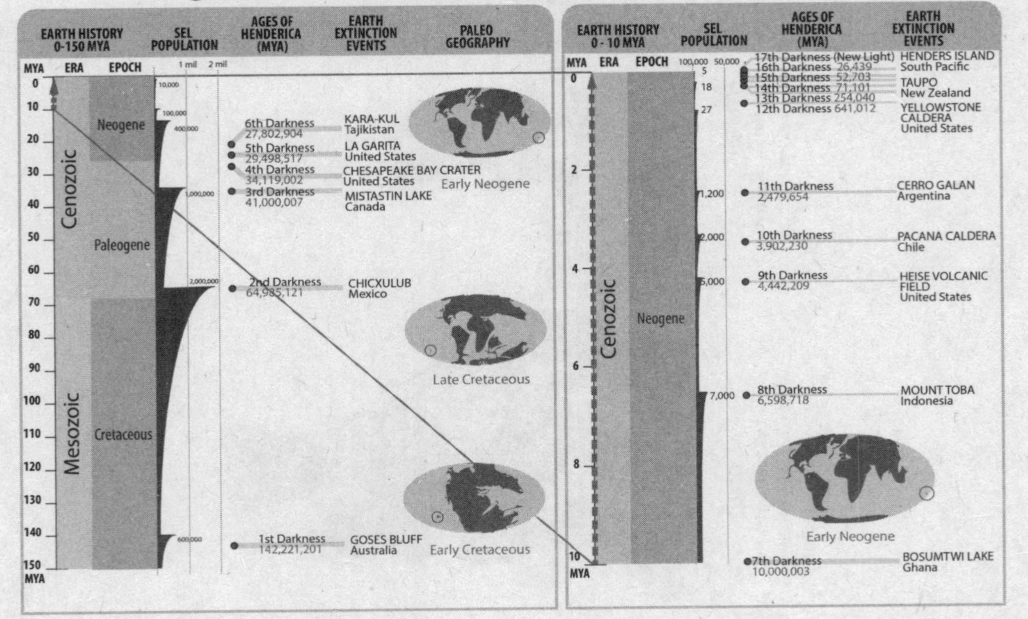